Because of You

KYLA FAYE

ALSO BY KYLA FAYE

Down We Go Series
Dollhouse (Book #1)
Ashes (Book #2)
Ace (Book #3)

Part Of Me Series
Our Way Back (Book #1)
Because of You (Book #2)

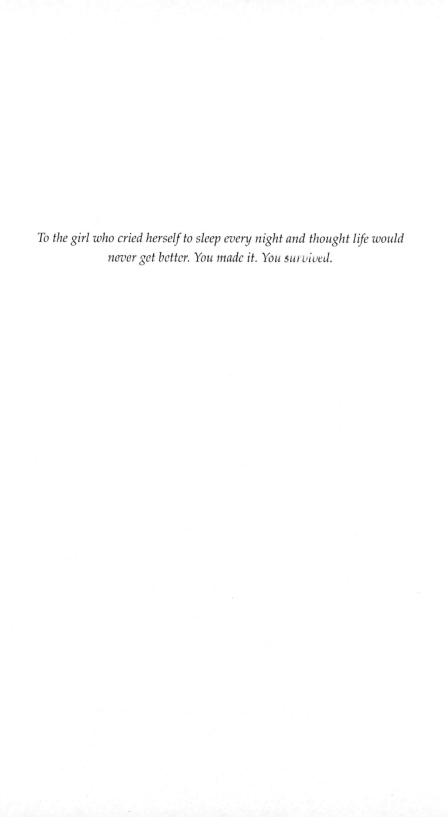

To the girl who cried herself to sleep every night and thought life would never get better. You made it. You survived.

To the ones who have begged someone to choose them over their addiction.

The ones who had to grow up before they should and had to become the parent.

The ones who have cried themselves to sleep at night.

The ones who wanted their pain to end, and prayed to never wake up.

This is for you.

WARNING

This book contains situations that may be uncomfortable for some, including child loss, depression, mentions of CSA, drug and alcohol use, overdose, death, and suicide.

For a complete list of content warnings visit kylafaye.com

Thank you so much JRea, Audrey, Mariah, Clara, Lucy, Emily, Jackie, Britt, Shae, Cecilia, Jamie for your support

patreon.com/kylafaye

PLAYLIST

"Dancing With The Devil" – Demi Lovato
"Sober" – Demi Lovato
"Save Me" – Jelly Roll
"Hate Me" – Blue October
"Relapse (Stripped)" – Cap Carter
"Falling Apart" – Papa Roach
"Best For Me" – Joyner Lucas & Jelly Roll
"Never Too Late" – Three Days Grace
"If I Surrender" – Citizen Soldier
"Iris" – The Goo Goo Dolls
"Lullaby" – Nickelback
"Loved By You" – Kirby
"Touched By An Angel" – Charlie Wilson
"You Don't Belong" – Daughtry
"Lost In You" – Three Days Grace
"Love Like Heroin" – Hollow City
"In My Veins (feat. Erin McCarley)" – Andrew Belle
"I'd Rather Overdose (feat. Z)" – honestav
"Love in the Dark" – Adele
"loml" – Taylor Swift
"I Can Fix Him (No Really I Can)" – Taylor Swift

PROLOGUE

Declan

NOISE.

All day there's been too much fucking noise in my head.

The voices inside my head are screaming. Colors are too bright. Voices are too loud.

My hands have been shaking with the desperate need to reach for the one thing that has the power to calm me down. But I've been fighting the urges.

For her. For him.

For my family.

They don't deserve to be burdened by a worthless excuse of a husband and father. A man who can't remain sober for one fucking night.

One night. I can do it. I've done it before. Sure, it's been a while. But I can do it.

I can. I have to.

My suit is too tight.

My eyelids are heavy.

I need something.

Anything.

My heart races as if it's mere seconds from beating out of my chest.

In the distance, I hear someone calling my name, but I'm unable to determine if it's in my head or not.

Not until it gets louder.

The voice calls, "Yo, Dec!" The tone is familiar and getting closer.

The voice calls out my name again, and this time I look up. Sliding one hand in my pocket, I use the other to remove the cigarette hanging from my lips.

My eyes land on the one person who can provide me with the relief I need. The one person I shouldn't be seeing. It's as if I summoned him to me. He knew I needed him, so he came to deliver.

Came to feed my demons.

Unable to control myself, laughter spills from my lips at the sight of my savior's new hairstyle.

His big head is buzzed on the sides, and there's a patch of bright neon-green hair that contains so much fucking gel it'll take him a year to wash it out.

Tommy's appearance isn't what you'd expect from a drug dealer. But then again, how is a drug dealer supposed to look?

"Hey man." I toss my cigarette to the ground of the alley and stub it out with my boot, lifting myself away from the brick wall I'd been leaning against.

"Long time no see." We bump fists by way of greeting. "What are you up to these days, man?" He leans against the brick wall and reaches into his pocket for a pack of smokes. After removing one from the pack, he places it between his thin, pale lips and lights it up.

Unease washes over me. I'm not in a good headspace and haven't been for a while now. It's been three months since I returned home from Riot's latest tour, and each day has been a fucking struggle. My wife watches my every move like a hawk and never lets me be. She's been holding my balls so fucking tight, and I need her to let go so I can breathe. Just once.

Thankfully, Tommy is the key to helping me feel better, but it'll come at a price.

If I take the type of help he can offer, Camille will be furious with me. One of these days, she'll make good on her threats to leave my sorry ass behind.

"Yo! Are you okay?" he asks, drawing me away from my thoughts.

"All good man," I tell him. "Just thinking." I step away from him, shoving my hands into the front pockets of my black pants. "I got my wife and kid inside the restaurant. I should get back to them."

"Alright man. It was good seeing you." He extends his fist to me, and I bump it with mine as I give him a nod.

I'm halfway down the alley when my legs stop moving, and my feet melt into the pavement, keeping me rooted in place. A knot forms in the pit of my stomach. I know what I'm about to do, and the thought enrages me. Knowing what I need to feel better disgusts me. I'm going to let my family down.

I always do.

I'm so fucking weak.

I don't want to be this person. I've always wanted to be better than my drug-addicted parents. Better than all the stereotypes that were pushed onto me.

Most importantly, I want to be better for those that matter most to me.

My wife and son.

Camille doesn't know I have these demons that I struggle to fight daily, and I can never tell her. Not when I already feel her slipping further away from me day by day. I promised her time and time again that I'd clean up my act. Sometimes I mean the words, but most of the time I stare into her captivating green eyes and know it's nothing but a lie.

The lies taste like acid on my tongue, but they always come easy.

Three weeks ago, I looked her in the eyes and promised I was

3

sober. The second she turned around, I downed a bottle of cheap vodka to make myself feel better for lying to her.

She doesn't love me anymore, and it's one of the worst feelings. We're more roommates than husband and wife. Four years married, and it's not getting better. Day after day, it only gets worse. I know it's my fault, but instead of doing anything to help save our marriage, I'm allowing it to fall apart.

All thanks to my addiction and lies.

I'm not a good husband. I'm not even a good person.

Most days, I think about how much better off those around me would be if I ended it.

Camille doesn't tell me she loves me anymore. She doesn't smile when she sees me, and she doesn't kiss me spontaneously anymore. The only time she allows me to touch her is when she's climbing on my dick. And that's only after she gets so fed up with me and begins screaming at me.

Five minutes into a screaming match, I end up buried balls deep inside of her, and our fight is a thing of the past. It's the same routine. We're going in circles and getting nowhere.

Tonight, I saw that look in her eyes. The same look that tells me she's tired. Tired of me. Tired of our life together. I've been selfishly sucking the life out of my beautiful girl for four years.

Bile rises in my throat as I walk toward Tommy, clearly deciding what I'm going to do. I'll get a fix just one more time, and then I'll stay clean and focus on my marriage and being the best father to Luca.

Just once. That's all I need.

The face of my wife and son are all I see behind my eyelids as I feel my inner demons threaten to ruin me.

"Tommy!" I call out, turning around to face my savior. "You got some blow?" I ask, resigned to face my fate.

A sinister smirk spreads across his thin lips. "I got you, man. Just got some new shit in that I think you'll like."

What a fuck-up I am.

I don't deserve the life I have—or my family.

I deserve the white powder Tommy slips into my hand after I give him cash from my wallet.

"Take it easy, Dec. I'll see you around." Tommy walks off, a wide fucking smile on his face.

Soon, I'll be the one smiling.

I waste no time opening the baggie, dipping my car key inside, and snorting the white powder.

My fix hits me, and suddenly I'm floating on cloud nine.

My happiness is back.

I'm myself again.

Nothing is wrong.

I'm happy now.

This is what I needed.

Just one more time.

I'll quit after this.

I promise.

I meet my family back inside the restaurant. I'm just in time to pay the bill as they finish their meal and pack up.

I see the way Camille looks at me as we leave. She's angry that I disappeared for who knows how long. She's trying to ruin my high, but I won't allow it. I'm too happy to let her fuck it up this time.

She always ruins my high.

Doesn't she want me to be happy?

The sky rumbles with an angry roar of thunder just moments before wet droplets land on my cheeks. There's a moment of calm before the storm, and I stand there watching Camille place Luca into his car seat, watching her red painted lips move, unable to make out the words.

One second, I'm standing there dry and warm, and the next, my hair is slick with wetness against my face, the cold raindrops soaking through the fabric of my clothing, and a chill settling in my veins.

Nothing good ever happens when it rains.

An ominous feeling washes over me as the devil whispers in my ear.

Get into the car!

Fingers snapping in my face draw me away from my stupor. "Declan!" Camille hisses, her annoyance with me rising. Can't blame her for being irritated with me. I haven't been listening to a single thing she's said.

"Give me the fucking keys!" Her awaiting palm is between us, but I push it away.

"Get in the car, Cam. It's fucking cold." I climb into the driver's seat before she has a chance to protest.

I'm sure I could try a little harder to pay attention to what she's saying as she climbs into the passenger seat, but it's hard to focus when I'm seeing two of her. I'm feeling things I've never felt before from the magic white powder friend that's burning a hole in my pocket. I feel like I'm floating, and my body feels heavy.

Maybe I shouldn't have taken so much. I don't feel good anymore.

Dizzy. I'm so dizzy.

I should've let her drive. That's all I can think of as I hear the crushing sound of metal on metal. It's followed by her piercing scream and tires squealing.

My body jerks, crashing through something hard, and then I'm flying.

Flying through the night with cold, wet air on my face.

The world spins around me, and I feel weightless.

Free.

I'm flying...

And then I collide into the darkness and hit rock bottom. I realize I should've given my wife the one thing she asked for.

Instead, I was selfish and refused her.

I'll never get the chance to make it up to her.

I refused to give her what she deserved, and because of me, I killed the one person we both loved the most in the world.

Our son.

ONE

Declan

Four years later

I'M A FUCK-UP, AND I RUIN EVERYTHING.

Everything I do.

Everything I touch.

I ruin it all.

My hands were made for destruction.

I wasn't always this way; I once had my shit together and had the perfect life. Or, at least as perfect a life as someone like me can ever have.

I had a fucking bombshell of a wife. I had a son who my world revolved around, and he saw me as his hero.

My life was great.

Dream job, dream family, dream life. But dreams never last. Eventually, we have to wake up, and before you know it, you're a shell of the person you once were. Now I hardly recognize the person staring back at me in the mirror.

I'm a fuck-up.

I let my perfect life slip through my fingers. I let my demons control me. They told me I wasn't good enough, that I didn't deserve my perfect life, and once I believed them, I woke up from my dream.

Goodbye wife. Goodbye son.

Now I'm struggling to hold on to the only thing I have left.

My career.

Some days it seems like I'm struggling to hold on to my fucking sanity.

After all I've lost, you'd think that would be enough to make me snap the fuck out of my stupor and get my life back on track. But I'm too weak to do that. I don't *want* to do that. I like to wallow in self-pity and numb myself when it all becomes too much.

Giving in to the voices in my head makes me feel at ease.

I gave in last night, as I've been doing every night since the ink dried on my divorce papers nearly two years ago.

Sure, I've had extended periods of sobriety since then, and by that, I mean my drug use hadn't been as frequent. As for my drinking, that's been a daily occurrence.

Last night started with one drink, and that turned into another and another, followed by a pretty girl who had more to offer than what's between her legs. Vaguely, I remember snorting lines of white powder off her silicone tits, but with my memory lately, I can't be certain if it was the woman from last night or a week ago.

The days and women all seem to blur together.

Wandering hands roam over my back, followed by a trail of wet, fervent kisses.

"Baby," the woman whines, her tongue tracing over the shell of my ear. "I want you. Please fuck me."

Since she asked so nicely, fuck it. With my erection growing, I quickly sit up and pin her underneath me. Within seconds, I have my dick wrapped in a condom, and I'm shoving myself into her wet pussy. I love the way her cunt stretches around my thickness. I have no mercy as I fill her to the hilt, and she takes all I have to offer like a champ.

I'm fucking the nameless blonde six ways to Sunday when I hear the door of my hotel room suite slam shut. From somewhere in the room, a light flicks on, encasing the room in a soft yellow glow.

With a groan, I turn my head to see Benny, my manager, standing at the foot of my bed and shaking his head at me.

This isn't the first time he's found me balls deep inside a random woman, and I know it sure as fuck won't be the last time.

My eyes burn from the light, so I close them and focus on the feeling of having a pussy around me. I don't lose momentum as I fuck the woman. Her porn star moans are too fucking much, but that doesn't stop me from getting what I need.

"Really, Declan?" Benny huffs, and if I open my eyes, I know I'd find him rolling his eyes and shaking his head. "Hurry the fuck up and get in the shower." I crack my eyes open, giving him a playful smirk.

He walks away, disappearing into the living room of the suite.

Two minutes later, I'm filling the condom with a load of cum and pulling myself out of my nameless fuck, not caring that she didn't finish. She can get herself off while I shower. I got what I needed.

Disappointment flashes in her eyes, and I have to look away because it's too fucking early to see that look—especially from someone whose name I don't remember and I'll never see again.

From the living room, Benny yells, "You've got fifteen minutes. Take a shower, and I'll get you some coffee. Get the fuck up!"

I grab the gold dress from the floor and toss it onto the bed. "Sorry doll, you need to get dressed and go." I turn my back on her, make my way into the bathroom, and remove the condom. After flushing it, I step into the shower. The cold water from the rainfall showerhead hits my heated skin, cooling my temperature and shocking my nervous system.

I never fuck without protection, but I don't trust the women that fill my bed enough to leave them with my used condom. I never take it off until I have a chance to flush it.

There's no need to worry about the woman stealing anything from me, because I know Benny will check her before she leaves and make her sign an NDA.

Ever since some random groupie recorded us having sex and partying, leaked it to the media, and then gave several interviews on our time together, Benny has insisted I make all my women sign an NDA. I never remember it beforehand, but I can make sure I get their signature before they leave. With Benny here, he can do it for me.

He wishes I were more careful. I'm already well-known, the last thing I need is having my name dragged through the media again. I should be careful, especially considering my career is already on the line.

Everyone is tired of my shit. Hell, I'm tired of my shit.

It's exhausting constantly letting everyone down, but I can't seem to stop.

It's who I am.

I'm Declan Valentine—the fuck-up. I'll never be anyone different, so there's no point in wishing for it.

THIRTY MINUTES LATER, I'M SITTING IN THE STUDIO ALONGSIDE MY band mates, Adam, Damon, and Cole, remaining silent as we conduct our first interview in nearly a year.

Now that Riot is making a comeback and making moves, it's time to control the narrative regarding the bad press we've been receiving, starting with being open and honest. Our fans have had many questions, and they've all gone unanswered for far too long.

The last few years have been hard.

Today is already hard enough.

I've tried to pretend I didn't know what day it is, but no matter how hard I try, I'll never be able to forget.

Today marks both the best and worst day of my life.

Eight years ago, it was the best day.

Four years ago, it became the worst.

On the drive over, Benny warned me to be professional and not say anything that could be used against our band. I've been on my best behavior since arriving, my hands in a white-knuckle fist, nails biting into my palms as I try to get through the day until I can drown myself in a bottle of vodka and forget about my cruel reality.

"It's been nearly a year since Riot's last tour and just as long since you've released any new music. Why did you decide to make a comeback now?" the nosy reporter asks, her blue eyes looking directly at me, a sign that she expects me to answer. Everyone knows I'm the reason we had to cancel our tour and postpone our album release.

"Well, Alyssa"—I mentally pat myself on the back for remembering her name—"as you and everyone else know, I went through a dark period." The reporter, along with everyone else with eyes and social media, knows what happened to me.

Three months after my divorce, my entire life had been exposed, and the media found out a lot more than I'd ever wanted revealed.

The media found details about Luca's death and about my time in rehab. I'd tried to keep it quiet, but I should've known better. They don't know I was high that night, but everyone now knows I was the one driving. They assume I lost control of the wheel because of the rain.

For once, I'm thankful to have the media printing lies about me.

They say I developed an addiction after the accident because of the painkillers the doctor prescribed. They say from there, I fell into a downward spiral of drugs and alcohol until one day

13

my wife left me. It's partially true, except that's not when my addiction began.

For months, they printed my entire life in full color, and my face was on the cover of every magazine around the fucking world.

I'm the reason my band, Riot, has been having such a difficult time lately. I haven't been able to write, and since I'm the lead singer and songwriter, without me, there's nothing. My band-mates and best friends have been suffering because of me.

Yet another reason I'm a fuck-up and failure.

Shockingly, they've all stood beside me. They could've kicked me out of the band and found a new lead singer, but none of them wanted to do it.

As teenagers, the four of us started Riot. We're in this together.

"Yes, I heard about that… and I see you've had quite the media attention recently." She sits back in her seat and scrolls through her iPad with her perfectly manicured finger. "The death of your child, rehab, divorce, and most recently your sex tape was exposed." I hold my breath, my heart beating rapidly in my chest at the mention of my child. Today of all days?

I adjust my posture on the stool I'm sitting on, nails breaking the skin on the palms. My jaw clenches, teeth grinding together painfully as I attempt to ignore the feeling of my skin crawling, my mind racing and begging for a drink in order to be silenced. The woman continues speaking, unaware I'm doing everything I can to remain calm.

"I've been a Riot fan for years, and I never knew you had a child. You once said you enjoy being transparent with your fans, and yet, no one knew you were a father until recently."

Fuck.

It's time for the questions I hate and always try to avoid.

This is a perfect example of why you cannot believe the media and what you see online. It's time to stop being a fucking pussy and control the narrative. They've printed so much false shit about me. The timeline is fucked up, and no one seems to know what's fact or fiction.

Inhaling, I close my eyes and slowly uncurl my fists, wiping my bloodied palms on my black jeans. For the first time, I calm myself and think before I speak. "My son, Luca, died four years ago today. Today is his birthday. He would've been eight. After his death, I couldn't cope and did things I'm not proud of. It led to rehab, and then my wife and I divorced. We were both young when we had him, and we wanted the best for him, which is why we got married. We've always been better off as friends rather than husband and wife." I've rehearsed what to say with Benny a thousand times. I know how to react when Camille and Luca are mentioned. "My ex-wife and I wanted to keep our son out of the media, and that's why his existence was kept private." For years, there was speculation in the media about whether I had a wife and child. I never confirmed or denied the rumors. Cam and Luca never joined me on tour for this exact reason.

As soon as we found out Camille was pregnant, we agreed to keep our son away from the hungry media vultures. We were successful for years.

"As far as the sex tape goes, that was recorded without my consent and directly violates my privacy. My lawyer is happy to answer questions you may have about it, but I will not as there is an open case." I lie easily, giving the blue-eyed reporter a threatening smile, daring her to challenge me.

Truth is, I was high as a fucking kite when I agreed to let some random chick I met at a club record herself sucking my cock. She said she wanted to make her ex-boyfriend jealous, and I happily dropped my pants. I was too high to remember the NDA, and sure enough, three days later, it was posted online. My face isn't visible, but you can sure as fuck see my tattoo-covered arms and hear my voice. The bold *RIOT* tattoo across my knuckles was visible while fisting her blonde hair and telling her how good her mouth felt around me.

There's no denying it's me. My face didn't need to be visible.

"What message do you think that sends to your fans? They should trust you, but you couldn't trust them with the truth about your family," the reporter says, brushing a piece of dark hair from her slender shoulder.

Don't get me wrong; I love my fans, but I'm not obligated to tell them every fucking thing about my personal life. I decide what to share with the public. I don't owe anyone anything.

"Can your fans trust you to remain sober?" she continues, the question making me want to laugh. I'm not sober, but she doesn't need to know that. In fact, if I had it my way, I'd be drinking myself into a blackout right now.

Thank fuck, Adam cuts in before I respond. "We are all brothers, and we stand behind each other completely, no matter what happens. Declan went through a lot, and with love and support, he's back and better than ever. Right now, we are preparing for our move and in the process of writing our new album." He pats me on the back, his hand squeezing my shoulder reassuringly. He knows what today is and how hard it is for me.

Over the years, Luca's birthday and subsequent anniversary of his death has become easier to manage. I used to spend the day sending my fists through walls, mirrors—anything, really. Then, I'd bury myself in a mountain of coke.

This year, I'm going to drown myself in a bottle of liquor.

I'd say that's progress.

As you can tell, therapy has been working for me.

Adam stands up from the stool he was sitting on. "We are happy to be working on a new album and get back on tour soon. We appreciate your time and hope to see you at one of our shows." Leave it to my best friend to swoop in and save me and end the horrible fucking interview.

Benny ushers the woman out of our studio, and only once she's gone can I breathe. I hate answering questions about myself. I'm thankful I kept my cool and refrained from doing something I'd later regret.

With shaking hands, I swipe a bottle of water from the mini

fridge and twist the cap off, chugging the cold water down as Adam walks over to me.

"You good, bro? I know Cam and Luca are your soft spots." I don't make eye contact, but I nod.

Adam and I met when we were sixteen. We were in the same group home for about six months before we ran away together. We're more than best friends—we're brothers—and sometimes this fucker knows me better than I know myself, which is why I don't want to look at him. I know what he'll see on my face.

My palms are sweaty, my skin is pale, and my hands are shaking. I'm itching for a fix. I'm too sober to deal with this shit.

Too fucking sober to be reminded of what a failure as a husband and father I was. I killed my son and drove my wife away. I'm trying to move forward, but with today being the four-year anniversary, I can't deal with it.

Not sober, at least.

"I'm fine." I grunt, tossing the empty bottle into the recycling bin.

"Speaking of Camille, she's been trying to reach you. She called me when you didn't answer. Her flight lands soon. Are you going to pick her up or send a driver?" Fuck. I forgot all about Camille coming to New York today.

When we visited our son's grave for the first time together, we promised each other that we'd meet and visit his grave every year. Today is his birthday, another year of him being gone, which means we're supposed to see him.

Sensing my sudden panic, Adam places his hand on my shoulder. "Don't worry, brother. I'll go pick her up. Are you still at the same hotel?"

"Yeah," I mumble, scrubbing my hands over my face. I've been staying at a hotel for a while now. Camille and I decided to sell the penthouse we once shared. When the realtor came to view our house, I had no choice but to escort her inside. It was my first time stepping foot in the time capsule since being divorced. A place we once called home.

17

She'd opened the door to Luca's room before I could stop her. A fresh wave of emotions had come over me, undoing all the progress I'd made.

That was the day I walked out the front door to get high after being sober for nearly a year, and I haven't stepped foot in the penthouse since. I haven't been able to return when I'm in an active addiction.

Not when I'm the reason the bed with the Paw Patrol sheets is empty.

My addiction killed my son. *I* killed my son.

Without making eye contact and without another word, I rush out of the studio just as quick as my long legs will allow.

My palms are clammy, I'm sweating, my chest is tight, and my vision is becoming blurry. I can't tell if my hands are shaking or if it's just my vision.

Everything is too much. Too fucking much on today of all days. I can't do this. Not sober. I'm feeling too much, and I don't want to feel anything.

I can't.

I can't.

I fucking *can't*.

TWO

Declan

"YOU LOOK LIKE SHIT." THOSE ARE THE FIRST WORDS I HEAR FROM my lovely ex-wife the moment I open the door to my hotel suite.

With an eye roll, I step aside and allow the feisty raven-haired beauty to enter my space. We may be divorced, and she may be seeing someone else now, but I will not lie and say the sight of her doesn't cause my dick to twitch. Camille has always been a knockout.

Her small waist is hidden underneath her oversized zip up jacket, but her perfect, peachy ass is displayed nicely in black leggings. Her thighs are a little thick, but they still make my mouth water. I've spent countless hours with my head between them, and sometimes when I'm feeling lonely at night and touching my dick, I remember what it was like to taste her.

"Earth to Declan! Focus!" she yells, snapping her fingers in front of my face. With a chuckle, I shake my head and let the door slam shut. I wrap my arms around her small frame, inhaling the sweet and familiar scent of her perfume.

"Sorry, baby girl. I was busy checking you out." With a snort, she quickly pulls away and makes herself comfortable by removing her sandals and plopping onto the couch. "Where's

Dean?" Surprisingly, I have a civil relationship with my ex-wife and her boyfriend. Which is something I never thought would've been possible, considering they had an affair behind my back after I got home from rehab.

After Camille and I divorced, Dean flew out to New York to see me. He wanted to talk man to man and apologized for having an affair with my wife. Then, instead of asking for her father's permission, he asked for mine to marry her.

I laughed in his fucking face, but once I finished laughing, I bought him a beer.

Although, I was the one who had the last laugh when I heard that Camille turned down his proposal.

Our relationship is unconventional. Who the fuck is friends with the man their wife cheated on them with? It's fucked up, but I want Camille to be happy, and I understand I'm not the one who makes her happy. I was twenty-three when I married her all because of two pink lines. She'd been twenty-two, just graduated college, and had backstage passes to my concert. A few days later, I asked her to come tour with me, and then our life was flipped upside down not long after when she missed her period. We've always known we were better at being friends than husband and wife, but we didn't want our son to be torn between two homes, so we stayed married, putting on a happy face for our child and fighting in private.

I have no ill feelings toward Camille. She's my best friend, and I want her to be happy—which means accepting Dean. Last I heard, she's been taking things slow with him. They reconnected a few months ago, and for now they're only dating, although Dean is ready to marry her the moment she agrees. During the time Camille and I were separated, she and Dean had ended their affair when he found out his wife was pregnant.

Long story short, Dean's ex-wife lied. She was pregnant, but not with his baby. They divorced, and several months later, he and Camille reconnected and have been dating ever since.

"It's just me. He had to go to Canada for business, so I came alone. It works out, because I want to talk to you." She tucks her feet underneath her little body and brushes her dark, silky hair away from her heart-shaped face.

"What's up, is everything okay?" I sit beside her on the couch and turn to face her. I watch with confusion as Camille inhales and slowly, so fucking slowly, unzips her jacket and lets it fall open, revealing a pink tank top that perfectly hugs her curves.

My eyes take in the sight of her cleavage and slowly lower until I see what she'd been hiding.

Holy fuck.

At the sight of her swollen stomach, my jaw drops, and my eyes nearly pop out of my fucking head. "Y-y-you're pregnant," I stutter, staring at the proof.

With glossy eyes, she nods her head and rubs her manicured fingers over her bump. "Yes, I'm pregnant. I didn't want to tell you over the phone." Shrugging out of her jacket, she stands and begins pacing the room, her hands on her hips.

"Fuck! I know the timing is terrible. It's Luca's birthday for crying out loud, and here I am, announcing my pregnancy." She wipes the tears from her face and turns to face me. "I swear I didn't mean for this to happen. I didn't plan to ever have any more children. I'm not trying to replace Luca and what you and I had. Please believe that." Her bright green eyes glisten with sincerity as her soft, vulnerable voice shakes.

Standing, I walk toward her and wrap my arms around her shaking body, rubbing my hands soothingly down her back. "It's okay, baby girl. I'm happy for you. I am. I don't think you're replacing me or Luca; you never could." Pulling back, I look down at her blotchy face.

"I was so worried to tell you. I wasn't sure how you'd take it," she explains, wiping away the tears still streaming down her face. "It's a girl. I'm due in five months." Taking a step back, I watch her hands rub over her belly.

My chest tightens, my heart aching with a mixture of emotions. After we lost Luca, I wanted to have another baby for months. Camille said no every time, and I understood her reasoning. Luca hadn't been planned, and she didn't want to replace him. She swore she'd never have another baby, but I've always known she was meant to be a mother and she'd have another child eventually, even if I wasn't the one who would father it.

It's bittersweet seeing her happy. Bitter, because I'm not the reason for the smile on her face, and I couldn't give her the things she needed. But sweet, because she deserves happiness. We were toxic together, and sweet Camille is too beautiful and pure to be dragged down with my toxicity, addictions, and demons.

She truly deserves everything she's getting now.

Camille lets out a sigh of relief, shoving my shoulder playfully. "I was so worried to tell you! I didn't know how you'd take it." I understand where she's coming from. But I'm happy for her and Dean. She may be my ex-wife, but she'll forever be my best friend. We have ties that can never be severed. "Say something so I know you're not mad."

Wiping a hand over my face, I clear my throat before speaking, "Are you two getting married? Last I heard, you wanted to take things slow."

"No, we're not getting married. At least not now. We have a lot of time to make up for, so we are taking things slow. I was on birth control, but this still happened." She points to her belly. "We're not even living together. We'd just started dating when I found out." She wipes her tears away, then pins me with a bright smile.

"Okay, I'm done crying. I'm starving and ready to eat."

$\mathmusic$

AFTER TWO LARGE PIZZAS AND A NAP, CAMILLE AND I LEAVE THE hotel to visit the cemetery where our sweet boy is laid to rest.

She brought yellow roses and a toy, as she does every time we visit.

I'm ashamed to admit that I only visit once a year with her. She doesn't live in New York anymore, yet she visits more than me. I just can't bring myself to stand and stare at Luca's headstone when I'm responsible for his death. I hate being here, but for her, I suck it up.

I see the distraught look on her face when she sees his beautiful angel headstone, and the weather damaged toys from her last visit. I don't have the heart to tell her I haven't been around to visit our boy, but based on the look on her face, I think she already knows.

My chest aches, my eyes instantly becoming glossy with tears. Cam drops to her knees and starts talking to the headstone, as if Luca can actually hear her. I obviously don't know what happens or where you go when you die, but I'd like to think my boy is watching over his mother and can hear her.

If my boy can see me, I don't want him watching the way I'm living my life right now. It's shameful, but the past haunts me. New York haunts me, and I can't get over the damage I've caused in my life.

I hold so much guilt. I let him die because I was too stubborn and wouldn't let Camille drive. Had I been sober or even handed over the keys, he'd be alive right now. Celebrating his birthday with us.

"Dec, come talk to our son." Camille's emotion-filled voice breaks me from my pity party, and I take her small hand and allow her to pull me toward her. I kneel beside her and place my palm on the photo of our son that's etched into the headstone.

"Hi little man. It's daddy." My voice cracks as emotion clogs my throat. "I miss you so much. I'm sorry. I'm so fucking sorry." My tears spill as I choke out a cry.

She strokes my back gently, allowing me to hold her tightly and let out all the tears and emotions that I'd been holding in for too long.

"I'm sorry, son. I'm so fucking sorry that I did this to you." My vision blurs as my body shakes with my sobs. Camille holds me tightly against her body, her own tears silent as they stream down her flawless face.

"Forgive yourself, Declan. It was an accident. Please, forgive yourself." Cam truly believes it was an accident. She believed me when I said I was too tired and lost control because of the rain that night. She doesn't know that I was high, and I'll never have the courage to tell her. The truth might set me free, but it would also ruin us. If she knew, we'd be beyond repair. She'd never speak to me again.

Camille would hate me as much as I already hate myself.

That night, when the ambulance came and rushed the three of us to the hospital, no one ran a blood test on me to check for drugs or alcohol. They ruled it an accident.

No one knows what really happened.

No one but me, and I'll never tell.

I know she deserves to know, but telling her now, after all this time, will only cause her more pain. She has a new life now, and she doesn't deserve more tragedy in it.

This is a secret I'll be taking to the grave.

One I'll never forgive myself for.

It's my burden to bear.

♪♪♪♪♪

CAMILLE SPENT THREE DAYS IN NEW YORK WITH ME, AND WITHOUT fail, every day we visited our son and spent two hours with him. She had a lot to tell him, and I loved to sit there and listen to her. Her green eyes are no longer filled with sadness but with life and happiness. The look on her face is a look I'd only seen directed toward Luca: pure happiness and love. A look that I've wanted to see on her face for years.

It was a great visit, but now it's time for her to return home to

Seattle—to her life with Dean. She has to leave soon, but before she goes, she wanted to pay a last visit to our penthouse, which is where we are right now.

Camille dug out our old photo albums and a few boxes from the hallway closet, and now we're in the living room while she goes through them, deciding what she wants to keep. We signed the papers this morning, and come next week, this place will no longer be ours. A new family will move in.

"Don't forget that guys from the donation center will be here tomorrow to pick everything up. Are you sure you don't want to keep anything?" she asks, glancing at me from where she sits on the floor.

I've already gathered my clothes and the few personal items I want to keep. Everything else can go. I can't stand the fact that strangers will go through Luca's room and his stuff will be sold to someone else, but I know it's for the best. It can't stay here. We can't keep this time capsule forever. It's not healthy.

"I'm sure. I already have everything I want to keep," I reply.

She nods. "So, I talked to Adam." She slams the photo album shut, shoving it into her oversized purse. What the is with women and having such huge purses? What do they even keep in there? "When did you plan on telling me you're moving to Las Vegas?" She crosses her arms over her chest, glaring at me.

Fuck. Adam has a big mouth.

"I planned on telling you once I got there."

Her bright green eyes widen. "Seriously, Dec? You were going to move and not tell me?"

"We're not married anymore, Camille. I don't have to tell you anything about where I live. Besides, we just sold this place. Where do you expect me to live?"

"Well, I thought you were staying in New York. I didn't know you were leaving." I open my mouth to speak, but she cuts me off. "I think it's great. It's a fresh start without any terrible memories. It could be great for you. The change you need." She stands, her red lips curling into a smile. "I just want to see you happy. That's all I want for you." She sighs, looking at the phone in her hand.

Yeah, she and I both, but I know I don't deserve to be happy.

"I've got to go now. My car is here. I'll call you when I land." She gathers her purse and suitcase, and I stand, following her to the door.

"I love you, baby girl. Be safe," I say, wrapping my arms around her, hugging her soft body to me.

"I love you too, Dec. I'll call you later. Be good out there in Vegas. Maybe Dean and I will visit you soon." We say our final goodbyes, and then she's gone, leaving me alone with the little devil on my shoulder telling me to call my dealer and get myself another fix.

Fuck my life.

THREE

Declan

SIX MONTHS AGO, COLE BROUGHT UP THE IDEA OF THE BAND moving. His girlfriend is from Las Vegas, and her mother has been sick, so she needed to go back home to care for her, and he didn't want to be away from her. We're all New York born and raised, and the city is where we formed Riot. It was a lot to process, but the idea of a new city and a fresh start felt needed for all of us, because we all have our own demons that haunt us in the city.

After months of working with our manager, Benny, we successfully transferred everything related to our band from New York to Nevada.

Adam, Cole, Damon, and Benny moved to Vegas first. They left right after our interview; it was the same day Camille came to town.

That was three weeks ago.

While they've been there, I've been here in New York, attending therapy three times a week and as many NA meetings as possible.

This time, I've been sober for three weeks, and I'm determined to stay that way. After Camille left, I'm embarrassed to admit that I threw myself a pity party and drank until I passed out.

The next morning, despite my hangover, all I wanted was another drink. I was in the kitchen, bottle in my hand, when I caught my reflection in the microwave. The sight of my disheveled appearance was enough to give me pause.

That moment I realized I was tired of relying on drugs and alcohol to make it through the day, and I'm tired of wallowing in self-pity day after day.

The day Camille left New York was the day I decided to be someone new. Be someone that I can be proud of, be someone that Luca could be proud of if he were still here.

I can no longer sit around waiting for someone to save me from myself. It's time I save myself and grow the fuck up. I'm thirty-one years old, and I'm a fucking mess.

"My assistant will give you the information for the doctors I recommend in Nevada. Promise me you'll continue therapy and NA meetings," Dr. Chen says, tearing me away from my thoughts. I look into her hopeful brown eyes and nod, fully intending to stay on track.

Today is my last therapy session with her. In three hours, I'll head to the airport and get on a plane to Las Vegas, where I'll get a fresh start.

It'll be good for me. It's what I need. I only hope this time will be different.

"Thank you for everything, Dr. Chen. I will look at those recommendations and schedule an appointment with someone once I get settled in." We both believe the lie on my tongue.

Immediately after leaving her office, I head to the airport, eager for what'll await me.

♪ ♪ ♪ ♪ ♪

THE SIX-HOUR FLIGHT WAS SMOOTH, THANKS TO THE FACT THAT I'D taken a sleeping pill to ensure I could sleep the entire time. The band took our private jet when they came out here, so I flew commercial.

Adam was there at the airport to pick me up the moment I landed. The fucker was wearing a blond wig and mustache. He held up a sign that said, *Welcome home from prison!*

Mother fucker.

Luckily, no one seemed to recognize us, or else I'm sure his stunt would cause a media frenzy, and rumors about me being in prison would be surfacing.

Now we're at his and Damon's rental house, and I'm kicked back on the large sectional in the living room, listening to Damon rave about the two girls he brought over last night that gave him the "best pussy of his life."

He says that shit every night. He claims every new woman he fucks is the best he's ever had.

"Alright, fuckers. I need a nap, so which room is mine?" I ask, just as the front door slams shut and Benny comes walking in. He's dressed casually in a pair of khaki shorts and a blue button-down shirt.

My eyebrows jump to my hairline at the sight of him. The man always wears a suit, so this is new. Once, I knocked on his hotel room door in the middle of the night, needing a condom, and even at 3 a.m. he was still in a suit.

"Well, fuck. Looks like Vegas life is already changing you," I tease, placing my hands behind my head.

He rolls his brown eyes. "Yeah, yeah, yeah, you little shit. Laugh it up. It's too fucking hot out here." Benny is in his mid-fifties, but with the way he cares for himself, you'd never tell. He's been with us for so long that I can't remember what it was like without him.

Before our band had a name, Adam, Damon, Cole, and I would play the songs I wrote and post them online. We'd used our fake ID's to perform at a local dive bar back in New York, and Benny was there in the crowd one night. He saw the potential in four moronic eighteen-year-old boys with chips on their shoulders and egos way too fucking big to handle.

No matter what we've been through—or what I've put them through—Benny has been here.

"Enough about my drip." He attempts to pop his collar and fails.

Instantly, Adam and I burst out in laughter.

"Your *what*?" Adam says at the same time I say, "Never say that again."

"My drip. Isn't that what the cool kids call it these days?" He scoffs. "Never mind. I've got a meeting, I just came by to make sure you made it okay." He sits next to Damon.

"I'm assuming no one told you about your... arrangements?" he asks cautiously, his eyes bouncing between Adam and Damon.

Sitting up straight, I look at two of my best friends, but neither make eye contact.

"What are you talking about? My arrangements?"

I watch as Damon nervously chew his lip ring. His eyes on the rug in front of us rather than me.

With a sigh, Adam speaks up. "Look, Dec. We all thought it would be a good idea, so don't get mad at Benny, but you're not staying here with us."

My palms begin to sweat. "What the fuck do you mean? Where am I going to live?"

Benny answers, "I booked you a hotel in Loganville. You're recently sober, and Vegas has too many temptations. For now, it's best to stay away. You'll have an on-call driver with you that'll bring you into the city as needed," he explains, maintaining eye contact while my two pussy best friends look everywhere but at me. "Take the next two months to focus on sobriety and writing new songs."

"Where the fuck is Loganville? I've never heard of it, and what, I'm supposed to be there for two fucking months?"

He nods, standing up. "There's two months until Riot's next

performance. Use this time to work on yourself. Relax, go to a meeting, write." He lifts his wrist, checking the time on his Rolex that we gifted him last year for Christmas.

"I've got to go. Your driver is already here, and we'll talk more later." Giving a nod toward the silent pussies next to me, he leaves.

Standing, I look at my friends, my dark eyes narrowing in a glare. "What the fuck, guys? No warning or anything?"

Damon put his hands up in defense. "Sorry, man. But if you knew beforehand, it wouldn't have gone over well, and you know this."

"Where the fuck is this stupid ass town?"

This time Adam speaks up, "It's about an hour and fifteen minutes away." I can tell there's something else they're not telling me, but I'm too pissed to speak any further to them.

Without another word, I grab my duffle bag and suitcase from the floor, stomping my way to the front door.

"Dec! You don't have to leave yet."

"Yeah, come on, man. Hang out for a bit," Damon says to my back, but I don't spare them another glance.

"Fuck you guys!" I call out, slamming the door behind me as I step outside, the desert heat hitting me in the face.

I spot a black SUV idling in the driveway with a familiar face sitting behind the wheel.

David.

He's been my driver a few times when I've been here. Benny always uses the same company whenever we're in Vegas.

Spotting me, he instantly climbs out and fixes his suit, hitting a button inside the vehicle to pop the trunk.

"Nice to see you, Declan. I'll be your personal driver. I can get those bags for you."

Waving him off, I place them inside the trunk myself. "Hey, man. Nice to see you, too. Let's just go."

Climbing into the backseat, I cross my arms over my chest,

huffing in annoyance at the situation. I'm aware I'm acting like a pouting child, but I don't fucking care.

They don't trust me.

It feels like I've been banished from being around my friends, because they don't trust me enough to remain sober while living in the city.

They're probably right, but that's not their decision to make. If I'm going to get better, I can't hide. No matter where I go, I'll always find a trigger.

Addiction doesn't stop just because you hide away in an unfamiliar city.

This is the time I need friends and support more than ever.

♪ ♪ ♪ ♪ ♪

WE'VE BEEN DRIVING IN SILENCE FOR NEARLY FORTY MINUTES WHEN I finally decide to stop pouting.

Pulling my phone from my pocket, I do a quick search of Loganville to check out the unfamiliar city and see exactly what I have to look forward to.

A humorless laugh leaves my lips.

Loganville, NV.
Population: 3,500
Location: Middle of fucking nowhere.

The more I scroll, I learn that there is nothing in the small town.

There's exactly one grocery store, two gas stations, a few restaurants that seem family owned, a 24-hour fast-food restaurant, a bar, a rundown motel, and one hotel that doesn't look too bad.

I say a silent prayer that Benny booked me the hotel. The images of the motel looked fucking awful.

Locking my phone, I slide it back into my pocket.

"Hey, what do you know about this middle of nowhere place we're going to?"

David looks up, his eyes meeting mine in the rear-view mirror, a grin on his lips. "It's everything you'd expect from a small town. It's mostly families and old folks out there. One of those towns where everyone knows everyone because they're all related."

"Great. Just fucking great," I mumble my response, getting a laugh from him.

Fuck this.

The exit sign for Loganville catches my eye as David flips on his blinker to turn, taking the road that'll lead us to my prison for the next two months.

I fucking hate small towns. I enjoy the noise of the city. The crowd. The energy.

You don't get that in a small town. It's too quiet. And quietness means it's too easy for me to lose myself in my head. The demons that speak to me become too loud, encouraging me to use drugs to silence them.

The farther we drive, the darker it seems; I notice when he turns the brighter headlights on the vehicle. There are no streetlights or light from any buildings around us.

We're alone in the dark on a lone two-lane road in the middle of the desert.

Great. This is when one of the town hillbillies jumps out and skins us, using our flesh as decoration.

I'm pretty sure this is where they filmed *The Hills Have Eyes*.

Who the fuck willingly lives out here?

After a ten-minute drive through the desert, the first light comes into view. The closer we get, the brighter it gets, until eventually we pass it and I realize it was one of the two gas stations this town has.

David mumbles under his breath, but I hear it. "Shit's creepy out here at night."

"Sure as fuck is."

A few minutes later, we've reached our destination. He pulls the SUV into the parking lot of a red-brick hotel that doesn't look too terrible.

Thank fuck Benny booked this and not that seedy motel.

I notice the rooms on the first floor are accessible from the outside, and the rest of the rooms on the second through fourth floor are all indoor.

Weird, but it'll work. Hopefully I can request a first-floor room so I can smoke easily.

"Are you staying here, too?" I ask David as we climb out of the car. I stretch my long limbs, tired of sitting in the car and on the plane earlier in the day. It's 9 p.m., and all I want is a shower, a smoke, and a fat ass burger.

My stomach grumbles at the idea of food.

I can't remember the last time I ate.

"Not at this hotel." A slow grin spreads across his face. "I live here."

What the fuck?

I think I said that out loud, because he throws his head back and laughs. "I know, I know. But I love the small-town life." I thought he was from Vegas. Never would I have guessed he's from this town.

"Trust me, this town will grow on you, and you'll love it. Call me if you need anything, I'm on call 24/7."

Shaking his hand and thanking him, I carry my luggage into the lobby as he drives away.

Two things I know for certain.

This town will not grow on me, and I can't fucking wait until the two months are up.

FOUR

Declan

THE CHECK-IN PROCESS AT THE HAMILTON INN HOTEL IS FUCKING torture. The blue-haired girl behind the counter is so busy giving me googly eyes and giggling about everything that it drags out the process. If she fucking giggles one more time, I swear I'm going to take her pens and stab them in my ears.

Her name tag reads *Lila*, which is a perfect fit. Her mother must've expected she'd be easy when she grew up.

"You'll be in room 107. First floor, right out those doors." She sets a packet of room keys on the granite countertop. "I put you close to the front desk if you need anything else. I'll be here until eleven." She leans forward, her blue eyes batting seductively and her pink tongue peeking out to lick her thin lips.

Normally I'd invite her to my room and give her what she wants, but the thought of fucking yet another random, desperate woman isn't appealing to me tonight. Maybe it's the hot Nevada air. My mind has been fucked up from the moment I landed and discovered my best friends were banishing me to *The Hills Have Eyes* county. Grabbing the keys and handle of my suitcase, I grunt a quick "Thanks" before taking off through the double doors she pointed to and heading out in search of room 107.

Staying in a hotel isn't ideal, and I sure as fuck wouldn't have selected one that is so fucking far away from Las Vegas. I want to stay in Vegas with the rest of my band mates, but they feel it'll be best if I stay in the small town of Loganville. Apparently I'm less likely to be recognized and less likely to be tempted.

I've been to Vegas enough times that I know where to go to get my next fix. But in Loganville, I don't know anyone. I'm pretty sure the entire town is a retirement village based on the internet search I performed on the drive.

This town doesn't even have a movie theater, for crying out loud.

Not that I go to the movies, but that shows how small this town is.

What the fuck have I gotten myself into?

The girl at the front desk appeared young enough to know who I am, but I don't think she recognized me. I just think she found me attractive and hoped I'd show her some attention. I probably disappointed her.

I'm good at that.

The moment I get to the room, I'm thankful it's clean. Tossing the keys on the nightstand, I leave my luggage in the middle of the room and flop on the bed, pulling my phone from my pocket, instantly calling Adam.

He answers on the fourth ring. "Hey, man. Did you make it in okay?"

"Fuck this town. I'm so far away from everyone out here." I huff, pinching the bridge of my nose. "What if coming here was a bad idea?" I've never felt like I belonged anywhere. Never felt like I belonged in New York, even though that's where I was born and raised. Didn't feel like I belonged in Seattle while living there with my ex-wife. Now I'm in Nevada, and even though it's only day one, I still don't feel like I belong.

Will I ever find my place in this world?

That's why I love touring. Different cities every night. Never having to figure out where I belong because it doesn't matter since the cities I visit are temporary.

For all thirty-one years of my life, I've been lost, floating through life without a place to call home. Perhaps a part of me prefers it that way. I'm not good at being tied down.

Adam's chuckle breaks me away from my inner pity party. "Quit complaining like a little bitch. Get some beauty sleep, eat, and the town will look better in the morning. We all need time to adjust." I scoff. "Easy for you to say. You have Damon and Cole there to get through this change." I'm aware of how whiny I'm acting, but I don't care. I thought I'd have support around me while I struggle to remain sober.

"Get unpacked and try to relax. Come to Vegas in a couple of days to see us, or we'll come to you. We're not that far apart, Dec."

Maybe it's the fact I haven't been this far away from any of my support team in a while that has me on edge.

Or maybe it's the fact I desperately need a drink.

Sighing, I suck it up. "Yeah, you're right. I think I'm just tired and will feel better after I get some sleep. Night, bro."

"Night, man. Let's talk tomorrow."

Ending the call, I toss my phone next to me on the bed and roll onto my back. After a few deep breaths, I force myself to get up and unpack my toiletries before jumping into the shower to wash the long day of travel off my skin.

Two months.

I can do this.

All I have to do is remain sober and write new songs.

I can do this.

FIVE

Andy

I'VE SPENT ALL TWENTY-ONE YEARS OF MY LIFE LOVING MY MOTHER more than she's ever loved me. I like to think she cares for me in her own way, but getting high has always been her priority.

Pills.

Meth.

Heroine.

It doesn't matter; she doesn't discriminate.

She's spent the last twenty-one years blaming her parents for the person she is. She said her battle with addiction began when my grandpa died. She blames him for dying. How dare he have the audacity to get pneumonia and die at sixty-seven?!

Everyone is at fault for her life being the way it is—everyone except her.

She blames my father for leaving her while she was pregnant, making her raise a child all by herself. Sometimes she'll claim that's when her addiction started. After I was born, she was stressed having to take care of a child while still living at home and working part time at a gas station.

When in reality, her addiction began long before that.

Long before I was born.

I've always heard the stories about the person she was prior to my birth, back when I was still a sperm in my dead-beat dad's ball sack.

I wish I could've met that person. The person she was before life got to her.

I've seen pictures, and she was beautiful. Lucious, long pin-straight chestnut colored hair and bright-blue eyes that don't match mine. She has her daddy's eyes, and I have mine. Every time I look in the mirror, I see him. The man who gave my mother a choice. Get an abortion and stay together or have a baby and be a single mother.

Obviously, I'm certain one can guess which option she chose.

Through years of drug abuse, she's lost her youth and beauty. Her hair is shoulder length, thin, and often kept in a low bun at the nape of her neck. She keeps it short because she says it's too hot. That's a lie; it's because her hair is so thin it's see-through.

I think it's also because she's tired of cleaning the vomit out of it during the one week a month she's forced to be sober. That last week of the month, before the first when her debit card will receive her monthly government deposit and she'll be able to purchase more drugs.

Truth is, I don't know when my mother's addiction began, but I know the only way it'll end is when she overdoses and I have to bury her.

When my mother is six-feet under, that'll be the only way to end her addiction.

I've always wondered how a mother could look at their precious innocent child and choose drugs over them.

While I was in my filthy crib crying for her while wearing my two-day-old diaper full of shit that was ready to explode, she was busy in the bedroom with her newest boyfriend of the night, sucking him off in exchange for her best friend, Crystal. Crystal meth.

Thank fucking God my grandparents chose that day for a visit and rescued my two-year-old self. Grandpa gave me a bath in our brown-stained bathtub while grandma tried to talk some sense into my mother and make her realize how terrible she was —and how poorly cared for I was.

Mom didn't care. She let my grandparents take me, and I'll forever be grateful for that. A week later, she was evicted and moved in with us.

Unfortunately, grandpa died too soon, and grandma missed him so much that she followed him a few years later.

Even though my mother lived with us, she was more my sister rather than my parent. She was absent. I was constantly begging for her attention, and always coming up short because the only thing that was ever important enough to her to warrant her attention was her precious pipe.

You'd think that a woman that was never supposed to have children would be the greatest fucking mom ever. I'm a miracle, after all. Not only was my mom told by multiple doctors that she'd never be able to conceive, but when I was born, I wasn't breathing. The cord had been wrapped around my neck, and I was blue. The doctors were ready to call my time of death when my grandma grabbed my cold blue hand, said a prayer, and I suddenly squeezed her finger.

That's why grandma always called me her "little miracle."

I know what happened because it's all on video. One of Mom's best friends recorded the entire thing. Proof that I'm a true fucking miracle.

I was fourteen when grandma died, and the only home I'd ever known was sold. Mom and I were forced to the streets with nothing more than a few dollars in our pockets from the sale of my beloved camera, and the boxes of things we could fit in our trunk. A week later, I'd managed to find us an apartment, no thanks to Mom. I'd sold anything of mine with any value to afford it. Mom was an only child, so I didn't have any aunts or uncles who could take me. I was fourteen, living with a drug addicted stranger.

A stranger who I am now desperately needing help from

because I have no other choice until my new apartment is ready to move in on Sunday morning.

I had the perfect place. A basement apartment that I'd been renting for five years from a retired widow who spent her free time babysitting children of women around the neighborhood who couldn't afford daycare.

Like I said, I had the perfect spot.

Unfortunately, she passed away, and her asshole of a son served me an eviction notice that same day, saying he needed to sell the house immediately.

Damnit, Linda Baker. Why'd you have to die?

Thank fuck, I'd been able to find a new apartment quickly, but it's not available until Sunday.

So, here I am. Standing on the doorstep of my mother's faded, yellow trailer, looking over my shoulder to watch my back every two seconds while I'm here in this sketchy ass trailer park.

"Can we stay with you for the weekend? We'll be gone Sunday," I say, the words like acid in my throat.

My mother sits on the porch in her stained recliner, a cigarette hanging from the side of her mouth, her eyes never leaving mine.

She's unable to hide her amusement, and I know she loves seeing me so desperate that I'm coming to her for help for once.

If I had other options, I wouldn't be here, but I used all my money to put down a deposit and first and last month's rent, leaving me broke until my next payday.

"Well? Can we stay here?" I ask again when she doesn't make an attempt to answer, instead staring at me with a smug look of satisfaction.

She blinks, looking away from me long enough to put her cigarette out in the ashtray beside her chair.

"You know you can." Using the back of her hand, she wipes away the beads of sweat that line her forehead thanks to the

Nevada heat. "I don't understand why you bothered getting another apartment when you could've just moved in here."

Of course she doesn't understand my reasons for not wanting to live with her again. Especially now. In her eyes, she's perfect and does nothing wrong. If you ask her, she'll tell you she was the best mother, and that she did anything and everything she could to support her daughter on her own. It's always everyone else around her that has the problems.

It's my fault for having a problem with her doing drugs.

It's my fault for having a problem with all the sketchy men she brought around when I was younger. I should've been okay with registered sex offenders sleeping in the room next to mine, because she was only trying to pay rent by renting out the room. Every night I slept with a knife under my pillow and a chair in front of the door, the back lodged under the doorknob.

Each time I saw movement beneath my door, I'd hold my breath, watching the handle shake, too afraid to move. I wouldn't breathe until the shadows disappeared, promising to return.

It's my fault we don't have your typical mother/daughter relationship.

Nothing will ever be her fault, because Diane Harris is fucking perfect.

It's been years since I lived here in this trailer with her. I moved out the first chance I could when I was sixteen, and I haven't looked back since. Any time I've seen her, it's been out in public or at my house during the times she's dropped by unannounced to ask for money.

I don't come here anymore to the trashy trailer that haunts my dreams and contains memories of my upbringing that I'd rather forget.

Under her roof, I was alone. I was busy parenting myself and working full time while she was the loudmouth stranger in the room next door, locked inside with her friends while they got high. She never even noticed that I'd dropped out of school in order to work two jobs.

Diane's blue eyes widen. "Where's Maxie?" she asks. I've been here for twenty minutes, and she's just now realizing that my daughter isn't with me. "Did you leave her in that fancy car of yours?" She squints, looking toward the driveway where I parked my gray 2007 Nissan Pathfinder.

My car is far from fancy. The miles are high, the tires are bald, the AC barely works, the transmission slips, and I'm past due for an oil change. Despite it all, it gets me where I need to go while I save for the repairs.

Actually, car repairs are the last thing on my mind. After paying rent each month, I have little left over. What I have left goes toward groceries, utilities, and anything else Max needs.

"No, Diane. I didn't leave my daughter in the hot car. She's at school." I roll my eyes. More stress piles on my shoulders at the reminder that today is Max's last day of school. Soon, I'll have to pay for childcare. Another expense I'll need to budget for during the summer break.

"Can't blame me for asking. I left you in the car a time or two, and you turned out fine." She waves her hand in front of me, standing from her chair, her bones cracking and popping as she does.

"Yeah, how could I ever forget the time you left me in the car in the middle of summer while you went into the casino? Thank fuck someone saw me and helped get me out." I was six, and she'd placed child lock on the doors, so I wasn't able to get out. A man was walking by and spotted me. Within seconds, he was breaking the window and getting me out. I'd been red and drenched in sweat.

"Bastard broke my fucking window because of you." She scoffs, opening the front door with a creak. I choose not to respond. It'll lead to an argument because, like I said, Diane Harris is perfect and does nothing wrong.

I stand in the doorway, scrunching my nose at the smell of sweat, mold, and mildew that assaults me.

"We'll be over around seven. I still have some packing to do," I say, shoving my hand in the back pocket of my shorts, pulling out my car keys.

"Fine. I'll have dinner ready."

Without another word, I pull the door closed and rush down the steps, going toward my SUV. Unlocking it, I climb behind the wheel and start it, wiping away the sweat from my forehead.

I fucking hate the idea of us having to stay here until Sunday, but I don't have any other options. I have no friends or any other family. My mom is my only option, and for my daughter, I'm willing to bite my tongue if it means a roof over her head. I'll be by her side the entire time, and we'll be okay as long as we remain in my old bedroom.

For my daughter, I'll put my feelings aside for the weekend to ensure she has a warm bed to sleep in.

Unlike Diane, I'd do anything for my child.

♪♪♪♪♪♪

AFTER PACKING THE REST OF OUR BASEMENT APARTMENT, MAX AND I make a trip to her favorite fast-food place for dinner and bring it back home, wanting to enjoy one last meal in the only home she's ever known.

Mom said she was going to cook dinner, but I'm not willing to eat her food. Knowing her, she'll bitch and complain and charge me for anything that I eat, even when she offers it. Plus, I don't trust her cooking. She acts like she's a five-star chef when in reality, eating out of a dumpster would be better. Not that she cooked often. My diet mostly consisted of frozen meals, Ramen, and anything else from the freezer section at the dollar store.

Have you ever had chicken from the Dollar Store? I wouldn't recommend it, but sometimes you have to do what you have to do. Even if that means sticking the package of frozen chicken breast under your shirt and walking out.

Luckily for me, George, Linda's asshole son, agreed to let me keep my stuff here until Sunday. I had nowhere else to store it, and I refused to take it to my mother's trailer, even though she offered her storage shed to me.

I had hoped we could stay here until Sunday, but George took our keys and said the power will be disconnected come morning.

Sunday morning, I'm supposed to meet him here, and he's going to unlock the basement so I can move all my stuff out, and then I'm getting my security deposit back.

So, that's something to look forward to.

I already plan to use that two grand to buy furniture for my new apartment, since the furniture in the basement were items that Linda had let us use while we lived here.

We may be getting a new apartment, but we're starting over. It's not like I'm not used to it. Sleeping in a bed has always been rare for me. There were many times I had to sleep on the floor because we had to leave my bed behind during one of our many moves. Before the trailer, we were getting evicted a lot thanks to Mom's constant parties, but when I was fifteen, Mom heard about this trailer park from a friend and we moved in.

I'm lost in thought, tearing apart my chicken nuggets when my phone rings, interrupting the cartoon that Max is watching.

My sneaky girl tries to swipe the call away, but I catch her eyes before she's able to ignore the call.

With an eyeroll and huff of annoyance, my sassy five-year-old slides my phone over to me.

Checking the caller ID, I click the green accept button and bring the phone to my ear. "Hi, Maggie."

"Hey, boss," Maggie says, coughing into the phone. "I'm sorry to bother you at the last minute, but I won't be able to work tonight. I'm not feeling any better."

I sigh, closing my eyes and pinching the bridge of my nose. Fuck.

Just what I fucking need is someone calling off work when I already have a shit ton to deal with right now. "Did you find someone to cover your shift?" I already know the answer, but I ask anyway.

If she had someone to cover her, she would've sent me a text to tell me. She's calling, which means I'm the lucky one that'll have to cover for her.

"No one is available. Toby covered it last night, and he can't cover it again."

Great. I took today off to pack since I have to work tomorrow morning, but now that Maggie is unable to work her graveyard shift, it means I'll be working a double.

Fan-fucking-tastic.

I shouldn't complain because I need all the hours I can get, but it's hard to do things on a moment's notice when you're a single mom.

"Okay. I'll cover it. Feel better."

"Thanks, boss. You're the best!" Before Maggie hangs up, I swear I hear giggling in the background. I'm willing to bet she's not even sick. She's so unreliable, but when she does show up for work, she's the best employee.

Setting my phone on the floor beside my box of nuggets, I look at Max. "Baby, mommy has to work tonight."

Excitement fills her brown eyes. "Can I come?" My baby girl loves going to work with me.

"No, baby. You'll go to grandma's and sleep, and I'll be there to take you to school in the morning." Without responding, she takes my phone from my hand, unlocks it, and returns to watching her show.

Great. I'm going to have to leave her alone with my mom overnight. The thought makes my stomach ache.

It's times like this I wish I wasn't doing this whole *parenting* thing alone.

Being a parent is hard enough when you have a partner, but doing it alone makes it a dozen times harder.

"Eat up, kiddo. We're going to grandma's."

SIX

Andy

"MOMMY HOW LONG ARE WE STAYING AT GRANDMA'S HOUSE?" MAX asks. Her big, innocent brown eyes stare at me, a frown on her lips. She hates being around my mom as much as I do, but there's nowhere else for her to go, and I can't have her with me at work for sixteen hours.

On the drive over, I called into work to see if there were any rooms available, but our small hotel is completely sold out, which I should've known. Besides, even with my employee discount, the rooms are too expensive.

"Only for the weekend, baby. We get to move into our new place on Sunday." Her eyes light up at the mention of our new apartment. My girl loved our previous apartment, but it was a studio, so we had to share the small space.

Our new apartment has two bedrooms, and Max has been looking forward to finally having her own room. She's slept with me since the day I brought her home from the hospital, so I'm not sure how I feel about her being away from me.

"Do you pinky promise I can get a princess bed?" she asks, holding up her tiny pinky to me. The moment she found out she'd be getting her own room, she'd been asking me for the four-poster canopy bed she saw in a furniture magazine we got in the mail.

I may not have a lot of money, but I make sure my baby is well taken care of and has everything I never had.

Since we've always slept together in my bed, she's never had her own. Now that she'll be getting her own room, I've been saving to buy her a bed, and it may not be perfect, but I'll find a cheap canopy and make her the best princess bed. I can do anything on a budget.

"I promise." I loop my pinky with hers, an easy smile spreading across my face.

"You're the best mommy ever!" she shouts, pure happiness radiating from her. "I will tell all my friends at school that I'm going to have the *bestest* bed in the world."

Smiling down at her, I brush an escaped curl from her hair and tuck it back into her powder-pink silk bonnet. I don't know why I bother putting a bonnet on her, because with the crazy way she sleeps, it always comes off during the night, but I'm hopeful it'll stay on so that her curls aren't too wild in the morning. I know my little diva only likes to wear one because I do.

Everything I do, she has to do.

My beautiful girl is the perfect image of me. Sometimes looking at her feels like I'm looking at an image of myself at her age and it makes my heart hurt, because how could my mother look at that sweet face and choose to turn away and get high? I'll never understand it.

Max has my wild, brown curly hair, my big, rounded brown eyes, and full, pouty lips. She didn't get her small button nose, round face, and deep dimples from me. Her complexion is also darker than mine. I'm biracial, half Black and half white. My skin is more caramel while hers is more of a deep bronze.

Sometimes, I hate myself for being so promiscuous and not knowing exactly who her father is. One day she'll ask and be old enough to know the truth. And I'll have to tell her.

My baby girl is gorgeous, and when she smiles and I see her

dimples, my heart aches because of how perfect she is. She's everything good in my life. I may have been a wild teenager, desperate for the attention of men, but I wouldn't change anything because one of those men I freely gave myself to, gave me my daughter.

I'll never regret her, or the fact I got pregnant at sixteen.

"Get some sleep, sweetie. Mommy has to go to work now." I give her the brown teddy bear that I bought the day I found out I was pregnant. She hugs it to her chest, and I pull the blankets over her small body and tuck her into the small twin bed that I used to sleep in. I brought our own bedding here because I didn't trust the sheets Diane provided. It's bad enough that I'm leaving my daughter here overnight.

"Do you know how much I love you?" I ask, kneeling beside the bed once I have her as snug as a bug in a rug.

Her face lights up. "With all your big fat purple heart."

"That's right." Leaning forward, I press a kiss to her forehead. "Go to sleep, baby. I'll see you in the morning." I stand and turn on the lamp beside the bed and walk toward the door, turning the overhead light off.

"Goodnight Mommy, I love you so, so, *so* much."

"I love you baby, sweet dreams." Quietly closing the door, I step into the hallway, taking in a deep breath to calm myself.

God, I hate having to leave her alone. Leaving her with my mother of all people.

She's never been very good at hiding her addiction—or when she's high. I've always been able to tell, which is why I came to her face-to-face this afternoon rather than calling. I needed to look into her eyes to know what kind of day she was having. Needed to know if she was sober and had people over.

Diane has been calling me and claiming she's sober, but she's said that many times before. The one week a month she was sober, she'd cry to me, begging me to give her another chance at being my mother, promising she was going to remain sober to be the parent I deserve. Promise after promise was made, yet every first of the month, without fail, she'd use her social security check to purchase drugs. All those promises meant nothing.

I learned a long time ago that words are useless. A person can say anything they want, but unless they have the actions to back it up, they're simply wasting air by speaking.

That's why I don't trust anyone. The only person I can rely on is myself.

I cannot count the times I've found Diane's glass pipe laying around or seen her passed out with a needle still sticking out of her arm because she got so fucking high that she wasn't even able to pull it out before passing out.

She never cared about putting her own child in those situations, but she's never been that way toward her granddaughter. Any time she knows Max is going to be around she cleans herself up and is always sober. Not that she spends much alone time with my daughter. In fact, this is only going to be the second time I've ever allowed Max to stay over.

The first time was when I was running late from work because I got stuck covering a shift and needed her to get Max from school until I could get home. I was in a panic the entire time, fearing the worst.

When I called her for help, I was desperate. I hate asking for help.

To my surprise, when I arrived, Max was thrilled to have had time with her only family member, and she even showed me her pink fingernails that Diane painted for her.

She never would've done that for me.

I'm glad she treats Max better than she ever has me.

"Don't ya need to get to work?" The sound of Diane's voice snaps me away from my thoughts, and I realize that I'm still standing outside of my old bedroom, my hand gripping the door handle.

"Are you sure you're okay to watch her overnight?"

She rolls her eyes. "Yes, you perfect princess. I'm capable of taking care of my sleeping granddaughter."

I ignore her insult. "And you're sure that no one is coming over tonight?" My anxiety is rising. My heart is pounding. I can't do this. I can't leave my baby here in the same bed where I used to lay in fear watching the door.

For a small moment, I think Diane's going to say something to answer my question and ease my worry, but her eyes drift off and that's when I know she's full of shit.

She's never able to look at me when she's ready to lie.

I should've known better than to count on her. Even for a single fucking night.

"Fuck this." Turning my back, I return to the bedroom and instantly lock eyes with my girl who is lying there wide-eyed, hugging her teddy bear, looking every bit as innocent and pure as she is.

The pain in my chest intensifies.

"Mommy?" She sits up, love and happiness filling her eyes at the sight of me.

"Damnit, Andy. Leave her be. She's fine here tonight." I ignore my mother, grab Max's backpack, and slip one of the straps over my shoulder.

"Put your shoes on, baby. You're coming with me to work." I kneel down to help Max into her pink fluffy slippers.

Clapping her hands, Max cheers. "Yay! I love going to work with you, Mommy."

Once her shoes are on, I pick her up and leave the trailer and my shit-talking mother behind.

I'll never forgive myself for almost leaving my child there.

Tears sting my eyes at the thought of my child ever having to be in the same situations as me.

The moment I pull into the parking lot, I'm rushing to get Max from her car seat in the backseat along with her backpack. I'm fifteen minutes late, and Lila has already been blowing my phone up with texts asking when she's going to be relieved of her front desk duty.

I hadn't planned on responding, but by her fifth text I had to, so I told her I'd be covering and was on my way.

She sent three more texts after that.

It's fifteen fucking minutes.

Carrying Max in my arms, I rush into the lobby, sweat beading on my forehead from the Nevada heat.

Good thing I'd taken the time to apply more deodorant while in the car.

Stepping into the hotel lobby, the AC instantly cools me down, causing a shiver to race down my spine from the chill.

Lila must have turned it down, because it's never this cool in here. It feels good, but I know the owners will complain so I make a mental note to change the thermostat as soon as I can.

Seeing me, Lila instantly perks up. "Hey, boss. What happened to Maggie?" I don't answer her until I make my way into the back office and set Max down on the chair at the desk.

"She called in." Setting down the pink backpack on top of the desk, I unzip it and bring out Max's snacks and blanket, setting them in front of her and wrapping her in the blanket.

My sleepy girl rubs her eyes, letting out a big yawn. It's past her bedtime.

Mine, too.

I'd love nothing more than to cuddle beside my girl and go to sleep, but thanks to unreliable employees, here I am. Stuck working a double shift because no one else wanted to work.

"Thanks for staying a little bit later. You can go ahead and clock out now," I tell Lila while quickly signing into Netflix on the computer and turning on a show for Max.

Once my daughter is set up with snacks and a show, I walk through the door that places me directly behind the front desk and sign in on one of the computers, scrolling the list of guests currently staying at the hotel, hoping to find a vacant room.

"Did all reservations check in?"

"Yup! The last one checked in a couple hours ago, and I placed him in 107, which was the last room we had available."

Nodding, I turn my attention toward her. "Thanks again, Lila. Have a good night. I'll see you tomorrow."

She disappears into the back office then leaves, waving goodbye as she crosses through the lobby, heading toward the entrance.

Grabbing the white cordless phone from the counter, I slip it into my back pocket so I'll have it with me in case anyone calls, and I won't have to rush back to the front desk. Stepping back into the office where Max is still sitting, I watch her for a moment. Her small fists rub her tired eyes, a wide yawn escaping her, yet her attention is fixated on the computer screen.

"Baby girl, I'm going to go make some coffee. Do you want to come with me?" I ask, checking the security cameras to do a scan of the hotel property, my brown eyes bouncing between the different screens in front of me that are displayed on the wall.

When I don't get a response, I look over my shoulder. "Max?" Her nose scrunches, and I know she can hear me. "Max? Look at me."

With a huff and eyeroll that matches mine, my daughter finally looks at me. I'm never able to be upset with her attitude because I'm the one she gets it from.

She's my mini-me in every way.

"I'm watching my show, Mommy."

"Yes, but I asked you a question, so you need to answer me." She blinks. "Do you want to come with me into the kitchen?"

She shakes her head, causing her dark curls to bounce with the movement. She pulled her bonnet off while in the car, so I left it. Her hair will be a frizzy mess come morning anyway.

"Can I go to the snack machine?"

"Sure, baby." Grabbing my wallet that I placed in her back-pack so I wouldn't have to carry my purse, I grab some cash and place it in her outstretched, awaiting palm.

Every time she comes to work with me, she loves going to the vending machine and selecting a snack. Each time, she gets something different. She tells me it's what she wants, but I know it's because she doesn't quite understand how to select the corresponding numbers to get the exact item she wants. I've tried to help her, but she wants to do it independently, so I let her.

After checking the cameras once more, I turn to her and help her to put her shoes back on before getting her down from the chair and leading her out of the office, her small, soft hand in mine.

"Get a snack for me too, and come right back here, okay?" She nods, her smile wide as she holds one dollar in each hand.

Max skips off toward the vending machine, and I watch her go. Once I see her reach it, I walk in the opposite direction to the kitchen.

From where I stand in the dining area, I have a good view of Max, and I watch her stand on her tiptoes to reach the machine, inserting a dollar and then pressing some buttons.

A smile spreads across my lips at the sight.

She's my world. Everything I could ever ask for.

Every day I worry that I'm not good enough for her, not giving her everything that she deserves in life.

Many nights I have laid in bed, watching my baby while she slept, silent tears streaming down my face because I don't understand how my mother could turn out the way she did. How she could look at her daughter and still choose to bring the pipe to her lips or stick the needle in her vein is something I will never understand.

The trauma I have because of her shakes me to my core.

When the machine beeps, signaling the small pot is brewed, I turn my attention away from my girl long enough to reach for a cup and add French vanilla creamer and sugar to my liking before pouring in the coffee.

More liquid creamer than coffee, but I like it sweet and hate the bitter taste.

I should've brewed a larger batch, but I don't want the stomachache that'll come along with having too much coffee.

With my cup in hand, I grab a granola bar from the counter

then leave the dining room that we use for daily continental breakfast and make my way across the lobby and back toward the office.

When I glance outside, I no longer see Max, so I assume she's back in the office.

"Alright, baby, what snack did you get for mommy?" I ask, pushing the office door open, my eyes landing on an empty room.

"Max?" I call out, setting the Styrofoam coffee cup and granola bar on the desk where she was sitting. Looking around, I continue calling her name, my anxiety rising the longer I go without hearing her voice.

Leaving the office, I run to the bathrooms to check in there. Maybe she had to go potty. Usually, whenever she has to, she asks me to go with her, which is why I'm not surprised when I find all the bathroom stalls empty.

"Max? Baby?!" I call out, rushing through the side lobby doors that'll take me to the vending machine where Max had been only moments ago.

Only there's no sign of her.

Why the fuck didn't I go with her?

I'm so fucking stupid.

SEVEN

Declan

IT'S BEEN A FEW HOURS SINCE I CHECKED INTO MY HOTEL ROOM, AND although it's after midnight, I'm too fucking wired to sleep.

Not like I ever go to sleep this early anyway.

I had hoped the shower would tire me out and relax me enough to sleep, but all I ended up doing was lying in bed for nearly an hour, staring at the ceiling.

All I want is a fucking cigarette. My skin is crawling, begging me for a taste of nicotine. It's been nearly twenty-four hours since I've had a smoke, and if I don't have one now, I might not be able to relax for the rest of the night.

What I really need is a cold drink and to slip inside of a warm pussy.

Giving into the urge, I sit up in the bed, push the covers off my body, drop my feet to the pale-pink carpet, and stand. Quickly pulling on a T-shirt, sweats, and shoes, I grab my pack of Marlboros from the nightstand along with a room key and exit the room.

The door slams shut behind me as I take a few steps forward, bringing a cigarette to my lips and light it, inhaling the nicotine deep into my lungs.

Just what I needed.

My eyes close, my head tilting up toward the night sky as I take a moment to enjoy the quiet night, something I'm not used to having lived in New York.

Quiet nights and a sky full of stars is nonexistent in the city.

I bring the stick back to my mouth and suck, the ember glowing in the night as the nicotine fills my lungs.

A high-pitched squeal has my eyes instantly popping open in search of the noise, suddenly on high-alert.

Great.

Just what I need is to be harassed by a screaming fan.

Hearing the noise again, I continue scanning my surroundings, my line of eyesight lowering until I land on a small figure.

A child.

Instantly looking around for the girl's parents, I come up empty, not seeing anyone else outside aside from the two of us.

What the fuck is a little girl doing out here alone?

The little curly haired girl's brown eyes widen when I look down at her, noticing the bag of chips and candy bar she holds in her hands.

Stepping toward me, she says, "I know you!" She yells louder than necessary.

My fingers twitch with the need to continue filling my lungs, but I'm not going to smoke around a child.

"Stranger danger, kid," I mutter. Clearly she was never taught not to talk to strangers.

Tossing the cigarette to the ground, I stomp it out then lean down to pick up the butt.

The girl looks at me again before speaking. "You're not a stranger. I know you."

"But I don't know you, and I don't talk to strangers." Setting the butt on the windowsill, I cross my arms over my chest, staring down at the kid.

She mirrors me, a grin on her lips.

My heart aches at the sight. She appears to be around Luca's age when he died, maybe a little older. A painful reminder of what I lost because of my actions.

"I'm Max, so now you know me too." An unwanted grin tugs at my lips at her logic.

"Where's your parents, Max? You shouldn't be out here alone talking to a stranger."

Her brown eyes continue staring at me, her little nose scrunching up. "I told you already that I know you!" She's a persistent little thing.

Her parents may have one of my albums, and she's seen me on the cover.

Regardless, she's out here alone, and I'm still a stranger. "Where's your mom?" I repeat, looking behind her toward the lobby that I was in earlier.

"My mommy is making coffee. When you came outside, I knew it was you. I wanted to say hi."

"Hi, kid. You should get back to your mom."

"My name is Max. Say *hi, Max*," she corrects me, and I can't help the laugh that bellows from me. God damn. This kid is going to give her parents a run for their money with her attitude.

"You're right, I'm sorry. Hi, Max." I nod toward the snacks in her hands. "Looks like you've got yourself some pretty good snacks."

She nods her agreement, raising the hand with the snickers bar. "This is for my mommy. I bought it for her. Well, she gave me the money." She holds up the other hand that holds a bag of Cheetos. "This is mine."

"Nice." Shifting my weight from one foot to the other, I ask, "What room are you in? I'll walk you back. You shouldn't be out here alone." I'm aware I'm being awkward, but I'm really fucking uncomfortable. The last child I spoke to was my own, and that was the night he died. Other than that, I don't have experience with children. Especially talkative little girls outside all alone.

69

Her face lights up with a mischievous smile. "I'm not alone. I'm out here with my new best friend."

She reminds me so much of Luca that it pains me to see her innocent smile and wide eyes staring up at me as if seeing me has made her entire night. She's just a child that doesn't deserve me being rude to her.

That's one thing I always loved about Luca.

His innocence.

Children have a happy way of viewing the world because they're too young to be jaded, or to understand how fucked up the world is. They're happy, and all it takes is a simple gesture for them to look at you like you hung the moon.

Squatting down until I'm closer to her height, I hold out my hand to her. "Miss Max, it was great to meet you, but you should be getting back to your mom. She must be waiting for that candy bar." Without hesitation, she shifts the candy bar from one hand to the other and places her small hand in mine, a blush coloring her bronze cheeks.

"I am your biggest fan, Mister Declan." She bounces from one foot to the other, excitement radiating off her. "Your biggest fan!" I silently judge her parents for allowing their child to listen to my music because it is certainly *not* child friendly.

What the fuck is wrong with her mother? Better yet, where the fuck is her mother?

My silent question is answered when I hear a feminine voice yelling, "Max!"

The girl lets go of my hand and looks over her shoulder, her lips twitching at the sound of her name. Her small shoulders curling in as her pouty bottom lip pokes out, knowing she's been caught doing something she's not supposed to be doing.

I know that look. It's the look of someone about to get in trouble because she is not supposed to be out here talking to a stranger.

The voice comes closer, and I look up, my dark eyes landing on the frantic figure that's quickly approaching us.

The woman's dark eyes narrow into slits. Sure, she probably means for it to be intimidating, but I glare right back because why the fuck wasn't she watching this child?

Based on how young and soft her features are, I'm assuming she's Max's older sister that was supposed to be babysitting.

"Max!" the woman hisses, making the girl look between the two of us as I stand to my full height. "What do you think you're doing?" She grabs her hand, tugging her behind her back protectively.

"I'm sorry, Mommy. I was with my new friend," Max defends, batting her eyes as she looks up at her mother.

Hold up.

Mother?

There's no fucking way this is Max's mom.

I don't believe it, and I voice it, "You're her mother?"

She continues glaring at me, as if I'm the one who did something wrong when she's the one who left her child unattended. "Yes, I am."

I shove my hands into the pockets of my black sweats, my eyes roaming freely over her appearance without caring if she notices or not.

I take in her appearance, from the boring black dress pants that are suffocating her thick thighs, all the way to the white cardigan that hangs loosely off her thick figure, hiding the squishy curves I know I'd find underneath.

It's hot as fuck, so I know she must be sweating like crazy in the heavy cardigan, despite having the sleeves bunched up to her elbows.

The woman's dark, curly hair is untamed and semi-frizzy, as if she hasn't washed it in a few days. Her honey-brown skin is lighter than her daughter's, but equally as beautiful. It's soft and blemish free, and strangely enough, I want to reach out and run a finger along the softness.

Who the fuck thinks shit like that?

My eyes travel from her cleavage to her face, memorizing her small nose, plump lips, soft jaw, and those angry, dark eyes that are so full of hurt.

When you're in pain, it becomes something you easily notice in others.

She wears her pain like a shield of armor, that much is obvious.

Her beauty is ethereal, but I get the sense she doesn't know it. I wonder if she's ever been truly worshiped.

My cock stirs at the thought of showing her how beautiful she is.

She's dumb as fuck for leaving her child alone, but beautiful nonetheless.

"Mommy, I got your candy bar. Eat it so you won't be upset." Max breaks our silent standoff, offering the Snickers bar to her mother.

A pink blush colors her cheeks, likely from embarrassment. Her hands tug at the bottom of her awful cardigan to adjust it.

For an unknown reason, I feel the need to ease the embarrassment from her, even if I do think she's an idiot for allowing her child to be outside alone. "That's my favorite candy, too." She stares at me like I'm stupid, and she can't believe I just said that.

Her daughter may be a fan of mine, but it's clear that her mother isn't.

"Here, take it." She shoves the candy at my chest, a chuckle erupting from me at her pissy attitude. "Max, let's go." She tugs her away, but the girl remains rooted in place.

"Alright, well, I'm glad you decided to come looking for your child. It's not smart allowing her to be out here alone." Turning my attention away from her, I look down at the girl behind her, winking when her eyes meet mine. "Goodnight, Max." Without waiting for a response from either of them, I turn and walk back to my room, hoping like hell I'll be able to get some sleep and that irritating woman will be checked out come morning.

"Goodnight, new best friend!" Max calls out to my retreating back, a smile tugging at my lips from her words.

Back in my hotel room, I toss the candy bar on the nightstand and shed my clothes before climbing under the covers.

With my eyes closed, I slip my hand down to my hard cock, replaying the memory of a scowling face and thick ass thighs as I jerk off.

Fuck. Me.

EIGHT

Andy

WHAT THE FUCK JUST HAPPENED?

My eye twitches, annoyance heating my skin.

Who the fuck does that asshole think he is talking to me like that about my child? I'm aware it was shitty to let Max go to the vending machine alone, but I'd made sure I could see her. She was in my line of sight most of the time, except for the few seconds I turned away to pour creamer in my cup. That must've been when she saw him and wandered off.

It's impossible to watch your kid 24/7, no matter how much you try.

Two seconds. I looked away for two seconds.

A lot can happen in two seconds.

Leave it to my social butterfly child to find the biggest asshole around and strike up a conversation.

The moment I laid eyes on the tall, dark-haired, tattooed covered man who literally oozes sex from his pores, I knew exactly who he was. But you'll never get me to admit it.

Especially to him.

I'll never admit how many nights I've cried myself to sleep with his voice flowing through my earphones, as if he were speaking directly to me through his lyrics. Or the fact his songs resonate with me so much that just hearing them gives me chills and is enough to make me choke up.

Declan Valentine writes music that is raw and filled with so much pain. In his lyrics, he's vulnerable, and just as fucked-up as I am.

I'll never forget the first time I heard his voice.

I was fourteen, radio playing in the background, crying alone on my bedroom floor, a bottle of sleeping pills in one hand and a vodka-filled water bottle in the other. Black mascara coated tears were streaking down my face, and all I wanted was for my life to end. I was tired of existing. I wanted to disappear. To be free.

I'd just swallowed the pills when the lyrics to his song, "It's Over Now" filled my ears for the first time.

His smoky, hauntingly beautiful voice rang out, filling the silence of my room and providing me with a comfort I hadn't known was possible.

The next day, I was a little less pissed at the world when I woke up. I'd slept most of the day away, and once I came to, I spent two days puking my guts out.

Guess that's what I get.

Attempted suicide. Just another thing that makes me even more fucked-up than I already am.

Then again, all I did was overdose on sleeping pills I'd bought from Walmart because I hadn't wanted to feel physical pain. So, how hard did I actually try?

Maybe a part of me wasn't ready to die.

Declan's music speaks to me. It's as if his lyrics were written for me. As if we're the same, and he understands my trauma.

Hearing him makes me feel a little less alone.

Although I love his music, I don't like him as a person. I'm aware the media is full of shit, but I've yet to see one positive thing reported about him.

He's a manipulative, womanizing player with a drug problem.

And now he's here... at my hotel.

The first thing I do once I'm behind the desk, safe away from deep brown eyes that caused my heart to skip a beat, is check the name associated with the room I'd seen Declan go into.

The room is registered to Benjamin James.

A quick internet search of the name leads me to finding out that he is the manager for Riot, Declan's band. The room is booked under his manager's name.

My shoulders slump a little at that fact.

Obviously, Declan wouldn't use his name, but part of me wanted to see his name typed out in black and white on the computer screen. That way I know it's real.

As I'm typing, hoping to find out the reason he's here, Max comes to stand in the doorway. She knows she's not allowed to be directly behind the desk. "Mommy, I'm tired." She rubs her eyes with her small fists, her bottom lip pouty and sticking out.

Locking the screen, I turn away from the computer and turn my attention toward my daughter. "Come on, baby. Let's get you set up for bed." I follow her back into the office and begin arranging a space for her to sleep.

I know we can't go back to my mom's house, and I hate myself for being willing. Tomorrow, I'll figure out something else, but for tonight, she'll be fine.

Taking two office chairs, I position them in front of each other and spread a blanket out and add a pillow. Picking up Max, I place her on the chairs and help her scoot down, holding onto the chairs so they don't slip away.

Once she's in a comfortable position, I use her pink blanket that I brought with us and cover her up, tucking her in. I would put her bonnet back on, but her curly hair is already wild and there's no hope. I'll have no choice but to wet it to tame it come morning.

"Sweet dreams, baby girl." Kissing her cheek, I resume playing the show on the computer then flip the office lights off.

"Night, Mommy." She sighs, her eyelids heavy and fluttering.

Leaving her be, I return to the front desk, just as the phone rings. Remembering I have the cordless phone still on me, I pull it from my pocket and check the screen before answering, chills shooting down my spine at the sight of the room number that's calling on the screen.

Gulping, I answer the phone. "Front desk."

That deep voice from earlier fills my ears. "Can I get four pillows?" God, his voice has me acting like a bitch in heat.

I may not like him, but I'm not afraid to admit that his voice is sexy as fuck, and I'll be thinking about it next time I have enough privacy to stick my hand between my legs.

Clearing my throat before I begin panting into the phone, I quickly agree, telling him I'll be there soon.

After locking a sleeping Max in the office, I rush to the laundry room to gather four pillows before taking them to room 107.

Holding two pillows under each arm, I hesitate for a moment before kicking my foot against the thick door with a little more force than necessary.

The door swings open, revealing a shirtless Declan standing in the doorway, black briefs sitting low on his hips as if he was in a hurry to put them on and didn't have enough time to pull them all the way up.

Good fucking lord.

This man radiates sexual energy, and the worst part is he knows it. I'm willing to bet he rarely bothers looking in a mirror, because he's that attractive and doesn't need to pick himself apart like I do.

Taken by surprise, my wide eyes shamelessly roam over his bare chest, taking in the defined muscles and tattoos that cover his tan skin. The intricate artwork decorates his neck and continues down both arms, ending at his hands. His tight toned stomach is free from ink, but small doodle like art decorates his chest.

The veins in his arms become prominent when he flexes, his arms hanging by his side while his fists clench and unclench. I knew his hands were inked, but up close, I'm able to make out the letters that are tattooed across his right knuckles in bold black letters.

RIOT.

Slowly, my eyes make their way to his face to find a smirk on his pink lips that tells me he knows damn good and well I was checking him out.

What can I say? It's been a while since I've had any action, and the guys I've fucked were never half as attractive as *the* Declan fucking Valentine.

I'm sure most women would fawn over the fact they met a famous musician, but for me, I couldn't care less. I can separate the art from the artist.

He wipes the side of his mouth, motioning for me to do the same, and stupidly I fucking do.

Great. Not only had he caught me dazed and ogling him, but he made it known that I was nearly drooling over him.

Asshole.

"So, you work here?" he says, breaking the silence, and just like that, I'm back to reality and the spell is broken.

I look him in the eye when I speak. "No, I'm wearing this uniform and bringing you pillows for fun." I deadpan, my eyes narrowing into a glare.

"You have a smart fucking mouth. But I'm sure I'm not the first person to tell you that." He's not.

One thing I know how to do is run my mouth. It's something you learn pretty quickly in order to defend yourself when your drugged out mother was constantly bringing around her junkie friends. I've always known how to stand up for myself, and I've never been afraid to do it. She would never protect me, so I had to learn to protect myself.

Declan steps aside and waves me into the room. "You can put those on the bed." With a roll of my eyes because clearly, he's too good to take the pillows, I step inside the room.

I never go inside of a guest's room. Considering I work the

79

morning shift, if a stay-over guest ever needs anything, I have someone from housekeeping deliver the item. On the rare occasion I've had to deliver an extra item to them, I give it to them without ever crossing the threshold.

Yet, here I am, standing inside of Declan's room, inhaling the clean scent that lingers in the air. The smell is fresh, like a cold winter morning, and something else that I'm unable to make out, but I don't think it's his cologne. It's him.

Declan sticks his head out the door, looking around before he turns his attention on me, letting the door close behind him, "Where's Max?"

The question takes me by surprise, though I'm sure my face shows it.

He's asking about my daughter?

For a moment I think about giving him a smart-ass remark, but the look on his face is one that I can only describe as worry, so I settle for the truth.

"She's sleeping." Realizing I'm standing in his room with the door closed, still holding the pillows, I jump into action and set them on the king-sized bed then walk to the door.

Declan steps in front of it, his arms crossing over his chest, eyes pinned right at me in a glare. "And you left her alone?"

Oh, hell no.

This fucker will not intimidate me and make me feel like a shitty parent.

Mirroring his stance, I glare right back at him. He may be taller than me and a wall of muscle, but I'm not small by any means. I stand at six-feet tall, and if he wants to get smart, I can take him.

"Somebody requested pillows because the four already in their room weren't enough. Would you prefer I wake her up to bring her with me?"

"I'd prefer you watch your fucking child and don't leave her alone." Is he fucking serious right now?

Stepping closer, I raise my finger in his face. "You of all

people do not get to tell me how the fuck to parent." If I thought he was angry before, the look he's giving me now is downright murderous. I don't think he'd hurt me, but I still take a step back.

If looks could kill, my time of death would be called right here right now.

Rest In Peace, Andy Harris.

The girl who could never keep her mouth shut.

Behind the anger in his eyes, I see a hint of something soft, and that's when I realize what I said to him.

Oh, fuck.

He had a child, too.

The name tattooed across his left collarbone stares back at me, showing me how much I fucked up.

Luca.

His son's name.

I open my mouth to apologize, but before I can get any words out, Declan steps aside, grabs the handle, and yanks the door open so roughly I'm surprised the hinges remain intact.

Way to go, Andy.

"Get the fuck out," he grits out, his jaw clenched tight.

On the way out, I spot the wrapper of my Snickers bar on his nightstand. Knowing he ate the candy bar I gave him makes my stomach flutter, though I know it shouldn't. How silly.

Looking up at him, I open my mouth in another attempt to apologize, but he slams the door in my face, and I hear the lock click into place.

Great.

See what happens when you don't think before you speak?

Back in the office, I pull up a chair and sit beside Max, watching the security cameras in front of me so I can be prepared for a guest if they wander in.

My stomach rumbles, reminding me it's been a while since I've eaten.

Fuck.

I wanted that candy bar, and I gave Max my last two dollars.

My size eighteen waist says I didn't need it, but damn, I wanted it. I should've never given it to Declan, but when I saw him staring me up and down, I knew what he saw when he was looking at me and I was embarrassed.

Not that I'd ever want to be one of his groupies, but it would be nice to pretend that a man like that would ever want a girl like me.

Girls that look like me don't get guys that look like that.

Fucked up, damaged girls like me, with years of trauma to sort through, don't end up with a happy ending.

NINE

Declan

THE FIRST TIME I WATCHED MY MOTHER GET HIGH WAS WHEN I WAS five years old.

I remember sitting at the coffee table in the living room of our small apartment, watching cartoons and eating stale cereal that tasted like cardboard, but I was so hungry that I ate it anyway.

She was forgetful. Most of the time, she forgot she was a mother.

Many times, she'd forget me as she'd walk out the door, not coming home for days. I knew days had passed, because every morning when the sun came up, I'd sit in front of the window, waiting for her to remember me and return.

Once, I spent four days waiting for her. When she walked in, I was so excited to see her. Instead of acknowledging me, she went straight to her bedroom with the man she brought home, and they made noises I didn't understand at the time.

After the man left, my mother was happy and took me for ice cream.

Since that day, I learned not to be picky with food, or eat too much, because I never knew how long I needed it to last.

My mother had been sitting next to me, which I remember because it made me happy. She never noticed me, so the fact that she was sitting beside me—paying me attention—made me happy.

I remember showing her my race car that one of the men who often visited had brought me and asking if she'd play with me.

"Not now, Declan. Mommy isn't feeling well." She'd said, patting my head. I wasn't sure what was wrong with her, but I felt special because she was around me.

I remember hearing the knock at the door, and seeing her face light up when she let the man in. My young self was terrified, on the verge of tears, that she'd be leaving me again.

I hated when she left me.

Instead of going to her bedroom or walking out the front door, she and the man sat on the couch, and he smiled at me with yellow teeth as he brought the flame of his lighter to the spoon in his hand.

At the time, I hadn't understood what was going on, but I remember watching them. Watching him load the needle and give it to my mother, then I watched as she brought it to her vein.

It looked painful, but the look of instant relief that came across her pale, sweaty face was a look that stuck with me for many years.

After that day, she hadn't bothered locking me in my bedroom anymore. She didn't mind if I saw what she did, and neither did I.

I hated being in my bedroom because she'd turned the door-knob around, placing the lock on the outside. Many days, I'd wake up to discover she'd locked me inside. And since she often forgot about me, that meant she forgot to unlock the door. Being inside of my room meant there was a possibility of being trapped there for days, and my tiny bladder and hunger couldn't handle that.

Not hiding in my bedroom also meant I was privy to her drug use. I had a front row seat every time she stuck the needle in her arm.

I was twenty-seven years old the first time I stuck a needle in my vein, filling myself with the same poison that killed my mother.

I'd always told myself that I'd be better than her. Sure, I drank, smoked weed, snorted coke, swallowed whatever pills I could get, but that was okay, because in my fucked-up mind, it was better than heroin. I was better than her, because I wasn't filling my veins with that shit.

And then I killed my son.

I wanted an escape, and my dealer was out of the white powder I'd been snorting any chance I got.

He'd said, "I've got something stronger you should try." And I knew what he meant. I hadn't rejected his offer, because at that moment, the memory of my mother's pale face flashed before me, and I'd wanted the same relief she had each time she got high.

I'd handed over the cash, then went home and loaded the needle, as I'd seen my mother do many times.

The relief was instant.

I was floating.

The pain in my chest was gone.

I could breathe.

One time was all it took me to begin a new addiction.

One that consumed my life.

Consumed my mind and body, until one day I tried to let it claim my life.

That was the day Camille found me.

Needle in my arm, nonexistent pulse, blue lips.

The woman I loved and vowed to protect had to find me during an overdose. She saved my life, when I had tried to end it.

Rehab came after that, and I haven't touched the drug since.

That doesn't mean I don't miss it, or haven't used other drugs, because I do, and I have. But I can't allow myself to get low enough to the point where I'd return to it.

I can't be that person again.

It'll kill me, and right now, I'm not sure if that's what I want anymore.

For a year after Luca's death, I was ready to die. I wanted to be buried beside him, but now, as much as I miss him, I want to live.

To fight.

I may not deserve to live because of my sins, but until the devil himself collects me, I'm going to continue living.

Ever since that curly headed spitfire left my room hours ago, I've been seething, pacing back and forth in my room that I'm sure I'm running the light-colored carpet bare. My hands have been clenching and unclenching, my heart pounding, and memories racing in my fucked-up head.

Memories of my mother.

All I can think about is how I never wanted to be like her. Never wanted to be the type of parent she was. The addict she was.

Many times during the night, I contemplated finding that curly headed big mouth and giving her a piece of my fucking mind, but I tend to lash out when I'm angry, and my words have a way of wounding someone. Not that she doesn't deserve it, but therapy has taught me to remain calm when I feel triggered.

Too many times during arguments, I lashed out at Camille, and she never deserved my spiteful tongue. She'd tried to hide the tears in her emerald eyes, but I saw them every time.

Every single fucking time I said something cruel, I watched her eyes become glossy, and I hated myself even more for it. All she ever tried to do was save me from myself, but I never wanted to be saved. I'd wanted to drag her to hell with me, but she was too strong for that.

She fought back, and in the end, I lost her; it's all my fault. I'm trying to be a better person. I'm fucking trying, though some days it seems impossible, like I haven't changed a bit.

Up until a few weeks ago, I was that person.

God, help me.

Some days I wish my mother would've left me to drown in that motel room pool when I was six. It was my first time ever swimming, and I had no idea how. I'd been touching the water when I fell in. Unable to reach the bottom, I kicked my legs and screamed, my small body heavy and sinking beneath the water.

The chlorine burned my eyes as I sank, but I remember seeing my mother's cold brown eyes stare at me, disgust on her face at the sight of me. For a moment, looking at her, I thought she would let me die. I'd heard screaming, then strong arms were in the water pulling me out.

A man staying at the hotel had seen me and jumped in to save me.

That night, my mother let her boyfriend of the week beat me black and blue for making them look bad. Then, I was locked in my room for days. Without a bathroom, I was forced to relieve myself on the floor, and I cried each time.

The smell of that small, piss-filled bedroom will forever haunt me.

Even now, I have to breathe through my mouth in any bathroom.

It's been a while since I've thought about my mother or anything regarding my fucked-up childhood, but thanks to some smart-mouthed woman, I can't seem to stop.

My feet don't stop pacing until I notice sunlight peeking through the blinds, filling the room with its warm golden rays.

Great. I've been up all fucking night, and I'm not even tweaking.

My shoulders rise with my inhale and lower with my slow exhale. "Fuck it," I mumble, going toward my open suitcase on the floor.

After quickly dressing myself, I step toward the vanity to brush my teeth and wash my face, hoping that my demons aren't lurking in my dark eyes and that it's not noticeable that I've been up all night going down my haunted memory lane.

Stepping into a pair of shoes, I grab my phone, wallet, and room key before leaving. I don't bother to check my phone for any notifications, because I don't care if anyone has messaged me. I'm on a mission, and nothing will slow me down. If I stop, I might not do what I need to.

Entering the lobby, my eyes instantly land on the dining area in the corner. It's full of guests helping themselves to the continental breakfast. I'm sure the check-in girl told me about it, but to be honest, I tuned her out.

I'd hoped for room service, but I should've known that wouldn't be offered here.

Turning away from the dining area, I walk to the front desk, offering a smile to the short girl standing behind it.

"Good morning, sir. How can I help you?" she asks politely, and I take a moment to watch her eyes, seeing if I catch a hint of recognition, but thankfully, I don't.

Not surprising.

I'm sure this small town lives under a rock, and no one will know who I am. Well, except for the little girl I met last night who deemed herself my new best friend.

"Morning, I'd like to report an incident with one of your staff last night. Pretty sure she's a housekeeper." It's petty as shit to report the smart-mouthed housekeeper in hopes she gets in trouble, but fuck it.

She wasn't wrong when she told me I shouldn't be giving parenting advice. I killed my son, but somehow, I felt compelled to call her ass out for leaving her child alone.

Twice.

I never left Luca alone.

The woman behind the desk scrunches her blonde eyebrows, her mouth opens, but I cut her off before she can speak. "Is there a manager on duty I can speak with?"

Closing her mouth, she stares at me for a beat before nodding.

Her blue eyes dart behind me as she says, "Here she comes now."

Turning around, my eyes land on the feisty woman from last night. The one I'm here to report.

Her brown eyes, filled with fury, land on me, and her strides are quick thanks to her long, thick legs, still covered in those hideous black pants.

Great.

Fixing her with a glare, I look down, noticing the smiling face of the little girl walking beside her.

At the sight of me, she drops her mother's hand and comes running over. "Declan!" she screeches, the excitement evident in her voice. She barrels toward me as if she wants to throw herself in my arms, but as she gets closer, uncertainty comes over her and she holds herself back, nearly tripping over her small feet.

"What are you doing here?" she asks, instantly following up with another question before I have a chance to speak. "Are you here to see me?!" Her big eyes are full of hope, her small fingers intertwining as she tucks them under her chin, looking up at me as if I'm someone important.

It's such an innocent look that nearly knocks me to my ass.

Her mother reaches us and stands behind Max, but her eyes are locked on me.

"Hey, boss," the woman behind the counter cuts in. "This gentleman asked for you. Something about an incident regarding housekeeping last night."

Boss? What the fuck.

My head snaps up at that, my attention momentarily stolen from Max.

Why the fuck did she call her boss?

As if seeing the question on my face, Max's mom raises a perfectly sculpted dark eyebrow, as if she's daring me to say something.

"Thanks, Jane. I'll take care of it. Can you refill the coffee in the dining area?" she instructs, and the blonde behind the desk gives a nod before disappearing into what I assume is a back office. She walks out of a side door and disappears across the lobby into the busy breakfast room.

"So, you have an incident to report?" She crosses her arms over her chest, pushing up her cleavage that I can't help but glance at, and she pops one of her wide hips. The corner of her mouth twitches, as if she's fighting to hold back a grin.

Tearing my eyes away from her infuriating face, I return my attention to the child between us, ignoring the scowling woman. "Good morning, Max. As a matter of fact, I am here to see you." I kneel down so I'm at her level when I speak.

Her eyes sparkle as a blush tints her cheeks. "Really?" She looks up at her mother, then back at me. "I knew you wanted to be my friend." I risk a glance at the woman behind her, taking note of the guarded look I see in her eyes as she watches me like a hawk around her daughter. It's a look of caution, as if she's on damage control and needs to protect her daughter's feelings.

Interesting.

"Mommy says I shouldn't bother you like I did last night. Or talk to strangers."

"You didn't bother me, Max. But your mom is right, you shouldn't talk to strangers."

She crosses her arms, unknowingly mirroring her mother. "Yeah, but you're my friend and not a stranger."

With a chuckle, I shake my head. This girl is just as quick as her mother. "Max, what's your mom's name?" I don't look up at the woman, but I can still feel her heated glare.

"Andy," Max answers with a wide smile.

Andy.

I repeat her name in my head a few times, wondering how the name would feel on my lips.

Preferably I'd be panting her name as she drops to her knees and wraps those pouty lips around me. Bet she wouldn't have such a smart mouth when her throat is full of my cock, and I'm holding her life in my hands. Deciding if she deserves to breathe or have me forced deeper down her throat.

My lips twitch with a smirk as I force the thoughts away, reminding myself that I'm around a child and shouldn't be fantasizing about her mother down on her knees.

"Is that a nickname? Like Max?" I ask, her small face scrunching up in confusion.

"What?" She shakes her head, pointing a thumb at herself. "I'm Max," she says, emphasizing the *A* and dragging it out. "My mommy is Andy," she repeats, also dragging out the *A*.

With a grin, I look up at the woman, who thankfully understands what I was asking. "Nope. It's just Max and Andy. Not short for anything."

Smirking, I stand to my full height, stretching out my long limbs. "Okay, just Andy." Fuuuck. Her name feels good on my lips.

She rolls her eyes, and for a quick moment I'd like to see her do that while she's impaled on my cock and I'm gripping her soft, wide hips.

Fuck, I wish I could see more of her body instead of that ugly fucking oversized cardigan that's hiding it away.

Based on the way she keeps tugging at it, I'm certain she's uncomfortable, but I'm not sure why. She doesn't have a single thing she should be embarrassed about.

Andy is a beautiful full-figured woman with a body that I'd love to explore, but I'm aware that can never happen.

I'm not the type of man that'll buy a woman roses and stick around after a fuck. I'm the type that'll keep you around long enough for us to have some fun, then send you on your way once we're both thoroughly satisfied. A one-night guy is who I'll always be.

Never anything more. Never again.

That isn't something Andy needs, especially when she has a child. I may not know her, but I know that she doesn't deserve to be dragged into my fucked-up life. That much is certain.

"I'm waiting to hear your complaint about housekeeping," she speaks, and suddenly I become aware that we've been standing here entrapped in a staring contest.

Who can blame me when her chocolate-brown eyes are so deep and dark, they look like they hold the secrets of the world.

Reluctantly pulling my gaze away from hers, I shove my hands into my front pockets, rocking back on my heels. "Never mind."

She raises a dark eyebrow. "Nothing to say now?"

"Nope." I look down at Max, who stares between us, her head moving back and forth each time one of us speaks.

"Are you sure?" she presses. "I'd be happy to take your complaint." The twitch returns to her lips, but this time she doesn't fight it and allows her plump lips to form a grin.

Did I come here, pissed off, prepared to tattle on her about her attitude last night? Abso-fucking-lutely I did.

Instead of brushing it off, I straighten my spine. "You had a bad attitude last night."

She scoffs, her hands falling from her chest to her sides. "So, what? You came here to speak to my manager?" She snarls, looking at me with either annoyance or disgust. I can't be too sure when it comes to her.

Turning her attention away, she looks down at the child between us. "Max, baby, go into the office and wait for me," she says, giving her daughter a soft nudge to move from where she remains rooted in place.

"But Mommy!" she begins to protest. "I want to stay here with my new best friend."

Shaking her head, soft brown curls bouncing, Andy gives her another gentle nudge. "Now, Max. I'll be there to do your hair in a minute."

Her small shoulders fall, her head dropping in defeat. "Fine." She sighs, stomps her little foot, and slowly starts walking away. She mumbles a quiet, "Bye, best friend," to me before disappearing into the back office.

With her out of ear shot, Andy stands straight in front of me, her hands on her plump hips. "What the fuck is your problem?" My head snaps back, and I'm momentarily taken back by her harsh words.

The fuck?

"Is this how you treat all your guests? Or am I just special?" I mirror her stance, placing my hands on my hips the same as she does. She's so fucking tall, yet I still have several inches over her.

"Don't flatter yourself."

"Tell me what the fuck your problem is."

Shaking her head, her brow curls bounce again. "I don't have a problem."

I scoff. Yeah, okay. She's had something up her ass since last night. Maybe this is her personality, but somehow, I doubt that. "You've had a problem with me since last night. You want to know what my problem is? Well, I want to know what the fuck *yours* is. You don't know me, yet you're acting like I ruined your life." Her expression never wavers, her eyes in slits as she glares. "You act like I fucked you, then broke your heart, but I know for a fact I've never fucked you, so I can't figure out why you're acting this way toward me." The words leave my mouth harsher than expected, causing her to rear back.

Andy's head drops, her features softening, shoulders slumping as she stares down at her shoes. Her fingers tug that ugly ass cardigan away from her body. She allows herself a brief moment of vulnerability before she puts her guard back up, returning her mask into place, and then she gives me a smile that doesn't meet her eyes.

"You're right." She tugs the sweater, and I wonder if she's even aware she's doing it. It seems to be a habit at this point. "I'm sorry for how I've treated you." *Tug.* "Sorry for Max bothering you, too." *Tug.* "Enjoy your stay, and don't worry, it'll be pleasant from here on out." *Tug.*

She forces another smile before stepping around me, holding

her head high as she walks past me, leaving me standing there to wonder what the fuck just happened.

It isn't until I return to my hotel room minutes later that I realize what I'd said, and how harsh it sounded.

The way my words came out made it sound like she wasn't good enough for me, when that's not at all what I'd meant.

I shouldn't care about hurting the feelings of some chick with a smart mouth, but for some reason strange reason, I do.

Fuck.

Way to go, Declan.

TEN

Andy

FOR AS LONG AS I CAN REMEMBER, I'VE BEEN INSECURE ABOUT MY body.

I've always been the biggest one in the room.

Taller than my teachers, even in elementary school.

My body frame is usually the largest, too.

I was in third grade the first time my grandma put me on a diet to help me lose weight, which was the beginning of my downward spiral. Diet culture is extremely fucking toxic, and no child should ever worry about their weight or be forced to drink meal replacement shakes.

Every time she'd serve me the chalky, purple meal replacement shake, I'd have to plug my nose to choke it down. The package the powder came in claimed it was berry flavored, but it tasted like grass.

All these years later, and I still remember the taste.

Portion control, weight loss programs, diet bars and drinks—I've tried it all. Yet, week after week, the scale never changed. No matter what I did.

After my grandparents were gone, I'd been alone and desperate for attention. Desperate for someone to notice me.

So I turned to meeting grown men from Vegas online when I

was only fifteen years old. I gave them my address, and let them pick me up and take me away to fuck in the desert. They would drive over an hour from Vegas to see me, and I felt special. All I wanted was to feel wanted, even if only for a night. I was young and naive, with no parental guidance, and confused lust with love.

My body image issues were tearing me apart, and the only time I felt attractive was when those grown men had their hands on me, telling me how much they wanted me.

I was fourteen when I lost my virginity to my former best friend's boyfriend. She encouraged it, telling me I needed to get laid. She waited outside my bedroom door while we did it. Afterward, she gave me a high five and left with him, promising to text me later to compare sex notes.

Three months later, she was dating someone new and forgot all about me.

At the time, I couldn't blame her. I'm easy to forget. I'm no one special.

Even the men I stupidly allowed bareback inside of my body at such a young age, didn't want me for more than a night. I was foolish enough to not give them pushback when it came to the discussion of a condom, and it's amazing that I've never had an STD.

I should regret my decisions, but I can't because one of those men blessed me with Max. And I'll never regret her.

Having her was the best decision I've ever made in my life.

I've been trying to love myself. I really have. Everyday Max and I have been going on walks, and I always run around with her at the park. It's too expensive to eat as healthy as I wish, but I no longer binge eat. It is a massive step in the right direction for me, considering I've been binge eating since childhood.

Shoveling food in my mouth until my stomach was so full it ached was something I did often. It became worse after Grandma died. After her death, I never knew where my next meal would come from, so I'd eat enough in one sitting for four days.

My lovely mother was unreliable when it came to keeping groceries in the house. Food didn't matter when you were high.

Point is, I was doing better, until Declan looked at me.

His dark eyes looking over my body had made me uncomfortable, to the point where I convinced myself he was judging me for my size.

I'm not stupid. I know the obvious difference between us. Yeah, he's taller than me, but he's pure muscle. He's someone who takes pride in what goes into his body. Well, apart from the drugs he does, of course.

I've seen photos of him with women online, and I've seen his ex-wife. She's a fucking dark-haired bombshell. Easily the most gorgeous woman I have ever laid eyes on.

Declan has a type, and there's nothing wrong with that. His type isn't me, which I already knew, but having him point it out really dug the knife in deep.

He told me he would know if he had ever fucked me.

Of course, he'd remember something like that.

Not like it would ever be possible. He's so far out of my league, it's hilarious.

Though knowing that didn't stop me from being embarrassed. My cheeks burned with embarrassment, my eyes stung, and my heart raced. I couldn't get away from him quick enough.

Though it's been hours since our interaction, I'm still unable to get his words out of the back of my mind.

I'm sitting at the desk in the back office with Max, where I've been hiding all day in hopes of not having to see Declan again, when Jane walks back with a smile on her face.

The girl radiates sunshine, which sometimes makes me want to tell her I killed a puppy so she'd do something other than smile and be happy.

Horrible, I know, but misery loves company and all that shit.

"Hi, Max." She waves, taking a seat in front of the desk I'm sitting at. My daughter waves her hand in response, too focused on her coloring book to give my coworker much attention.

Jane has worked here for two years. She was the first person I hired to help me with the front desk once I received the promotion of general manager. At the time, I'd been thrilled, since I've been working the front desk here at this hotel since I was sixteen. Don't get me wrong, I am grateful to have this job. I only wish it paid more.

The owners live in Dubai and have several hotels all over America, and they're rarely here, leaving me in charge of all daily operations. The only time we speak is when they email or call me whenever they need something. Which is rare.

They have so much money it's hard to comprehend, yet they don't pay well. The times they have visited the hotel, which they do at least twice a year, when they come here as a family on their way to Las Vegas for vacation, they're always dripping in designer brands.

Literally.

Sara, the owner's wife, has a purse worth more than a brand new car. Yet, when I asked for a raise so I wouldn't have to choose between paying my electric bill or putting gas in my car, they told me they couldn't afford it.

Meanwhile Sara unboxed a new pair of shoes feet away from me, while her husband, Amir, wore a watch equivalent to what I earn per year.

I know I shouldn't be ungrateful, and I'm not, because this is the highest paying job in this small ass town, but I'm tired of living paycheck to paycheck. Many people who live here travel to Vegas every day for work, but that isn't realistic for me when I have a child, an unreliable car, and no gas money.

One day, I hope to save enough money to move into the city.

So far, I have forty dollars.

Oh yeah, Andy, you'll get to Vegas in no time.

Shaking myself away from my inner pity party, I return my

attention to Jane, noticing her lips moving but not hearing a thing she's been saying.

"Sorry, Jane, what did you say?"

She pauses, takes a breath, then speaks, "I asked you if everything was okay with that guest this morning. The one with the complaint. What happened?" She'd asked me earlier what happened, but I'd brushed her off, telling her I had to finish the night audit and get it emailed to Amir.

Since then, she's been working in front behind the desk, while I've been hidden away in the back office.

Deciding to play it off, I shrug. "Yeah, everything is fine. Simple misunderstanding."

Her blue eyes stare at me, her teeth biting into her bottom lip as she contemplates if she wants to say what's on her mind. The thing about Jane is that she always questions herself, instead of coming out and saying exactly what she wants to.

She's the complete opposite of me. I don't have a filter and am blunt.

Finishing the audit report and quickly sending it to Amir, I give her my full attention, "Say whatever it is that you're thinking."

A slow grin creeps across her face. "That guy is Declan Valentine. The Declan Valentine!" she gushes. The mention of his name sends chills down my spine and has Max perking up, clearly finding the conversation interesting enough to deserve her time.

"It is Declan!" Max confirms, shoving her coloring book aside and standing, walking toward us to stand beside where I sit. "I bought him a candy bar last night."

My eyes roll remembering the Snickers bar I gave him, because I'd been too embarrassed when he was eyeing me up and down, and the candy bar in Max's hand, which she happily pointed out, was for me.

"That was sweet of you, Max. Did you have him sign anything for you?"

My daughter scrunches her dark eyebrows, looking at Jane as if she were crazy, "He's a singer, not a signer, silly." She giggles, nudging my legs apart to stand between them. Her small arms wrap around my thighs as she leans against me.

A faint smile tugs at my lips at the position. When she was a baby and learning to walk, she'd always stand between my legs, trying to balance herself and get used to pulling herself up. Now she does it without realizing, because she loves touching me.

Max's love language is physical touch. She is a touchy child and shows her affection by touching. Whether it is by holding your hand, rubbing your arm, or playing with your hair, she has to have physical contact with the ones she loves.

The list of people she loves is small. I hate that I don't have a family to give her.

A father to give her.

Having a fatherless child was never something I wanted. I know first-hand what it's like to have your first broken heart be because of an absent father.

History wasn't supposed to repeat itself.

I was never supposed to walk in my mother's footsteps and make her mistakes.

At least I'm sober and have never done drugs.

Something small I remind myself of daily.

"Right, Mommy?" Max tilts her head back, giggling as she looks at me upside down.

I don't admit I allowed myself to get lost inside my head, instead, I nod. Leaning forward, I press a kiss to her forehead, "Sure, baby, whatever you say."

Jane laughs, standing from where she was sitting, "You've had a long shift, I bet you can't wait to go home and sleep." The mention of sleep causes a yawn to slip past my lips. It's nearly three p.m., which is when I'll finally be off after working a sixteen-hour shift.

"Actually, we haven't moved into our new apartment, so mommy doesn't have anywhere to sleep." Max simply states, putting my business out on display and throwing me under the bus.

Fuck. For a moment, I'd forgotten about our living situation. Not sure how that happened, considering I never forget things I need to do. The stress of moving and needing a place to stay for a few days has kept me up at night.

Another thing I need to figure out.

I'd love nothing more than to crawl into bed and sleep, but considering we're now homeless, I can't do that.

Sure, I could swallow my pride and return to my mother's, but that isn't my first option. I'd asked her yesterday because she was the last resort, but today is a new day. I'll figure something out, like I always do.

Figuring shit out is what I'm good at.

"Max, I'm almost off, so get your stuff packed up so we can go as soon as Lila gets here." She nods, stepping away from me to pack her coloring books, pencils, and toys into her backpack.

Jane stares at me with worried eyes from where she stands by the door, "If your apartment isn't ready yet, where are you staying?" I'm sure if she had the space, she'd offer us to stay with her over the weekend. That's the type of person she is, but she lives in a studio apartment.

Avoiding eye contact, I stand and begin cleaning up the desk. Then I fold the blankets I brought for Max to sleep with and gather our belongings, shoving them into my tote bag. "We move in on Sunday and will stay with a friend until then."

Setting my neatly packed tote on the chair, I look over at her just in time to see the sympathetic look she gives me, "Are you sure, Andy?" No. I'm not fucking sure. But what can I say?

Today is Friday, which means I'll need a place for my daughter to sleep for the next two nights. Having to suck up and go to my mom's seems like the only option. At least I'll be there with Max, so she won't be alone.

"Of course. We'll probably even spend a night with my mom so she can see Max." I give her the best forced smile I can muster up so she doesn't worry. Luckily for me, no one knows about the strained relationship I have with my mother. I never talk about myself at work, so apart from my employees knowing my work ethic, they don't know much about me. It's what I prefer, considering I've been too trusting of people in the past and have always been hurt.

Everyone leaves me in the end.

"Good! I'm glad you'll have a place." Jane's positive energy radiates from her blonde head. She reminds me of a sunflower— bright and beautiful.

Unlike me, she's new to town. She moved here a few months before she began working here, which at the time I remember thinking was strange because no one moves to Loganville.

This town has three types of people...

The ones that graduate, marry their high school sweetheart, and start a family.

The ones who leave for college and return home right after.

Or the rare, lucky ones that move away after high school and never return, wanting more out of life than this small town.

Well, I guess there's a fourth type, which would be me. The one who didn't finish high school, got knocked up at sixteen, and has never left this town.

Point is, no one moves here unless you're from here. Which Jane isn't.

Two years later, and I'm still curious why she moved here of all places. But her secrets are her own, just like mine.

♩ ♪ ♫ ♪ ♩

By the time Lila clocks in promptly at 3pm for her swing shift, Jane clocks out and leaves while I stay behind for a few minutes to finish up a couple emails to vendors. Since I'm off the next two days, I like to make sure everything in my work basket is completed.

Fridays are always the busiest days for me, and today was no exception.

I'm sending my final email at thirty minutes after three when Max drops my phone on the desk with a loud thud, followed by the most dramatic sigh she can possibly come up with.

"I want to leave already," she whines, her small hand rubbing her stomach. "Mommy, I'm hungry and tired. So, *so* starving."

Laughing at her dramatics, I log out of the computer and lock the screen, grabbing the backpack and tote bag when I stand.

"Alright, little drama queen. Let's get you fed." She grabs my phone and rushes to my side, taking my hand in hers. Truth is, I'm not in any rush to leave considering we have nowhere to go.

Hand in hand, Max and I leave the hotel, waving to Lila on our way out, wishing her a good night, and promising to see her Monday morning when I return to work.

After loading our bags into the back of my SUV, I help Max into her car seat, then climb into the driver's seat.

A beeping coming from my car instantly causes my ass cheeks to clench, knowing that life is about to fuck me a little harder.

The shining orange gas light stares at me, the gauge that was barely above the *E* is now under it.

Great.

Now I need gas. More money I don't have to spare.

"Mommy, can we get McDonalds?" My daughter's voice is hopeful, the sound instantly easing my fears and calming me. For her, I'll survive. I can do this.

She is my reason for existing.

"Sure, baby. We can even go inside and play."

Max shouts her excitement from the backseat as I switch the car into reverse to pull out of my parking space.

While I drive, she babbles on about her excitement for the McDonald's playground, and I feel a little more at ease, choosing not to worry about my lack of funds.

At least for the time being.

ELEVEN

Andy

As I sit at the table inside McDonalds, watching my daughter inhale her nuggets, all I can think about is my mother and life after my grandparents were gone. How much we struggled for money because she deemed herself *unable to work*, when it really meant that working would interfere with her carefree lifestyle and drug use.

Thinking about the past is something I seem to be doing a lot of lately. It's hard not to when I stare into the eyes of my daughter, feel the soul-consuming, unconditional love I have for her, and I question why my mother was unable to feel the same way.

Diane Harris looks at drugs the way I look at my daughter.

Like we would do anything for them.

The older I get, the more I realize the trauma I carry with me daily. It consumes me, and at times, it feels suffocating. I know it's toxic and I should be in therapy or even read a fucking self-help book, but I'm not sure if I'm ready to let go of the resentment and anger I feel toward her. It's not healthy for me, but if I forgive her, what does that say about me? That it's okay that she treated me the way she did? That she should get a second chance? Well, more like a one millionth chance, considering I've been giving her *second* chances since I could walk.

With a sigh, I sink down into my chair, my eyes never leaving my beautiful girl in front of me.

My growling stomach causes her dark eyes to look up at me and away from her nuggets. "Why aren't you eating, Mommy?" she asks, taking a long drink from her cup of Powerade.

Because I only had twenty dollars and still need to get gas.

I refuse to touch my credit card unless I absolutely have to. I've been in debt before, and it's not fun trying to pay it off. I took nearly two years to pay off the small $500 limit. And I'd rather miss a meal than use it. It's too easy to fall back into debt —even with one small purchase.

But I don't tell my daughter the truth, because I'll never place the burden of finances on her small shoulders, so instead, I lie to her. "I'm still full from breakfast." Every morning that I work, I eat breakfast at the hotel, and this morning wasn't any different. I fed us both, and then when Max got hungry in the early afternoon, I reheated some leftover pancakes for her.

Sitting back in her seat, she places a hand on her stomach and rubs it. "My tummy is full. Can I go play?" I nod, and she runs toward the playroom, nearly tripping over her feet, which makes me laugh.

She'll be hungry later, and I can't afford to eat out again today, so instead of eating her remaining five nuggets and fries like I'd usually do, I place them in the brown to-go bag and set it inside my purse to save for later.

This phase of life is only temporary.

One day, money will not be an issue and I'll be able to give my daughter everything her little heart desires.

One day.

♪♫♪♫♪

WE SPENT TWO HOURS AT McDONALDS BEFORE I SWALLOWED MY pride, bit my tongue, hid my resentment, and called my mom. I could barely keep my eyes open, and Max was whining because she was tired.

Out of options, I called Diane and asked if we could spend the night. Of course, she said yes, and I hung up immediately after so I wouldn't have to listen to her talk shit about my asking.

That's where we are now...

Standing on my mother's porch.

My pulse races with anxiety as I wait for her to open the door.

The moment she does, I regret my decision to come here... yet again.

Twice in a week. Surely this is a new record.

Dull blue eyes stare back at me, different from the bright, ocean-blue eyes she used to have. Before the drugs took her youth and beauty, she had the same eyes as her father, my grandpa, the greatest man I've ever known. But drugs have ruined her, and her eyes are now soulless.

Empty.

Her pale skin is wrinkly and dry, and despite being in her forties, she looks nearly twenty years older.

Another thing she has to thank the drugs for.

Those dull eyes look from me and down to Max, a genuine smile spreading across her thin chapped lips at the sight of her granddaughter.

"Hi, Maxie girl. Come inside." She steps to the side, allowing us to enter the trailer that somehow always manages to smell like a wet dog, even though she doesn't have a dog, and she always has a new wax melt in her wax warmer.

Apple pie spice mixed with wet dog.

Smells like home.

While Max talks to my mom, catching her up on the difficulties of being a five year old, I take our bags into my old bedroom, the same room where I'd tucked Max in last night.

It's almost seven p.m., and it's been nearly forty-eight hours since I've slept. At this point, I'm running on fumes. My eyes are dry and burn, and all I want is to close my eyes for the night and get a solid ten hours.

I know that's impossible, though. I haven't slept more than five hours since I started working two full-time jobs, eighty hours a week, when I was only sixteen. Then came Max, and any chance I had of sleeping for a long period went out the door.

I'm used to it, but I also know I won't be able to completely relax here. Not until we're moved into our apartment on Sunday, and I'm back in my own space.

When I check on Max to make sure she's okay with my mom, I find them baking cookies, so I choose to leave them alone and return to the room to take a quick nap. I'll be fine once I rest my eyes for a few minutes.

Twenty minutes, that's all I need.

Biggest lie of my life.

Four hours later, I wake up to a small warm body crawling over me then curling up beside me. My eyes pop open, and it takes several blinks for me to adjust to the darkness of the room.

"Max?" I wrap my arms around her small body, hugging her to me. "What were you doing?"

She yawns, her curls ticking my nose. "Grandma made cookies that I got to help with. Then she needed help eating them, so I helped her eat them. And I got to watch cartoons." If she weren't exhausted, her voice would be filled with more excitement than what it currently is.

"Sounds fun, baby," I mumble, keeping my arms around her as we fall asleep together.

♪ ♫ ♪ ♫ ♪

SATURDAY MORNING, I WAKE WITH A STIFF NECK AND MY ARM asleep and tingly from my daughter using it as a pillow all night.

Groaning, I carefully unwrap my arms from my sleeping daughter and climb out of the bed, stretching my stiff limbs as I stand.

The worn mattress we slept on was uncomfortable, but I'd been too tired to complain. Not that I would anyways since it's a bed. And considering I don't have one of my own currently, I have no right to complain about anything.

Tomorrow morning, we will meet Heather and get the keys for our new apartment. For the first time in a while, I have something to look forward to, and am excited to be in our new home. The rent was more than what I'd previously been paying, and I'll need to find someone to look after Max once she gets out of school after summer is over. That will be tomorrow's problem. Today, I'm going to take my girl to the thrift store to go shopping for furniture since we don't have anything for our new apartment.

One more fucking day until we're home.

We're so close.

While Max sleeps, I quickly change into a pair of black leggings that hug my thick thighs like a second skin, along with a faded Nirvana crop T-shirt that is short enough to reveal my legging covered belly and a sliver of skin. After slipping on my socks and second-hand black converse, I go into the bathroom connected to the bedroom to brush my teeth and wash my face.

Years ago, when Mom and I moved into this trailer, I demanded the master bedroom. We fought over it, her telling me that she deserves it because she's the mother and the one paying rent.

"I'm the one that has to pay the fucking rent while your ass gets to go out and party all day." She had screamed in my face, her stupidity pissing me off. Every day I went to work, even though she convinced herself I was "partying." Mothers are supposed to pay rent and provide a roof over their child's head. That is the bare minimum that a parent should do, yet she always threw it in my face that she was paying rent.

Never mind the fact I was the one paying for everything else.

She sold her food stamps each month to have money for drugs, so it was my paycheck that paid for groceries, which I was often unable to afford.

Another thing we fought over.

Every month we'd stand in line at the food pantry to get a free box of food. When I wasn't able to afford anything else, that's the only food we'd have for the month.

When the kitchen is always empty, you really learn how to make a packet of Ramen become a gourmet meal.

Knowing my mom and the company she kept, I hadn't wanted any more exposure to them than necessary, which is why I demanded the master bedroom. As soon as I'd return home from work, I'd lock myself in my bedroom, only coming out if I had no other choice.

I hated being around her friends. The gross men with pick marks and scars on their aged, leather skin, their beady eyes lingering on me for too long, always standing too close; the feeling of their hot, rancid breath on my skin still haunts me.

I shudder at the memory.

Being here has memories resurfacing that I'd rather keep out of my mind. It's ironic, considering I allow my past to keep a constant noose around my neck. As long as I continue holding onto my anger there will never be any room for healing. No room to move on and let go.

I badly want to be free and let the little girl inside of me heal and have a happy ending.

I am not defined by my childhood trauma.

One day, I will heal and be free.

After going through my morning routine of brushing my teeth, washing my face, and applying tinted sunscreen and mascara, I bend at the waist to shake out my frizzy curls that desperately need to be washed. My hair is wild and should probably be in a bun, but I'm on a journey of loving my hair.

For too many years, my curly hair was subjected to chemical

hair straightening treatments and relaxers because no one in my family knew how to properly care for a Black child's hair.

There were a few times my grandma took me to the salon with her to get my hair cut just like hers—so my hair was short and my curls would be looser and easier to manage.

It was difficult growing up in Loganville as a biracial child.

I was always too white to be Black, and too Black to be white. Anywhere I looked, no one looked like me. My family didn't, and neither did the people in town. Even the dolls I used to play with didn't look like me.

For so long I felt like an alien who was sent here from a different planet. Maybe my real alien family forgot me on earth and Diane mistakenly brought me home.

That idea went out the window when she showed me a photo of her and my father, and I learned that I look just like him.

I've always wondered if that's why my mom always secretly hated me. I know she loved my father, and their relationship was ruined when she discovered she was pregnant.

Because of me, they're not together anymore.

"Mommy?" Max calls out from the bedroom, confusion and panic in her voice from waking up in an unfamiliar space without me next to her.

Popping my head out of the bathroom, I meet her eyes and smile, watching her shoulders visibly relax at the sight of me. "Hi, sleepy girl." I wash my hands before going into the bedroom and sitting on the bed beside her.

She climbs on my lap the moment I sit, her arms around my neck and legs around my waist. "How did you sleep?" I ask, rubbing her back.

"Good, but I'm hungry." Her hair tickles my nose, using the hand not wrapped around her I smooth down her mess of curls.

"Let's get you ready then you can eat. We're going to have a fun day today." The promise of doing something fun grabs her interest and perks her up. Her small body pulls back, and wide brown eyes look at me, and I swear they sparkle with excitement.

Squealing, she climbs off my lap and rushes toward the bathroom. "What are you waiting for, Mommy? Let's go!" It doesn't take much to excite my little girl.

With a smile spread wide across my lips, I rush after her, feeding off her innocent energy.

One more day, I remind myself.

Tomorrow, we'll be starting a new chapter in our lives.

TWELVE
Declan

I DEBATED ALL DAY FRIDAY WHETHER TO RETURN TO THE LOBBY AND talk to Andy. The sad look in her brown eyes haunted me, but I forced myself to stay away. Even though I had willingly gone to the lobby to report her bad attitude, I wasn't willing to go back in and risk causing another scene by pulling her away from her work.

Something told me that if I did, she'd hate me forever, crushing any hope I had of getting to know her. Yes, I'm being hopeful as hell that she'll allow me to explain myself and apologize for the way my words came out. Though, something about Andy tells me she's not the forgiving type.

The only time I've seen her let her guard down and look carefree is when she's with her daughter. With anyone else, even her blonde co-worker, her steel walls are back in place.

She's going to be difficult to reach, but for some strange reason, I want to try. That realization alone surprises me. I can't explain why I want to get to know this woman when every interaction we've had has been terrible, and I've never been the type to pursue a woman before. It could be that I recognize the hidden demons behind her eyes, but I can't be sure. All I know is there's something about her that makes me want to learn everything there is to know about her, to find out why she's so guarded and exactly what trauma is behind those chocolate eyes.

Who hurt her? And why do I care? Maybe I just like the fire in her eyes and arguing.

This morning, when I woke up, I went to the lobby for breakfast. I was hoping to see Andy again after having a chance to sleep on my thoughts. No such luck finding her. I asked the front desk woman, and she told me Andy was off and would return to work on Monday.

Great. Two days until I can speak to her and apologize.

I should call my former therapist and tell her that I realized what I did was wrong. I bet she wouldn't find the humor in that as I do, and I'm sure she'd give me some *therapy is helping* bullshit like she's done in the past. Never before have I willingly wanted to apologize for hurting someone. Sure, I've apologized to Camille many times before, but those apologies came after I severely messed up and she threatened to leave. Horrible, I know, but I don't claim to be a good man.

After breakfast and my dashed hopes of seeing Andy, I returned to my hotel room and flipped through the few cable channels the hotel offered. I quickly grew bored and wasn't ready to talk to my best friends—the ones who plotted behind my back to dump me out here in *The Hills Have Eyes* County, so I called David to ask him about the town. After finding out everything was within walking distance of the hotel, I showered and headed out for the day, which brings me to where I am now.

I walk the streets of Loganville, getting side-eyed by everyone passing me. I don't miss how women clutch their purses tighter, how they grab their children's hands to pull them away, or how the men scowl at me before moving their wives out of my way. As if I want anything this city has to offer. They're clearly not used to seeing outsiders here and have no shame in staring, either. It's human nature to judge. Anyone who says they don't is lying. However, this town seems open about doing it publicly. Not that anyone has said anything to me, but

I've been feeling the looks since I left the hotel property. Sure, my tattoos are on full display, but I don't know what it is that's causing people to turn their noses up at me. Is it the ink covering my skin, the fact that I'm a stranger, taller than every person I've seen, or how I'm dressed in ripped black jeans, a black T-shirt, and black boots? Yeah, I stick out like a sore thumb in this little colorful town. Living here will be fun.

Instantly, my mind races back to Andy, and I wonder what her experience has been like living here and if this small-minded town is where she grew up. I have so many questions about the curly-haired woman who seems to despise me.

By one o'clock, I find myself at one of the two restaurants in this town. Scoops is a local family-owned ice cream shop and café. The cool air soothes my heated skin the moment I walk in, and the sweet ice cream scent fills my nostrils. White walls surround me, each covered with family photos, some so old that they're in black and white. To the left is a massive display of all the ice cream flavors, signs for the flavors, and a display case showing the different types of waffle bowls and cones they offer. I've never had much of a sweet tooth, but seeing the different flavors displayed suddenly makes me crave the sweet, cold treat.

To the right, several wooden tables and chairs occupy the space, nearly full of patrons who all seemed to abandon their plates of food to fixate on me the moment I walked in. Their eyes on me make my skin crawl, and the urge to run causes my legs to twitch. I despise having attention focused on me; it makes me feel like I'm under a microscope. If these people scrutinize me too closely, they'll uncover the truth about me that I'm trying to keep hidden. This town is small enough that I don't need everyone to know who I am, because, so far, it's clear that no one does. Here, I can be a stranger. I can just be Declan—whoever he is. Maybe I can find out who he is while I'm here for the next two months.

Straight ahead, I notice the sign that says *Order Here* and a menu hanging on the wall behind the teenage girl working the cash register. Ignoring the nosy people staring and whispering at my expense, I plaster on a broad smile and approach the counter.

The teenage girl pops her gum, one finger twirling her brown hair. "Good afternoon, what can I get for you?"

My eyes quickly scan the menu and find mostly soups and sandwiches. I'm hungry, so I should order something, but I can't stop drooling over the ice cream since walking in.

"Can I get a banana split minus the bananas?"

She looks at me like I suddenly grew two heads. "You want"—she looks down at the register, then back to me—"a banana split. But without bananas...on the banana split?" she questions, her face scrunching in confusion.

Was my request that hard to understand? I'm not too fond of bananas, but I want the triple scoop of ice cream packed with all the toppings. "Yes, that's exactly what I want."

Rolling her lips, she punches some buttons on the machine and tells me the total. I hand her a twenty, telling her to keep the change.

"Come over here and tell me which flavors you want." She walks behind the ice cream case, and I stand before the display, carefully looking over each flavor.

"Cookies n' cream, please."

She nods, then scoops the ice cream into the bowl. "What else?"

"Just cookies n cream." Mumbling something under her breath, she places two more large scoops into the bowl, then piles it up with hot caramel, fudge, whipped cream, and sprinkles.

I haven't had one of these since I was a kid. The last day I spent with my mother before she abandoned me and I was placed into foster care. She'd taken me to a local ice cream shop and bought me a banana split—minus the bananas, because even as a child, I hated them, and we sat outside while I ate the frozen treat.

"Be a good boy, and stay right here, Declan," Mom says, her brown eyes glossy with unshed tears.

"Mommy, what's wrong?" I ask, getting an uneasy feeling in the pit of my stomach. She's been acting strange the past few days, and I don't understand why.

Taking a napkin, she wipes away the whipped cream from my mouth. "Nothing, baby. Promise me you'll be a good boy and remember that I love you." She hugs me tightly as a sob rips from her chest. "I'm sorry, Declan. I'm so sorry." My hands cling to her tank top, desperate to keep her arms around me. Hugs from my mother are rare. Her remembering me and taking me out for treats is rare, so I want to savor the day. Savor the feeling of my mother's arms around me and hearing her tell me she loves me.

This morning, she woke me up and told me we could have ice cream for breakfast. I shouted with glee, thrilled to spend one of Mom's good days with her. It wasn't often she had good days.

When she didn't have her needle or glass pipe, she was sick in bed for days.

"Stay here, it'll be okay." Before I can ask her anything else, she rushes off, leaving her eight-year-old son alone.

My mother often forgets me, but she always returns. So I stay there like she said and finish eating my ice cream.

By the time the sun goes down, she still hasn't returned, and the ice cream shop has closed. The owner called the police when he noticed me still sitting outside.

A red-headed officer approaches me, asking where my mother is, and my response is, "Mom said to stay here. She'll be right back."

"How long has she been gone?" he asks, and I carefully shrug, not wanting to get Mom in trouble for leaving me outside, but I don't want to be out here anymore. I'm hungry and have to pee badly.

When the officer doesn't get the answer he wanted, he asks, "Do you know what time you came here?"

That was a question I could answer.

"We came here for breakfast."

A look of shock flashes over his face, and then a moment later, he's speaking in code into the radio strapped to his shoulder. I don't understand what he's saying, but the next thing I know, I'm sitting in the front seat of a police car heading back to the police station.

For a moment, I panic, thinking I'm being arrested, but then Officer Griffin lets me push the buttons for the siren and gives me a shiny police badge sticker. When I hesitate, he assures me I'm not in trouble and promises to help me find my mother and get me back home.

He lied.

I never returned home.

Three days later, my mother was located, and I learned she signed away her parental rights. She didn't want me anymore. It was as simple as that.

All it took to give your child away was a signature.

A piece of paper.

Snapping out of the unwanted memory that assaulted me, I blink back into reality to find myself sitting on a bench outside the café. One hand holding the banana-less banana split while the other is closed tightly in a white-knuckle fist.

Fuck.

I hate thinking of my childhood. Of my mother.

After she abandoned me, I was placed into one foster home after the other until I was fourteen. Then I was transferred to a group home after getting kicked out of my final foster home for assaulting my foster father. That fat fucker deserved worse than a broken nose.

The group home was where I met Adam when we were sixteen. We ran away together, started playing music, then two years later met Damon and Cole and formed Riot. Now the rest is history.

Years later, when Riot became popular, my mother found me. She'd shown up at one of our shows, apologizing for leaving me, begging for money.

She was so thin and frail that I hardly recognized her. I hated her, but I also hated seeing her like that. I'd given her all the cash in my wallet, and afterward, she thanked me, promising she'd come to meet me for coffee the next day.

I should've known better, but foolishly, I showed up at the coffee shop we agreed to meet at. I'd spent all day waiting for her, hoping she felt guilt for leaving her child, but I was wrong. That way of thinking gave her too much credit because she wasn't sorry. All that I was suitable for was an ATM.

I never made that mistake again.

Even as she tried to contact me through the years, I ignored her until the day I learned she died.

Camille thought it was harsh that I hadn't attended the funeral, but I didn't care. She may have given birth to me, but she was never a mother.

The ice cream in my bowl is now melted, thanks to the hot Nevada sun and the unwanted trip down memory lane.

Being sober, I don't have the drugs or alcohol to numb me and suppress the memories and emotions I've had tucked away for so long. Everything I'd rather forget and keep buried deep rises to the surface, forcing its way out, and trauma has a weird way of sneaking in and triggering you when you least expect it.

Thinking about my childhood will not do me, or anyone else, any good. If anything, it'll only lead me to drinking again. Which will inevitably end with me hitting rock bottom in an endless supply of coke and pussy. And I can't be that person ever again.

Tossing the untouched, melted ice cream into the trash, I wipe my hands along my jeans before shoving them into my front pockets and walk along the sidewalk, my feet taking me farther and farther into the dreadful city that is my home for the next few months.

I walk until I run out of the sidewalk and find myself standing in front of a white and blue thrift shop.

I'm ready to turn around and begin my walk back to the hotel when a dark head of curly hair catches my attention. A slow smirk spreads across my lips at the sight of Andy.

She's dressed casually in black leggings and a faded crop top displaying her legging-covered belly. It's short enough to reveal her lower belly but insufficient to show soft skin. Her curls are wild and frizzy but still appear smooth and in perfect ringlets. This version of her is much different from her at work—hidden beneath a baggy cardigan.

Despite wearing a crop top, I can see the way she sucks in her stomach, visibly uncomfortable by the short shirt.

She looks hot as fuck and doesn't even know it.

My feet decide for me. My brain takes a minute to catch up, but I realize I'm walking in her direction once I do. We're only feet away when her big eyes look up and notice me walking straight toward her.

Andy's eyes widen, and I can practically see the wheels spinning in her head. The debate between whether she should run away from me or face me is evident in her stare.

Despite her scowl, a smile spreads across my face. It's unclear why she wants to hate me so desperately, but little does she know that I already hate myself, so her hatred doesn't bother me.

Lies.

I'll change her mind. I don't know why I want to, but I will.

THIRTEEN

Andy

CAN I NOT ESCAPE THIS ASSHOLE?

How long will he be in my town?

I swear, every fucking time I turn around, there he is.

Declan Valentine in all his six-foot-something sex appeal glory.

At this point, I'm going to stop turning around.

My features narrow into a natural scowl at the sight of him, and to my surprise, he grins instead of returning my childish scowl. A small dimple appears on his left cheek with the movement of his mouth, and his heated brown eyes lock right on me, each step bringing him closer and closer.

For a second, I wonder if I can shove Max back into the car, then hurry and drive away before he'd get to us. My hands twitch with the urge to bolt.

As if he can sense that I'm considering fleeing, his steps quicken until he's near my car. All while my eyes never leave his.

Noticing that I have turned my attention away and am staring at someone, Max pushes my hands away from the buckles of her car seat and finishes removing the straps and climbing down from the chair.

My daughter's curly head pops out of the backseat to investigate what or who has my attention. At the sight of the man she claims is her new best friend, a broad smile takes over her features.

"My best friend!" she squeals in excitement, grabbing my hands to help her out of the car. Unlike the last time she saw him, she doesn't hold herself back. She runs full speed at him, barreling straight toward him with her arms raised and stars in her eyes.

He doesn't hesitate to bend down and catch the five year-old, taking her into his arms. My girl looks so tiny wrapped in those muscular, ink-covered arms, and for a moment, I allow my scowl to fall and look at them, taking in every detail of them.

Max has never had a male figure, so I'm not surprised she's clung to Declan after meeting him once. Obviously, she doesn't understand his music, but she's been listening to him from the backseat from the moment she was born.

Wrapping her arms around his neck, she hugs him tight, which he returns without hesitation. The sight brings a smile to my face and breaks my heart simultaneously. I shouldn't encourage them because one day he'll leave, and my little girl will be heartbroken when that happens.

Once again, I hate myself for not being able to give my girl the father she deserves.

My first heartbreak was my father, but I was lucky enough that I had the most fantastic grandpa to step in and fill that fatherly role for me. Max doesn't have that, and it's one thing I wish I could give her.

Every day, I try hard to be everything she needs me to be, but I'm not naive enough to think I'll ever fill that void. No matter how hard single mothers try to make up for their children not having a father, we'll never be able to.

It's impossible.

One day, she'll feel the void and have questions.

All I can do right now is be happy that I don't yet have to

deal with questions about where her father is. She has never asked me about him or expressed any interest for as long as she's been alive. But I know that she's still young. Being with me constantly, she doesn't yet understand what she's missing.

A family.

A father.

Things I can't give her.

Max turns to look at me with one arm around Declan's neck as he holds her with one arm. "Mommy, look! My best friend is here."

"I see that, baby." Grabbing my purse from the backseat, I pull the strap on my shoulder, shut the door, lock my car, and then toss the keys into my tote bag. "We should get going, Max. We have shopping to do."

Her frown is instant, her wide eyes looking at the man she's claimed. "Best friend, you can come shopping with us, right?" she asks him with hopeful brown eyes, her bottom lip stuck out in a hopeful pout.

Catching Declan's eyes, I say. "Max, I think your friend has other things to do today." I give him a look that begs him to let her down easy. No way am I going to go inside a thrift store with the Declan *fucking* Valentine. I'm not embarrassed about my financial situation or the fact I'll be shopping for pre-owned items; I just don't want him here. I don't want to spend time with the man with the horrible reputation that exudes everything I hate.

I shouldn't even allow him near my daughter, let alone hold her, but my girl was so happy when she laid eyes on him that I didn't stop her from running to him.

After today, I'll put distance between them, I promise myself, genuinely believing it. Max will end up loving him because she has such a big heart and is desperate for more people. Which I can't be angry about because I understand.

I'm desperate for someone in my life, too.

I want to be loved as much as anyone else.

"Actually," Declan begins, giving me a wink before looking away from me and giving Max his complete attention. "I don't have anything to do today." He sets her down on her feet, but she quickly takes his hand. "What are we shopping for?" he asks her.

"My bedroom!" she announces, bouncing on the balls of her feet. "Mommy and I are moving, and I'm getting my own room!" Happiness radiates off her, and I can't keep the smile away from my face. I love seeing my girl happy.

Max rushes ahead, dragging Declan along with her and into the store, leaving me behind to grab the small handbasket and follow them.

I may not have fast food money, but that's because I budget every penny I receive. Every check I put money aside for bills, gas, groceries, savings, and anything else I must have funds available. I'll admit, my gas budget is never huge. But that's not a requirement when this town is so damn small, and I rarely go anywhere besides work.

Since finding out we'd have to move and start completely over with furniture, I've been saving as much as possible to afford the necessities. I plan on getting a little today, but I need to check the prices for a bed and couch.

When I lived with my mother, I slept on the floor for months until I could save up enough money from babysitting jobs to afford to buy my own bed. Diane slept on an air mattress and didn't care what I was sleeping on.

An air mattress that I bought her.

I'd bought myself one, too, but after a month of sleeping on it, a hole formed, and despite patching it, it grew bigger and bigger, tearing each time I laid down. When I woke up one morning on the floor, the flat mattress underneath me, I said fuck it.

I continued sleeping on the floor for months until I had enough saved to buy a used bed.

I'm back at square one and need to buy a bed. I'll buy one,

and Max and I can share until I can afford one of my own. It'll be fine.

It's not the first time we've had to make do with what little we have.

I follow Max and Declan inside the store as my girl leads him directly to the toy aisle. One place in this store that she never seems to forget where it's at, and every time we come here, she always runs right to it and spends way too long picking out the one toy that she decides is "the most *perfectest* toy to ever exist." She has an entire box of perfect toys, yet I never deny her when we come here.

Letting go of Declan's hand, Max begins digging through the shelves, searching for the toy we'll inevitably take home.

While she searches, he turns to face me. His hands shoved into his pockets as he steps closer to me until we're toe to toe. "Look, Andy," he begins, sighing. A minty breath of air escapes him and fans over my lips. "I owe you an apology. What I said yesterday... that wasn't how I meant it."

Goosebumps rise on my flesh at our close proximity and the feel of his breath on my lips.

He looks over his shoulder to check on Max, and then he returns his attention to me. Max is still occupied with searching for toys and paying us no attention.

Lowering his voice, he leans into my ear, his nose pressed against my curls. "What I was trying to say was that if I had the honor of burying every inch of myself inside of you, I'd remember it." My lips part with a silent gasp at his words as his tattooed fingers play with my curls. "There's no way in hell I wouldn't remember having a goddess on my cock," he whispers, his warmth radiating off of him and waking a part of myself that has been dead for so long.

Desire.

It's been so long since I've felt anything other than emptiness. I haven't been fucked since the week before I found out I was pregnant. Sure, I've made myself come with the showerhead at night after Max is fast asleep, but that doesn't compare to the feeling of being touched by a man.

The feeling of having your pussy weep for a hard cock, then being stuffed and coming while squeezing the length, is such an extraordinary feeling, unlike the showerhead.

God, I miss having a sex life.

My thighs squeeze together at his words and the memories of what it's like to be touched by someone.

With a devilish grin on his lips and darkness that I assume is desire in his eyes, Declan rests his forehead against mine for a brief moment, then pulls back. "What are you two doing after this?"

When I don't answer him immediately, he speaks again, "Andy." The way his smoky voice says my name sends a rush through me.

Fuuuuck. I want to hear him say my name when I'm on my knees for him, gagging on his cock.

His moans would be music to my ears as I look up at him with tears streaming down my face, my throat full of his length.

My eyes widen at the thought.

Woah, down girl.

Where the fuck did that come from? He whispers one dirty thing in my ear, and suddenly my inner whore is awakened and ready to beg.

He raises his dark eyebrows expectantly, waiting for my answer.

Breathlessly, I say, "Nothing." My heart pounds in my chest, the pulse between my legs throbbing. "We're not doing anything."

"Spend the day with me." He doesn't ask. He commands. Any other day, I'd fight him and refuse to be submissive, but the only other option is to return to Diane's. I'd rather run over my foot than spend unnecessary time at her trailer.

Knowing I'll regret it later, I give in to him anyway.

Fuck being rational.

"Okay."

FOURTEEN
Declan

AFTER ANDY AGREED TO SPEND THE DAY WITH ME, I HAD TO EXCUSE myself so I could go to the bathroom and adjust my aching cock, which threatened to tear through my pants.

I wasn't sure what came over me when I invaded her personal space and whispered in her ear, but the moment her eyes stared into mine and her sweet, cherry-vanilla scent invaded my senses, I was a goner.

All rationality left me, and I could only think about being around her longer. Getting to see her let her guard down for me and let me see the demons she dances with and the scars she wears like a shield of armor.

Her brown curls tickled my nose, and my mind went blank. All I could focus on was her, which surprised us both. Something tells me that she's not used to having someone genuinely want to spend time with her just because they like to be around her.

Once my cock is adjusted, I return to Max and Andy, finding them now in the furniture section. In the basket Andy holds is a pink karaoke machine, which makes me chuckle.

The sound causes Max to look back at me with a broad smile across her innocent face. "Best friend, look what I got!" She points to the small machine in the basket. "We can sing together," she announces, bouncing on her tiptoes the way I noticed she does when she's excited.

Andy rolls her eyes, shaking her head.

"I can be like you!" the little girl exclaims with glee, punching me in the heart with her innocent, pure words. Once upon a time, Luca had said something similar, and the thought of him ever becoming like me was a nightmare.

My son had only seen the good in me and wanted to be like me. So fucking bad, I wanted to be the hero he looked up to. A good man who didn't battle demons every fucking day, who had to take drugs or drink to cope with living. To him, I was every-thing, and he loved what I did.

Luca spent hours sitting on my lap or at the table with me as I wrote lyrics, giving me a thumbs-up each time I figured out a bridge I loved. He didn't understand the meaning of the words, but he still looked at me like he did.

No matter how many verses I came up with, he'd give me a thumbs up and say, "That's it, Daddy! That's the best song in the world." His pure spirit had always calmed me.

Until my demons begged me to let loose and snort some shit I shouldn't have.

Not a day goes by when I'm not reminded about what I did or stole from Camille. From myself.

Because of me, a mother will never watch her son grow up.

She'll never get to see him graduate high school.

Hear about his first kiss.

Watch him go to college.

Walk him down the aisle at his wedding.

Witness him become a father.

The possibility of Luca ever having a future is over because of me.

Because I'm worthless.

Because I'm weak.

Because I'm unable to say no.

Weak. You're so fucking weak.

My mother was weak, and I never wanted to be like her.

You already are.

No. No. No.

It should've been me who died that night. A mother shouldn't be living without her child.

It should've been. It's not too late.

I'm fucking spiraling.

My hands clench and unclench, my jaw locked tight.

A warm hand rests on my forearm, dragging me away from where I stand. "Look at me," a voice commands, yanking me out of the darkness that threatens to consume me and bury me alive.

With a blink, I'm staring into big brown eyes.

My eyes connect with the smart-mouthed girl working her way under my skin.

"Breathe, Declan." Her fingers pry my fists open until she's holding both of my sweaty hands in hers. Her eyes never leave mine as she takes deep breaths, pausing each time until I follow along, breathing with her.

How fucking embarrassing.

I want to get high, yet this stranger is giving me fucking breathing lessons, forcing me to return to reality instead of continuing on my downward spiral.

My veins ache to be stabbed with a needle and injected with the poison that nearly claimed my life.

"Tell me three things." She squeezes my hands. "What do you see, hear, and smell?"

Her words surprise me, but her voice is the only thing anchoring me right now. I need some fucking air.

She squeezes my hands again when I don't answer.

"Tell me, Declan. Don't think, speak."

I do as she says, focusing on her as I respond, "I see you. Hear you. Smell you." She keeps my sweaty palms against hers, anchoring me to reality when I only want to float away and allow myself to sink further into the dark hole I've spent my life trying to crawl out of.

Her permanently stiff posture around me softens with a heavy exhale. "I'm here, Declan," she whispers, her fingers tracing invisible shapes on my skin.

After a few more deep breaths, my heartbeat returns to normal, and my heavy breathing is now silent and uneven. Instead of darkness creeping in and my demons whispering in my ear, all I can see is Andy.

Andy is holding my hands.

Andy staring into my eyes.

Andy helped me through the darkness rather than leaving me to go through it alone.

Andy. Andy. Andy.

The one who can save me.

Clearing my throat, I stare at her, committing every feature to memory.

The freckles across the bridge of her nose and the tiny freckle on her right eyelid. Plump pink lips that appear so fucking soft and sweet.

At this moment, I know without a doubt that if I'm not careful, she'll become my new addiction. And it'll be one that I'll never recover from.

"Mommy? Best friend?" A small voice breaks us away from our moment. At the sound of her daughter's voice, Andy pushes my hands away like I burned her and practically jumps away from me.

"Hey, baby." She greets her daughter, squatting down to kiss her cheek.

Worried brown eyes find mine. "Are you okay, best friend?" Concern is evident in her eyes, which shatters my heart a little more, knowing she's concerned for me.

"Baby, Declan will spend the day with us. Would you like that?" Max cheers, her hands clapping while she jumps up and down.

A protest is on the tip of my tongue. I got triggered over something so fucking simple that she said. How can I be around them right now? How can Andy allow me to be around them when it's clear that my state of mind is questionable?

Andy looks at me over her shoulder as if she can sense my thoughts. "It's okay," she whispers. "You shouldn't be alone."

Without another word, Andy takes Max to the counter to pay for the karaoke machine while I go outside to grab some much-needed gulps of air.

When they return, Andy places the shopping bag and her purse in the backseat, then loads Max into her car seat, all while I fixate myself by her side. Something about her is comforting, and although she scowls at me and might hate me, she calms my racing mind.

I fucking need that right now.

Closing the door, she looks at me. "I'm not going to ask if you're okay because it's obvious you're not. Right now, I can tell you need someone."

"Why?"

"Why what?"

"Why are you going to spend time with me and help me?"

Sadness fills her eyes, making me desperate to find out everything about her and why making sure I remain in good mental health is important to her. "Because I know what it's like to need someone and not have anyone. Loneliness hurts, so if I can be that person to be there for you when you need someone, then I will." She pauses. "Even if I have been judgmental and possibly rude."

"Possibly rude?" I scoff. "You've been judging me from the moment you laid eyes on me."

Her eyes soften. "I'm sorry." Her white teeth bite into her bottom lip, her gaze fixated on her shoes. "I guess I allowed the media to fill my head with stories about you and bought into them. They don't paint a good image of you, so I believed it. Gullible, I know, but I admit it."

"So, you do know who I am?" That gets her attention. Her beautiful eyes return to mine.

"Of course I do." Her lips twitch with a smile she's trying to fight. "Your songs have helped me through some of the darkest moments of my life."

That's news to me. When we first met, I searched her eyes for any hint of recognition and found none. Not to be cocky, but typically when I encounter someone who knows who I am, they're starstruck.

"Do I need to worry about you being an obsessed fan and taking me hostage? Maybe you'll sell my location to the tabloids?" A playful grin spreads across my lips. "Maybe this was all part of your plan. Get me in your car, drive me to your house, then tie me up."

That earns me an eye roll and a slight grin. "Absolutely." She nods. "That is what I'm going to do. Better hurry and get in the car. Don't want to keep me waiting." Blessing me with another of her small smiles, she climbs into the driver's seat and brings the car to life.

"Fuuuuck." I exhale, discreetly adjusting my dick, before walking around and getting into the passenger seat.

This girl is going to fuck me up.

FIFTEEN

Andy

THANK FUCK DECLAN GETS IN MY CAR AFTER THE LOW FUEL ALERT stops beeping. I didn't stop for gas yesterday like I needed to or even this morning. It's wishful thinking, but I've been hoping that I'll magically have a full tank when I start my car next time.

Yeah, I know, not fucking possible.

"Where are we going, Mommy?" Max asks from the backseat, too excited that her new best friend is sitting in the passenger seat, ready to spend time with her.

I don't know what compelled me to agree with his request for us to spend time with him. Right after agreeing, I'd been thinking of any excuse to come up with to back out of it. An excuse was right on the tip of my tongue when he had his freak-out.

I'm not sure what triggered it, but I noticed him spiraling. He spiraled the same way I have many times. As I stared into his vacant brown eyes, I felt desperate to bring him back to reality and see the spark of life shining in his eyes. At that moment, I knew if he were to leave, he would go and do something that he'd regret.

His eyes showed loneliness, and I wouldn't say I liked it. A knot had formed in my stomach, and I was afraid for him. Fearful of what he'd do to himself if he were left alone.

Little does he know that he's been the person to bring me back from the edge many times before. His music has often been the only thing to keep me centered.

If only he had known that I'm alive because of him.

"Yeah, Andy, where are we going?" Good question.

Considering I'm nearly out of gas, we won't be able to go very far. I could stop and put gas in, but then he'd see that I could only afford to put in ten dollars, which would be equally embarrassing. It wouldn't be nearly as embarrassing as running out of gas with him and my daughter in the car.

So, I swallow my pride and drive toward the closest gas station.

"Need to get gas first, then we can go somewhere." Maybe I'll get lucky, and he won't notice that I can't fill my tank.

During the two-minute drive to the gas station from the thrift shop, Max convinced Declan to get food and then go to the park and picnic. When she was a baby, I'd always take her to the park and lay out a blanket for her to play on while I fed us. It's been a few years since we've done that, and she was too young to remember, so I'm not sure why she wants to do it now.

Buying food and eating in front of Declan isn't something I'm looking forward to, but my girl always gets what she wants.

Parking at an open pump, I slide my SUV into park, then twist the key to shut off the ignition. "I'll get gas quick, then we can go into the store and find something for lunch." Suddenly, I'm flustered with awkwardness and unsure how this will work out.

Thankfully, Max saves me, "Mommy, I have to pee really super-duper bad!" She kicks her legs against my seat, whining like always when she needs to go potty.

"Go," Declan says, unhooking his seat belt. "I'll wait for you, then we can get some food."

Quickly, I take Max out of her car seat and rush into the store with her, knowing that if she has to wait, she'll likely have an accident, and I don't have an extra change of clothes for her.

Once we've washed our hands, I hold her tiny hand and lead her out of the bathroom and back onto the store floor. Thanks to his height, Declan is easy to spot. His eyes find mine, a smile spreading across his face as he makes his way toward us, his hands full of snacks.

My eyes widen at the sight, silently hoping we can pay separately, and I won't have to pay for everything he's getting.

"I wasn't sure what you two would like, so I have yet to get you anything. If you tell me what you want, I can grab it."

"Thanks, but we can do it," I say as Max pulls her hand away, waiting for permission to run and pick out a treat. "She likes to pick out her snacks." Looking at my daughter, who is already staring up at me patiently, I nod, and she runs toward the candy.

"We'll be quick. Just going to grab some sandwiches." I notice in his hands that he already has two turkey and cheese sandwiches, chips, water, and sour gummy worms.

Stepping away, I search for my lunch. Opting for water and the same turkey sandwich as Declan. I grab a peanut butter and jelly sandwich with apple juice for Max.

"Mommy! I got some yummy snacks." She holds the bag of chips in one hand and the bag of mini donuts in the other. No matter what, my girl must always have a sweet and salty treat. She does the same thing whenever she's with me at work, and I allow her to visit the vending machine.

Sometimes, she does things that make me wonder where it came from. Is it random? Or did she get it from the unknown man she shares DNA with? I have more of a salty tooth than a sweet tooth, so I know she didn't get it from me.

I know it's likely random, but the thought still crosses my mind more often than I'd care to admit.

Max follows me to the checkout stand with our food in hand and places her food on the counter beside mine. Joining us,

Declan empties his hands, setting his items next to ours, and my stomach drops.

Oh, fuck. This will be more than expected, especially considering I still need gas.

Gulping, I watch the cashier ringing up the items and tossing them into a bag. The number on the screen is increasing.

As if I weren't spending enough, Declan grabs two Snickers bars from the candy bar display underneath the counter, winking at me as he hands the items to the cashier to scan.

"Your total is $56.75. Cash or card?" the cashier asks, her blue eyes looking between the both of us.

Reaching into my purse for my wallet, I'm prepared to tell her I'll be using my card when Declan steps in front of me with his card in his hand and taps it against the card machine.

It beeps with acceptance, and before I realize what just happened, he's shoving his wallet back into his pocket and grabbing the bag.

"Let's go." Max takes his hand, and the two walk out, leaving me behind with my jaw hanging open.

What the fuck just happened?

No one does anything for free, so what does he want in exchange for buying my daughter and me a gas station lunch?

With my signature scowl back in place, I rush after them, suddenly stopping when I see the nozzle of the gas pump inside my tank.

What the fuck did he do?

"What did you do?" I demand, hands on my hips.

Helping Max into the car, he looks from me to the gas pump I'm staring at. A low chuckle leaves him, his attention turning toward me after Max and the shopping bag are secured in the backseat and the door is closed.

"I left the gas pumping while we were in the store. Figured it would save time."

"You paid for it?" He nods. "Why?"

"Why what?"

"Why did you pay for my gas and our food?"

"Andy"—he steps toward me with a sigh, as if he's already tired of being questioned—"it's food and gas. It's not a big deal. You're letting me intrude on your day, so it's the least I can do." His words are sweet, but I can tell that he wants something. Men always do. No one does anything just because.

"What do you want in exchange for it?"

He takes a step back as if my words had knocked him off-balance. "What the fuck are you talking about?"

"Nothing comes free. So, what do you want? Are you expecting me to suck your dick in exchange for a sandwich?" It wouldn't be the first time that was expected. Before Max, the first and only date I've ever been on, after buying me pancakes at Denny's, he expected to get his dick wet at the end of the date. I hadn't known that until after I thanked him for dinner, and we were in his truck, and I was ready to go home. That's when he began touching and kissing me, telling me that it was the least I could do since he bought me dinner.

Since then, I've learned that nothing comes free, and I'm careful about accepting things because I know everything comes with strings attached.

"Holy fuck, Andy." He shakes his head, exasperated. "Your company is all that I want. You don't know how fucked up my head is right now, but instead of leaving me alone, you're taking time on your day off to spend it with me. That's all I want." He appears genuine, but my guard is too fucking high to know for sure.

"I'm a man, so yeah, I'm always down to have a beautiful woman suck my dick, but that's not what I want, nor do I think that's going to happen. Truly, I want to be around you and Max. That's it." Without waiting for my response, he climbs into the car, staring at me through the windshield.

Fuck.

How can I believe him when I don't even know him? Since he is a stranger, letting him in my car and spending the day with him is the last thing I should do. But to get to know him, I need to spend time with him to do precisely that.

Despite his freak out at the store, which resulted in us leaving early and not getting anything we came for, I don't believe he's a danger to Max.

If anything, he's a danger to himself.

For that, I worry because I can already tell that Declan is someone who has the potential to change my entire life.

For better or worse, I'm not yet sure.

Only time will tell.

SIXTEEN

Declan

As soon as we arrive at the park, Max runs toward the playground when her tiny feet touch the ground after Andy takes her out of her seat. She had grabbed a blanket from the back of her car, and then I helped her spread it over the grass before spreading out the food we bought.

It's obvious that Andy has never had anyone do anything for her just because. That became clear in how she reacted to me buying our food and filling her car with gas. Money isn't an issue for me. The millions I earn from Riot sit in my account and are only used for hotels. A hefty amount was once used for drugs, but not anymore.

Camille hadn't wanted anything during our divorce, so I didn't have any other payments apart from legal fees.

Apart from money from my music career, I have several investments deposited directly into a savings account, which has been accruing interest for years. I'm at a place where a price tag doesn't matter. Meanwhile, Andy is squirming over fifty dollars and a tank of gas, which I understand because I remember what it's like to be broke.

Growing up, I was a poor kid. The kid that went to school with holes in my clothes and pants that were too short for my tall frame. My mom often forgot to send me lunch money or submit the paperwork each school year to qualify for school lunch assistance. She'd always said our finances were our business, and she didn't need everyone at my school to know how much she made. Her pride was more important than her child having a hot free meal every day.

Occasionally, when she was passed out from taking too many drugs, I'd steal money from her wallet to buy myself lunch. I never took more than five dollars, but it was worth it to have at least one hot meal a day. Even if it meant having to lie and gaslight her when she asked what happened to the money. I'd tell her I didn't take it and assure her she miscounted or lost it.

After Adam and I started Riot, we struggled, taking gigs at bars and even bussing tables in exchange for a few bucks or free food.

By the time I got married, my financial situation had improved, but Camille and I struggled initially until Riot got a big break and she started her business.

The point is, I know what it's like, so I'll never fault someone for having to budget and not having anything extra.

A sandwich thrust in my direction steals my attention, suddenly bringing my focus to the woman holding the wrapped food. I take it from her just as my stomach grumbles with hunger. Quickly, I tear into the packaging and take a massive bite.

"Max! Come eat," Andy calls, opening the peanut butter and jelly she picked out for Max and the bottle of apple juice.

A disappointed child approaches, her feet shuffling in the grass as she nears us, brown eyes rolling, "But Mommy, I want to play." She groans, collapsing to the spread blanket with a small thud.

"Eat first. You can go play after." The three of us eat in silence.

When Max is done, she takes off running to the empty playground, climbing up the slide.

"So," I break the silence, hating that the woman who has never had a problem putting me in my place is suddenly silent and seemingly shy. "Come here often?" Her brown eyes look at me, and I wiggle my eyebrows.

Throwing her head back, throaty, deep laughter erupts from her. Dark curls bouncing when she shakes her head. "You're ridiculous."

"But I made you laugh, so I'd consider myself a winner."

"Do you need a prize for making me laugh?"

I think momentarily before answering, "Actually, I do."

"Alright. Pick your prize." I know exactly what I want. Just hope she gives it to me.

"Tell me why you instantly hated me. You know who I am, claim you're a fan, yet you hated me immediately." I've been wondering about it since the other night when we met. Sure, I'd understand if she hated me because I was a stranger talking to her daughter alone at night, but there seems to be more to it than that. Her feelings toward me seem personal.

Andy's shoulders rise with an inhale, her eyes shifting between her hands and Max playing on the playground.

A long moment of silence passes. She clears her throat and speaks when I think she won't answer me.

"I've already admitted the media doesn't paint the best picture of you." She chews her bottom lip, fingers nervously playing with the rose gold ring on her right index finger, "I know you're an addict." The confession hangs between us, thick in the air.

That's not a secret. Everyone knows I'm an addict and have been to rehab, but what they don't understand is accurate details or timelines of my addiction. They've labeled me a recovering addict and act as if I'm healed and am not at risk of relapse.

Considering this woman is still a stranger to me, I should protect myself and not give her any personal information, especially since she hasn't signed an NDA. Many women I've encountered have sold less to the tabloids than I'm about to tell her. But for some reason, I don't think she's that type of person to sell things she learned about me. So, I confirmed what she already knew about me.

Running a hand through my hair and tugging it gently at the roots, I shift my body until we're sitting face to face, and she has no other option than to look me in the eye, "I am, and I always will be, even if I'm no longer using or drinking. You don't stop being an addict just because you're in recovery. Addicts will always have an addiction, which means I'll live with it for the rest of my life. All I can do is wake up each morning and choose to be sober. Choose life instead of being a half-dead, drugged-out zombie." My Adam's apple bobs with my swallow, my hands resting on my bent knees.

"Are you?"

"Am I what?" She eyes me carefully, looking over my exposed skin as if she's expecting to see fresh track marks or some sign that'll reveal I'm lying.

"Are you sober? How long has it been since you've used?"

I appreciate that she asks me exactly what she wants to know instead of beating around the bush. "Yes. I have been sober for three weeks now. It's hard as fuck, but I wake up every day and choose to fight." Why does talking to this woman make me feel better than talking to a therapist ever did?

"How long are you staying here in Loganville, and why are you here?"

"Two months. The rest of the band is in Las Vegas. They think I should be here while we have some downtime, and I'm... newly sober." The admission tastes sour on my tongue, "Eventually, I'll join them and move to Vegas." Two days ago, I couldn't wait to leave this place and join my best friends, but now, since meeting this mother-daughter duo, I don't mind being here for now.

That realization shocks the fuck out of me. It makes no sense, considering I just met this woman and know nothing about her.

Maybe it's the fact that she isn't trying to hop on my dick and doesn't want anything from me. This is the first time in a long time I've been around a woman without any expectations. There's no pressure about letting her down or fulfilling a promise. I don't have to be anything other than myself.

Dare I say there's a chance I could have a friend? A friend other than Max, of course. Since, according to her, we've been best friends.

Andy stares at me, chewing her plump bottom lip. Her eyes narrow as if deep in thought, yet unsure what to say. We've been doing good so far with this whole honesty thing. I don't want her to stop now.

"So, you're only here for two months?" I nod to the confirmation she seeks.

With a heavy sigh, she brushes her curls behind her ears, and I feel I won't like whatever she has to say. I brace myself for impact when she opens her pretty little mouth to speak, "Two things will happen. I'm not sure which will come first." She shifts, sitting a little bit straighter.

"Either you'll leave and break my daughter's heart because she already considers you her best friend and will notice your absence. Or you'll relapse before you leave. It will happen one day because I know it always does." The softness from her eyes disappears as she stares at me.

What the actual fuck?

As if she hadn't twisted the knife hard enough, she opens her mouth to stab me again. "I can't allow an addict around my daughter." There's finality in her tone. It is as if she's been thinking about this for a while and has decided.

I scoff. "So much for being honest with you, right?" my jaw twitches, and I bite my tongue to keep myself from lashing out at her like I've always done whenever I'm hurt.

"Your honesty was appreciated, but I have to protect my child. You've only been clean for three weeks. You're dangerous for her."

She thinks I'm dangerous for Max.

Just like I was dangerous for Luca.

The backs of my eyes sting, and the way she's staring at me makes me feel even more pathetic than I already am. She looks at me as if I'm beneath her. The gum stuck on the bottom of her shoe.

It's a look I've seen many times before. A look that tells me I'm not good enough and never will be. No matter how fucking hard I try, my past will always define me. I will never be anything more than the man who used to stick needles in my veins, constantly chasing a higher high.

Worthless. So fucking worthless.

It should've been me that died.

It should've fucking been me.

Die. Make the world a better place.

Swallowing back the emotion clogging my throat, refusing to allow myself to be any more vulnerable than I've already been, I stand on shaky legs.

"Hurt people, hurt people, Andy," I manage to say through gritted teeth. "I hope one day you heal from whoever hurt you."

Emotionless brown eyes continue staring at me, but I don't spare her another glance before I turn my back on her and walk away, biting the inside of my cheeks to keep myself from displaying any emotion currently clawing its way under my skin.

"Best friend!" a small voice yells, but I don't turn around. I can't. I fucking can't.

I'm dangerous.

"Hey, best friend!" Max screams. "Wait! Best friend!"

With my hands curled in tight fists, I walk toward the hotel.

It isn't until I hear a horn and a yelled "fuck you" that I realize I've been walking in the middle of the road, but I don't care.

Maybe I'll get lucky, and one of these small-town fuckers will put me out of my misery.

When I reach the hotel, my heart is racing, and my hands are aching from where my nails cut into my palms. Bloodied crescent moons reveal how tightly I've had my hands balled into fists.

The way Andy looked at me was the same way Camille used to look at me when she'd come home to find me passed out or high out of my fucking mind. The look of disgust and resentment was evident in her eyes.

Thinking that anyone could look over my past and see me was foolish. See the man behind the addictions and demons. The man who is trying every single fucking day to do better and make up for my sins.

Am I not worthy of redemption? Do I not deserve it?

Have I fucked up so goddamn bad that I don't deserve to be given another chance?

It wasn't like I was trying to marry her. All I wanted was friendship. Someone to talk to. Someone who wouldn't judge me for my past.

It's all wishful thinking.

I'll never deserve a second chance.

This is who I am. This is all I'll ever be.

A burden for everyone.

My best friends and bandmates don't even want me around. They're the only friends and family I have.

My mother didn't want me, so what makes me think that anyone else ever will?

A humorless laugh escapes me as I stare at my reflection in the bathroom mirror. Tears that I hadn't noticed streamed down my face.

Look how fucking weak you are. Crying like a little bitch.

My laughter dies down as I study myself in the mirror, staring into the eyes of my reflection.

I fucking hate what I see.

I hate it so much that I send my fist through the mirror, shattering the glass.

"You're a fuck-up!" I scream, repeatedly hitting the shattered mirror. My body is so numb that I'm unable to feel the glass shards that wedge themselves deeper into the broken skin of my bloodied knuckles.

Droplets of blood run down my hand to my elbow, dripping in the white porcelain sink.

"Fuck you! Fuck you! Fuck you!" I yell until my voice becomes hoarse and my knuckles a torn mess.

Choking on my sobs, I collapse to my knees, hugging my bloodied fist to my chest.

My fingers twitch. I need something to put me out of my misery. Maybe I'll get lucky, and the next time I shove a needle in my veins, it'll be a fatal dose.

I'm constantly torn between life and death. I don't want to live with my sins, and I don't deserve to live for what I've done to my son. But I also don't want to die. I don't want to float away into the abyss and disappear into the darkness of my mind and addictions.

I don't want my loved ones to find my body and be forced to bury me.

I don't want to look up at them from my place in hell as they wear their best Sunday clothes and speak through tears, sharing their favorite memories of me.

Luca's face appears behind my eyelids, and then, Max's face follows soon after.

Fuck.

No. No. No.

I refuse. I can't be that person again.

I don't want to be that person again.

I want to fucking live! I want to wake up with clear sober thoughts, feel the heat of the sun warming my skin, and breathe air into my lungs.

I'm trying so fucking hard to be better. Why can't anyone see?

Why doesn't anyone notice me? Why can't one person see that I am trying so fucking hard to be better? To do better.

With a racing heart and spiraling mind, I shuffle into the

room to the nightstand, reaching for the only thing I must rely on right now to calm myself.

Opening the leather notebook to a blank page, I pull the pen cap off with my teeth and pour my heart out on the blank pages, leaving behind bloody streaks and drops of tears as I frantically write.

I am not broken beyond repair.

SEVENTEEN

Andy

It was impossible to miss the broken look in Declan's eyes when I said what I did to him. Hearing him admit what I already knew and then finding out how long he's been sober had made me furious. It's been over a year since he was in rehab, yet he's only a few weeks sober.

Which proves my point.

He's been to rehab, yet he's relapsed since then. It would be irresponsible to allow Max around someone like that. He'll be gone in two months, but we'll still be here. It's best to cut ties now before my daughter gets her heart broken. She clings to anyone she can, which she already does with Declan. She's known him for two days. I can't imagine how she'd react when he leaves after spending two months together.

I can't do that to her.

I'm a firm believer in the saying, "Once an addict, always an addict." I don't believe addicts can change.

If they can, then why didn't my mother change for me? Was I not worth it?

My entire life, I've always been the one who was supposed to forgive her for letting me down. When I refused to have her toxicity around me, I've always been met with dirty looks and given the "but she's your mother" speech.

Yes, she's my mother, but who told her to clean up her act because I'm her daughter? Who was giving her the "but she's your daughter" speech?

I've come second to a pipe my entire life.

School plays, dance recitals, parent-teacher conferences, everything she should've attended; she was never there because she was too busy getting high. Too busy forgetting about me. Luckily, my grandma was there for me and could step in.

Even though my grandparents raised me, and I consider them my parents, the ache is still very much present and always will be.

Why wasn't I enough?

Why wasn't I fucking enough for her to fight her addiction and be sober. Didn't I deserve that?

Before I was even born, my father made the decision he didn't want me. My mother made the decision that drugs were more important than me a long time ago.

I've lost count of the times I've cried to her and begged her to notice me. Want me. Love me. Spend time with me. Every single fucking day, I fought for her attention, but she never saw me. All my mother could ever see was the pipe in her hands.

Who needed a child when they had meth or heroin.

Not Diane Harris. She had all she needed.

Am I jaded? Absolutely.

Do I view all addicts the same because of my mother? Yes.

Did I judge Declan and assume the worst of him because of my own trauma? Possibly.

However, in my defense, I already know what to expect, and I won't allow him the chance to hurt my daughter. No one will ever have the opportunity to hurt her the way my mother hurt me.

I wish I were able to say that I've come to terms with the fact I'm unwanted, but then I'd be lying. My grandparents wanted me, but they died when I needed them the most. Since they've been gone, all I've felt is like an unwanted burden, which is why I've tried to take my life. Many times, I've wanted to end it.

Living is so fucking hard. If it weren't for Max, I wouldn't be here.

I'm aware of the power words have. And that if Declan goes and does anything stupid, it'll be directly my fault because I pushed him. He's here in Loganville trying to remain sober, going to therapy and meetings. He's fucking trying, which is more than I can say for my mother. But my pride won't let me apologize. All I can do is hope he doesn't do anything stupid, but I'll accept responsibility if he does.

Though, if he does, it'll only prove me right.

Max noticed him the moment he began walking away. He left, leaving me to deal with my heartbroken girl. Can't blame him, considering I was a bitch to him.

When he was out of sight, I packed the remainder of our failed picnic and loaded it into the back of my car. I'd told Max that he had things to do and had to get back to his hotel, but she didn't believe me. She pouted and ignored me the entire drive back to my mom's house.

Luckily, when we arrived, she was gone, so I used the key she hid under her flowerpot and let us in.

We've been here for hours, and Max still hasn't spoken to me. For the first hour, I tried to get her to talk to me but eventually decided to let her have space.

Now she's in the living room playing with the few toys I brought with us while I'm in my old bedroom, lying on my back on my bed, staring up at the white popcorn ceiling, replaying my interactions with Declan from the moment he walked toward us at the thrift store.

Something happened at the store that triggered him. He'd been ready to shrink into himself and bolt, but I was the one that stopped him. I helped him through his panic attack, then an

165

hour later, turned on him and told him his relapse was inevitable.

What the fuck kind of person says shit like that? I can't take the words back. But fuck am I remorseful now.

I'm unsure how long I've been there staring at the ceiling, replaying our conversation, when I hear voices in the living room.

Goosebumps form along my skin, the hair on my arms rising at the nasally voice I remember all these years later.

In the time it takes to blink, I'm up on my feet and running to the living room, grabbing my daughter from the floor and pulling her small body protectively into my arms.

Catching sight of me, the tall, bald-headed man beside my mom smirks. "Andy! Is that you?"

"Andy, baby, you remember Gus?" Mom claps her hands together, swaying back and forth on her feet, her pupils dilated and skin paler than usual.

Great. She's fucking high.

"We're leaving," I announce with a snarl, burying Max's face in my chest, holding her tight as she fights against me, wiggling and crying for me to put her down.

She can continue being upset with me later. Right now, we need to fucking go.

I don't put her down as I grab her backpack and my purse from the floor, quickly gathering up the few belongings we brought with us the best I can manage with one hand.

Footsteps creak down the hallway, stopping outside my open bedroom door, a shadow filling the space. One look over my shoulder tells me it's my mom, but that doesn't ease my worry.

"What the fuck is your problem now, miss perfect princess?" My mother snarls, clicking her tongue as she watches me frantically pack our bags with one hand. I refuse to put my daughter down. I wouldn't bother packing anything if I could afford to replace whatever we'd leave behind.

"Quit acting like a little bitch. You're being rude to my

friend." At the bite in my mother's tone, Max tightens her hold on me, no longer trying to get free.

"We're leaving, Diane." Pulling the straps of our bags over my shoulders, I step up to my mother, who is still blocking the doorway with her arms crossed over her chest.

"Oh, now I'm Diane, again? I see how it is. You're only good enough to come here when you need something."

It's pointless to argue with her. She'll always be the victim, and I'll always be the disrespectful daughter. "Move." I step closer, bumping her arms with mine from the way I'm holding Max.

Throwing her arms in the air dramatically, she steps aside, yelling curses and telling me what a spoiled bitch I am as I rush out of the trailer, smoke invading my senses the moment I step outside.

With a snarl, I turn to see Gus standing against the side of the trailer with a cigarette hanging out of his mouth.

"Climb in your seat and strap yourself in," I whisper in Max's ear, placing her in the backseat before closing the door, then I quickly throw our bags into the trunk of my SUV.

"Where ya running to, sweet Andy?" Gus speaks, using the nickname he gave me years ago that I fucking hate.

I first met him a few months after we moved into the trailer. I woke up, went to the kitchen to find something for breakfast, and found him sitting on the couch drinking a beer like he owned the place. It was nine a.m., but I was sure he'd been up all night. My mom was gone, so I couldn't ask her who the fuck the strange man was. I was used to her bringing random people around our house to party all night, but they were never there when she wasn't.

Thank fuck, Diane had returned soon after, but when I asked about the man, she informed me he was our new roommate. She spent her money on drugs and needed help with the rent, so she rented our third bedroom to a man who was a friend of a friend.

She met him one fucking time before allowing him into our personal space.

The second I learned his full name, I searched for him online, quickly finding out that the forty-five-year-old man was fresh out of prison for molesting a child. The man that slept next door to my room is a pedophile and on the fucking sex offender registry.

Of course, Diane didn't care. She told me that the little girl who accused him of touching her had lied, and he was only convicted because they believed the little girl over him.

I knew it was a lie. He went to prison because he was guilty.

How can a parent not care that a registered sex offender is sharing a house with their underage child? I was fourteen.

He's the reason I started sleeping with a knife under my pillow and a chair in front of my door. Ever since he snuck into my locked bedroom while I was showering and began stealing my panties.

When I told my mom, she said I was making up lies.

One day, when I got in the shower, my bedroom door had been locked. I'd undressed before my bed and left the dirty clothes on the floor. After my shower, I discovered my bedroom door was unlocked, and one thing was missing from my pile of dirty clothes.

My panties.

Over the next few months, several more pairs of panties went missing while I'd been doing laundry. And every chance he got, he'd find some way to put his hands on me. My mom thought it was sweet when he wanted to give me a shoulder massage and yelled at me for being rude when I pushed him away from me.

When he tried to spank me, I was the ungrateful child because he'd brought burritos for dinner and I had declined the food. Which is why he wanted to spank me.

Fuck her and fuck him.

Four months later, he was gone. Apparently, he knocked up a

seventeen-year-old, and they moved away together. I'm unsure why he's back, but I don't care.

Tears stream down my face as I drive, unsure of where to go. Glancing in the rearview mirror, I find Max staring at me, and for once, I'm thankful she's not asking questions. I never allow myself to cry in front of her, but right now, I can't seem to control myself.

I feel so fucking defeated.

We're so close to having our own space again and not having to rely on anyone. One fucking night. That's it.

In the morning, we'll meet with the landlord to get the keys to our new apartment. Everything will be fine come morning, but until then, I need a solution.

Most people have friends or family to help them when they need it. I don't have anyone. What a fucking fool I'd been to think Diane would be capable of being the person to help me when I needed it. A part of me will always be hopeful that one day she'll be capable of being the mother I need, the mother I deserve.

Maybe it's wishful thinking, but the little girl inside me aches for her mother.

Staying at her house last night had been fine, but now she's high and with Gus. There is no way a warm bed is worth risking my daughter around that creep.

I drive aimlessly around our small town for nearly thirty minutes before Max begins complaining she's hungry. Instead of worrying about money, I order food from the dollar menu and find myself in the parking lot of my work.

The hotel is completely booked, so staying there isn't an option, but I do park around on the side where guests or employees are less likely to spot us. The parking on the West side of the hotel is rarely used since the parking spaces are the furthest away from the rooms. The only people parking here are guests traveling with oversized vehicles and trailers.

Making sure we're out of sight of cameras and prying eyes, I keep the car running for the AC and get out to go around to Max's side and get her out of her car seat. Taking a pair of her pajamas from the trunk, I quickly help her change her clothes before setting up a comfortable area with blankets and pillows. Then, I set out her food and let her use my phone to watch cartoons while she eats.

While her attention is elsewhere, I stand outside with my back against the car door, allowing myself a moment of weakness.

Heavy tears streamed down my face, and silent sobs lodged in my throat.

It's okay. We can do this. One night, that's it. We'll sleep in the car for tonight, but everything will be okay again in the morning. This is just a rough patch we're going through. Things will get better.

Life will not always be this hard.

I can do this.

I will get through this.

EIGHTEEN

Declan

SATURDAY NIGHT WAS SPENT WRITING LYRICS UNTIL THE PAGES became too bloody to read. My knuckles throbbed, and my hand ached from the tight grip I'd had on the pen, spending countless hours holding it in a tight fist as I knelt beside the bed, filling page after page with the dark thoughts that lived inside my head. Blood coated the white sheet beneath me, everything I touched becoming smeared with crimson.

Once I finished writing, I cleaned myself up, opting to shower and allow the hot water to wash away the monster in my mind. After I cleaned my knuckles, carefully removing shards of glass, I wrapped my hand in toilet paper until I could get to the front desk. Luckily, they had a first aid kid with everything I needed to bandage my hand.

I didn't bother telling them the bathroom mirror would need replacing. I figured when it came time to check out I'll let them know then and pay for the damage. However, I did ask for a change of sheets that I immediately put on my bed once I returned to my room, rolling up the bloodied sheets into a tight ball and shoving them into the trash can.

With clean sheets and a fresh mind, I climbed into bed and lay there restlessly for hours before finally falling asleep.

173

By seven a.m., I'm awake. My hand hurts like a bitch, but I deserve the pain. I'd rather feel a throbbing hand than nothing at all. Too many times, I've numbed myself, burying my emotions when they became too much because I was too weak to deal with the pain. Not anymore. I can't do that anymore.

Feeling any type of pain is inevitable, whether physical or emotional. Whatever it is, I welcome it because it's a reminder that I am alive.

I am fucking alive.

Cradling my bandaged right hand to my chest, I reach the nightstand with my left hand to grab my phone, bringing up my text thread with Adam.

ME

I'm ready to get back in the studio. I've got some new shit.

Adam is an early riser, so I'm not surprised when he texts back almost immediately. Sometimes, I wonder if he ever sleeps. There have been many nights when I've texted him at different hours, and his replies always come quickly.

ADAM

Fuck yeah! I knew a change of scenery would be good. Whatcha got so far?

ME

I came up with two new songs last night. Working on a third.

ADAM

Proud of you, man. I'll hit up Benny.

ME

I'll send you what I have.

Sitting up, I grab the black leather notebook I carry to jot down lyric inspiration whenever it hits and take pictures of the bloodied pages from last night, sending them to Adam.

My phone lights up five minutes later with an incoming Face-Time call from him. Rolling my eyes, I click the green button.

"What the fuck happened? I know you pour your soul into your writing, but what did you do? Try to cut out your heart?" My best friend's voice eases some of the aches in my chest. Out of my friends, Adam is the one I'm closest to. He is the only one who truly knows my darkest parts because he was there with me during those moments. He's the one I confided in when my addiction got worse and through all the shit Camille and I were going through. He knows it all and has never judged me.

"Nah, man, yesterday was rough," I confess, sighing at his green eyes studying me closely. "I met a girl, and she said some shit that fucked me up."

"Declan." Concern is evident in his tone. He rarely calls me by my name. "Don't worry about some chick. Your mental health and staying sober is what's important. Not some pussy who will end up becoming a crazy bitch when you inevitably kick her out of your bed."

I chuckle, shaking my head. "It's not like that, bro. She's not interested in me. We only met because of her kid."

His eyes widened at the mention of Max. "She has a kid? Abort mission. That's too messy. You're not staying in Logan-wherever the hell you are."

"Yeah, she said that. She doesn't want me around because…" I hesitate, my cheeks heating with embarrassment. "Because I'm an addict. She thinks I'd be a danger to her daughter."

Adam's eyes soften, but it's not a look of sympathy. He knows that I love kids and that being a father was the greatest gift I ever received. Despite my bullshit, I was the best fucking dad to Luca and always put him first. Up until the night I ruined everything, I'd never been high around him. Countless nights away on tour, new city, new bed every night. I was too fucking lonely being away from my family. Too much time on my own to think and send myself spiraling.

I'd always start with a drink and wouldn't stop until I was high out of my fucking mind. After each tour, I'd clean myself up and then return home. But the last tour before Luca died is what fucked me up the most, and I don't know why.

Our tour ended in the UK, and I stayed behind for two weeks to withdraw and get better, but I couldn't. By the time I went home, Camille and I were fighting nonstop, and all I craved was the carefree high that I'd experienced every day during the six-month tour.

The night Luca died, I'd caved and bought drugs in an alleyway outside of the restaurant where we were celebrating his fourth birthday.

After burying my son, I no longer felt the need to be sober. I spiraled every single fucking day until I hit rock bottom.

My wife cheated on me and then left me.

My friends were disappointed in me.

I hated myself.

Now, I'm fighting daily to prevent myself from falling that low again.

"You're a good man, Dec. If this chick will lead you to send me pictures of bloody pages, leave her alone. She's not worth it if she makes you do stupid shit."

"I think she's just as fucked up as me," I admit, remembering the way Andy looked at me when I confirmed her assumptions about me being an addict. The way her plump lips curled and her brown eyes narrowed will forever be engraved in my mind. She looked at me with disappointment. Like I was going to eventually be another person to let her down.

Andy doesn't strike me as someone who relies on anyone, but for some strange reason that I don't fucking understand, I want her to be able to depend on me. I want her trust. To give me the chance to prove her wrong.

Leaving her alone isn't something I want to do. Only after she's even given me a chance to prove myself.

"All I'm saying is be careful. Don't let this chick fuck-up the progress you're making." It's going to be hard as fuck to break down Andy's walls, and I shouldn't want to, but for some unknown reason, I do.

Perhaps it was the look in her eyes when we met. Beyond the scowl and sour looks is a vulnerable shy woman, that something tells me she's got more issues than I can fathom. Putting together the fucked up puzzle that is Andy isn't something I should want to do, but I'm unable to stop myself.

Did she say hurtful shit to me yesterday? Absofuckinglutely.

Am I going to forgive her for it? Not easily.

Do I want to see her again and force her to give me a chance? Yes.

Am I a dumb fuck for wanting these things? 100%.

Adam and I talk for a few more minutes, then end the call with me promising to send him any other songs I can come up with.

♪ ♪ ♪ ♪ ♪ ♪

LEANING MY BACK AGAINST THE BRICK WALL OF THE HOTEL, I BRING the lit cigarette to my lips, inhaling the minty nicotine deep into my lungs.

Pushing off the wall, I keep the cigarette pinched between my lips as I walk along the sidewalk around the building.

One hand in my pocket, I keep my damaged knuckles close to my side, the broken skin itching. It wouldn't be the first time I've busted open my knuckles. Every time I do it, I swear it'll be the last time because the healing process sucks. Yet here we are.

At this point, my skin is going to be permanently scarred.

Kicking a rock with the toe of my Vans, I stop when I see a lone car parked in the empty lot. A gray Nissan Pathfinder, looking identical to Andy's. I was in the car yesterday, excited to get out of the hotel and spend time with someone other than my thoughts.

I'd been so fucking excited when she agreed to spend the day with me, but once we got to the park, she ruined it by opening her mouth. Not going to lie; it was embarrassing as fuck having her look at me with those judgmental eyes and her pretty mouth telling me it was only a matter of time until I relapsed.

For the first time in a while, I was so fucking excited, then she crushed me.

Adam is right. I should stay away from her, but my mind and body must not be communicating because suddenly, I'm walking toward the car, stomping out my cigarette as I go.

At first, I'm not sure it's hers, but as I get closer, it becomes clear.

Standing beside the driver's side, I peek into the car, eyes widening at the sight of Andy lying back in her seat, a small pink blanket across her chest, eyes closed, and long black eyelashes fanned across her cheeks.

What the fuck? Did she sleep in her car?

Gently tapping on the window to not startle her, I cup my hands around my eyes and peek into the backseat in search of Max. Her tiny body is visible, cuddled up with blankets and pillows.

I check the handle.

Locked.

Tap.

Tap.

Tap.

I knock again, brown eyes shoot open, lips parting as if she's gasping, but I can't hear it. Andy wipes her eyes, turns her head to the side to check on a sleeping Max, and then brings up the back of her chair. Stepping back, I allow Andy space to climb out of the car.

A light-red paints her heated cheeks with embarrassment,

and her eyes look everywhere but at me as she wraps her arms around herself.

I take in the sight of her, noticing she's wearing the same clothes she wore yesterday.

Hoping to ease some of her embarrassment, I attempt a joke, "Stalking me, I see. Knew you were an obsessed fan."

Finally, her eyes meet mine, shock and appreciation filling her brown orbs. She's still embarrassed, but I'm unsure if it's just because I found her sleeping in her car or if she's also embarrassed about what she said yesterday.

Hopefully, it's both.

Shifting on my feet, I run my bandaged hand through my hair, catching her eyes and ending our silence.

"What happened to your hand?" she asks, her morning voice raspy and sexy as fuck.

I could make up an excuse, but why should I? "Didn't have a very good night." She continues staring at my hand, and then, slowly, her eyes met mine. This time, hers are full of remorse.

Good.

"Declan." She sighs, and my pants grow tight at the sound of my name on her lips. "I'm so fucking sorry," she whispers, her shoulders dropping. Her arms fall to her sides, defeat filling her face. "So fucking sorry. You didn't deserve that. My problems are mine, and I had no right saying that shit to you." I get the feeling that apologies are rare for Andy. She strikes me as the type of stubborn woman who'll justify anything to keep herself from muttering the words, *I'm sorry.*

I was once the same way, but through therapy, I've learned that apologizing isn't a sign of weakness. It's okay to admit when you're wrong.

"No, I didn't deserve that, Andy. Was pretty fucked up of you to say that shit considering you don't even know me."

She nods. "It was. Especially after you've done so much for me." What have I done for her? She must notice my confusion because, thankfully, she clarifies, "The gas and the food."

"That was nothing."

"It wasn't nothing," she states firmly. "No one has ever done anything like that for me before."

I'm both surprised and pissed that no one has ever done something so fucking simple for this girl.

"I ruined our day."

"Yeah, you did," I state, not willing to let her off the hook so quickly for the shit that happened yesterday. Six months ago, I would've kept my feelings to myself and pretended it was fine until one day, I blew up, admitting it wasn't okay. But I'm not that man anymore. At least, I'm trying not to be.

I'm trying to be better at communicating.

"Come to my room." She steps back, taken aback by my request.

"Why?"

"Because you slept in your car, and I'm sure you'd like to be able to change your clothes and brush your teeth." Wrapping her arms around her waist, she thinks momentarily before opening her mouth, agreeing quickly.

"Thank you. We won't be very long. We're moving into our new apartment today, so we'll be going to pick up the keys soon.

When she grabs Max's sleeping body from the car, I stop her and tell her I got her. Carefully, I pick up the small girl, holding her against my chest while Andy grabs a bag from the back of the car.

"Lead the way." She gestures, so I do.

Max stirs in my arms after we enter my hotel room, her brown eyes widening when she sees me holding her.

"Best friend?" She groans in equal confusion and excitement, unsure if she's still dreaming. Her small fists rub her eyes, a yawn leaving her little mouth.

"Good morning, Max." She smiles, throwing her arms around my neck and hugging me tight.

"You left me, best friend." She sniffles. "You never said bye." My heart aches. I never meant to allow my anger to impact her. I should've known she'd be left confused by my sudden departure.

"I'm sorry, Max. It won't happen again." She nods, and I set her down.

"Come on, baby. We'll use Declan's bathroom to get ready for the day and pick up our keys." That causes Max to jump and cheer with excitement.

"Best friend, you get to see my room!" She squeals.

Andy's quick to rain on her parade by saying, "He's not coming with us, Max."

"Actually," I interject before my new mini-best friend is ultimately defeated. "I don't have anything planned today. Do you need help moving in? I'm sure you have more stuff to move."

"Are you sure?"

"I wouldn't have offered if I wasn't." A small smile spreads across Andy's face, one that she tries to keep hidden but fails.

Goddamn, she's beautiful when she smiles. Wish she did it more often instead of scowling.

"That would be great. I don't deserve it after yesterday, but thank you." Nodding, I turn my attention to Max.

"Looks like I'll get to see your new room after all." While she cheers her way into the bathroom after announcing she has to go potty, I return my focus to Andy, standing directly in front of her so she's unable to look away from me this time.

"You owe me because of yesterday." She gulps but nods, the movement causing a stray curl to fall in front of her eyes. Without thinking, I raise my non-injured hand and brush the soft curl away, tucking it behind her ear.

"Get to know me, Andy," I whisper, keeping my fingers in her soft, dark hair. "Not the version of me you think you know from the media. The real me. Give me a chance to prove I'm not a total fuck-up."

"You're leaving in two months, Declan."

"I'm not asking for you to marry me. I'm asking you to put

your guard down and allow yourself to get to know me. As a friend."

"As a friend?" she whispers, her voice warm against my lips from our closeness.

I nod. "As a friend. I think we could both use one right now."

"Okay."

Little did I know, her agreement would seal my fate.

NINETEEN
Declan

It's been two weeks since Andy agreed to control her poisonous tongue and agreed to be friends. After she and Max used my room to prepare for the day, we stopped at a drive-thru to grab breakfast before going to their new apartment to pick up the keys. She signed the papers and handed over a check, and the smile that formed on her face after receiving the keys to her new apartment is one I'll never forget. I've never seen such pure joy on her face in the few days I've known her. It was much different from the constant scowl she seemed to have when it came to me.

Afterward, we went to her former apartment and loaded all their belongings into her car. Since none of the furniture had been hers, it had only taken two trips. They didn't have a lot, but over the next two weeks, Andy has been able to decorate her and Max's apartment and make it feel like a home.

We even had a repeat of the day at the thrift shop and went back to pick out furniture. I tried to buy her a new couch as a housewarming gift, but she turned me down, telling me the small gray sectional she picked out for seventy-five dollars was all she wanted. The couch had a massive stain and had been covered in animal hair. It had taken her three days to clean it before anyone could sit on it, but now it looks like a brand-new couch.

During the last two weeks, I have seen Andy every day. I go into the lobby every weekday for breakfast, and she's behind the desk. Whenever she's not with a guest, I make it a point to stop at the desk and chat with her. She helped me to find an NA meeting, which I can proudly say I've been attending twice a week at the local community center.

On the weekends, I've taken her and Max out for breakfast, and then we usually go for a walk or to the park, which leads us to get lunch and ice cream at Scoops afterward.

The weekends give me something to look forward to.

I was right about Andy. She's so fucking guarded and doesn't let people in easily. When she speaks, it's never about anything personal, and I haven't pushed her to either, in fear of how she'd react when her back is up against the wall.

So, I've been taking things slow. I am navigating our friendship at her pace. Though I can't say it's not frustrating. All I want is for her to trust me and to open up, but it's clear that's not something she does effortlessly. Especially when every day she has made it a point to bring up the fact I'll eventually be leaving. It's almost like she's reminding herself and using that as an excuse not to get too close.

It's a sad way to live. But I recognize it because it's how I've been living, too. Too damn afraid of letting someone truly in.

Even during my marriage, there were parts of me that I kept to myself, afraid to reach that depth of vulnerability.

Today is Saturday, and Andy texted me a few minutes ago to let me know she was on her way to pick me up. Seeing her name on my screen was enough to put a smile on my face and have me bouncing in anticipation, anxious to see the two girls responsible for brightening my days and making my time here bearable.

Slipping my checkered Vans on, I shove my room key and wallet into my back pocket before stepping outside the room. The heavy door slams shut behind me as I lean against the cement wall. Quickly pulling out the pack of smokes from my pocket, I place one between my lips and light it up, inhaling the smoky menthol deep into my lungs.

The familiar gray SUV pulls into the parking lot, stopping in the empty parking space in front of me. A smiling Andy sits behind the steering wheel, causing my lips to curl into a smirk.

Tossing my cigarette to the ground, I step it out before walking toward the car and climbing in, the cold AC instantly cooling my heated skin. One thing about this town I have yet to get used to is the heat. The desert heat is no joke, and constantly suffocating no matter the time of day.

"Hi, best friend!" Max shouts from the backseat, her voice filled with excitement.

Looking over my shoulder, I smile at my little buddy, reaching my arm back to partake in the special handshake she told me we needed last weekend. We'd been sitting at Scoops eating ice cream when she grabbed my hand and said, "Best friends need special super-secret handshakes." We spent the next thirty minutes trying to develop something that she deemed unique enough.

"Hi, Max. I'm happy to see you finally." Andy brought Max to work with her last week, but she's started her new daycare since then.

"I missed you so much!" Max wasn't happy about returning to daycare, but Andy told me two days ago that she was making friends and now looks forward to going each day.

"I missed you too, little buddy. Good thing we're going to spend the day together." Turning my attention toward Andy, I see her sitting back in her seat, watching Max and me interact with a smile. I love how much she smiles now. She's too beautiful to always be angry and scowling. If she's not careful, she'll end up getting premature wrinkles from doing all that shit.

Unable to help myself, I reach across and brush away the stray curl that always finds a way to fall into her eyes. "Hello to you, too. I also missed you."

A soft blush tints her cheeks before she clears her throat and looks away, placing the car into reverse and backing out of the parking spot. "Hi," she says quickly, eyes darting forward to focus on the road.

"So, what are we doing today, ladies?"

"Mommy said we're going to the fruit festival," Max chimes in from the backseat, her tablet long abandoned and her focus fully engaged in whatever conversation is going to happen.

"The Cherry Festival," Andy corrects, looking at me from the corner of her eye. "It's something this town does every summer. They have a lot of vendors, food trucks, face painting, dancing, and live entertainment." She pauses, an amused look coming over her. "Although, I doubt the entertainment would be anything compared to you. It's mostly local bands. Usually garage bands with teenagers, and middle-aged dads."

"So, a farmers market?" I clarify. She shrugs.

"Eh, I guess. But several stands sell cherry everything from cherry pie to cherry jam and cherry-infused lip balm. You'll find it there if you can use cherries to make it. Max loves all the cherry candy." she pauses, a soft smile spreading along her plump lips, "It's a town tradition. I've been coming with my grandparents since I was a baby. When they died, I continued going, and after Max was born, I started taking her every year." I sit silently while Andy speaks, appreciating that she's opening up to me when it's rare for her to do so. Until now, I had no idea her grandparents had passed away. She's never said anything about her family, but I've been curious. About where her family and Max's dad are, but I've never asked. I've been keeping my questions to myself.

Before I could ask her any other questions, we stopped on a dirt path beside several cars.

"Don't know why, but people come from out of town to attend the cherry festival." She laughs, shaking her head as if she doesn't understand why people would travel to some small-town cherry-themed farmers' market.

Fucking strange. Have I ever mentioned how much I hate small towns?

Hand in hand, Max and I follow Andy to the entrance of the Cherry Festival, which is located inside an art museum. That makes it even stranger, but I can't deny that I'm amused by this quirky little town.

With my phone in hand, I snap pictures of the inside of the gallery and remind myself to send them to Spencer, my ex-sister-in-law, later, knowing that she'll be horrified about seeing all the vendor booths set up inside the museum.

Spencer owns an art gallery in Seattle, and her love of art is something I'll never understand. After Camille and I got married, she quickly became one of my best friends. After the divorce, we've continued to keep in contact. In fact, I stay in contact with both of Cam's parents, too. The dynamic isn't typical, but it works for us. Apart from my bandmates, they're the only family I have.

Spencer has often tried to teach me about art and share what she sees in it, but I will never understand how a canvas of shapes and random brush strokes can have a deeper meaning.

"Come on, let's start outside, and then we'll come back," Andy says, leading us through the building until we reach the back doors that are propped open, people coming in and out.

Before we step outside, Andy points down a long hallway, a smile on her lips. "Down that hall is a dance studio. I took ballet when I was a kid." A ballet studio in an art museum? Oh, God. There's something really weird about this town.

As we walk through the building, I take in all the booths, promising myself to return to check them out despite how weird I think this whole thing is.

We make it outside, and Max instantly starts cheering when she sees the bouncy house, begging Andy to let her go and play.

To my surprise, Andy agrees. Not needing to be told twice, Max drops my hand and runs toward the bouncy house. From where we stand, I watch as she climbs inside and starts jumping around, instantly falling into giggles as the other kids jump with her.

Andy watches her daughter with a content smile, genuine happiness, and calm coming over her.

While we walked around, exploring more of the outdoor activities and even more booths, I wanted to learn more about what she said in the car.

Feeling hopeful that Andy might be willing to continue opening up and giving me pieces of herself like she did in the car, I ask, "Did you come here with your parents, too?"

The question catches her off guard. She stares at me, blinking, and just when I think she's about to shut down and push me away, she shakes her head. "My grandparents were my parents. They raised me." She turns away and walks in front of me. Her shoulders are tight with tension, her face set in an unreadable expression as if she's having an internal battle with herself.

I fall into step behind her, allowing her to set our pace and work out the thoughts in her pretty head before speaking or pushing for anything further.

Finally, she slows her pace until I'm beside her, then shares more of her story with me, "My dad left when my mom was pregnant. He didn't raise me or want me."

"Have you ever met him?"

She nods. "Once. When I was pregnant. Found him online. He lives in Vegas." She scoffs, her brown eyes rolling. "An hour away. Can you fucking believe that?" she laughs a humorless laugh.

"He has a wife and son. I have a half-brother I've never met, and he doesn't know about me. I was seven months pregnant but drove to Vegas to meet him. He couldn't even be bothered to meet me halfway or come to me." The way she speaks is as if she doesn't give a fuck, but the look on her face, the hurt in her eyes, tells me otherwise. She feels the rejection of her father, and it makes me angry for her. Furious that the piece of shit was able to produce such a beautiful daughter but wasn't man enough to stay and raise her or even get to know her when she reached out to him. Fuck him. He doesn't deserve her.

"We met at some run-down diner off the freeway. You should've seen the way he was dressed. Way too overdressed for that shitty diner. Some fancy designer suit. When it was time for the check, he requested two. I mean, really, he wore a fucking Rolex and drove a Mercedes but couldn't buy me a twelve dollar meal." She shakes her head, hurt shining in her eyes. "He showed me pictures of his son and talked about him and his wife. Never asked me any questions about myself. When he noticed I was pregnant, all he said was, "Oh, wow. I'm going to be a grandpa." As if he has any right to claim that title. A tear that she'd been trying so hard to hold back escapes, rolling down her cheek.

Andy angrily wipes that tear away, continuing her story, "He didn't even know my name. He called me Andrea, and when I told him it's Andy, he laughed and said he was using my full name." Her dark eyebrows pull together. "Andy is my real name. I know it's usually a nickname for people, but it's not for me. I told him that, but he didn't care and quickly started talking about his son." She wipes another tear away.

"I realized that it wasn't that he was incapable of being a father. It was that he didn't want to be my father. He chose not to be my dad. Meanwhile, some other kid got to grow up in a normal two-parent household with a dad who loves them. A dad who can fucking be there. Who wants to be there." Tears stream down her face, but she doesn't wipe them away. She looks me in the eye, and for the first time, I see hurt and vulnerability staring back at me. The walls she keeps around her heart crumble one by one, just enough for me to be able to climb over the wall.

"Why didn't he want me, Declan? Why does he want to be a dad to someone else but not to me?" Her bottom lip quivers, and my heart fucking breaks for this girl. The girl is wearing her heart on her sleeve for the first time. The girl who is allowing me to see an unhealed piece of herself that will never recover from that childhood trauma.

Stepping closer to her, our toes bump together, her breasts brushing against my chest as we stand so fucking close, sharing the same breath. "Fuck him. It's his fucking loss." Brushing her hair behind her ears, I place my hands on the sides of her face, tilting it back so she's staring directly into my eyes. "He doesn't deserve you. You didn't do anything to deserve an absent father, and I'm so fucking sorry. But don't you dare think you did anything wrong." Her lips parted as her breathing quickened, minty breath fanning across my lips.

"Tell me, baby. Say it's not your fault." Using my thumbs, I wipe her tears away, hating that she's crying over how unworthy she feels because of the weak man who is nothing more than a sperm donor.

"It's not my fault," she whispers, eyes never leaving mine. Her body steps closer, her hands fisting the sides of my T-shirt at my waist. We're so close that I can feel her heart beating against my chest.

"Louder."

"It's not my fault." She raises her voice, brown eyes shining. "Fuck him." She smiles, her nose inches away from mine.

"That's my girl."

"Declan," she whispers my name in a desperate plea, her nose rubbing against mine, her eyelids slowly closing as she presses herself against me, lips parting as she approaches.

With a racing heart, I fight the urge to strip her bare in front of all these people and bury my cock in her warm pussy, pounding into her until her eyes roll back into her head and I'm the name she's screaming.

I want to fuck her so hard that twenty years from now, when she's having mediocre sex with her husband and using her vibrator after he falls asleep, I'm the one she's thinking about.

I want to implant myself so fucking deep under her skin that

I'll leave my mark on her and make sure there's no possible way she could ever forget me.

But I can't do that, because she's too good for me. So, instead of giving in to what I want, I clear my throat and pull away.

"We should go find Max." I don't miss the hurt and rejection that flashes in her eyes.

I feel like a piece of shit instantly, but I'd feel like an even bigger one if I were to lead her on and am unable to give her what she wants. She's vulnerable, and I was there, which is why she tried to kiss me. It's not because I'm special. It's because I was there.

She'll realize I was doing her a favor. Had I allowed our lips to connect, there's no fucking way that would've been enough for me. I would take from her until there's nothing left, and I can't do that to her.

She doesn't deserve to have another man break her.

TWENTY

Andy

OH MY GOD. I'M A FUCKING IDIOT.

Not only did I cry in front of Declan, but I tried to kiss him when he'd just been trying to comfort me. Like a fool, I read the situation wrong and wanted to shove my tongue in his mouth. He was so close to me, smelling so damn good, and he was there comforting me when I revealed how I felt about the man I share DNA with. I've never talked about my father before because I've never had anyone to discuss him with.

My mother was so against me meeting him that she wasn't even willing to go to Vegas with me when I begged her. I promised that she wouldn't have to see him. I was willing to let her use my car to go anywhere else and even offered her money. All I'd wanted was someone to be on that trip with me, but she couldn't do that.

Instead, she cussed me out for wanting to meet him. Telling me I should forget about him because he didn't want me. He left us and knew where I lived for sixteen years, yet never once chose to reach out to me.

Before I blocked him on social media, I saw we even had mutual friends. Mutual friends! Yet he never cared about reaching out to me or getting to know me.

I could tell during our dinner that he wasn't interested in being there. He was humoring me in hopes I'd never reach out to him again. Meanwhile, I was fighting a silent battle while I sat across from the man who didn't want to be my father. It was a mindfuck seeing how many features we had in common. I've always known I didn't look like my mother, and seeing the man in real life whose features I share meant a lot to me.

Unfortunately, it didn't mean anything to him.

He couldn't wait to get out of there quick enough. There was no promise to keep in touch, nothing. All that I got was a wave as I was left alone at the table to pay for my meal and drive my pregnant-self home, all while tears streamed down my face the entire time.

Sometimes, I feel guilty because my grandpa was my everything. He was the only father figure I've ever known, and he was the man who showed up. At any school function, he was there in the audience.

He was there for every book fair, *Bring Your Dad to School Day*, and *Dads and Donuts Day* at school. But despite having a fantastic grandpa, I'd always been curious about my biological father. Even more so after I got older and lost my grandpa.

I'm terrified that Max will grow up and have the same feelings. She doesn't have any father figure in her life, but one day when she's old enough, I want her to know that I tried so fucking hard to give her someone.

That's partly why she's clung to Declan the way she has. She asks about him daily, lighting up whenever she sees or talks to him.

The day after he gave me his number, I woke up to find her FaceTiming him because she missed him. No matter what I do now, she will be heartbroken when he leaves in a month and a half. I tried to prevent it, but it's bound to happen because she already loves him.

I can't blame her. Declan is amazing with my daughter. He's a natural with children, but I see the sadness in his eyes every time they interact. He's never opened up about losing his son, but I can't blame him for that, considering each time he's tried for us to get to know each other better, I've been the one to stop him. I'm too afraid to get close and let him see the real me.

Guess what? It doesn't matter now, considering I was vulnerable with him today. Getting to know him would be a good idea. But how can I keep my heart out of it? That's the problem. I have a terrible habit of falling for all the right words too quickly. I'm too desperate to have someone and not be alone, and I'm at risk of falling in love with the next man to offer me any attention.

God, I'm such a fucking mess.

Wiping the corners of my eyes with a napkin, I stare at my reflection in the mirror. After the failed kiss, I'd run into the bathroom while Declan checked on Max. I've been in here for over ten minutes, so it's considered avoiding him now.

With a slow breath, I dry my face and dig into my purse for my makeup bag. Taking out the pink sheer lip gloss, I run the sticky gloss over my plump lips, then swipe some mascara over my dark lashes.

"No more tears, Andy. So what if he doesn't want to kiss you. Don't act weird about it." I mumble, forcing myself to smile at my reflection, hoping the embarrassment and rejection will vanish from my eyes at the action.

Huffing out a breath, I toss my makeup bag back into my purse, then pull the strap over my shoulder, forcing myself to pull on my big girl panties and exit the bathroom.

Spotting Declan in the crowd is almost instant. Our eyes have become magnets over the past two weeks spent together. It's like we can feel when the other is looking for the other because, in a matter of seconds, our eyes find each other.

Just like now.

With a smile, he waves his hand as if I'm not staring right at him. He turns to face me completely, and laughter bursts from me at the sight of him carrying Max on his shoulders while she eats from a bag of popcorn.

Popcorn pieces fall from Max's tiny hands into Declan's face, but he doesn't seem bothered by it. Meanwhile, my girl shoves the cherry-coated goodness into her mouth by the handful.

When he turns to pay the vendor at the stand they're currently at, I take a moment to quickly whip out my phone and take a picture of the two of them.

Approaching them, I can't contain the grin spreading across my glossy lips. "She's going to be so hopped up on sugar that I'll never get her to sleep tonight. I should make you come over and be the one to put her to bed."

He chuckles, one hand holding onto Max's leg while the other has a bag of chocolate-covered cherries. "I'm up for the challenge." Taking a candy from the bag, he holds it out to me between two fingers.

He pulls his hand away when I reach for it, guiding the candy toward my mouth. Eyes on his, I part my lips, allowing him to place the chocolate-covered cherry in my mouth.

Declan feeds me the candy, his finger running along my tongue, my lips closing around the thick digit. He smirks, pulling his fingers away and shoving them into his mouth, "Delicious."

The pulse between my legs throbs as I watch him, my thighs clenching together and begging for relief. I've been one horny bitch since meeting him, and I don't see that ending anytime soon. His appearance alone is enough to make me want to jump on his dick, as I'm sure most women do.

But one thing I know for sure about Declan is that I'm not his type. I'm not the type of woman he's been photographed with. The women he dates are all beautiful enough to be models and are physically fit. None of them are as big as I am. Which I've come to accept.

I have a love-hate relationship with my body, which I always have and always will. I won't wake up one day and be a size six. This is the body I have, so I'm going to love it because it's the body that grew and gave birth to my daughter.

Every day, I try to remind myself to be kind to myself.

One day, someone might tell my daughter she looks like me, and I don't want her to be ashamed of herself because of the way her mother talks about herself. Max hears everything, and the last thing I ever want her to hear is how I speak and think about myself.

It's hard when you don't like what you see in the mirror, but I'm trying. Part of accepting myself is realizing that not every man is attracted to bigger women, and that's okay. We all have our preferences, and I'm not Declan's. Do I think that's the reason why he rejected my kiss? No. He's not that shallow. But it did sting and create doubt.

Mixed signals are more like it, considering he just fed me candy, touched my tongue, and then licked the finger that touched my tongue.

What was that about?

Regardless, it was hot. He'll be a great fantasy.

I can't wait to think about him and this moment tonight in bed while I finger myself.

♪ ♪ ♪ ♪ ♪

WE SPENT THE ENTIRE DAY AT THE CHERRY FESTIVAL. MAX GOT A pink and purple glitter butterfly painted on her face, then went to the temporary tattoo station and got a couple airbrush tattoos because she wanted to be like Declan.

She managed to talk him into trying all the treats, despite my protests, and since my girl has him so wrapped around her finger, he gave in and bought her everything she wanted.

A new stuffed animal, non-toxic, peelable nail polish from one of the vendors, and way too much candy. They made it their mission to visit each booth and buy everything that was either cherry-scented or flavored.

Max also wanted Declan to wear cherry-flavored lip balm, so

he bought one for himself. The three of us have enough cherry products to last the rest of our lives.

At one of the booths, she pointed out the red bottle of perfume I have at home sitting on my dresser. "That's your perfume, Mommy," she'd said with a smile, proud of herself for remembering.

Declan's response was to lean in and sniff me with a smirk, nodding when he said, "I knew you smelt like cherries."

Five minutes later, I was walking away with a bag containing two more bottles of the perfume I buy yearly, along with the matching shower gel, lotion, and body spray. I tried to protest, but Declan didn't want to hear it and bought it anyway.

I raised an eyebrow in question when I saw that he purchased an extra set for himself but otherwise kept my mouth shut.

We ate our weight in food, and now that the sun is going down, we're leaving.

Holding Declan's hand, Max skips toward the car, still hopped up on her sugar high. She ate more junk food than ever before, and with all her energy, I'm hoping she crashes when we get home. It's been a long day. The last thing I want is to get home and fight her over going to sleep.

"Did you have a nice time?" I ask Declan once we're in the car and leaving.

"I did, actually. I'll admit it's surprising. I didn't have high hopes for this festival, but it proved me wrong." From the corner of my eye, I can see him staring at me. "Helped that I had great company, too."

I gulp, nodding at his words. Sometimes, I can't tell if he's flirting with me when he does or says certain things. That's another thing about me. Be nice to me, and I'll think you're flirting.

Delusional.

There have been several times over these last two weeks that I could've sworn he was flirting or had lust in his eyes when he looked at me, yet when I tried to act on that feeling and tried to kiss him today, he rejected me.

Remembering that is enough to cool my heated body. I'd been so embarrassed but played it off the best I could, pretending it didn't bother me. Neither of us brought it up, instead choosing to focus on Max and going everywhere she wanted to go and trying everything she wanted to try. But now that the day is ending and I can't use my daughter as a protective shield, the awkwardness has returned between us.

After several minutes of silence, Declan ends it by clearing his throat. "I think Max is passed out," he says, looking into the backseat. One glance into the review mirror tells me he's right.

My girl has passed out in her car seat with a bag of candy on her lap and chocolate smeared on her face. Her lips are parted, and tiny snores escape her as the sugar high finally catches up with her.

A small laugh escapes my lips. "Good. It's hard to get her to sleep when she's hopped up on sugar. I was dreading having to put her to bed tonight. She becomes a cranky monster when the rush starts to wear off." I glance at the sleeping girl in the backseat again. "Wish I could sleep as peacefully as she does."

"Are you not sleeping well?" he asks.

Declan hasn't been back to my apartment since the first day he helped us move in, so he's unaware of our sleeping arrangements. My priority was getting Max a bed, and I had enough saved to buy her a new twin bed. I even found the perfect canopy at the Dollar Store and hung it around her bed, giving her the princess bed she had requested.

Meanwhile, I'm still saving up for a bed and sleeping on an air mattress, but I was smart this time and purchased one with the highest weight limit. That way, I'll be able to sleep on it for a while without having to worry about holes.

Declan doesn't know any of this because I'm willing to bet if he did, he'd offer to buy me a bed. The last thing I'd ever be able to accept from him is a bed. Besides, my sleeping situation isn't any of his concern.

"Nope," I say.

"Why not?" he asks, but I won't be honest.

What can I say? I'm sleeping on an air mattress that sucks, and I miss having a real bed, but I'm also okay with it because I've slept on the floor before, so it's nothing new. Yeah, not going to tell the hottest guy I've ever met that embarrassing fact.

"Probably just adjusting to the new place." He seems to buy my answer because he moves on.

Looking back at Max again, he chuckles. "I can always carry her in for you."

"How would you do that?"

"Well, we'd go to your place, and I'd carry her inside for you." The thought of not having to carry her up three flights of stairs makes me groan with relief.

"Wait, how would you get home?"

"I can walk." Quickly, I look at him, then blink my eyes back to the road.

Why am I considering this? I shouldn't be.

Especially when my body is still on fire for him.

"Take me to your place, Andy," he says in a gruff, commanding tone, causing my body to heat and my thighs to clench.

Holy fuck.

I'm taking him home.

TWENTY-ONE
Declan

WHEN WE ARRIVE AT ANDY'S APARTMENT, SHE PARKS IN HER assigned parking space and gets out without glancing at me. Nervous energy had been radiating off her from the moment I told her to take me home with her, but I ignored it because I was determined to tear down her walls one way or another.

Was it wrong of me to use Max as an excuse to go home with her? It's possible. Do I regret it? Not one fucking bit.

Following Andy's lead of getting out, I open the door to the back seat and carefully remove the sleeping child from her car seat, holding her with one arm while I use the other to grab the shopping bags, which seemed to have multiplied.

"I don't remember having this many bags," I grumble, keeping a firm hold on Max to prevent her from slipping.

Andy smirks, closing the trunk after grabbing her purse. "Pretty sure you bought out the entire festival."

I shrug. "What can I say? It was impossible to deny Max whenever she asked for something." Each time we reached a new booth, she'd look up at me with her big brown eyes, and I was putty in her hands. It was impossible not to tell her yes. I'm not sure what she's going to do with half the shit I bought, but I'm sure her imagination will find use for it.

"You could've limited the candy," she says with a grin, gesturing toward one of the bags that's filled with boxes of chocolate and other cherry-flavored goodies.

"That's your job, Mama. I get to be the fun buddy who spoils her rotten." I wink, side-stepping her and walking toward the stairs, leaving her gaping at my back.

She mutters something under her breath that sounds a lot like *asshole*, but I don't look back as I take the stairs two at a time, keeping the bags and Max secure in my arms.

When we reach the third floor and Andy unlocks the door, my heart is racing inside my chest, not from the physical activity but from the fact she's allowing me inside her private space for the first time in two weeks.

She's sent me pictures of the decorations she's thrifted and different areas of her apartment as she's been decorating, but seeing it all come together in person is so intimate. Like she's trusting me enough to allow me inside of her shell.

The moment I cross the threshold, the sweet, warm cherry vanilla scent fills my nostrils, and I take a moment to inhale, breathing in the smell of Andy deep into my lungs.

Fuuuuck. She always smells so damn good.

Andy turns on a couple of lamps, encasing the apartment in a warm glow before locking the door behind me. After taking the shopping bags from my hand and placing them on the kitchen table, she turns toward me, and I watch as she removes her shoes and places them on the shoe rack beside the door. Her red-painted toes dig into the light colored carpet as she scrunches them, and a smirk forms on my lips as dirty thoughts invade my mind.

Bad Declan. Now is not the time for that.

Clearing my throat, I step out of my Vans, leaving them by the door, and remain in my white socks.

"You can just put her in her room," she says, following me down the hallway as I walk toward Max's bedroom, carefully lying her down on the soft white and pink princess bedding.

Andy removes Max's shoes and then pulls the blanket over her before pressing a kiss to her forehead.

Despite Max being asleep, Andy still whispers in her ear, telling her how much she loves her. Seeing them together has me mesmerized, yet I feel like it's a moment I'm intruding on, so I step out into the hall to give her some privacy.

Andy joins me in the hallway a second later, shutting the door behind her. "She'll be out for the rest of the night." All I can do is nod. My words suddenly lodged in my throat.

Usually, I always have something to say, but right now, I can't bring myself to make any smart-ass remark. Especially when Andy is standing there practically eye fucking me.

She bites her bottom lip between her teeth, fingers slowly brushing her hair behind her ears, eyes never leaving mine, "Do you want to hang out for a little bit?" she asks, nervously playing with the gold ring on her right thumb.

I've been waiting for her to invite me over, so there's no hesitation when I nod in agreement. That movement caused a shy smile to appear on her pink, plump lips, her body visibly relaxing as if asking the question and not knowing my answer had stressed her out.

"Give me the tour of your apartment now that you're unpacked," I say, shoving my hands into the front pockets of my black jeans to prevent myself from reaching for her and pulling her curvy body against mine. I've wanted to run my tongue along every curve and mark of her body since the day I laid eyes on her, and that hasn't changed.

I can look but can't touch. Never can I touch. Not when I know that my touch would taint her beautiful golden skin and leave her dirty and even further fucked up. I'm incapable of anything more than friendship. Don't deserve it either. The only thing I have left of myself to give a woman is my body. And Andy means too much to give her my body when I know what'll happen the next morning.

Andy waves her arms out. "This is the hallway." She smirks,

nodding toward a closed door at the other end of the white hall-way. "My room, but you already know that." She walks away, wide hips swaying with the movement. My pants tighten at the sight of her round peachy ass jiggling beneath the black biker shorts she's wearing.

Like an awestruck boy, I follow behind her, watching her as she points out everything in the apartment she's added since moving in. Her smile is vast and full of happiness as she speaks, proud of the home she's creating for herself and her daughter, but I can't focus on anything besides her.

I don't give a fuck. I don't care about the crème-colored place-mats she found at the thrift store for two dollars for all four. Nor do I care about the kitchen rugs she was gifted from a neighbor who no longer liked the color. All I care about is her. I love the sparkle she gets in her brown eyes whenever she speaks about something she loves or something that excites her. But my sole focus is on her, not the objects and rooms she's showing me.

Without realizing it, I find myself standing right behind her, so close that the scent of her floral shampoo invades my scents, and the frizzy curls tickle my nose.

Not realizing how close I am because she's busy showing me the apartment, she steps back, bumping into me as she does, her bare foot stepping on mine. Turning to face me, she looks at me with a slight grin. "Sorry. Didn't mean to step on you."

She must notice the look in my eyes because the grin quickly fades from her face, her eyes widening as she stares back. All humor is now long gone. Looking at her, I can tell there's only one thing on her mind.

"Declan. Why are you looking at me like that?" she whispers, her throat moving as she swallows.

I step toward her until her back is against the fridge, and there's nowhere else for her to go. My pants strain against my dick, but I fight the urge to pull down my zipper and relieve some of the pressure.

"I'm trying to be a good man," I rasp, jaw tight as I fight the urge to show her exactly what I've been fantasizing about doing to her. "You're making it really fucking hard."

Her lips part, eyes rapidly blinking. "How am I making it hard for you to be a good man?"

"Because you are so fucking tempting." Pulling my hands out of my pockets, I place them on the stainless steel fridge beside her head, caging her in, my forehead resting against hers as I allow myself a few seconds of breathing in her sweet scent.

"So fucking tempting, Andy, and you don't even know it."

"How am I tempting you, Declan?" she asks innocently, playing with fire.

"All I've wanted to do since the moment I laid eyes on you is tear you apart. I want to force your tight little pussy down on my aching cock, and keep you there until I spell my name on your walls with my cum." She gasps, goosebumps spreading across her flushed skin. "You have no idea how badly I want to drown in your juices. Bend you over every surface in this goddamn apartment and fuck you until your mascara is running down that beautiful face, and you're begging me to stop." She stills, and I'm sure she stops breathing.

"The things I want to do to you, I have no right thinking. You have no idea how depraved I can be. How badly I want to ruin you and carve my name into your ass so the next man who bends you over will be forced to see it." I press my body flush against hers, allowing her to feel the hard length straining in my jeans as I push it against her.

"But I'm trying to be a good man, so I can't do any of that. No matter how fucking badly I want to."

Her breathing quickens, and I'm willing to bet if I were to slip my hands inside her panties, she'd soak my fingers with her wetness.

"Why not?" she asks, her voice breathy and higher than usual.

"Because you deserve more than a dirty fuck from a man who doesn't know how to be gentle. Or how to care for you afterward." I hate that I have to admit it to her. So fucking bad I wish I could be the type of man she deserves. But she deserves someone who can commit to her and doesn't come with a semi-truck full of baggage.

I'm an addict with five weeks of sobriety who is trying like hell every day to fight the urges, but it's hard as fuck. The only thing that has kept my mind off walking into the bar and downing a bottle of vodka or finding a dealer and snorting a bag of cocaine is the woman in front of me and the little girl sleeping down the hall. The promise of getting to see them has been helping me through this time, helping me fight the late-night urges when I'm unable to sleep.

"Go on a date with me," she blurts out, brown eyes widening in surprise as if she hadn't meant to say that out loud.

Smirking, I pull my head back from her forehead to see her stunning face better. "Andy, did you just ask me on a date?"

Straightening her spine, she nods. "I did." She breathes, minty breath fanning my lips, "Go on a date with me. Give us a chance to get to know each other properly."

This is a disaster waiting to happen, and I should say no, but when I open my mouth, I cannot form the words no. Instead, I agree.

"Next week? Choose when and where. I'm going to Vegas Monday to meet with my band to get started on the new songs I've written."

"Friday night? I'll leave Max with the sitter and take you to Mesquite. It's a town bigger than this, about thirty minutes away."

"Friday night," I confirm, pressing a kiss against her forehead, my lips lingering against her soft skin. "I should go before we do something we can't return from."

She nods, pulling her bottom lip between her teeth long enough for me to groan, then lets it go. "You should. Will we see you tomorrow?" There's hopefulness in her tone, and internally, I cringe. Tomorrow is Sunday when we normally have breakfast and go to the park, but I have to get ready for meeting with the boys Monday.

"Sorry, baby, not this week. I'll see you Monday before I leave, and I'll be all yours Friday." A few days ago, Benny called me and said he wanted me to meet up with Adam, Damon, and Cole and play them the songs I've been working on. Since sending Adam the first two I came up with, I've written four more over the past two weeks. And now it's my chance to see my friends again and play them the songs I've been working on.

I've been nervous as fuck about it because I know what comes along with new music. Touring. And that's where it gets tricky, because I don't believe I'm strong enough to tour right now. I'm taking it slow. The first step is to return to the studio, which I've been dying to do. My sanity needs to get behind a piano's keys and feel the guitar's strings.

My fingers twitch with the anticipation of being with my brothers again, doing what we love to do.

Music will heal me. It's what I need right now.

"Please stop in on Monday and say bye," she asks, arms firmly against her side. "How long will you be gone?"

"Probably a few days. I'll be staying with Adam, so don't worry about me. It'll be good." Concern flashes in her eyes, and I feel she doesn't believe I'll be coming back.

"I'll be back in time for our date." She nods, but the look in her eyes doesn't fade. People may have let her down in the past, but I can only promise I'll return. Which I will. There's no way in hell I will ghost her when she's finally willing to give me a chance.

Pushing off the fridge and stepping away, I fix her with a smirk.

"Goodnight, Mama. Dream of me."

TWENTY-TWO

Andy

I was an anxious mess yesterday. I was looking forward to getting back to work. Usually, I enjoyed the weekend and dreaded having to return on Monday, but I've also spent the last two weekends with Declan. I see him briefly throughout the week, but the weekends have been unofficially reserved for our time together.

After he left Saturday night, I ripped my clothes off and jumped into the shower, then used the showerhead to give myself multiple orgasms until I was panting and my clit was throbbing. The things he'd said to me had left me hot and bothered and with an ache that I know only he can fill.

Declan has awakened my inner hoe, and I don't think I'll be satisfied until I get some relief. It's been a long time since I've been fucked. Never have I wanted it as badly as I do now. He drove me so crazy with his words that I was ready to throw caution to the wind and beg him to take me right then and there. But the rational side of myself didn't do that. Instead, I remain horny, even after all the orgasms I've given myself since then. My touch hasn't been able to come close to the touch of someone else.

It's Monday morning, and as much as I hate leaving Max at

daycare, I was thrilled to get to work. I know it's ridiculous to be excited over seeing him or even asking him out on a date, especially considering I know that his time here is only temporary. He assured me Saturday that his trip to Vegas would only be a few days and he'd return, but eventually, that trip would become permanent. He's already said he'll be moving in a month and a half, but foolishly, I've wanted to ignore that fact and pretend that we're just an average man and woman getting to know each other and having their first date.

There's no future for us. No chance of a relationship, I know that. Yet that didn't stop me from asking him out. One day, he'll leave, and I'll just have been someone for him to pass the time with while he goes on to live his exciting rockstar life.

That thought alone is enough to ruin my mood. I'd been so excited, but now I'm upset and hoping he doesn't come to see me before he leaves.

Fuck the fact that I'll never have a happy ending. I'll never be anything other than a page in someone's story. Someone they leave in their rearview mirror as they move on and begin a new chapter in their life. It's happened too many times to me. No one has ever wanted me for more than a night.

We should've hooked up on Saturday. That way, he could begin putting distance between us after getting what he wants, and I wouldn't be too invested. I could've given him the green light. Could've begged or told him how badly I wanted him. Instead, I kept my mouth shut, hoping he'd be willing to get to know me and wanted to spend time together as just the two of us.

Fuck my life.

Rolling my eyes, I click away on the computer at the front desk, compiling a list of room assignments for when the housekeepers come in to start their shift so they'll know the status of each room the hotel has to offer.

Seeing movement from the corner of my eye, I turn my head

just in time to see Declan standing outside smoking a cigarette. The ember glowing as he inhales, his dark eyes already on mine.

My heart stops at the sight of him. God, why does he have to be so damn attractive? His dark hair is longer on the top and shorter on the sides, the perfect length to tangle my fingers in as he's between my legs, using his tongue to spell his name on my clit.

Nope. Not going there this morning. I will not get horny while at work and be forced to be uncomfortable in wet panties all day.

After stomping his cigarette out, Declan walks inside the lobby, a smile already on his face at the sight of me. He's dressed in black jeans, black boots, and a white, perfectly ironed T-shirt, so crisp and free from any wrinkles.

He winks at the sight of me, leaning his forearms on the counter as he looks at me. "Morning, Mama." He greets me in that raspy morning voice that has me swooning.

Ironically, I hate the smell of cigarettes, but smelling them on Declan doesn't bother me. The smoke mixed with the clean scent of his cologne has me leaning toward him and inhaling discreetly, needing to fill my lungs with his scent as much as possible.

"Hey." I brush my hair away from my face, noticing the designer duffle bag down by his feet. The smile falls from my face at the sight of yet another reminder that his time in my life is only temporary.

"Don't do that."

"Don't do what?"

"Don't start thinking this is goodbye. I promise I'll be back." Promises mean nothing to me anymore. Too many people have made me promises they never intended to keep.

My mother promised all the time she'd quit doing drugs for me. Pinky promised that she was going to get her shit together and be the mother I deserved. She lied. She never got sober or got her shit together. Every single promise she made was broken the very next day.

My grandpa promised he'd be okay and come home the day he went to the doctor to have his two-week-long cough checked out. He lied. He never came home. Instead, he went to the hospital and died three days later from pneumonia.

My grandma promised that she'd be at my high school graduation one day. She lied, too. She missed my grandpa so much that she went to sleep one night, dreamed of the man she loved, and never woke up, leaving me to find her cold body the following day.

The point is: everyone who has ever mattered to me has broken their promises. Actions speak louder than words, and that's all that matters to me. Words are pretty. You can say anything.

"It's okay, I get it, Declan. You have a job to get back to. A band and fans that need you." Sometimes I forget that the man standing before me is the Declan Valentine, the lead singer of Riot, the most popular rock band in the world. The man whose voice I fell asleep to on many nights and whose lyrics have imprinted on my soul, buried themselves deep into my heart and helped me through the darkest moments of my life.

Luckily, Loganville lives under a damn rock and is too much of a religious town to listen to rock music, and no one has figured out who he is. Though, I'm sure that's only a matter of time. One of these days, I'm sure someone will figure it out.

To me, the man standing in front of me is the man who took my car for an oil change last week while I was working because I briefly mentioned I didn't have time to do it. He's the man who carries my daughter on his shoulders and runs around the park playing with her. The one who holds her hand while she gets her face painted and then buys her new toys. The man who climbed onto a jungle gym and squeezed himself onto the slide because Max asked him to go down with her.

The man standing in front of me is nothing like the drug-addicted, womanizer portrayed in the media. Perhaps I have been too hard on him and should give him a chance. It's the very least that he deserves.

Looking at me, his eyes narrow. "I'm coming back, Andy. I'm not sure how long I'll be gone yet, but I promise I will be here for our date." He reaches out and takes my hand, "You'll see."

"Okay, we'll see what happens."

"Sure will." Bringing my hand to his mouth, he presses a kiss to the back of it, a faint smile on his lips as he pulls away.

"My driver should be here, so I've got to go. Say hi to Max for me." I nod, watching as he grabs his duffle bag and leaves.

Before stepping outside, he looks over his shoulder and winks, then disappears, making my heart skip a beat.

Holy fuck. Falling for that man will be easy, but I already know he will destroy me. He's going to be the worst heartache I'll ever have.

After my shift ends, I pick up Max from daycare and take her home. She's playing in her bedroom with the new toys Declan bought, and I'm in the kitchen preparing our dinner when my phone pings with a new text message.

Considering I have a small contact list, I pause momentarily before grabbing my phone, an instant smile spreading across my face at the sight of Declan's name on the screen.

DECLAN

Arrived safely. Sorry I didn't let you know sooner. Been catching up with my buddies since getting here.

ME

Don't be sorry, I figured you were busy.

DECLAN

What are you doing?

ME

Cooking dinner. You?

DECLAN

What are you cooking? I'm waiting for Damon to stop eye fucking himself in the mirror so we can go eat.

ME

Spaghetti and garlic bread. Are you all going out tonight?

DECLAN

Yum. We are, but not like you're probably thinking. We're going to some new sushi place Adam has been crying about trying.

ME

I've never had sushi.

Incoming FaceTime call from Declan

QUICKLY STRAIGHTENING MY POSTURE AND BRUSHING THE HAIR FROM my face, I answer the call, unable to keep the smile from my face at the sight of Declan on my screen.

"You've never had sushi?" he asks, seemingly alarmed by my answer. As I shake my head, I can't contain the laughter that escapes me.

"Never."

"Friday night. I'll take you for sushi."

"I'll look, but I don't think Mesquite has any sushi restaurants. They're mostly steak and seafood."

"Do you want a steak, Mama?" My insides become gooey every time he calls me that. A light blush tints my cheeks.

Not going to lie. Thinking of a perfectly cooked medium-rare steak with some lobster makes me want to drool. But I also want to try something new with the man on my screen. "I'll try sushi."

He smirks. "Good. I'll plan everything then. I'll pick you up on Friday at five. Does that work for the sitter?"

"That's perfect." There's yelling in the background, and then I watch as a pillow is thrown at Declan's face, knocking the phone from his hand.

His deep chuckle comes through the speakers moments before he picks up the phone and blesses me with another sight of his face. I watch as he throws up his middle finger to someone off-screen.

"Fucking Cole," he grumbles, a broad, relaxed smile on his face. "We're getting ready to go, but let me say hi to Max quickly."

Nodding, I quickly carry my phone into my daughter's room and hand it to her. At the sight of Declan, her eyes light up, and she quickly grabs the device, bringing it right to her face, "Hi, best friend! I missed you!"

"Hi, Max. Are you being good for your mom?" he asks.

She nods frantically, "So super-duper good!"

"That's good. I miss you two, but I'll see you soon."

"Okay! If I continue being a good girl for mommy, will you bring me a new toy?"

"Max!" I hiss at the same time Declan chuckles and says, "Yes."

"Yay! Thank you, best friend." She returns the phone to me, and I bring it to my face just in time for him to see my dramatic eye roll.

"You're going to spoil her." He shrugs, flashing me his panty-dropping grin.

"I've got to go now. Let's talk later."

"Okay, Declan. Have fun tonight."

"Later, Mama."

♪ ♪ ♪ ♪ ♪

I'VE JUST FINISHED MY NIGHTTIME ROUTINE WHEN MY PHONE pings with a new text message. It's nearly ten p.m., and

Max went to sleep two hours ago, but I stayed up cleaning the house, then took a shower and did my skincare routine.

Dressed in my fluffy black robe, I grab my phone from the counter and swipe up, my body heating at the sight of Declan's name.

DECLAN

Hey, Mama. Are you up?

ME

Yeah. I was just getting ready for bed.

DECLAN

Oh yeah? What are you wearing?

I hesitate momentarily before channeling my inner flirty hoe and being honest. Sure, I'm wearing a robe, but underneath, I'm naked.

ME

Nothing.

DECLAN

You're killing me.

ME

What are you doing?

DECLAN

Laying here in bed, trying not to imagine you also in bed... naked before me and spread out.

ME

Why wouldn't you want to imagine that?

DECLAN

Because my best friend is in the room next to mine, and I'd feel weird about jerking off. I have a hard time sleeping in new places.

ME

You've never slept at his house before?

DECLAN

Not here in Vegas. This is my second time here since we all moved out here. The day I got here was the same day I went to Loganville. It even took a few nights before I felt comfortable sleeping in the hotel, too.

ME

Try some hot tea and honey. That always helps me sleep.

DECLAN

Fuck no. Tea tastes like hot piss water.

ME

LOL. I assume you've drank warm piss water before.

DECLAN

Fuck no, I haven't. I just hate the taste of tea and assume that's how hot piss water would taste.

ME

You're ridiculous. Be a baby then and stay awake all night.

DECLAN

I hate not having my own bed to sleep in. It's too quiet here at his house. Noise is the only thing that helps calm my racing mind. It's hard to sleep without it.

ME

How do you sleep when you're at the hotel?

DECLAN

Ehhhh. I get a few hours each night, but it's not the same as having your own bed. It's been years since I've slept more than a few hours.

ME

That's not healthy.

DECLAN

LOL. I've done a lot of unhealthy things, Mama. Losing a little sleep isn't going to kill me. The drugs were more likely to take me out.

ME

How are you doing being in Vegas around your friends? Did you play your new songs today?

DECLAN

No, we just hung out today. We're going to the studio tomorrow. Honestly, I was worried for nothing. I felt embarrassed about seeing them again. I've done so much shit and am the reason for all our bad media attention. They were all there when our manager told me I wasn't allowed to stay in Vegas because I couldn't be trusted to not buy drugs. But seeing them again, everything was normal. I was worried for nothing. They're my brothers. I shouldn't have doubted them.

ME

That sucks that you were embarrassed. I'm sorry you felt that way, but I'm glad everything felt normal seeing them today. I don't want to be insensitive... but did you feel like using or drinking today?

DECLAN

Drinking, no. They ordered drinks at dinner, but I didn't feel the need to drink like I used to. But using... I know you won't like the answer.

ME

Be honest with me. Always.

DECLAN

I felt like using because I felt anxious. During the drive, I had myself convinced they'd think of me a certain way since I'm not staying in the same city as them, but once I realized it was all in my head, I felt better. Every day, I have the urge, but I fight it. I don't want to be that person anymore.

ME

I'm proud of you for resisting those urges. I know we never talk about it, but you can share anything with me. I understand more than you may realize.

DECLAN

I don't want you to be disappointed in me. I've disappointed too many fucking people in my life.

ME

I won't. You can talk to me.

DECLAN

Okay, as long as you won't think of me differently.

ME

My mom is an addict. I have unresolved childhood trauma because of her, and that's why I was so quick to judge you for being an addict. She always chose drugs over me and was okay with us struggling as long as she had drug money. My grandparents raised me because she was incapable, but they died, so it was just the two of us. I have no sympathy for her. It's easier for me to share my feelings over text rather than have to look someone in the eye and do it. I hate being vulnerable.

DECLAN

I figured someone in your life was an addict. I'm sorry, baby. That shit fucking sucks, and no child should have to deal with anything like that. My mother was an addict, too. She used to lock me in my bedroom while she got high, but one day, she stopped locking the door and encouraged me to sit with her while she shot up. I was a fucking kid watching his mother do heroin. I swore I'd never be like her. LOL. How pathetic am I?

ME

You're not pathetic, Dec. You're strong because you are fighting your addiction. I will help you however I can. Just promise not to lie to me. I can handle anything but lies.

DECLAN

I've broken so many promises. I broke every promise I made to my ex-wife, so I don't want to give you false promises. All I can do is tell you that I will try my fucking best every single day to be the man who can be trusted. To be the type of man a woman like you deserves.

ME

Lying is my dealbreaker.

DECLAN

I got you, Andy.

ME

Don't make me regret anything.

DECLAN

I'll do my fucking best.

ME

Goodnight, Dec.

Incoming FaceTime call from Declan

With butterflies in my belly, I hesitate a moment before answering the call and quickly adjust my position in bed, ensuring my robe is closed and my red bonnet is out of my face.

Clicking the green *accept* button, I smile, seeing Declan's face lighten up my screen. The room around him is dark. His face only lit up from the light on his phone. The phone provides enough light that I'm able to see him lying on his back, his arm propped behind his head, and his chest bare.

"I wanted to hear your voice before I went to bed," he says, eyes on my face on the screen.

After being so open with him while texting, I was a little worried about how I'd feel seeing him, but now I realize it was all in my head. He makes me feel comfortable, even when I'm vulnerable. What I shared about my mom is something I've never shared with anyone.

"I'm glad you called. It's nice to see your face."

He squints, bringing the phone closer to his face as he studies the background. "Why does it look like you're on the floor?"

I swallow. Fuck. I did not plan on telling him about my sleeping situation.

"Um, I don't know. That's weird." I shrug it off with a little white lie, hoping it is too noticeable.

"Andy," he says my name firmly, shifting his position to lean against his pillows.

"Ugh, fine." I roll my eyes. "I'm using an air mattress until my bed comes in." Another minor white lie. Wasn't I just telling him I don't like liars?

Pot meet kettle.

"Did you order a bed?"

Rolling my lips, I keep silent, nodding instead. Another lie. Damn, I'm on a roll tonight.

"Why didn't you tell me you didn't have a bed?"

225

"It's not a big deal, Dec. I've slept on the floor before when my mother could not provide me a bed. It's not a big deal."

He shakes his head. "You should've told me."

"Why are you so concerned with my sleeping situation?"

"Because I care about you."

"Appreciate that, but it's fine. It's not like I can do anything about it at this hour. So, let's just go to bed."

He smirked but didn't say anything else about my sleeping situation.

"Goodnight, Mama."

"Goodnight, Declan."

TWENTY-THREE
Declan

ME

Tell me three things about yourself.

ANDY

Good morning to you, too.

I'm a Scorpio. My favorite color is red. Reading is my favorite hobby, but I need more time to do it.

ME

I love that, but dig deeper. Open up to me, mama. Let me see you.

ANDY

I bet you would like to go deeper.

ME

LOL. You already know I'd like to get as deep in you as possible.

ANDY

Creep.

ME

You started it.

ME

I'm serious. Open up to me.

ANDY

What do you want me to say?

ME

What's your biggest fear? What are your hopes and dreams? What are you thinking about when you're in bed alone at night?

ANDY

I should say something happening to Max is my biggest fear, but that's obvious. So, I'll say... being alone. I'm terrified of spending the rest of my life without someone who loves me. When I'm in bed alone, I think about my life. About the present and the future. I worry that this will always be my life, but sometimes, I fantasize and pretend I have everything I've ever wanted. As for my hopes and dreams, they're silly and unrealistic.

ME

You're not going to end up alone, Andy. That's not what you deserve, and I know you are destined to get everything you deserve. You're going to have it all. Your dreams aren't silly. Tell me what you want to be when you grow up.

ANDY

A writer. I've always loved books and used to dabble in writing stories. In a perfect world, I'd be a famous romance author and married to the love of my life.

ME

One day, mama. It'll happen.

ANDY

Wish I had your confidence.

ME

Yeah, most people do ;)

ANDY

So fucking cocky.

ME

Can't wait to show you how COCKY I am.

ANDY

Goodbye. I'm blocking you.

"DECLAN! ARE YOU GOING TO SPEND ALL DAY SMILING AT YOUR phone, or are you going to get your pretty ass up and come play with us?" Cole smacks my shoe, causing me to remove my outstretched legs from the coffee table they'd been resting on.

"Keep talking shit, Cole, and I'll show you my pretty ass and give you something to play with." Adam and Damon chuckle while Cole flips me off.

"Who are you texting that has you smiling like that?" Damon asks, sitting beside me on the couch in our new studio.

"This girl I met." The mention of Andy is enough to bring another smile to my face. When I left yesterday, the look in her eyes had made me sick to my stomach all day. She doesn't believe I'll return, but I'm going to prove her wrong. There's no way in hell I'll be able to stay away. Not when she's finally starting to open up and let me in.

My inevitable departure is a problem for another day.

Adam looks at me, his worry evident on his pretty boy face. "The chick you told me about?"

"You told Adam about your girlfriend? You didn't tell us about her." Cole pouts, acting hurt that he was left out of the loop.

"Have you fucked her yet?" Damon asks, because, of course, that's all he'd care about. He's the biggest playboy I've ever met.

I'm sure there's not a woman in this world that would ever be able to tame his whorish ways.

"She's not my girlfriend, and no, we haven't fucked. She's just a friend that I'm still getting to know."

"All you need to know is how tight her pussy is," Damon says, patting me on the back with a smug look. Of course, sex is all that matters to him.

"Fuck off, man. Your biggest concern should be making sure the woman you're trying to get with is single." I flick his nose. It's lined with purple bruises. He flinches, slapping my hand away and making me laugh.

Last night at dinner, while Adam, Cole, and I were getting ready to leave, a woman sitting at the bar caught Damon's eye. Unable to stop himself, he approached her and gave her his number just as her boyfriend came. The man confronted Damon, telling him the woman was his, but that didn't stop him. He made a few provocative comments that resulted in the muscle head boyfriend punching him in the nose. Luckily, it's not broken, but it did leave an ugly-looking bruise.

Serves him right for going after an unavailable woman. Not that it's ever stopped him before. In all the years I've known him, I'm surprised that a punch in the face is the worst thing to ever happen.

"Enough," Adam chimes in, standing from the stool he'd been sitting on. We got to the studio a couple hours ago and have been sitting around playing with the songs I've written, trying to find the right tune and adjusting the lyrics. "Benny will be here soon. Let's get this shit ready for him."

Benny had meetings this morning but promised to meet us at the studio to hear the new songs. The man was fucking thrilled when he heard that I'd been writing again and had new songs for him.

"Alright, pussies. Enough about my love life. Let's get started on this shit." Standing, I flip off Cole and Damon on my way into the recording room.

Black padding lines the room's walls, and a black and red drum set sits in the corner, waiting for Damon to do what he does best. Adam's custom PRS guitar sits in the stand beside Cole's bright red bass.

They join me in the studio, grabbing their equipment and getting into position. Placing the black headphones over my ears, I nod to Frank, the studio engineer, through the glass, signaling that we're ready to get started.

The red recording light above the door turns on, and he gives us a countdown with his fingers before we get started.

Holding my leather lyric book in my hand, I open my mouth and pour my heart into the songs I've been writing.

The pained words rasp out of my lungs, filling the space with my smoky, haunting voice, blending perfectly with the beat of Damon's drums, tangling with the electric sound of Adam's guitar.

Cole's bass cuts in, mingling perfectly with my voice and the other instruments.

I do what I do best. I tear my heart out and leave myself bleeding on the studio floor, offering the bloody organ to anyone who can relate to the music. To the lyrics that tell the story of my fucked-up mind.

Hands gripping the stand of the microphone, I close my eyes and allow the music to consume me, filling my veins with the only drug I can have.

Music.

By the time the first song ends, I'm panting, my heart beating against my chest, and I have to slam my fist against it to ensure it doesn't beat out of my chest.

"Fuck yeah!" Damon yells out as the final note of the bass rings out into the air. "That was fucking epic!"

"Not bad for the first time we've practiced it together," Cole adds with a proud smile. I know they're just as happy as I am to be back in the studio doing what we all love to do.

This is more than a career to us. Music is our everything. It's what saved each of us from our fucked-up lives. The day our first album went platinum was the night we had our *I made it moment,* and all four of us got matching tattoos.

We all have *Riot* tattooed across our knuckles. Over our left pec, we have the notes to the chorus of "Rockstar"—it's the first song we ever played together and performed live.

We're in each other's veins.

Without us, there is no Riot.

With shaking hands, I remove the headphones, turning to face my brothers with a big ass grin on my face.

"That was electric," I say, fingers twitching with the need for a cigarette to take the edge off. I can't remember the last time we played together. It's been too fucking long, and that's all because of me and my shit. The look in their eyes tells me they missed playing just as much as I did.

"We're fucking back, baby!" I shout, pumping my fist into the air.

"We're back! Let's fucking do this!" Adam chimes in with a roar as the three of them rush toward me for an awkward-ass group hug.

God, it feels good.

We exit the recording room just as Benny walks in; he's dressed to the nines in his custom-tailored Armani suit.

"Good job, boys. I heard you in the hallway. Can't wait to see that magic." He smiles proudly, looking like a dad who is proud of his four heathen sons who finally managed to get their shit together and act right. "It's good to see you, Declan." He places his hand on my shoulder and gives me a reassuring squeeze.

"You too, man. Missed your old ass."

He scoffs, removing his hand and running it along his jaw. "Watch your mouth. I'm still a handsome devil." He waves his arms out to the side, doing a slow spin in front of us. "Look at me. I'm young and well-dressed."

"Whatever you say, old man." Cole smacks his shoulder.

"Okay, Dad." Adam laughs, earning the middle finger from Benny.

"Fuck off. All I'm hearing is jealousy. You four wish you could be this good-looking when you're my age." As much as we enjoy giving Benny shit, we all know he doesn't look his age. The only sign that he's older is his salt-and-pepper hair. Otherwise, the man could easily pass for forty.

"Jealous little shits," he mutters under his breath, one hand smoothing over his hair. "Anyway, I have news, so sit down, shut up, and buckle up."

We do as he says. Adam and I sit on the couch while Damon and Cole sit on the arms of the sofa, our attention on our manager, the one man who believed in us when we were nothing and supported us every second.

We owe Benny everything, which is why no matter what bomb he's about to drop, we'll agree.

"Riot needs some good media attention right now. Fans miss you, and your ratings are dropping. You're losing followers and people are asking about you," he says coolly, looking between us, but we all know it's my fault. "Until your album is done and we can lock down dates for your tour, I've booked you a few shows to make up for the tour we had to cancel." My heart stops, and my stomach knots at the casual mention of a tour and performing again.

As good as it felt to play with my band, the fact is that I'm an addict and afraid to tour. I'm worried about being backstage at a venue where I know there's going to be drugs and alcohol present.

Going to a rock concert and not finding drugs and alcohol is like going outside and expecting the sky not to be blue.

Fuck. How am I going to manage this? I was supposed to have two months before I had to step on a stage in front of thousands of screaming fans.

"Where are we performing?" Adam asks.

"They'll be local shows here in Vegas. I've also confirmed the arrangements and dates for your shows in about a month. I've emailed the cities and dates to each of you."

Frantically, I reach into my pocket for my phone and find the email from Benny, finding our performance schedule.

Two weeks.

Four states.

Seven cities.

Eleven shows.

Holy fuck.

Beside me, Adam looks over at my phone to see the schedule. I turn my screen so he's able to view it.

"Declan, I know we agreed for you to stay in Loganville, but it might be easier for you to be here in Vegas so you'll be available to rehearse. The first local show will be next Friday. That'll be enough time for you four to get prepared and for tickets to be sold. Short notice, but your true fans will show up. My goal is for all the shows to be sold out." He speaks casually, unaware that I'm sitting here with a racing heart and anxiety creeping under my skin.

How the fuck can I do this?

Next weekend, I'll be on the stage again. In a month and a half, I'll be spending two weeks on the road, performing eleven shows. Then, once our album is completed, I'll be on tour next year.

Each show is going to be a challenge. A challenge I'm not yet ready for. The temptation to use or drink will be constantly there in my face.

Am I strong enough for this?

As if sensing my inner turmoil, Adam touches my back. "You got this, man. We've all got you. We're going to crush this shit sober."

Cole nods in agreement, squeezing my shoulder.

"We all got this," Damon agrees.

Turning to Benny, I find his worried brown eyes looking down at me as if he'd just noticed that I was struggling.

Giving him a reassuring nod, I stand, shaking out my nerves to try and reassure myself, "Fuck yeah, I got this. It'll be fine. Let's do this shit," I say, hoping like hell my words will be true.

ME

You didn't ask, but I'll tell you my three things anyway.

My biggest fear is that I'll spend the rest of my life waking up and not recognizing the person looking back at me in the mirror. I don't have hopes and dreams anymore. Everything good that happens to me ends up crashing down around me, so I try living in the moment and not thinking about the future. When I'm in bed alone at night, I think about my son and how much I miss him. I think about how he was the one good I did in my life, but I fucked up and he's gone. Every night I think of what a piece of shit I am and how I don't deserve anything good.

I especially don't deserve you.

TWENTY-FOUR

Andy

DECLAN

You have a delivery.

ME

What are you talking about?

I HIT SEND ON THE TEXT JUST AS THERE'S A KNOCK AT MY DOOR. Placing my phone into my back pocket, I walk toward the door and look into the peephole, finding two men wearing yellow vests on the other side.

What the fuck?

Usually, I wouldn't open the door for a stranger, let alone two strange men, but I do it anyway because Declan texted me and seemed to know what was happening.

Cautiously, I unlock the deadbolt and open the door. "Hi. Can I help you?"

The tallest of the two men takes a step forward, a clipboard in his hands. "Good evening, ma'am. We have a delivery for Andy Harris." Scrunching my face in confusion, I shake my head as I look between the two men.

"There must be a mistake. I haven't ordered anything."

The tall, bald man looks down at the paperwork in his hand

and then turns it to face me, "Is this your name and address?" he asks, and I nod after reading it.

"Great. No mistake. We have the bed frame right here and can get that set up. The installation has already been paid for."

My jaw drops. "You're bringing me a... bed?"

Baldie nods. "Yes, ma'am. We have a bed frame, box spring, and mattress."

Fucking Declan.

Moving to the side, I allow the men into my home, watching as they carry inside a box that I assume is the bed frame they will assemble.

"I'll show you the bedroom." I guide them toward my bedroom, quickly pulling the plug on the air mattress to deflate it.

The men set the box beside the wall. "We're going to grab the other two items and will be right back." Nodding, I let them see themselves out while quickly picking up my room in preparation for my new bed.

"Mommy, who was that?" Max asks, peeking her little curly head into my bedroom.

"Come here, baby. Jump on the air mattress and help me get the air out." Her eyes light up, her hands rubbing together as if she's been preparing for this Olympic moment her entire life.

Max runs toward the mattress, arms and legs spread out like a starfish as she jumps, landing with a slight thud. The air whooshes out, a small hiss filling the air.

Max giggles, rolling back and forth on the bed, living her best life. She's not allowed to jump on her bed, so I'm sure she's loving every moment of this.

Once the mattress is flat, I gather all the bedding and pillows into a pile, shoving them into my closet until my new bed is assembled.

A quick peek at the box tells me it's king-size. Thankfully, so was my air mattress, so I can use the same sheets.

Fuck yeah.

When the men return with the mattress and box spring, I excuse myself into the kitchen to prepare dinner for Max and me while they work.

ME

How do you know my last name?

DECLAN

Steven at the front desk.

ME

You really asked my night shift employee for my last name?

DECLAN

Sure as fuck did.

ME

Why? Thinking of stealing my identity or stalking me?

DECLAN

I don't need your last name to stalk you.

ME

That's... creepy.

You didn't answer me about stealing my identity or not.

DECLAN

Ha, I promise not to steal your identity.

I assume you got my gift?

ME

I did. It's way too fucking much, but I won't pretend like I'm going to fight you on it or try to give it back. It's currently being assembled in my room, and I can't wait to sleep on it. So, thank you so much.

DECLAN

You're welcome, mama. I hope you sleep good tonight.

ME

I hope you do, too.

DECLAN

Unlikely, but thanks.

ME

Still can't sleep at your friend's house?

DECLAN

Nah. Got a lot on my mind too.

ME

Talk to me.

DECLAN

Let me gather my thoughts first, and then I will.

ME

Whatever you need, whenever you're ready, I'm here.

DECLAN

I know, mama. Enjoy the bed.

THREE HOURS LATER, MY BRAND-NEW KING-SIZE BED IS ASSEMBLED, and the pillow-top mattress looks heavenly beneath my new sheets. After it was assembled, they informed me new bedding had also been ordered and was included in the delivery.

Not only do I have a brand new bed, but I also have brand new Egyptian cotton sheets, silk pillowcases, and a comforter that feels like a cloud.

I may have gotten teary-eyed when I saw the silk pillowcases. I'm not sure how he knew it's what I needed for my hair, but he did.

Be still my heart.

After the new sheets were on, I snapped a picture and sent it to Declan, thanking him again for the expensive gift.

Tomorrow is Friday, but he hasn't said anything about when he's coming back. If he's coming back. Or anything about our date.

I have yet to bring it up either; I'm afraid to hear his answer in case he doesn't plan on returning or if he forgot about our date. Just in case, though, I scheduled a babysitter and bought myself a nice outfit from the thrift shop. They rarely have my size, but whenever they do, I always grab the items regardless of whether I like them or not. If I don't like it, at least it's my size, and I can style it somehow that I will like. But I got lucky and found a stunning midnight-blue velvet dress. The ruffles in the velvet lay smoothly over my belly, so I won't have to wear shapewear with it.

God, Declan. Please don't stand me up.

I've been looking forward to going out with him. He has been the first person I talk to every morning and the last person I talk to before I fall asleep. Every day that I wake up, there's a text waiting from him. Sometimes, he asks simple questions, like my favorite book series or favorite flavor of ice cream.

My favorite book series is *Down We Go* by Kyla Faye, and I love the Superman ice cream from Scoops. He thought it sounded ridiculous, but I said I'd take him and he could try it before he judges it.

Other times, he'll ask me about my childhood and what it was like growing up in Loganville. I told him it was challenging because everyone knew me as the granddaughter of Max and Claire Harris, whom they raised because their daughter Diane was too busy doing drugs.

I never had friends because parents didn't want their children playing with the girl who had a drug addict for a mother. They weren't allowed to come to my house, and I wasn't allowed at theirs.

When kids in my class were handing out invites for their birthday parties, I was always the one who was excluded. I was the outcast that people liked to stare at and whisper about.

I told Declan all of that.

He told me about how he was in foster care because his drug-addicted mother left him outside of an ice cream shop. He shared that he was eventually transferred to a group home when he was sixteen, where he met Adam—his best friend and bandmate.

For the first time, I've found myself having something new to look forward to daily. A break in my regular, mundane routine. It's refreshing to have someone new in my life to talk to. To share my day and thoughts with.

Someone who doesn't care about what I've been through and isn't judging me for the sins of my mother. Or judging me for being a high school dropout.

Declan doesn't care about any of that. I'm convinced it's me that he cares about.

Once Max is asleep, I quickly shower, going through the steps for my typical night routine. Excitement courses through me until I'm bouncing on my feet, ready to get between the sheets and sleep on the memory foam mattress I tested out briefly earlier.

Wanting to feel the softness against my bare skin, I don't bother putting clothes on. Instead, I turn off the light, encasing my bedroom into a soft purple glow thanks to the purple Halloween lights I bought and hung around my walls.

My naked body slips beneath the cool sheets, a groan of satisfaction releasing from my lips at the contact and the content feeling of sleeping on something besides a hard air mattress.

Bringing up my phone, I take a picture of the empty side of my bed and send it to Declan.

ME

This bed feels fantastic. Thank you again.

His response is instant.

DECLAN

> If you're going to send a picture like that, make
> sure you're in it.

FEELING MORE CONFIDENT THAN USUAL, I FLIP THE CAMERA AND bring the phone to my face. Tucking the blanket underneath my arms to cover my breasts, I smile and snap a picture, sending it instantly to Declan before I can stare at it and criticize everything about myself.

For once, I want to do something without overthinking it and picking myself apart. I don't care if my double chin is showing or if I didn't force my collarbones to show. It doesn't matter if my cleavage isn't perfect because my breasts aren't high and perky.

It's fine. He knows what I look like.

DECLAN

Do you always sleep naked?

ME

> No, but tonight, I wanted to be comfortable and
> feel the sheets beneath my skin.

DECLAN

You're killing me, mama.

ME

> Why did you get me silk pillowcases?

DECLAN

> I read that it's best for your hair. I know you
> wear your bonnet, but I thought the pillowcases
> would help, too.

ME

> Did you read it, or you know from experience dating a lot of black girls?

DECLAN

> I don't date.

> You were the only one I was thinking about.

ME

> What are you doing?

DECLAN

> Sitting in Adam's backyard, working on new lyrics. Got to come up with a few more songs for the album.

ME

> Can you share any of the new songs with me?

Incoming FaceTime call from Declan

PROPPING MYSELF UP ON THE PILLOWS, I DOUBLE-CHECK THAT MY breasts are covered before answering the call. "Hey, Dec." A smile finds my face at the sight of him. I take in his appearance, his hair disheveled as if he's been running his fingers through it.

"Hey, mama." He breathes a sigh of relief, but I'm not sure why he's relieved. "You have no idea how much I needed to hear your voice."

"Why? What's wrong?"

He rubs a hand down his face, his stubble prominent. The last time we were on video chat, he was freshly shaved, but that was a couple days ago.

"I'm stressed as fuck," he admits.

"What's going on?"

"I learned a few days ago that we will perform next Friday.

My manager, Benny, booked us a few shows here in Vegas beginning next week. Then, in less than two months, we will do a few shows in four states."

My heart sinks, dread filling my stomach. "Are you going to move to Vegas so you can be with your band?" The question is like acid on my tongue. I hold my breath, dreading the answer.

He shakes his head. "I don't fucking know. I'll be gone for shows for two weeks, then we'll be on tour, either the end of this year, or beginning of next year. Benny is anticipating this year."

"Your plan was always to go to Vegas after two months here. Why not go now, since you'll be playing in Vegas? It might be easier. Less commute."

"The commute isn't an issue." Maybe not to him, considering he has a personal driver. But that hour might as well be six to me.

"What's the issue?"

"Performing again. We've been playing all week, and it feels so fucking incredible. But the last time I was on stage, I celebrated by snorting a line of coke off a pussy." I cringe, but he doesn't apologize. Not that he should because he's telling the truth. I asked for honesty, no matter how ugly it can be.

"You're worried that you'll be tempted to use," I clarify. He nods.

"During the times I was performing, it was the worst for me. Having that adrenaline in my veins, being hopped up from hearing the crowd going wild for me, all I wanted after I stepped off that stage was a cold drink and a little white line waiting for me. I'm not sure how to play sober or party with my bandmates while remaining sober," he confesses, many emotions swimming in his dark eyes. "I don't want to do any of that."

"What if you have someone there to help you? Prevent you from using," I suggest.

"Like a babysitter?"

I shrug. "I read that sometimes labels will hire a sober coach for their artists when they're struggling with addiction."

"You just happened to read that? Or you looked into it?"

"I knew this day would come. The day you'd be back on stage, so I looked it up."

He sits straight in the chair he'd been slouched in, a smile tugging at his lips. "You surprise me, Andy Harris."

"Don't read into it. It's not a big deal."

"It is," he whispers, quickly clearing his throat. "You want to hear one of the songs I've been working on?"

Holy fuck, yes! Like the rest of the world, I've been waiting for Riot to release a new album. It's been a few years since they've released any new music. Trying not to seem too eager, I shrug. "I guess that would be okay."

He eyes me suspiciously. "We've never talked about it before, but you once told me you knew who I was when we met." Why is he bringing that up?

"Yeah, so?"

"Andy Harris, are you a fan?" He cocks his eyebrow, his dimple appearing deep in his cheek when the slow smile takes over his panty-wetting face.

"You know what, Declan Valentine, I am. There. I admit it. Riot is my favorite band."

He tilts his head back, exposing his tattooed throat as he laughs. "I fucking knew it. Why haven't you told me? We've talked about music before."

"I never told you because I didn't want your ego to get any bigger."

"Too late for that, baby."

"Whatever. Yes, I love Riot, and I'm excited for the new album, but I also understand the risk that comes with it." The risk of relapse.

"What's your favorite song?"

"'It's Over Now,'" I answer without thinking about it. That was the song that was playing the day I tried to take my life. The song that saved me.

"Damn, mama. That song is heavy as fuck." He's not wrong.

The song's beat is low and sung slower than his others. Listening to it is a personal experience. Anyone who can relate to it is someone who has been to hell and back. Someone who understands what it's like to feel so hopeless and broken that you want to die.

"One day, when I need a reminder of why I'm getting on that stage, I want you to tell me why that song is your favorite."

"Deal."

"Good. Now, lower your phone a little bit and lift the blanket."

I laugh, blushing at the insinuation. "Stop. We're not going to have phone sex."

He pins me with a look. "Who said anything about phone sex? I just want to see you."

"Not happening."

"Pussy," he grumbles.

"You're awful. I'm going to sleep."

"Goodnight, mama."

"Night, Dec."

His face disappears as the call ends. Reaching my nightstand, I plug my phone into the charger, then double-check that my alarm is set so I can wake up in time for work.

Another night was spent with a belly full of butterflies, and Declan as the last person I talked to.

Snuggling down in the sheets, I close my eyes, ready for sleep, when my phone pings with a new text.

DECLAN

I'll pick you up tomorrow at five.

Can't wait to see you.

I'll play one of the new songs for you then.

ME

You just saw me.

249

DECLAN

In person. A screen doesn't do you justice. I
need more.

ME

Tomorrow at 5. See you then.

DECLAN

Counting down the hours until you're in my
presence. Until I can feel your skin beneath my
fingertips.

Dammit. Lying on my back, I spread my legs, pinching my nipples before trailing my fingers down to my wet center, using one hand to text.

ME

Where do you want to touch me?

DECLAN

Go to bed, Andy.

Oh, I will. Right after I get myself off while rereading our text messages.

TWENTY-FIVE

Andy

DECLAN

Tell me three things.

> **ME**
>
> I don't think I'll ever be able to forgive my mom for choosing drugs over me. I want to experience what it would be like to have a partner who loves and supports me and can figure problems out with me instead of me doing everything alone. One day, I will put my fears aside and do something I've always wanted.

> Tell me three things.

DECLAN

Sometimes I sabotage my happiness because I feel guilty that I get to live when I've ruined so many lives. I want to hate my mom, and I think part of me does, but I also love her and miss her. My story doesn't end with a happy ending.

Have a good day, mama. Can't wait to see you tonight.

Friday morning, I woke to yet another text from Declan, just like I have each morning since he left. Nothing like starting your day with a smile on your face after reading a text from the man you masturbated to.

Shamelessly, I came so hard on my fingers last night just by re-reading our text conversations. It's easier to be vulnerable with someone when you don't have to see their expressions and look into their eyes. The thing I love about our routine is that he never gives advice or comments on what I say. He lets me confess what I need to say and I do the same.

Sometimes, a response isn't needed. Sometimes, you just need to be heard. To share your truth.

It's easier to say what I need to say when I'm sitting comfortably behind the screen of my phone.

I wonder if that's why people feel so comfortable talking shit online.

All day at work, I checked the time, waiting for 3pm when I could rush home and get ready for my first date with Declan. I'd be lying if I said I wasn't nervous but also incredibly anxious to experience my first ever date.

I know. How embarrassing. Twenty-one years old, and I've never been on a date before.

Unless you count the guy that took me to Denny's, but I don't, considering all he wanted was to get laid.

I'm new to dating, but what do you expect when you were a teen mom and haven't dated since your child was born? When I say "date," I use that word loosely because what I did in the past with men wasn't exactly dating. We hooked up.

Hit it and quit it is more like it.

I'd spend weeks talking to guys online, meet them in person, and let them fuck me the first-time meeting, then the moment they got what they wanted, they were gone, and I was blocked on all their accounts.

Whatever.

Fuck those guys.

Now that I'm older, I realize how wrong it was to be with them. They were grown men. Most of them were ten years older than me when I was fifteen.

By the time three p.m. came around, I was in a rush to get home and even ran a stop sign in the process.

My neighbor, Lucy, has a daughter the same age as Max. Lucy's little girl goes to the same daycare. Luckily, she agreed to pick up Max after daycare since she will be babysitting her tonight. Max begged for a sleepover with Lucy's daughter, Haley, and Lucy accepted.

I'd be lying if I said I wasn't a nervous wreck about leaving Max alone or allowing her to stay the night at someone else's house, but I've come to trust Lucy, despite being friends for a short amount of time. She never has anyone over, lives a quiet life, and since the day I moved in we've been texting and chatting nonstop. She reminds me so much of myself, and for once, I've felt comfortable enough to let my guard down and truly get to know someone well enough to make a friend.

She'd texted me to say she was taking the kids out to eat so I'd have time to prepare. I thanked her by sending her money on CashApp to cover Max's food. Like myself, Lucy is also a struggling single mother, so I wouldn't feel comfortable with her paying for my child.

The moment I rushed through the front door, I was immediately stripping off my clothes in a rush to get in the shower to scrub my body and shave. Luckily, I washed my hair yesterday, so that saved time. I wasn't about to go on my first-ever date with wet curls, and blow-drying would take too long.

Standing in front of the bathroom vanity in nothing by my birthday suit, I sway my hips to the beat of the music; Sam Cooke is turned up full-blast on my phone as I apply makeup to my round face. My blemishes and freckles disappear beneath the full-coverage foundation. The freckle on my left eyelid is covered beneath a dark, smoky eye and winged black eyeliner. With my makeup perfectly applied, I complete the look using matte dark red lipstick.

Makeup is something I wear infrequently. Never have a reason to. But damn, I must admit that it feels nice to dress up for a night.

Picking up the red bottle of lotion from my counter, courtesy of Declan, I squirt the thick white cream into my hand. After rubbing my hands together, I massage the creamy cherry vanilla-scented lotion into my brown skin, my dark eyes following the movements of my hands, looking over every naked inch of my large body.

My fingertips brush over the faint stretch marks along my breasts and down to the marks on my stomach and hips. I remember what it felt like to watch my already large body grow into something even bigger when I was pregnant. I gained weight, and new stretch marks formed. For the longest time, I hated what I would see each time I looked in the mirror.

Why couldn't I be skinny?

Why did I have to have acne as a teenager that left me with minor acne scars? They're not visible to most, but I've spent hours looking in the mirror and picking myself apart so I know exactly where they are. My pores are too large, and my skin too oily, but I'm human.

I used to spend hours scrolling social media, looking at pictures of influencers, and comparing myself to their photo-shopped and over-filtered photos. For so many years, I've hated myself, but now, when I look in the mirror, all I see is a human being with scars and flaws.

I see a woman who has an imperfect body that has been through one diet after another, one workout regime after the other, one starvation diet after the other. But this body grew, created life, and gave birth to a beautiful baby girl.

I see heavy breasts with dark nipples that hang lower than I'd like as a result of being large and having nourished a baby. For seven months, these breasts provided milk.

I see a woman who has been through darkness, and instead of giving in, she fights for life every day. The brown-eyed woman looking back at me may not be perfect. She may not be a model or be close to perfection, but she is beautiful and is worthy of great things.

She is worthy of love.

I am worthy of love.

Blinking back the tears in my eyes, I reach for the blue velvet dress hanging on the back of the bathroom door and carefully pull it over my body, smoothing the material with my hands as I stare at myself in the full-length bedroom mirror.

The ruffled material smooths away any signs of cellulite and the lines of my belly roll.

Holy fuck. When I die, bury me in this dress.

The dress is form-fitting yet loose enough to not stick to my skin and expose my imperfections. The neckline is low enough that it reveals a tease of cleavage but not enough to be too revealing or inappropriate for a dinner date, while the sleeves of the dress are long enough to cover my shoulders and the parts of my arms that I hate, going all the way down to my wrists.

Initially, I had worried the material would be too hot for the Nevada summer heat, but surprisingly, I'm comfortable. Besides, being warm isn't enough to get me out of this dress. Not when I look the way I do.

Never in my life have I felt more beautiful than I do right now. My confidence is at an all-time high, and I can't wait to see the look on Declan's face.

As time races by, quickly approaching five p.m., I complete the finishing touches to my look by spraying perfume on myself, fluffing my second-day curls, and adding a pair of cubic zirconia earrings I found on sale at Walmart one day while I was shopping there in Mesquite.

Yup, that's another telling sign of how small Loganville really is. The closest Walmart is thirty minutes away.

My phone pings, and I quickly check the time and the message.

LUCY

I'm coming over with Max to get her pajamas.

WITH A SMILE, I UNLOCK AND OPEN THE FRONT DOOR JUST IN TIME to see Lucy's door open across from mine. Then my daughter comes rushing toward me, her arms outstretched. "Mommy!" I bend down just as she collides with me.

I scoop her into my arms, hugging her close, inhaling the scent of her strawberry shampoo. "Hi, baby girl. I missed you so much."

Lucy steps out, and she's wearing her typical attire of cut-off jean shorts and a white tank top. Her blonde hair is piled high on her head, her smile wide, revealing a bright, white smile, "Wow, girl. You look good!" she compliments, and I blush.

Lucy is a knockout. She's petite—several inches shorter than me—but she's got long model legs that are perfectly toned. She is stunning, and for a moment, I hope Declan doesn't see her because she is precisely the type of woman I have seen him with online.

I hate myself for having that thought. He will be here to take me out on a date. If he weren't interested, he wouldn't be coming.

But he's not the one that asked for the date. I am. Oh, fuck. What if he only went out with me because I asked him to, and he felt he couldn't say no?

Great. Look at me. Wearing the most beautiful dress, and now feeling like shit because I'm allowing my fears to get the best of me.

"That man is going to be so lucky! Wow, you are beautiful."

Lucy continues feeding me compliments, unaware that I want to smack her for being the type of woman that Declan would be interested in.

How sad is that? All she's doing is being polite, and I'm mentally assaulting her. What a shitty person I am.

"You look pretty, mommy." Max smiles, kissing my cheek. Lucy steps out of her apartment and walks toward us, black flip-flops slapping against the heels of her feet as she walks.

"Thank you, baby." I nuzzle Max, holding my sweet baby tighter before putting her down on her feet. "Come in. I'll grab her overnight bag."

Lucy steps inside, standing in the doorway to keep an eye on her apartment where Haley is.

"Go pick out your pajamas, baby," I say, and Max nods before running off to her room.

"Do you know where y'all are going?" Lucy asks, her Southern accent thick in her words. She moved here from North Carolina six years ago to be with Haley's dad. After she gave birth, he left town, and they haven't seen him since. Lucy is only three years older than me, and unlike myself, who has lived here my entire life, she's active in the community. She's friendly with everyone, but from what she's told me, she's lonely, and I'm her only friend.

I've known Lucy since Max was a baby. We attended the same free mommy and me class at the local community center every Thursday. We'd share pieces of our life and bonded over being new young mothers, but our friendship never went beyond that. Sure, we'd chat each time we spotted each other around town, but it wasn't until Max and I moved next door that our friendship was kicked into high gear. I'd been struggling to carry all my shopping bags to the third floor while carrying a sleeping Max, who fell asleep in the car and refused to wake up, so she and Haley helped carry my bags. We got to talking, discovered our girls were friends at daycare, and we've been becoming best friends ever since. Lucy considers it fate that I moved in across from her, and maybe it is. Maybe the universe knew we both needed someone to share the crazy journey of motherhood with.

My first week living here, she invited me over for a glass of boxed wine after the girls were asleep. We spent hours sitting on her balcony sharing our stories and trauma bonding. We're more alike than I realized, and I think that's what draws me to her so much.

I'm twenty-one years old, and I just got my first friend. How sad is that?

First friend. First date. I'm really on a roll lately. Go me.

"Nope," I admit. "Well, I think we're going to Vegas, but I'm not positive. I know he mentioned sushi, and there are no sushi restaurants in Mesquite."

"Get it, girl." She winks. "You deserve it."

"I'm nervous as fuck," I confess, placing a hand on my stomach that has been full of fluttering nerves all day long.

"Don't be! You look hot as fuck, and he's lucky to have your company tonight. Don't worry about Max. She'll be fine." She steps closer to me and wraps her arms around me, pulling me into a hug, "Stay out late. Let him take you to pound town and enjoy yourself." I return her hug, needing the warmth of her embrace.

God, it feels good to have a friend.

Pulling apart, I give her a smile. "You're right. I got this. It'll be great," I say, trying my hardest to believe my words.

"I'm going to go get Max ready. Be right back." Lucy slaps my ass as I walk away, and when I look over my shoulder at her, she winks, making me laugh.

Once I have Max's pink backpack packed with pajamas, her toothbrush, and her favorite pink blanket she sleeps with every night, I hold her hand as I follow her into the living room, where Lucy still stands in the open doorway.

Guilt creeps in, keeping me rooted in place. "Maybe I should call and cancel. I don't feel right about leaving Max."

Lucy takes the bag from my hand, practically prying my fingers from the straps. "No way, girl. You're going. Max will be fine, I promise," she assures me, but it doesn't settle my nerves.

"I really want to stay with Haley, mommy!" Max pouts, staring at me with her wide brown eyes.

With a sigh, I lean down and give my daughter a kiss and a tight hug, "Be good, my girl. I love you and will see you tomorrow."

"I'll be so, so super-duper good, Mommy. Pinky promise!" She holds up her pinky, and I hook it with mine. Kissing her forehead, I stand, giving Lucy another thanks for agreeing to babysit her overnight.

After they leave, I shut the door and attempt to calm the butterflies fluttering around in my stomach.

Here goes nothing.

TWENTY-SIX
Declan

ONLY ONE THING HAS BEEN ON MY MIND ALL DAY.

My date with Andy.

It feels weird as fuck to be going on a date at thirty-one. It's my first date since I was twenty-three.

The last time I went on a date, I had a child and was married soon after. Although, I don't think Cam and I actually had a first date. Unless you count hooking up backstage, and then her joining me on tour as a date. But I've never asked a woman on a date before, nor have I put effort into it.

Andy is the one who asked me out, but I'm still counting it.

I woke up in Vegas this morning, thrilled to return to Loganville today. It's ironic, considering how excited I'd been about seeing my friends and going to Vegas, only to get there and find myself missing a small, middle-of-nowhere town.

It wasn't the town I missed. The two brown-eyed girls who made my days brighter were who I missed.

Texting isn't enough for me anymore. I need more of Andy. Need her presence around me and her scent infiltrating my senses. I'm not sure what shifted between us, but somehow, during our week apart and getting to know her better each day over text, I found my cold, dead heart thawing for the woman.

I want to be a better man for her. The type of man that she deserves.

Sure, I'd been tempted to drink over the week, but each time I thought about picking up the bottle, I saw Andy's face and realized that I didn't want to let another person in my life down. I don't want to let her down. Haven't I let enough people down?

No one expects anything good from me. Everyone knows I'm a fuck-up and expects the worst. I'm tired of giving them the worst. That's not the type of man I want to be anymore.

David, my personal driver, drove me back to my hotel in Loganville this afternoon, and once I arrived, I began getting ready for my date.

This morning, after breakfast, Cole had asked what I planned to wear and told me to dress nice. Apparently, ripped jeans and a T-shirt weren't the best outfits for a first date, so we did a quick morning shopping trip.

After my shower, I dressed in the new outfit Cole helped me pick. A pair of black dress pants, a white dress shirt, and a well-fitted black jacket.

A suit. I'm wearing a fucking suit for my date.

Jesus.

I wait outside for David, my fingers twitching with the need to reach inside my pocket and grab my pack of smokes, but I've been trying to quit, and I don't want to smell like cigarettes before my date.

Andy has never said anything, but I know she hates the smell. That's become apparent based on how I've noticed her scrunching her nose each time I get in her car after smoking or whenever I step away from her and Max to light up. I can't blame her; it's a nasty habit, but it's better than what I could be doing.

I've been smoking since I was thirteen, and it's become entirely too natural to me that I often find myself craving it. Especially when I'm feeling anxious.

My last cigarette was two days ago, but I keep them in my pocket at all times, just in case.

Once David arrives at the hotel, I climb into the back of the SUV and give him directions to Andy's to pick her up, as he'll be driving us to Vegas for our date.

I thought about renting a car to drive her myself, but I decided I wanted to have my sole attention on her without paying attention to the road. Luckily, David was down to add some more hours to his paycheck.

We make one stop along the way to a local flower shop that David told me about. During one of our conversations, Andy told me that she loves roses but is not interested in having them around because they die too quickly. She'd never received flowers before but said it was okay because they'd be dead the next day.

I've never been the hearts and flowers type of man anyway, but for some reason, I want to be for her.

"You can park here. I'll be right back with her," I tell David once we arrive at Andy's apartment complex. Then, I climb out, carrying the gift I have for her that I bought while in Vegas and the bouquet of a dozen red roses mixed with baby's breath. On my back, I carry my acoustic guitar held on by a black leather strap. It's been a while since I've played, but I promised Andy that I'd play her one of the new songs I've been working on.

Taking the steps two at a time, I reach the third floor and take a moment to calm my anxious mind as I stand outside the door.

"You got this," I mumble under my breath, needing some encouragement before I raise my fist and knock on the door.

Seconds later, the door swings open, and the sweet, sultry scent of cherry-vanilla assaults my senses, calming every worry I've had all week, putting my mind at ease, and making me feel like I'm home.

On the other side of the door stands a true fucking goddess. Andy is already a beautiful woman, but seeing her in the blue velvet dress with a slight smile on her dark-painted lips and the aura of confidence surrounding her is next level. My dick thickens at the sight, my pants becoming tight, and I refrain from tugging down the zipper to provide myself some relief.

"God damn, you are a true vision," I whisper hoarsely, my throat suddenly dry.

Andy steps to the side, allowing me to enter her apartment, the warm coziness enveloping me.

"Spin for me, mama. Let me see all of you," I request, needing to see every inch of her in that dress that has me wanting to rip it off her voluptuous body with my teeth.

Andy twirls for me with a shy smile, dark curls bouncing with the movement, eyes sparkling with giddiness.

I grab hold of the guitar strap around my body, carefully removing the instrument and set it against the wall.

"Well?" Andy waves her arms out. "Do you like it? It's new," she says, blushing.

I wonder if she bought the dress just so I could take it off. Bet it would look pretty nice on her bedroom floor.

Not so subtly, I reach a hand down and grab my crotch, adjusting my aching cock. This woman will be the death of me. Getting hard every two seconds was never a problem before her.

"There are no words to describe how you look." Grinning, she gestures toward the roses in my hands. "I assume those are mine?"

I chuckle, unable to keep my eyes off her body. "They are. Just give me a minute to catch my breath. You truly look incredible."

"Do I not look incredible all the time?" Andy is gorgeous any time of the day. Messy bun, sweats, no makeup, or dressed up like she is now. She's a knockout regardless.

"You are always beautiful, and my pants are always tight around you, no matter what you wear. Especially when you bend down in those little biker shorts you like to wear." I smirk. "The gray ones are my favorite."

"Are gray biker shorts the equivalent to men's gray sweatpants?"

I shrug. "Don't know, don't care. You're the only one who makes my dick hard from an article of clothing. They're see-through, by the way." I smirk, revealing a fact she likely wasn't aware of. "And you don't wear panties with them." The last time we took Max to the park, Andy wore a pair of little gray biker shorts. I had sat down before her, and when she bent over, I had a perfect view of her visible skin beneath the sheer fabric. The barrier of panties was nonexistent as I got an eye full of her peachy ass with the little rosebud asshole and the slit of her pussy.

I'd never been much of an anal fan before that day, but fuck, the sight made me want to eat both of her tight little holes before sticking my dick in each.

At the revelation, her face flushes red with embarrassment.

"Oh my god, you saw my asshole!" She squeals, covering her face with her hands.

"Fuck yeah, I did. Wanna know what I thought?" She shakes her head, but I give her an answer anyways. "I thought how sexy it was and if you'll come quicker when my fingers are in your pussy or your ass."

She scoffs, peeking at me through her fingers. "I'm canceling our date. I'm too embarrassed to go anywhere." I grin, walking closer to her. With my free hand, I gently pry away her hands from her face, causing her to lift her head to look at me.

Deciding to put her out of her misery, I say, "Here, mama. These are for you." I finally hand her the red roses she'd been eyeing and watch her eyes light up.

"Dec." She smiles, her shoulders relaxing. "I love them." She brings them to her nose and inhales the fresh floral scent.

Reaching inside my black jacket, I remove the gift I bought for her in Vegas. "Flowers die too quickly, I know that you're not a fan because of that, but everyone deserves to experience flowers at least once in their life." Extending my hand toward her, I present her with a red welded metal-shaped immortal rose. "This one is a rose that'll never die to remember our first date."

She gasps, taking the black stem from my hand, eyes becoming glossy as she stares at the flowers in her hands. Both real and fake.

"This is the sweetest thing anyone has ever done for me," she whispers, eyes glossy. That's sad. This woman deserves more than being impressed by some roses.

Andy sets the flowers on the counters while she fills up a large kitchen mixing bowl with water, turning to look at me with a shrug. "Sorry, I don't have a vase." She places the real roses in the water and then disappears down the hall with the fake one. I assume she's putting it in her bedroom, and that thought makes my heart swell at the idea that something I gave her would be so special that she'd want it on display.

Returning to the living room with her purse, Andy nods toward my guitar, as if she's just noticed it. "Did you bring that so you can play for me?" she asks, the corner of her lips curled in a grin.

Nodding, I step toward her. "I want to play you a new song I've been working on after dinner."

Her face lights up at the idea of getting to hear me play for her, but she covers the excitement by making a smart-ass remark. "You're assuming our date will go well enough for me to allow you back here in my apartment after."

I smirk, stalking toward her until we're standing toe to toe. "Whether you want me to stay or not, I'll have no choice but to come back up in order to grab my guitar."

She rolls her eyes, but doesn't say anything else. Instead, she steps back, giving me another playful twirl. "I'm ready to go now," she declares, hands on her wide, curvy hips.

Looking at the shoe rack beside the door, I pick up a pair of wide platform heels with black straps up the ankle and hand them to her. "Put these on, mama, and let's go."

She laughs. "I can't wear those."

I look at her in confusion. "Why? Are they not yours? They were with the other shoes here." I point, showing her where I picked them up from.

She stares at them longingly before taking the shoes from me to put them back. "They are." She sighs. "But I'm too tall to wear heels. We'd be nearly the same height in these."

"Baby, wear the damn heels." I pick them back up and hold them out toward her. "Who gives a fuck if we're the same height?" Andy is five inches shorter than me, standing at exactly six-feet tall. The heels on those shoes aren't five inches, so I'll still be taller, but it wouldn't matter to me even if I weren't.

"No, Declan. I'm too tall to wear them."

"Says who?" I demand. She shrugs.

"Fuck that. Put them on. We both know you want to." I take the shoes from her hands, dropping to one knee before her. Unlatching the strap on the right shoe, I carefully guide it on her foot, then fasten the belt around her ankle. Moving onto the other foot, I repeat the step until both shoes are placed on her feet.

Before standing, I trail my fingertips up the soft skin of her calves, slowly rising to my six-foot-five height in front of her.

"God damn," I whisper, staring into her dark eyes. "What a sight you are." My fingertips brush the loose curls from her face, and I slowly lean into her warm body, my lips placing a lingering kiss on her cheek.

I kiss from her cheek to her ear, smirking at the sharp inhale of breath she takes. "See, I'm still taller than you." I kiss the shell of her ear before pulling away, winking at the sight of her parted lips, flushed skin, and rapidly rising and falling chest.

With her hand in mine, I guide her carefully down the three flights of stairs and help her into the back of the awaiting black SUV, introducing her and David.

An hour and a half later, we're in Las Vegas at the recently opened sushi restaurant I visited with Adam, Damon, and Cole earlier this week.

Andy had planned on going to Mesquite for our date, but when she said she wanted to try sushi, I had to bring her here. I've never been to Mesquite, but we'll make that the destination for our second date.

We're seated within minutes of arriving and giving the hostess my name. We're sitting in the back in one of the dimly lit private dining rooms, Andy sitting across from me, looking like sunshine mixed with a wet dream in the soft yellow glow of the candle burning on our table.

She studies the menu, eyes looking at each item, uncertainty creasing her features.

"I'll be honest, I'm not sure what to get because I don't know what I'll like," she admits, closing the red leather menu and setting it on the black tablecloth-covered table.

"Would you like me to order for you?" She nods instantly.

"I got you, mama. I'll order for us." She gives me a shy smile, her shoulders relaxing somewhat, yet she still seems nervous. I don't know if she's nervous to be with me or just inexperienced at dating.

In an attempt to break the ice, I give her a confession. "This isn't typical for me." I wave toward my attire. "I don't do suits and fancy restaurants. Honestly, most days, I'm okay with a food truck. I don't need fancy shit."

"Why did you bring me here, then?"

"Because you deserve the finer things in life. And I want to be the one to give them to you."

"I always go to fancy restaurants." She smirks, sitting back in her chair. "Fly me first class to Greece for a week, and then I might be impressed."

I chuckle. "Only one week?"

She stares back at me. "Can you actually afford that?" she asks in a low tone, then scoffs, shaking her head. "Of course, you can. Sometimes I forget that you're literally a fucking rockstar." Her eyes widen with a sudden realization, then she gasps. "Oh my god, I'm on a date with a millionaire."

It's been a while since I've checked my bank accounts, but I know there are more zeros in that account than I'll ever be able to spend in this lifetime. After Riot's last album, my net worth skyrocketed to hundreds of millions.

"If you want to go to Greece, I'll take you. Max, too." She holds her hand up, giving me pause despite the wanderlust in her eyes.

"Let's see how our first date goes. I'm not the type of woman to get on a plane with a man I just met." She bites her bottom lip in an attempt to hide her grin.

"I think you know me pretty damn well, baby." It's scary how true that is. The things I've confessed to her this week, I've never admitted to anyone else. It's shocking how comfortable I feel with her and how much I want to remain an open book for her constantly.

When the waitress takes our order, I order nearly every roll on the menu. My girl doesn't know what she likes, so I will help her figure it out. She can try everything until she decides which roll she likes.

Once the waitress leaves, Andy's attention returns to me. "When do you move to Vegas?" Damn. We're jumping right into the topic weighing heavy on my mind all week and the conversation I've been dreading having with her.

Leaning forward, I watch the condensation drip down my water glass, my eyes tracking the movement of each drip of water slowly.

Inhaling, I lean back in my seat, slowly allowing my eyes to find hers across from me. Her face is set with a grim expression as she awaits my answer, no doubt preparing herself for the worst and trying to become detached. I only hope this time she doesn't push me away when she gets news that she doesn't like it.

"Fuck." I groan, scrubbing my hands over my freshly shaved face. "My manager, Benny, wants me to move now so I'm closer to the band whenever we need to rehearse. But it's not that far of a drive to come here every day and stay in Loganville."

"Why would you stay in Loganville? It's convenient for you to be here. Closer to your bandmates." Leaning forward, I reach across the table for her hand, and luckily, she places her golden hand in mine. My thumb mindlessly rubs along her soft skin.

"True, but I don't want to be away from you. Whatever the fuck is happening between us, I like it. Want it. Need it. Crave it," I confess, watching her face for a reaction. Her pupils dilate, red-painted lips parting.

"I have this feeling about you that I want to continue exploring. I'm not ready to give that up. How am I supposed to break down your walls if I'm unable to see you every day?" Her eyes soften at my declaration, shoulders relaxing as she exhales a sigh of what I assume is relief. Seems as if she'd been expecting the worst. Me to leave her.

"We haven't known each other long," she says. "Three weeks. Yet, I feel I've known you longer than that."

"That means we're soulmates." She bursts into a fit of laughter, pulling her hand away to place on her belly as she laughs.

Once she's calmed herself, she wipes away invisible tears. "You're ridiculous," she says with a broad smile, her eyes never leaving mine.

I can't remember the last time I enjoyed a carefree conversation with someone or the company of a woman. It isn't that I spent much time conversing with any though. I'd be with them long enough for them to hit on me, get to my hotel, and then I'd get them on their backs and they'd be screaming. Many tried to converse with me afterward, but I was never interested.

All I ever cared about was getting my dick wet and getting my next fix. But lately, I find myself caring about someone other than myself.

I care about Andy and want to claim her every thought and smile she has to offer. All it took was three weeks for her to become the light to my darkness.

Crazy how much can change in three weeks.

"Why are you staring at me like that?" Andy asks, breaking me away from my thoughts. She shifts in her seat, her dress clinging to her skin and rounding out her soft belly. Three weeks ago, she never would've worn a dress like this.

Three weeks ago, she would've constantly tugged at the fabric to get it away from her skin. Slowly, day by day, I've watched this beautiful woman grow into her confidence without realizing it.

If only she could see herself the way that I see her. She'd never have another negative thought again.

A small smile finds my lips as I realize I've been sitting there silently staring at her, fixated on the sight and intoxicating presence. "You make me happy, Andy. You and Max. It's something I never thought I'd feel again, and I sometimes feel guilty. I shouldn't get to be happy when I've done unforgivable things that I'll regret for the rest of my life. You are everything good about my day, and I worry that I'm going to let my demons ruin you."

She leans forward, elbows resting on the table as she speaks. "You deserve good things in your life, Declan. I know you think you don't. You think you're unlovable and unworthy of goodness, but I promise you that you deserve it all. Allow yourself to be happy."

If she knew what I'd done, she wouldn't look at me as she is. She's likely to slap me and run as far away as she can get and then hate herself for allowing her daughter to be around me. I want to confess my sins so fucking bad. Confess what I did to Luca. That I'm the reason he's dead because I was high while driving.

For the longest time, I blamed everyone but myself. Blamed Tommy for selling me the cocaine. Blamed whoever the fuck it came from for lacing it with who knows the fuck what.

Coke never affected me the way it did that night. And I knew better than to drive, especially in the rain, but I was so fucking angry at Camille for trying to ruin my high that I was trying to prove a point. To whom, I'm not sure.

That resulted in the car accident that claimed our son's life. I hadn't been wearing a seat belt and was thrown from the car the moment we collided with the semi. No one checked my blood, but I'm sure the reason I'm still alive is because I was under the influence. I'd laid there on the asphalt, vision blurry, body numb, unable to move or speak, as I heard Camille cry for our son.

Her screams of anguish had filled my ears as I succumbed to the darkness threatening my vision. I knew Luca was gone by the sound of her screams, and in that moment, I'd prayed for death.

The devil didn't take pity on me, and instead, days later, I woke up in the hospital, my wife by my side as she told me what I already knew. There was a car accident. Our son was gone.

Little did she know, it was all my fucking fault, and it wasn't an accident.

If Andy had known, she wouldn't think I was a good man or deserved happiness. She'd tell me what I already know. I'm a monster. A piece of shit. I should die for what I did. It wouldn't be anything new; it's things I tell myself daily anyway. Only I know the truth about the type of person I am.

I'm a fraud living on borrowed time until the devil is ready for me to pay for my sins.

Andy stands, eyes never leaving mine as she walks toward me, stopping beside me. She holds her hand out, and without hesitation, I place my palm in hers, standing when she tugs me up.

The way my tattooed flesh looks against her clear brown skin has my cock stirring in my pants and makes the little devil on my shoulder scream at me to corrupt her.

Mark her.

Scar her.

I want to forever taint her perfect skin with the devilish mark of me.

God, how I wish I deserved an angel like her. But I know our time together is temporary. My future and happiness with her aren't in the cards for me. The devil himself told me what he had planned for me, and it was a life full of sorrow and self-destruction. I was destined for that the moment I was born.

I'm living on borrowed time right now.

Meeting Andy and being with her only reminds me of what my future will never be like.

Being with her is only for a moment.

Not a lifetime.

We're temporary.

But I'll be damned if I'm not going to be a selfish prick and steal every moment with her while I can. Might as well soak it up with the beautiful woman before me.

This is yet another reason I know I'm not a good man.

"I don't care what you think. All you need to do is believe me because I'm a mom, and moms know shit. We're usually always right." She grins teasingly, taking a step toward me.

Her arms wrap around my neck, her breasts pressing against my chest as she hugs me tightly to her soft, warm body.

My body relaxes against her, and I wrap my arms around her waist, holding her so fucking tightly against my body. I'm afraid that if I were to let go, she'd disappear, and I'd wake up to find this temporary moment was just a dream.

My eyes close, nose buried in her curly hair as I inhale her cherry-vanilla scent.

Her body is soft and pliable against mine. She needs this just as much as I do.

It's crazy how a simple hug can relax your racing mind. Human contact sets off mood-altering chemicals in the brain.

I'm not sure how long we remain in the embrace, me holding her and her holding me right back like I'm her fucking lifeline, but we pull away and return to our seats when the waitress returns to our private dining room with our plates of food.

Plate after plate of sushi rolls and nigiri are placed on the table around us, not an empty spot in sight as we become surrounded by food.

"Sorry that our date turned out to be a little heavy," I say, forcing a laugh, suddenly embarrassed by the fact our date turned into an emotional confession instead of a lighthearted conversation I'm sure she wanted to have.

Andy shrugs. "I'll always want you to be real with me. I'd rather you tell me what's on your mind and how you feel rather than some bullshit. Doesn't matter where we are or how heavy the topic is." I nod, then pick up my chopsticks and focus on the food.

Deciding to start her off with something simple, I pick up the spicy crab roll and bring the bite toward her mouth. "Open." She obeys, opening her mouth wide enough for me to place the sushi roll inside. Slowly, she chews while I watch her expression closely.

Her expression shifts from skeptical to one of intrigue as mine shifts to amusement. "Good?" I ask, confirming what her face is portraying.

"Fuck, yeah." She takes a drink of water. "You just took my sushi virginity." She laughs and I join in.

Picking up another roll, I feed it to her, then feed one to myself while she chews.

We continue on like that. I feed her one piece of each roll before I eat one, and we go through all the plates, trying each one. Surprisingly, she seems to like most of them. The only pieces she doesn't like are the raw ones, but she's still a champ and tries them all.

By the time we're done sampling everything, we're both stuffed and sitting back in our seats. The waitress came to check in on us, and I have her package everything to go before bringing the check.

Andy declined dessert, and selfishly, I'd hoped she would've gotten it so we'd have more time together. I hate that our night is ending when I don't want it to. I'm not ready to say goodnight to her.

Not now. Not ever.

"What's your favorite food?" she asks the random question, taking me by surprise. One thing I've learned about Andy is you never know what to expect. One minute, she's asking what my favorite movie is; the next second, she's asking what conspiracy theories I believe in.

"Smash burgers. A food truck in New York makes the best smash burgers you'll ever have. They're always open late, so sometimes when I couldn't sleep, I'd get out of bed and walk a few blocks to get one."

"I've never had one before." That doesn't surprise me. Loganville doesn't have many dining options.

"One day, I'll take you to New York to get one," I tell her, trying my fucking hardest to believe the lie, knowing that it likely won't be in the cards for us.

"Deal." She agrees with an easy smile.

If telling her pretty lies keeps the smile on her face and the sparkle in her eyes, I'll continue telling her pretty bow-wrapped lies.

"Deal," I confirm, reaching for her hand, needing to touch her before I wake up from the dream.

TWENTY-SEVEN

Andy

THE DRIVE BACK TO LOGANVILLE IS FILLED WITH LIGHT conversation. Declan put up the privacy divider between David and us, and we spent the entire hour drive cuddling close, sharing facts about each other.

I learned that his favorite toy as a child was a red race car he got from one of his mother's boyfriends. I told him mine was a baby doll my grandpa had bought one day when we'd gone to the store together.

He asked what my favorite memory of my grandpa was, and I told him it was shaving with him every night. I'd been such a grandpa's girl that I always had to be around him, including when he shaved. I'd sit outside the bathroom door while he showered, and once he was done and dressed, he'd let me in. Every night, he'd set me on the counter, put shaving cream on my face, then give me a Q-Tip to shave with while he stood beside me shaving with his blue razor.

My grandma was never happy when she entered the bathroom to find the trash can full of Q-Tips, but it was mine and his routine.

When I asked Declan what his favorite childhood memory was, he said it was when his mother took him for ice cream. She left him the same day. He said that, before she left, he felt so damn excited and special to be out with his mom. Just the two of them.

He asked if I ever had any pets, and I shared that in elementary school, I had a brown hamster named Baby Boy and a black lab puppy named Macy. When he asked what happened, I told him. Baby Boy died in his cage somehow, and Macy ran away one day when the door was left open. We also had a massive fish tank full of goldfish because I once won one from the carnival one year. After that, I'd told my grandma I wanted more, and the next thing I knew, I had an entire tank and several more fish that we picked out together from Wal-Mart.

Eventually, I got tired of them, so she gave them to the neighbor with a son who had been wanting goldfish.

Besides, they weren't considered pets anyway.

Declan admitted he'd never been to a carnival, so I told him about the carnival that comes to town every year and promised to take him to the next one.

I loved how he held my hand and listened when I spoke. He absorbed every word as if he were engraving my words on his brain so he'd never forget a conversation.

I felt seen and heard for the first time in my adult life. He truly cared about what I had to say, which meant everything to me. I rarely get to converse with someone who cares about the words that leave my mouth.

When we reach my apartment, I realize the drive went by in the blink of an eye, and I don't want to say goodbye. I'm not ready to say goodnight and end the most incredible night of my life, my first date.

Undoing my seatbelt, I turn to look at the man next to me. "Want to come up? The night doesn't have to end." One look in his dark eyes tells me we both know what's on our minds and what the invitation insinuates.

Asking him if he wants to come inside is the nicer way of

saying, *Hey, want to fold me into a pretzel and fuck me ten ways til Sunday?* Still, I'm sure he's aware of what I'm offering.

For the first time since giving birth, I want to allow a man inside of my body. I want to share that part of myself, and he's the one I want to share it with. I've been horny for too fucking long, and I'm ready to submit and cry out his name.

Declan's eyes darken as he stares at me, a slow smirk spreading across his lips. "Let's go," he says. I climb out of the car while he tells David to go home.

He climbs out, holding the bags of our sushi leftovers. With one hand on the small of my back, he guides me toward the stairs as the SUV pulls out of the parking lot. The taillights fade into the distance as David leaves.

Once we enter my apartment, I toss my purse on the couch and lock the door behind us. Declan takes his shoes off before entering the kitchen and placing our food in the fridge, returning to me within seconds.

"Someone is eager to spend more time with me." I smirk, my back against the door as I watch him stalk toward me with dark, hungry eyes full of desire.

"You have no fucking idea." He growls, caging me in by placing a hand on either side of my head. "If you didn't invite me up here for what I think you did, then tell me right now."

"I thought we could play a board game. Maybe put together a puzzle," I tease, shrugging innocently.

He groans, his forehead resting against mine as his breath fans across my lips. "You drive me fucking crazy." He presses his hips into mine, allowing me to feel the hardness growing in his pants.

Holy fuck.

"You have five seconds to change your mind, mama. Tell me now," he commands, his voice strained as he uses all his willpower to hold himself back.

"Five." He begins counting down. "Four… Three…"

"One," I whisper, tilting my head up and pressing my lips to his; at the same time, he collides against me, his hands going into my hair and tugging at the roots, keeping my head firmly in place and slightly tilted as he devours my mouth.

God. If he fucks as good as he kisses, then I'm a goner.

My hands grip his hips, curling into fists as I bring his body closer to mine, desperate to feel him all over my aching body.

His lips devour mine, and his tongue dominates my mouth as he massages it against mine, tasting every inch of my mouth. I groan against his lips, my skin heating with the sensation as lust consumes me, my pussy weeping for him.

Declan's hands slip down from my hair to my ass, grabbing a handful of each cheek as he drags my body as close to his as he can get, closing any lingering gaps of space between us.

"Andy," he rasps against my lips, pulling his head away until he's looking into my eyes. "Are you sure about this? I'm not a good man, and I may corrupt you." He presses a wet, needy kiss against my lips, leaving me breathless, panting against the wall like a bitch in heat. "You are too fucking good for me. If you allow me inside of you, I'm going to suck the life out of you." He warns, his tone ominous. He's given me plenty of warnings that he is not the man for me or even a good one. Yet, I want nothing more than to allow him inside of my body.

Right now, there's nothing he'd be able to say that would be able to stop me from taking the next step with him. A step that I know I'll never regret.

No matter what happens between us, I'll never regret the time we've spent together—the time we've spent sharing secrets over text and getting to know each other. He may break my heart someday, but I'll never regret him.

I'd willingly cut my heart out and hand it to him if it meant getting another moment with him.

"Shut up and take me. You have my consent to do whatever you want to do. Fuck me, destroy my life, ruin me for any other man." One day I know these words will come back to bite me, but it's too easy to give in when you're thinking with your vagina rather than your head.

I'd hand over every dollar in my wallet right now if he wanted it. It wouldn't be much, but I'm too turned on to reason or deny him anything.

Declan's hands trail down past my round ass to the backs of my thighs, bunching the fabric of my dress in his hands until he has it around my waist and my legs are exposed. His fingertips firmly grip my bare skin as he lifts me, making me gasp in surprise.

"Declan! Put me down. I'm too heavy," I protest, pushing his shoulders to get free from him. His mouth takes mine in a savage kiss, his tongue lapping against mine, my legs automatically wrapping around his waist as the dark fabric of my dress pools around my waist, revealing my ass to the cool air.

Goosebumps rise on my skin, my heated pussy pressed against his stomach as he holds me firmly in his arms, confidently walking toward my bedroom, all while never breaking our kiss.

He lies me down in the middle of my king-sized bed, my legs unwrapping from him, as I lie there on my back staring up at him with parted lips, practically panting from how wound up my body is with desire for him.

His eyes never leave mine as he stands before me, tattooed fingers slowly unbuttoning and removing his clothing. Once he's bare before me, I prop myself up on my elbows to stare at his magnificent body, eyes drinking in every single inch of his skin, committing him to memory in case this is all a cruel dream that I'll be waking up from.

"You are so goddamn beautiful. I don't feel worthy of having the honor to look at you," he says, eyes drinking me in despite the fact I'm still dressed.

I've never been completely naked in front of a man before. I've always kept a shirt on, too insecure and uncomfortable to allow my belly to show or reveal my breasts that aren't as perky as I wish they were. They're heavy double D's, and without a bra, they hang a little lower. Don't get me wrong, they're not grandma-level saggy, but I have a child, so of course, they're not going to be as high as they were prior to having a baby.

Declan makes me want to bear myself to him despite my past and insecurities. I want to show him my body because that dark look in his eyes tells me he'd worship me.

The mattress dips beneath his weight as he places a knee on the bed, slowly unbuckling the black strap around my ankles from my heels. Once he has my shoes off, he tosses them across the room with a thud. His calloused hands roam up my skin, grabbing hold of my red thong and pulling it down my legs, tossing it onto the bed beside my head.

His eyes focus between my legs, on my very wet pussy that is no doubt glistening with my arousal. I've never been so turned on in my life. My eyes follow his movements as he undresses, my body humming with the need for him, desperate to have him fill me up with the hard cock bobbing between his muscular thighs.

"You have two seconds to take this dress off, or I'm ripping it," he says, his expression stoic. Surely, he wouldn't tear my dress.

When I don't make an attempt to move, he grabs the hem and balls it into his fists, "Okay! Wait! Fuck, don't destroy it." I quickly climb to my knees, turning to give him my back so he can unzip it.

Declan slides the zipper down my back, cold fingertips tracing over my heated skin, causing goosebumps and a rush of coolness. Sliding the dress off my arms, I quickly undo my bra and toss it across the room, turning to face him.

With my chin high, I shove the dress down my hips, exposing my less-than-perfect body to the God in front of me.

Where I am soft and have rolls and stretch marks, Declan is sculpted with perfectly chiseled abs and a sharp jawline. Mine is soft and sometimes hidden thanks to the double chin that appears at certain angles.

His eyes roam freely over my bare skin, the dark, lustful gaze making me feel absolutely fucking powerful.

For the first time, I don't want to hide. Not when he's looking at me the way he is. Like I'm the only woman in the world to him.

It doesn't matter that I'm not his usual type because right now, he's mine. He's here looking at me with dark eyes full of hunger only I can satisfy.

Declan climbs onto the bed, mimicking my position of standing on my knees. His rough, calloused fingers press against my heated skin, roaming down to my backside where he grabs my ass cheeks in each hand, forcing my body closer toward him with a rough yank.

"I want to fucking devour you, but that'll have to wait. I need to get my dick in you right the fuck now."

Our lips connect, and then suddenly, we're becoming a mix of limbs and frenzied kisses, unable to keep our hands off each other. My dress is removed, thrown across the room, then he's between my spread legs, his hard cock rubbing against my aching core with each grind of our hips. He's teasing me, denying me what I need.

He pulls away from my lips, looking down at me from where he lies above me, forearms on either side of my head. "Are you ready to become mine?"

I'm so delirious, desperate for him to fill me, that I nod frantically, unsure of what I'm agreeing to.

He buries his face in my neck, lips pressing against my skin. "I'm going to make you a filthy girl," he mumbles. "I'm going to fucking ruin you," he warns in a whisper so low I almost miss it.

Pulling back, he grabs my hips and sits back on his heels as he lines his cock up with my entrance and presses his crown against me.

"Count the inches. Let's see how much your greedy little

pussy can take." His eyes fixated on my core as he slowly moves his hips forward, his hard length pushing through my tightness. Thank fuck I'm wet enough for him.

My lips part, hands fisting the sheets beside me as he stretches me, forcing his massive cock inside of my body.

"Count," he demands, his voice strained.

Usually, I'd refuse to stroke his ego, but he feels too fucking good that I don't have it in me to argue. So, I give him what he wants.

"One... two... three..." His expression is pinched as he forces himself to hold back as he watches his cock disappear inside my body.

With another rough shift of his hips, he fills me all at once, forcing a gasp from my throat. "Ten," he says in a loud moan, moving his body above mine, taking my lips in a searing kiss that leaves me breathless and dizzy.

My pussy clenches around him, squeezing his length as I adjust to the intrusion of him inside of me. It's been years since I've had more than my own fingers.

Unexpectedly, he pulls out, causing me to whine at the loss of him, but it's not for long because a moment later, he's thrusting forward, filling me to the hilt and setting a rough, punishing pace, barely allowing me time to adjust.

Pretty sure my eyes roll so far into the back of my head that I spot my brain.

My lips part, and loud, uncontrollable moans seem to fly out of my mouth, my knuckles white from the tight grip on the sheets.

"Fuck!" He groans, his breathing heavy and uneven. "You're so fucking tight. Feels so damn good." His lips connect with mine as he takes advantage of my parted lips, and he shoves his tongue into my mouth, massaging it against mine.

He swallows my cries of pleasure, taking every moan and cry I have to offer.

I wrap my arms around his back, my nails digging into his

clear skin. My nails dig deep, leaving crescent moons in his flesh. My left hand claws and scratches, while my right remains dug deep.

The pain seems to spur him on, his thrusts becoming deeper. He grabs my left leg and wraps it around his waist, holding it against him as he continues pushing into me, giving me everything he has.

Our combined noises become louder, drowning out the sound of our skin slapping together and my headboard banging against the wall.

It's a good thing that my apartment is at the end of the hall, and my bedroom doesn't share a wall with a neighbor. If it did, I'm sure I'd hear someone banging on the wall, yelling at us to be quiet.

The new position has him sliding deeper, hitting the spot within me that has my toes curling and pussy clenching, shocks of pleasure racing through my sweaty body.

Declan reaches a hand between us and expertly finds my clit, applies pressure, and rubs it in a perfect steady rhythm that sends me over the edge, fireworks erupting around me.

Goosebumps rise on my skin, and before I know it, I'm tightening around him and screaming my release. It feels so fucking good that tears fill my eyes.

We kiss sloppily, and neither can focus on having our lips move in sync. The sloppy kiss matches his thrusts that become out of rhythm as he chases his building orgasm.

"Fuck, baby. Going to fill this pussy," he mutters against my mouth, body continuing to move against mine.

A moment later, he stills against me, roaring his release as warmth spreads through my body, his cum flooding me. He leans back onto his heels once again, eyes fixated between my spread legs as he slowly pulls his softening cock out of me, my pussy already mourning the loss of him.

Fascination is evident in his eyes as he watches his cum drip out of me. I clench my walls, forcing even more of it out of me.

"Fuck, that's hot." He groans. Swiping a finger through my swollen lips, he sticks it inside me, the invasion making me groan.

He swipes his finger through my core once more before bringing it to my lips, glistening with our combined release. Knowing what he wants, I open my mouth, and he shoves the cum-coated finger inside. The saltiness explodes on my taste-buds, making me hum and even more desperate for him and his taste.

My eyes never leave his as I suck his finger clean.

With a satisfied smirk, Declan pulls his hand away, places a final kiss on my lips, and then rolls off me, collapsing on his back beside me.

"Best pussy ever."

TWENTY-EIGHT

Declan

I'D PROMISED MYSELF THAT I WOULDN'T TOUCH ANDY. BUT I'M A liar, so I'm not surprised that I broke the promise and jumped on her the first chance I got.

I didn't want to taint her pureness with my demons. She's too much of an angel to be burdened with my sins. Yet that didn't stop me, and I don't regret anything. I'll save my regrets for another day when our temporary moment is over, and I'll be full of regrets, forced to live in the solitude of the sins of my past, remembering what it was like to have an angel beneath me.

Fucking her hadn't been planned, but thank God it happened because I've been wanting her for far too long.

Being with her had exceeded any expectations I could've had. The moment our bodies combined, it was magical. Sliding into her hot, wet, tight pussy for the first time was pure fucking sin.

God, she was perfect. The way she lifted her hips to fuck me right back. She gave as good as she got.

My dick twitches, already growing to half mass at the thought of getting to sink inside of her again. Before the night is over, I definitely need to be inside of her a few more times.

Her pussy is like a drug. I'm an addict, and once will never be enough.

We lie side by side, our breathing heavy and intertwined, the scent of sex heavy in the air. Perspiration lines my hairline, my skin feeling hot as if the flames of hell are rising closer, threatening to take me home.

"Want some water?" Andy's throaty voice breaks our silence, her voice raw and scratchy from all the screaming she was doing.

"Yeah," I exhale, finding my own voice to be husky thanks to my moans. "I'll get us some." Rolling over to my side, I wrap my arms around the angel beside me, pulling her naked body against mine, needing to feel her bare flesh against me once again.

As I roll on top of her, Andy shifts beneath me, a content smile on her face as she stares up at me, legs spread so I fit perfectly between them. I keep my weight off her with my forearms on either side of her head, staring down into her eyes.

"You were incredible," I rasp, pressing a slow lingering kiss to her lips, trailing my lips down to her neck, biting and sucking the delicate skin.

Beneath me, Andy lets out a low moan, her hips moving up toward me, trying to get my hardening cock to slip inside of her greedy little pussy again.

"You want my cock again so soon?" I ask as she smirks, moving her hips against mine. "Let me taste you." Pressing another kiss to her lips, I trail my lips down her bare body, capturing one of her little brown nipples in my mouth and sucking, flicking the pebbled peak with my tongue.

"God, Declan." She moans, her hands grabbing fistfuls of the crumbled sheets around us. I suck more of her breast into my mouth, pulling back with an audible pop before moving to the next one. My hand grabs hold of the breast I just left, fingers mindlessly rolling her nipple. Her heavy teardrop breasts are soft in my hands, and I make a mental note to talk her into letting me titty fuck her. She has the best tits for that.

Continuing my descent down her body, I scoot further down

on the bed, trailing my lips along her cherry-scented flesh. Andy's sharp inhale has me looking up at her when I reach her soft belly, watching how she bites her lip and watches me. She sucks in, clearly uncomfortable with having me so close to an area that she struggles to love.

"You're so fucking sexy," I assure her, biting at the skin of her belly. Whether she allows me to or not, I'm going to bite and suck every inch of her skin and leave my mark everywhere I can. I've never given a girl a fucking hickey on their stomach before, but the girls I've fucked in the past also didn't have enough meat on their bones to allow for that, either.

Andy has the perfect body to accept my mark.

I dip my tongue into her belly button, licking every inch of her in long strokes, then switch to kissing as I pay special attention to her stretch marks. Slowly, I press gentle kisses to the discolored marks, fingertips trailing over every one that lines her hips and the few around her belly button.

Pulling back, I look up at her, allowing her to see the sincerity in my eyes when I speak, "I wish you could see yourself through my eyes. If you could, you'd never have another negative thought about yourself again. You'd know how exquisite you truly are." My lips trail lower, getting closer and closer to her wet cunt where I know she wants me the most. "You, Andy Harris, are a true fucking masterpiece."

Before she can respond, I flatten my tongue and lick over her hard clit, wrapping my lips around it and sucking it like my life depends on it.

Andy gasps, her back arching as her fingers tangle in my hair, tugging at the roots. Without warning, I plunge three fingers deep inside of her needy pussy, going as deep as I can until I reach her g-spot, then begin massaging it.

"Declan," she cries out, body writhing beneath me as I feast on her pussy like a starved man at a buffet for the first time.

The sweet taste of her explodes on my tongue, my cock becoming achingly hard beneath me, precum beginning to bead at the tip and leaking onto the sheets beneath me. Andy's soft heels press into my back, her feet twitching and jerking back and forth against my skin as I attempt to satiate my hunger for her, knowing that I'll never be completely satisfied.

I'd been too desperate earlier to get my dick inside of her that I hadn't gone down on her. If I'm being honest, I'm glad I waited until now because I would've ended up coming on her sheets like an inexperienced teenage boy, so it's a good thing I was able to bust my load inside of her before getting to fill my mouth with her pussy juice and treat my taste buds to the most delicious thing I've ever fucking eaten.

It's a damn shame that some men don't like eating pussy. How the fuck can you not like it? The smell, the juices, the squelching noise as I fuck her with my fingers, her pussy becoming wetter with each thrust. Not to mention the moans from her pouty lips.

God. The fucking moans.

Andy's deep, throaty cries of pleasure are music to my ears. The most incredible sound I've ever heard. I should've set my phone up to record her so I'd be able to listen to it on repeat for the rest of my goddamn life.

Something to remember her by after she inevitably leaves me.

I'd turn the volume up and listen to it every single fucking day while I fuck my fist using the cherry-scented lotion I bought for her at the cherry festival.

I'm going to savor her taste.

Her pussy tightens around my fingers in a vise-like grip as I continue pumping them in and out of her, my pace quickening as her orgasm noticeably begins to build, her body twitching with the desperate need to come.

Flicking my tongue over her clit, I pull back to look up at her, watching her writhe in pleasure, her curly hair becoming frizzy with the frantic movements of her head. Her back arches, pushing her heavy tits into the air, little brown nipples pebbled and hard.

"Your pussy is so fucking greedy. Squeezing my fingers so tight." I smirk, leaning my head down to take another lick of her clit, flicking the hard pleasure pearl.

"Greedy, greedy girl. I wonder what it'll take for you to soak my face." Her eyes roll into the back of her head, mouth popping open as I continue massaging the spot deep within her that'll have her soon seeing stars and begging for God to save her.

"Let's find out. I wouldn't mind drowning in you." I dive back in, my mouth attaching to her clit and both sucking and licking in perfect rhythm with the movements of my fingers.

"Holy fuck, Declan." She groans breathlessly. "Oh, God. I'm going to—" I don't allow her to finish her sentence. Instead, I steal her breath, curling my fingers upward and giving her what she wants, what I've been teasing her with.

Release.

The first squirt of fluid sprays my chin and neck, juice continuing to drip down my face.

I bury my face in her soaked pussy, licking the length of her and groaning against her skin at the taste. She's my new favorite fucking flavor, and I want the taste of her on my tongue for the rest of my life. If I were to die right now, I'd die a very happy man.

Put my cause of death on my headstone.

Here lies Declan Valentine. The man who died while eating the best-tasting pussy.

What an excellent way to go.

Andy's body convulses underneath me, her nails scratching at my scalp and pulling at my hair, desperate to ease the sensation on her sensitive clit.

"Declan!" she cries, her thick thighs locking around my head. "Fuck! It's too much." Her whines only urge me on, making me force as much out of her as I possibly can.

When she's unable to share any more of her sweet nectar with me, I pull back, looking up at her with a wide grin on my soaked face. She winces when I remove my fingers, holding them up between us to show her how much cum she gave me.

She stares at me with horrified eyes, watching me closely as I suck them into my mouth, licking every trace of her off them. It may be a while before I wash my hands or shower. I want the smell of her lingering on my skin as long as fucking possible.

Sitting back on my heels between her spread legs, I wrap a fist around my angry heated cock, groaning in relief at the sensation. I don't think I've ever been this hard before, and if I don't come soon, there's a good chance my balls might actually turn blue.

I use my wet fingers and beads of precum to lube up my shaft, stroking myself root to tip as I stare at Andy's perfect pussy, spread wide before me and glistening with her juices. Beneath her, I notice the large wet spot that's formed and hold back a smug smirk.

That's my girl.

"I came so hard that I didn't think I was going to stop," she says, licking her lips as she stares back at me, face flushed and glowing with sweat.

Smirking, I remove my hand from my aching cock and place a hard quick slap to her pussy, hitting her right on her sensitive clit, causing her to yelp.

Before she can come up with a smart-ass response, I slap her clit again. "Either sit on my cock or put it in your mouth. Either way, you have two seconds before I choose for you."

Like a good girl, Andy climbs to her knees without needing to be told twice and gets down on her knees and elbows in front of me, giving me the perfect view of her peachy ass as she leans down and swallows my cock.

"Fuuuuuck." I groan, scooping her hair out of her face and holding it tightly in my fist like a ponytail.

Spotting her red lace panties still on the bed, I quickly reach across and grab them while she continues sucking my dick like a champ.

Bringing the wet crotch of her panties to my nose, I inhale, desperate for more, even though her scent is surrounding me.

Once I have her scent deep into my lungs, I quickly wrap her thick, curly hair up into a bun using the red thong to secure it like a hair tie. With the wild locks out of the way, I have the perfect unobstructed view of her face, and I watch her closely as she bobs in my lap, her eyes finding mine.

"You look like a beautiful little whore with my dick in your mouth. Made just for me." She hums her satisfaction, tongue circling my head as she pulls back to lick the white beads of precum before sliding her mouth back down, lips wrapping firmly around my shaft as she sucks.

She groans in satisfaction, the feeling vibrating around my cock as she relaxes her throat and swallows me down, throat tightening with each gulp.

"Just like that, baby. Such a fucking good girl." Spreading my legs wider, I press her head down, her nose touching the trimmed hair at my base.

Wide, glossy, brown eyes look up at me, drool spilling from the corners of her lips as she urges me to release. Her hand works my shaft in perfect movement with her pouty mouth.

"Fuck, I wish you could see yourself. Your mouth isn't so sassy when it's full of dick." She whimpers, picking up the pace, her head bobbing as her free hand moves between her legs to finger her greedy cunt.

"Damn, baby, did that greedy pussy not get enough?" Along with the sound of her gagging, I can hear the sound her wetness makes as she fingers herself.

A familiar warmth settles at the bottom of my spine, my release begging to be set free. The sight of her fingering herself while sucking my dick is too much to bear.

She's enjoying sucking me so much that even though her perfect cunt needs a break, she still needs more because my taste has turned her on.

What type of man would I be if I didn't ensure she was thoroughly pleased?

"I need to be in your pussy right fucking now. Get that ass up for me, baby." Andy pulls away with an audible pop, quickly shifting into the same position she was in to suck me off, except now her ass is directly in front of me.

Climbing to my knees behind her, I line myself up with her glistening entrance, grip her hips firmly, and roughly plow into her, filling her to the hilt in one thrust.

She cries out beneath me, her head lowering to the bed as her ass remains up high for me, hips being held in my tight grip.

"You want my come, baby?" I run my palm along one of her ass cheeks before slapping it, her body jerking with the movement. "Want me to fill this tight little pussy?"

"Yes!" she practically screams beneath me, one of her hands between her legs rubbing her clit, while the other plays with her tit, squeezing, rolling, and pinching her brown nipple in her fingers. "Make me come, Declan." She pants, her head on the bed as she looks at me over her shoulder.

"Come on this cock, baby. It's all yours." I slap her ass cheek again, my ass clenching as I pound into her. Tight warm walls surround me in a vise-like grip, her pussy becoming tighter as she gives into her orgasm. Her body shakes with her release, cries and screams of pleasure surrounding us.

Andy's pussy convulses around my shaft, practically milking my dick. With a groan, I give in to my own pleasure, holding still as I shoot my cum deep into her body, holding her hips as I force her to take every drop I have to offer.

We should've used a condom, but I wanted a part of me to be alive in her body, swimming around for days. Not that I want to get her pregnant, but I like knowing my sperm is alive inside of her, playing a game of Russian roulette. We've never discussed birth control, so we'll see if she gets her monthly bloody visit or not.

Andy drops to the bed, her body spent and shining with

sweat. Her body moves with each heavy breath from her parted lips. Leaning down, I stick my tongue out and press it against her skin, licking up from the bottom of her spine all the way to her earlobe.

I twirl my tongue in her ear, sucking the lobe into my mouth as she groans beneath me, eyelids heavy with exhaustion.

"Don't fall asleep," I warn, kissing her temple. "You know that you're mine now, right?"

Brown eyes shoot open and she stares at me, arching an eyebrow. "How do you figure?"

"Well, you know the saying, 'lick it and it's yours'?" I smirk, holding myself up above her. "I licked you, so you're mine." To prove my point, I slowly lick up her cheek. She giggles, wiping her wet cheek as she turns onto her back, staring up at me with a broad smile and hearts in her eyes.

"I told you, baby, once I get my dick inside of you, that's it. Game over." Leaning down, I faintly brush my lips against hers. "Tell me you're mine," I plead, needing to know she's in this as much as I am.

"I don't know what the fuck I have to offer you. It's selfish to want you, but whenever I'm around you, all I want is to be selfish." I've always been selfish, but that will not change now. Not when I have this beautiful woman beneath me who doesn't expect me to be something I'm not. She knows that I'm not a good person, but she still gives me her precious time and allows me into her life.

We're temporary, and until this dream is over, I want to spend every second with her as much as possible.

"Tell me you're mine," I beg, burying my face in her neck, keeping my weight on my forearms.

"Yes, Declan, I'm yours," she whispers, arms wrapping around my back, holding me firmly against her. "I'm yours," she repeats, two words setting our destruction in motion.

TWENTY-NINE
Declan

Feeling the sense of an empty bed beside me, my eyes pop open, blinking rapidly to adjust to the purple glow in the dark room thanks to Andy's strung-up lights. Without reaching out, I already know the side of the bed where she slept is empty. It's been a long time since I've slept with someone I cared about, and the last time I did, my body was so in tune with hers that I'd wake anytime she got out of bed.

It seems the same with Andy.

Sitting up, a yawn escapes me, my eyes glancing over at the closed bathroom door as I hear the lock flip seconds before the door opens, revealing Andy standing in the doorway in her fuzzy robe, the scent of cherries escaping the open door.

"Did you shower?" I ask, leaning against the headboard, blanket pulled around my waist. The last thing I remember was Andy and I holding each other, and then we must've fallen asleep.

She nods, a shy smile on her lips.

"What time is it?" I ask, watching as she walks to her night-stand and taps her phone to reveal the time.

"It's three in the morning," she says, climbing onto the bed beside me and looking everywhere but at me. The awkwardness between us is thick in the air, but I don't feel any differently than I did before we went to sleep, and I'm sure she's worried about it.

"Hey, mama, look at me." Reaching over, I grab her wrist, pulling her closer toward me, "What I said wasn't pillow talk. I want you to know that I'm all in. I meant every word I said to you tonight," I assure her, needing her to believe me and know that she won't turn her back on me.

Andy stares at me, a long silence passing between us before she sighs and speaks. "I've never been someone's girl before. I don't know how to act. And if you were saying those things in the moment, it's okay. I know that shit gets said during sex that guys don't always mean." Sitting up, I grip her chin, holding it firmly in my hand, not allowing her to look away as I speak.

"Fuck anyone who has said shit to you they didn't mean. I wouldn't say what I did had I not meant it. You're mine, Andy, and I'll do whatever I have to for you to believe that." Through her softening eyes, I can see the walls around her heart crumbling. "I think we're both pretty fucked up, but I think you might be my redemption." Perhaps she's an angel that's been sent to me for one last attempt to save my soul before I'm dragged to hell.

"Give me all of you, baby." With a slow smile, she nods, tears coating her dark eyes.

"I'll try," she promises, her soft hands trailing my forearms as I hold her face. "Please don't hurt me, Declan. I don't think I'd be able to take it if you did."

"You have my word that I will always do my fucking best." She kisses me, climbing into my lap, arms wrapping around my neck as she lets down the final wall around her heart, allowing me in the sacred gate.

For the first time in a long time, there's a flutter in my chest, a sign that the organ is still alive and beating.

The devil hasn't called me home yet, so until he does, I'm going to enjoy as much time as I can with my angel on earth.

ANDY RETURNS TO THE BEDROOM WITH TWO WATER BOTTLES, our bag of leftover sushi, and a familiar black leather strap around her body. The sight of my guitar peeking over her shoulder brings a grin to my lips as I sit up, adjusting myself so my back is against the headboard and the blanket covers my naked lap.

Still wearing her robe, Andy climbs onto the bed beside me on her knees and spreads out the food before setting a fork beside me. Carefully, she pulls the strap over her head, handing me the black guitar.

"Play for me." She sits facing me, the food spread between us as she grabs a fork of her own. I adjust the guitar on my lap, holding it in my arms as my fingers strum over the familiar chords, eyes never leaving hers.

"I didn't have chopsticks, so a fork will have to do," she says, brushing the loose strands of hair out of her face, a flash of red in her hair making me nearly choke on my saliva and burst into laughter.

She blinks, looking at me in confusion. "What?" She wipes her hands over her face. "Do I have something on my face?"

I shake my head, a smirk spreading across my lips. "Did you look at your hair while you were in the bathroom?" I know the answer before she responds. Of course, she hasn't because if she'd seen the red thong in her hair used as a hair tie, she would've thrown it at me after promptly removing it.

"What's wrong with my hair?"

"Nothing, baby, it's beautiful."

She scoffs, eyes rolling as she quickly removes her hair from the bun. Her eyes flash with confusion when she realizes what she thought was a hair tie isn't.

Unwrapping her curls from the red thong, she pulls the piece of fabric between us, eyes wide in horror at the sight. "What the fuck?" Her eyes narrow into a glare, and she tosses the fabric into my face, which I happily accept.

Catching it in the air, I inhale her scent to my nose. My cock comes alive beneath the sheet, ready for another touch or taste of Andy's sweetness. She watches me with wide eyes, blushing at the sight of me openly sniffing her used panties.

"Fuck, you smell so damn good."

"You're such a creep," she teases, and there's no conviction behind her tone.

"Look what your scent does to me." Holding up the guitar, I push the sheet off my lap and reveal my bare cock hard between my legs. It's laying on my stomach heavily. Dark eyes fixate on my length, her pink tongue coming out to lick her pouty lips. "Put that tongue away, baby. Might be tempted to make you put it to use and run it along this dick."

Andy's eyes meet mine, a slow smirk spreading across her lips as her tongue once again pokes out and traces over her lips, the action slow and so fucking erotic.

God, this girl is going to be the death of me.

Turning to face me, she leans in while allowing her robe to fall open, revealing her soft naked body. "Maybe if you're a good boy, I'll let you put this hard cock in my mouth," she says in a sultry tone, breath fanning across my lips as she speaks.

"I'll make you count the inches as I take you deep into my throat, licking and sucking your cock until you're begging for me to let you come." She leans closer to me and presses her lips against mine for the briefest moment, pulling away before I can return the kiss. "Only when you're begging me to come because you can't take it anymore, I'll decide if you've been a good enough boy to deserve it. You can fill my mouth if you do, and I'll swallow every drop." She presses her lips to mine, forcing her tongue inside my mouth.

She pulls back after a moment. "Mmmm, I can taste myself on your tongue." She kisses me again, then flashes me a smile before settling into her spot, her attention on the box of sushi she pulls onto her lap while I lay there stunned, trying to figure out what the fuck just happened.

Where the fuck did the shy girl go?

Andy takes my dick a couple times and suddenly becomes a filthy-mouthed little temptress who can put me in my place and leave me speechless.

"Play for me, Dec." She opens the plastic container and stabs one of the leftover rolls with her fork, bringing the piece to her lips that I'm aching to have around my cock again.

Damn, I'm going to have my hands full with this girl.

"You're going to just leave me... hard?" She turns her head to look at me long enough for me to see her roll her pretty brown eyes before turning her attention back toward her food tray.

Leaning into her, I press my lips against her bare shoulder, slowly pulling the robe down until it's around her waist, and her heavy tits are exposed. "That's okay, mama. Two can play that game." I trail my lips up her neck, satisfaction coming over me at the sight of goosebumps on her brown skin.

Once I reach her neck, her breath hitches, and I place a single kiss along her jaw before pulling away and returning my back to the headboard.

Clearing my throat, I adjust the chords, then slowly begin to strum the tune to a song I've been working on. Keeping my smoky voice low, I fill the silence of the room with the melody of my voice and guitar.

Your brown eyes are haunting me.
If I had a heart, it would be yours.
You're bringing me back to life to live a life I don't deserve.
If I had a future, it would be yours.

As I sing the words, my gaze never leaves the brown eyes staring back at me. My lips are parted as she takes in every word I say. Silently, I set the guitar on the side of the bed, propping it carefully against the nightstand, and then I grab the fork and dive into the leftover sushi spread out across the bed.

"That was beautiful, Declan," she says, gaze meeting mine again. A smile spreads across my lips, but I don't respond, suddenly feeling too vulnerable and desperate for a change in conversation.

We eat in silence for a few minutes before I clear my throat, moving my body to sit at the foot of the bed so I can have a perfect view of her bare tits. Her perfect brown nipples are pebbled and hard for me.

"So, Cole is having a barbeque at his house on Sunday. I was wondering if you'd like to go with me. Everyone would love to meet you." I should've invited her sooner when Cole told me about it, but I had wanted to wait until I could ask her in person. It's short notice and likely putting her on the spot, but at least it doesn't allow her time to come up with an excuse and overthink it.

"In Vegas?" She wrinkles her brows. "I don't think that's a great idea. I have work on Monday morning."

I nod, already having thought about her schedule. "I know, and we'll be back early enough that you'll get enough sleep. It's at noon." Cole's girlfriend works early on Monday as well and couldn't take the day off, so they decided to have it early enough that everyone would be able to attend.

I open my mouth, prepared to convince her to say yes, but she surprises me. "Okay, I'll go."

"Fuck yeah, mama. Are you serious?"

"Will all your bandmates be there?"

I nod. "Yup. Adam, Cole, and his girl who is bringing her sister and her kids, Benny, Damon, and whoever the fuck he brings. It'll be pretty chill with it just being us." Intimate gatherings with those I consider family is exactly what I fucking need, and it's important to me that these heathens know how special Andy is. How much I both want and need her in my life.

"What about Max?" she asks, grabbing the bottle of water, unscrewing the cap and taking a sip.

"She'll come with us, of course. Cole's girlfriend's sister has twins who will be there, so Max will have kids to play with. I'm unsure how old they are, but they'll have fun."

"Let's do it, as long as we're back early enough for me to go to bed." I place my hand across my chest, nodding sincerely.

"Yes, ma'am. Cross my heart, you will return in time for your six o'clock bedtime." She laughs, tossing the gray throw pillow at my chest. It lands in my lap, and I wrap my arms around it.

"I also wanted to talk to you about something you said the other night that got me thinking." Setting her fork down, she ignores the remaining sushi and gives me her undivided attention.

"Now I'm nervous. What did I say?"

"You mentioned that you were Riot's biggest fan and how much you've been stalking my band and fingering yourself every night while watching our videos." She snorts, laughter erupting from her. She flips me off, wiping away imaginary tears. "For real, though, I want you there. I want to see your face when I look out into the crowd Friday night."

She inhales sharply, her jaw falling open. "You're asking me to attend your concert?" I've been thinking about it since Benny dropped the bomb that I'd be back on stage sooner than expected. One fucking week until I return in front of a screaming crowd and have to give them a piece of my soul while remaining sober.

"I am, mama. I need you there. Need to know that you're watching me." When I get off that stage, I'm the most vulnerable, and all I want to do is be able to lose myself in my girl rather than drugs and alcohol.

"I'm honored that you'd want me there, Declan. That means a lot to me." A shy, hidden smile comes across her lips. "Can't believe I'm going to see my favorite band live." She pauses, seeming to think for a moment before continuing. "Actually, I can't fucking believe that I'm dating the lead singer of my favorite band."

"The concert will go pretty late. Can you stay the night in Vegas with me?"

She thinks for a moment, clearly considering her options for Max. Finally, she nods. "I'm pretty sure. I'll check and make it work." She laughs humorlessly. "Is this real life?"

Reaching over, I pinch her thigh. She hisses, pushes my hand away, and rubs the spot I just pinched.

"What the hell was that for?"

"Just making sure this is real life and not a dream."

"You're an idiot."

I shrug. "Maybe. But you agreed to be mine, so who is the real idiot?"

Returning to the sushi, she grabs her fork and resumes eating. "I'll ask Lucy to babysit."

"I'll pay her," I tell her.

She shakes her head. "No, I will. Max is my kid."

"Yes, but I'm asking you to visit Vegas with me and spend the night. I will pay for babysitting."

She nods, giving in easily. I don't mind paying. I know I have more money than she does, and I'm asking her to be there for me. It's not right that she should have to pay.

"Check with Lucy, and then let me know. I was thinking I could have David pick you up Friday after work, bring you to the venue, and then take you back Saturday afternoon."

"Shouldn't be a problem, but I'll find out. Lucy has offered to keep Max many times, and like me, she could also use the money."

Picking my fork back up, I dive into the sushi, the weight on my shoulders feeling lighter than it has all week.

There's no possible way I'll use or drink with her there. But that's not the only reason I want her there.

"Thank you, Andy."

"For what?"

"For being willing to make it work with childcare for me so you can be there for me. You have no idea how much that means to me." It's been years since I've had someone standing in the crowd just for me. Waiting for me. There to support me.

"You don't have to thank me, Declan. You said I'm yours, and that means showing up for each other." She shrugs, acting as if it's not a big deal. "Besides, I'm the real winner here. I get to watch my favorite band live for the first time," she teases, giving me a wink.

All I want is to remain in the bubble we've created tonight, by Andy's side, safe from the demons in my head and the voices from the outside world, but I know it's not possible because guys like me don't deserve a happy ending.

My hands were made for destruction, and everything I touch crumbles.

I ruined my family and stole my son's life because I was too selfish.

I don't deserve to live happily ever after.

Our downfall is inevitable.

THIRTY

Declan

S ATURDAY WAS SPENT LOCKED INSIDE A NDY'S APARTMENT WITH HER and Max. After we woke up and I ate her pussy for breakfast, she showered and then went over to Lucy's to get Max while I showered.

When she returned, she informed me that Lucy had agreed to babysit and that we were on for our plans next weekend.

Andy is showing up for me. She's going to my show to help and support me. She'll never know how much that means to me.

Facing my biggest fear won't be as hard when I'm able to see her face and remind myself to remain calm and sober. I must remain sober for her. For Max. They deserve it.

They're relying on me to keep my promise of returning to them, and I know Andy will never let that happen if I fuck up.

No pressure or anything.

It's Sunday, and we're in Las Vegas to attend Cole's barbecue. Before we left, she had tried to back out because she was nervous about meeting the ones I consider family, but after much reassurance, she agreed. Now, here we are.

"Do you think they'll like me?" Andy asks, her nerves becoming apparent as we approach our destination. I park in the driveway of Cole's new house, a massive three-story home within a gated community.

"They will because you're you, and you make me happy. It's been a while since these guys have seen me smile, so they've wanted to meet the one responsible for that." I place my hand on her thigh and give it a gentle, reassuring squeeze. I want to lean over and steal a kiss from her pouty mouth and slide my tongue along the inside of her mouth to get a taste of her until I'm able to spread her bare underneath me again and feast on her body, but I keep my mouth to myself.

For now.

Andy told me this morning that she wanted to wait to tell Max that we're together, so I'm doing my best to be respectful of her wishes by limiting our PDA. If it were my decision, we'd tell Max right now, but I understand that my being around is still new. Andy told me that she hadn't dated since Max was born, and she'd never had a male figure in her life.

Taking it slow is the responsible thing to do. We need to figure things out on our own before bringing an innocent child into the mix and risk confusing her.

"This place is like a castle!" Max chimes in from the backseat, and I look back to find her nose pressed against the window, eyes wide as she takes in the large house.

"Sure is! Let's go explore the castle." Looking at Andy, I give her a wink, then climb out of the car and open the back door for Max to climb out.

Andy was willing to drive us and insisted on it, but I didn't let her. Especially when her car is a piece of shit. It gets her to work, but that's about it. The tires were bald before I had a new set installed when I'd taken it for an oil change that was several thousand miles past due, the transmission is slipping, and there's no AC, which is unacceptable in this hot weather.

I ordered a rental and had it delivered to her apartment this morning, just in time for us to take it to Vegas. I booked it for a month and plan to let her use it during the times I'm away. After a show, the last thing I'll want to do is drive over an hour back to Loganville, which is why I have a driver.

Max skips ahead of us, excited to check out the house she considers a castle. Her curly pigtails bounce with each skip, and her yellow dress sways, her smile never leaving her face.

Andy walks beside me, fingertips lightly brushing against mine as we walk, not risking any PDA in case Max were to turn around suddenly and find us. She was unsure what to wear this morning and asked me to help her pick something out. Knowing everyone would likely be swimming, I chose a pair of ripped denim shorts and a black tank top to cover the red bikini top she has underneath.

She'd laughed when she saw the outfit, refusing to wear something so revealing, her insecurity controlling her, but luckily, thanks to a few kisses to her neck and sticking my hand down her panties and fingering her until she came, she agreed.

Yes, I took advantage of her post-orgasm bliss, but I got what I wanted, so who is the real winner here?

Once Max reaches the door, she rings the doorbell and stands on the black welcome mat, excitedly bouncing on her toes.

Before Andy can get too close to her daughter, I press myself against her back and whisper in her ear, "By the way, you look hot as fuck. Can't wait to pull down those shorts, bend you over, and fuck you." I don't wait for a response. Instead, I leave her standing in the driveway with parted lips and rush to Max, then open the large white door, knowing it would be unlocked.

Considering the party is in the backyard, no one would be inside to hear the doorbell anyway. Stepping inside, Max takes my hand and plasters herself to my side, suddenly shy. Andy follows behind us as I guide my girls toward laughter and children screaming.

The newly renovated backyard is so fucking huge that I stop to do a double take. I knew that Cole had purchased this house a while ago and spent a couple years renovating it, but this is my first time seeing the final result of the backyard.

Directly in front of us is a massive swimming pool. Off to the left is a basketball court where I see Damon and two identical blonde women playing. Of course, he picked up twins and brought his latest fucks to our little gathering. That's so typical of him.

To the left is the outdoor patio furniture, along with the outdoor kitchen and dining table. Cole stands at the grill, lighting the flame. Benny is beside him, and both men have a bottle of beer in hand.

Adam is the first to notice me as he makes his appearance from the door we've just come through. He slaps me on the back. "Sup, Dec? Good to see you." The mention of my name draws attention to us.

Andy squirms uncomfortably beside me, clearly feeling out of her element. Max must be feeling it, too, as she presses herself against my leg.

"Hey, man," I say in greeting just as the rest of my family joins us. The blonde twins remain on the basketball court while Damon jogs toward us, eyes on Andy and a telling smirk on his face.

If this mother fucker tries hitting on my girl, I'll lay him the fuck out. I've already warned him once to be on his best behavior.

"Well, hello there!" Benny greets, his arms out wide as he approaches Andy.

"Andy, this is our manager, Benny," I introduce them, suddenly finding myself nervous as fuck. My skin begins to feel like it's crawling. I shift my weight from foot to foot, uncomfortable in this situation.

Regardless of what these fuckers think, I'm going to keep her. Benny has told me many times that I should be single for a while, considering I'm newly sober and my divorce wasn't that long ago. It was easy to agree because I was never interested in dating anyone.

Then I met Andy.

Andy is polite as she introduces herself and Max to everyone.

While the introductions are being made, Cecelia, Cole's girl-friend, her sister Sara, and her six-year-old twins Maddy and Chloe join us.

"Andy! It's so great to meet you! I'm Cecelia, but everyone calls me Cece." She pulls Andy into a tight hug. It's been a while since I've seen Cecelia in person, and sometimes I forget how fucking tall she is. She's nearly as tall as Andy, though my girl still has a few inches over her.

I watch their interaction carefully, smiling as I notice my girl's shoulders visibly relax at Cece's embrace. "This must be your daughter." She squats to Max's level. "You are so pretty," she says, complimenting her and throwing a thumb over her shoulder. "Those are my nieces, and I bet they'd love to go play with you." Max's eyes light up, bouncing between us and the two girls waving at her across the yard.

"Mommy, can I go play?" she asks, crossing her fingers, hoping for a *yes*, as if Andy would ever tell her no.

Andy nods. "Have fun, and be nice." Max doesn't need to be told twice. She races off in the direction of the two girls, their mouths moving for a minute as they quickly engage in conversation that leads to giggles. Moments later, they race into the house hand in hand.

Sara joins Cece's side. "They're going into the game room. Don't worry about them; they'll be fine. I'm Sara, by the way."

Adam nudges my shoulder. "Let's go cook while the ladies chat," he says, and I nod.

Placing a hand on Andy's back, I guide her away from the small crowd, taking her to the corner. "Are you okay?" I ask, brushing soft curls away from her eyes.

She nods. "I am. Not feeling as nervous as I was. I'd like to get to know Cece and Sara."

"Okay, mama. Do the girl thing, I'll be over there with the guys." Taking her face into my hands, I press a kiss against her lips, quickly turning it deep and forcing my tongue into her mouth, needing to taste as much of her as I can.

"Get a room!" Cole yells out. At the same time, Damon whistles and catcalls.

Andy pulls away, cheeks pink as she grins at me, looking so fucking young and carefree right now in this moment. A look I wish I could see more often from her rather than the stressful look constantly in her eyes.

"Come to me if you need me," I say, stealing another quick kiss from her mouth. Breaking apart, I walk toward my best friends while Andy goes to the pool to join Cece and Sara.

Cole tosses me a bottle of water while opening another beer bottle.

From where I stand, I watch my girl. She sits on the edge of the pool beside Cece, takes off her sandals, and sticks her long golden legs into the cool water while Sara cannonballs into the pool.

"So, that's Andy." Adam breaks the silence, his voice amused.

"Yup," I say. "That's my girl."

"Don't fuck it up," Benny warns.

"She's hot as fuck," Damon says, earning a slap on the back of the head from Cole.

"That's his girl, man. Have some fucking respect," Cole chastises. "Go worry about your real-life blow-up dolls over there, man." He jerks his chin toward the adult twins that are jumping around the basketball court in a confusing attempt to play basketball or be sexy. I'm not sure what they're trying to accomplish.

"Don't have to tell me twice. Plug your ears if you hear screaming, and don't come looking for us later," Damon says, wiggling his eyebrows and chugging the rest of his beer. He sets the empty bottle down on the marble countertop, then jogs off toward the two women, who begin squealing at the sight of him approaching them.

"Fucking Damon. Bastard is going to fuck in my new house," Cole grumbles under his breath.

"What the fuck is that?" Adam grabs my hand, bringing it closer to his face to inspect my painted fingernails that I'd forgotten all about. Benny and Cole look over, like the nosey fucks they are.

Cole bursts out laughing. "Purple is your color, man."

Yesterday, after Max came home from Lucy's house after her sleepover, she squealed in delight at the sight of me. It had been over a week since I'd seen her in person, and she was so excited that she cried. I'd spent the entire day at Andy's apartment, hanging out with my girls, and at some point in the afternoon, Max had decided she wanted to play salon using the makeup and nail polish kit I had bought for her from The Cherry Festival.

I sat on the floor, and she stood behind me, brushing my hair, clipping it in butterfly clips, and twisting it in colorful rubber bands. Just when I thought the rough hair-pulling salon experience was over, she decided I needed my nails painted.

Max then painted my fingernails a bright neon purple, painting more of my skin than my nails. Thankfully, the polish scrubbed off my skin while I was in the shower. Seeing how proud she was of the paint job on my fingernails, I didn't have the heart to remove the polish even after Andy offered me some polish remover. My mini-best friend was proud of her work, so I gladly rocked purple nails.

Movement across the yard catches my eye. I watch Andy as she walks toward the sliding glass door, opening it to slip through, leaving it open as she disappears from my sight.

"You deserve to be happy, you know that, right?" Adam says, letting go of my hand. Not wanting to get into a deep conversation or tell him how he's wrong, I shrug.

"I'm starving. I'm going to grab some chips." Without looking at my friends, I walk casually toward Andy, needing to put my hands on her soft body and inhale her intoxicating scent.

Following the smell of cherries, it leads me to the hallway bathroom. Just as the door unlocks and begins to open, I rush in, forcing Andy to take a surprised step backward as she gasps.

"What are you doing here?"

Locking the door behind me, I turn to face her. "I need you."

Understanding flashes in her eyes. "Oh yeah? Are you that desperate for me?" she taunts, fingers already unbuttoning her little shorts, shoving them down her wide hips along with the red bikini bottoms.

"Fuck, baby." I rush toward her, and our lips connect in a frenzy, desperate for each other. Her fingers make quick work of undoing my pants and shoving them and my boxers down my ass far enough for my cock to spring free, hard, hot, and ready between us.

She wraps her hand around my shaft, squeezing me and earning a groan from me as she begins pumping me in her soft hand.

Moaning into her mouth, I tangle my tongue with hers, fingers brushing against the soft curls between her legs before spreading her pussy lips apart and diving in. I push two fingers knuckle deep inside of her, my other hand slipping underneath her shirt to grab her heavy tit, rolling her hard nipple between my fingers, pinching until she's crying.

"Fuck me, Declan. Right now. I need you inside me."

"Turn around, baby." She obeys me, turning to face the vanity mirror and stepping out of her bottoms. Placing her hands on the counter, she leans forward, spreads her thighs, and tilts her ass back toward me.

I give her ass a hard slap, and she yelps. The sight of the red handprint on her ass only urges me on, making my dick even harder. Grabbing one of her legs, I raise it up to set it on the counter to allow me better access.

Lining myself up with her entrance, I hold onto her hips, then with one rough thrust, I force into her, filling her to the hilt.

She gasps, eyes crossing as a loud moan escapes her open mouth.

"Quiet, baby. Your moans are mine. Can't have anyone else hearing them." I remove one of my hands from her hips and bring it to her lips. I shove the two fingers that I used to rub her pussy inside of her mouth, and she sucks without needing to be told.

"Rub your clit for me. This will be quick." While she sucks my fingers, soft tongue tracing the digits, I hold her in place and pound into her, my eyes never leaving her reflection in the mirror.

Skin-on-skin slapping fills the air, along with our panting and heavy breathing. The hand she slipped between her body and the counter rubs her clit vigorously.

Her tight walls suck me deeper, tight and warm around me. Her pussy is begging to soon be full of my cum.

I can feel the moment her climax nears. Her walls tighten, her eyes roll, and her mouth hangs open, forgetting about sucking my fingers as she drools. As her body jerks with the build-up, the movement of her fingers becomes sloppy and uneven.

Pushing her hand away, I replace it with mine, massaging the hard bud beneath my fingertips as she chases the orgasm.

"Keep those eyes open, baby. I want you to watch yourself. Watch yourself come and see how fucking perfect you are," I say into her ear, tone heavy and raspy.

She's so fucking wet that her clit is slippery beneath my fingers, but I keep my rhythm, fucking her in perfect sync with my thrusts.

My balls tighten, a familiar warmth returning to the bottom of my spine as we both chase our high. "Fuck, baby. We're almost there."

"Fill me up, Declan. Come with me." She pants, eyelids heavy, and stares at herself in the mirror, just like I told her to do.

Such a good fucking girl.

Her body twitches, a scream climbing up her throat that I

quickly silence with my hand as I reach my release, moaning heavily into her ear as I explode. My cock twitches, and I paint her walls with my cum. Buried so fucking deep inside of her that she has no choice but to accept every drop. Her greedy pussy throbs, milking me of everything I have.

I carefully pull out of her so I don't make a mess on the floor. She winces at the loss of me, slowly setting her leg down on the floor. Turning to face me, she stares at me as a slow grin spreads across her swollen pink lips.

Her grin glistens with drops of drool from sucking my fingers, so I lean in and lick it before pressing a kiss to her lips.

"You always feel so fucking good." I kiss her again. Grabbing some toilet paper, I pull up my boxers and pants, then kneel in front of her, prepared to clean up the glistening mess between her legs, but she stops me.

"I want to feel you inside of me all day. And we'll have to sit there knowing your cum is dripping out of my pussy," she says, raising her eyebrow as if she expects me to argue, but I don't.

"Yes, mama. Whatever you say." Pressing a kiss to the curls between her legs, I help her into her bottoms and then pull the shorts up to her hips as I stand.

"You are a filthy girl." Instead of responding, she flips her hair over her shoulder, unlocks the door, and struts out of the bathroom—leaving me stunned.

Fuck she's perfect for me.

THIRTY-ONE

Andy

Yesterday, I was nervous about meeting Declan's bandmates. I couldn't stop thinking about what would happen.

Would they like me?

Would they compare me to Declan's ex-wife?

How would they react knowing I'm not the type of woman that Declan typically goes for?

It turned out I was worried over nothing. The guys had been accepting, and Cece and Sara were amazing. During the drive home, Max couldn't stop talking about her new friends, Chloe and Maddy, Sara's six-year-old twin daughters. She'd run off with them right after they met, and the three of them were in a fit of giggles the entire party.

When they became tired of the game room where they'd been dancing around to Taylor Swift, they wanted to go swimming. I'd helped Max change into the swimsuit I'd brought for her, and then she was splashing around in the shallow end of the pool with her new friends while Sara, Cece, and I sat on the side of the pool, watching and talking.

By the night's end, the three of us exchanged phone numbers with a promise to keep in touch, especially since Cece shared that she often goes on tour with Cole.

Declan held true to his word about us leaving on time, but I was having such a great time that I did something I'd only done twice: calling into work. Considering I'm the manager, I had to email my boss to inform him I wouldn't be coming in, and then I had to text Jane, who typically works the morning shift with me, to give her a heads-up that she'll be on her own.

Can I afford to miss a day of work? Fuck no.

But I was having such a great time, and Declan leaves Tuesday, so I spent the day with him rather than at work. And thank fuck I did.

Today is Monday, and Declan woke me up with his head between my legs. He informed me that I was not allowed to get up until I came on his face as many times as possible.

Turns out five orgasms in a row is my limit.

With Max asleep down the hall, I had to bite a pillow to silence my cries.

By the time he was done eating my pussy like a starved man, I was sensitive and completely sated. To my horror, when he popped his head up, his mouth was drenched in my juices that were dripping down his chin.

While I showered to clean myself up, he tossed my sheets into the washer and made breakfast for us. Max was awake by the time I dressed, and we ate together.

Since then, I've spent the morning watching Declan interact with my daughter. When she wanted to listen to Taylor Swift and put on a concert, Declan was right beside her. He played her small pink keyboard and was backup vocals while she sang her heart out to "Shake It Off."

After her concert, she wanted to go swimming again. I wanted to show Declan another piece of this little town, so I invited him to the reservoir with us where everyone in this town visits during the scorching summer days. To us locals, it's known as *the resi*, and many people will set up tents and camp there near the water and start bonfires. I've been coming since I was a kid. My grandparents loved to dip their feet in the water and roast hot dogs when the sun went down.

"We'll have to stop by the hotel so I can grab my shorts," Declan says, coming to stand beside me in the kitchen, where I currently stand in front of the counter, spreading peanut butter and strawberry jelly over some bread, getting us a picnic ready for another day of swimming.

"You have shorts?" I ask in surprise, considering he wore jeans yesterday while everyone else wore shorts. I've never seen him in anything other than black jeans.

He rolls his eyes, swiping his finger through the thick peanut butter I'd just spread over one side of the bread. "Yes." He sticks the finger in his mouth, sucking it clean. "I do have a pair of swim trunks, actually." He looks over his shoulder, seeing Max is still away in her bedroom, changing into her swimsuit.

While she's gone, he grabs my hips, turns me to face him, then leans in and places a kiss so deep on my lips that it steals my breath and has my heart racing. "I'm going to miss you," he mumbles against my lips, arms wrapped securely around my waist.

Smiling up at him, I wrap my arms around his neck, needing him close to me and feeling his warmth. Tomorrow is the dreaded day. He's leaving for Vegas to prepare for his first show on Friday, and he'll be there all week to make it easier since the band will need to rehearse for several hours a day.

I won't see him until Friday, when Declan's driver, David, picks me up after work and takes me to the venue.

I'd be lying if I said I wasn't worried as fuck. Worried because he's voiced his concerns about performing to me many times. One thing I know for sure is that I will do everything possible to prevent him from doing something he'll regret.

I can be there for him. I can be his person. The one to keep him sober.

I can do it.

I was never enough to keep my mother sober, but I'm tempted to be enough of a reason for Declan.

"I'll miss you, too," I admit, hugging him tightly to me, nuzzling my nose into his neck, and inhaling his intoxicating scent deep into my lungs.

"I'm ready!" Max yells, her stomps becoming louder as she approaches, skipping down the hallway. My arms instantly fall from Declan's neck, and I attempt to pull away, but he holds me tighter, refusing to let go.

"Declan," I warn, placing my palms on his chest.

"I know, mama." He sighs, forehead resting against mine. "I just need to hold you another second." He places his lips against mine, stealing another lingering kiss before finally pulling away, just as Max joins us in the kitchen dressed in a purple one-piece swimsuit with green polka dot swim shorts. A towel is tossed over her shoulder, dragging on the ground, and pink sunglasses are on her face. Looking her over, I notice the blue sparkle flip-flops she's wearing on the wrong feet.

A slow smile spreads across my lips. "Wow, look at you. I love your style, kid." She pops her hip out and then places her hands on each hip.

"Let's go, guys!" She poses, clearly loving the mismatched outfit she chose for herself. I stopped choosing her clothes last year when she started throwing fits over the outfits I'd pick. Some days, she may wear a tutu, a tank top, and shorts, and other days, she may wear a dress with jeans underneath.

Little Miss Independent wears whatever she wants, and I love that for her.

"Your shoes are on the wrong feet." I point out, then grab the towel from her shoulder while she takes her flip-flops off and switches them. "I'll grab our beach towels, then we'll go." Taking the towel she uses for showers away from her, I exit the kitchen and return the towel to the bathroom. Instead, I open the hall closet and grab three large beach towels and my large beige tote bag I use every time we go to the resi.

Quickly, I step into my bedroom and change into the same red bikini I wore beneath my shorts and tank top yesterday at Cole's barbeque. I never got in the water or removed my clothes. The only part of me to get wet was my legs.

My pussy, too, if I'm being honest.

I slip on another pair of shorts and a white tank top, wanting to be comfortable but knowing that I won't be swimming or revealing my swimsuit to Declan. I may be comfortable enough to be naked around him, but I'm not about to wear a bikini in public and risk having other people see me. I'd be the talk of the town with how much of my skin I'd be revealing.

Once I'm dressed and ready to go, I return to the kitchen to find that Declan has packed the sandwiches in Ziplock bags, and all the food I'd gathered is packed into the little white cooler.

He meets my gaze, giving me a wink. "Are you girls ready?" he asks, and Max yells her response.

"Swimming lake pool, here we come!" She jumps, arms in the air.

Declan grabs the cooler from the counter and the tote from my hand and follows us out of my apartment.

Once we reach the parking lot, he unlocks the doors to his rental car and then pops the trunk, placing the cooler and tote inside. As if we've been in this car a hundred times, Max opens the back door and climbs into her car seat, already comfortable.

When the fancy white Range Rover was delivered to Declan yesterday, my jaw dropped. It's my literal dream car, but it is something I know I'll never have. Getting to ride in it was a fucking dream, and I won't lie and say that I'm not excited about getting to ride in it again today.

After ensuring Max is strapped in, I climb into the passenger seat, watching as Declan easily slips behind the wheel and presses the button to start the car.

Unlike my car, which grinds and clunks when starting, it comes to life smoothly and silently.

I watch Declan as he drives, leaning back in his seat with one hand on the wheel, confident in himself.

"I miss driving," he admits. "I've had a driver for so long. Sometimes I'd walk, but most of the time I was being driven."

"I hate driving."

He looks over at me. "It's a good thing you have me then. You can be my passenger princess." He smirks, his eyes returning to the road.

"Mommy isn't a princess!" Max chimes in, suddenly interested after hearing the mention of her favorite word, "I'm the princess, and she's the queen." She states as if we should've known.

"You're right, Max." Looking back at her from the rearview mirror, Declan says, "Your mom is a queen, and you are a little princess." I look over my shoulder at my daughter, watching as she nods in agreement with a broad smile at the mention of being a princess.

We arrive at the hotel, and he parks in an empty space in front of the door to his room. "Come in while I pack. I have to prepare my stuff for Vegas this week, too." He doesn't wait for my response before he turns the car off and gets out, already helping Max from her seat.

I follow him inside his room, instantly turning on the TV and finding a cartoon for Max to keep her busy. She curls up on the couch, eyes glued to the screen, and I follow Declan further into the room as he grabs his duffle bag and sets it on the bed.

"You can stay with me tonight," I offer, wanting to spend every second of his remaining time with him.

He grabs his toiletries from the bathroom, looking at me with a smirk. "I planned on staying anyways, but thanks for the approval." He grabs my waist with one arm, pulling me close to his chest as his lips find mine.

I want more than stolen kisses in the bathroom, but I'm afraid to tell my daughter I'm dating the man she decided is her best friend because part of me is still guarded and worried about the what-ifs.

Realistically, how can we work out long-term?

I'm not going to give myself false hope by believing that we'll be end-game because in the back of my mind, I know that all I am for him is a summer fling. He'll return to his fast-paced, famous rockstar life, and I'll be here.

I'll still be the single mom working at a hotel, struggling to make ends meet while he's touring the world and doing what he does best.

I'm a temporary phase for him while he's slowly becoming everything to me.

God, I wish I were able to protect my heart. One day, when he inevitably leaves, it's going to be so fucking brutal.

"Friday will be here in no time, mama. We'll be together then, and I'll spend the entire night worshiping this body." His hand roams down my backside, and he grabs a handful of my ass.

"Friday." I give him an easy smile and a quick kiss before pulling away, leaving him alone to pack. I join Max on the couch, but my eyes follow Declan around the room.

He meets my gaze, secrets and fear swimming in the dark pools of his eyes, forced away by the smile he plasters on his face.

He glides around the room effortlessly, packing up his belongings and returning the room to its vacant state. If I didn't know better, I would say that he wasn't planning to return.

He leads us out of the room with packed bags and back toward the car. I glance at the room, knots forming in my stomach at the empty sight.

He's taking everything.

Apart from the broken mirror, it's as if he was never here.

Ten minutes later, after I gave Declan directions, we made it to the reservoir.

Luckily, we found a vacant spot, parked on the dirt road, and hiked down the sandy path toward the water.

After I sprayed Max with sunscreen, put on her life jacket, and made sure it was secure, she went out into the water, splashing around near the shallow shore while I set up our beach towels.

Declan pulled his shirt off, revealing his inked chest and leaving him in a pair of black swim shorts. Then, he joined Max in the water while I sat on the towel, spraying myself with sunscreen and watching them together.

While they laugh and splash around, I discreetly pull my phone from my bag and take several photos and videos of them, wanting to remember this day for the rest of my life.

I will forever remember this as the day I started falling in love—against my will, of course, but falling nonetheless.

After several minutes of sitting there watching, Declan wades out of the water. He has a look of determination in his eyes as he walks straight toward me, a grin on his perfect lips revealing his single dimple.

"Get her!" Max cheers in the background, causing me to go on high alert.

Sand sticks to his wet feet as he stomps toward me.

"What are you doing?" I demand, putting my hands up in defense.

Ignoring me, Declan leans down in front of me, scoops my body in his arms bridal style, and takes off running toward Max in the water.

"Put me down!" I squeal, arms hooking tight around his neck, fearful that he'll drop me because of my heaviness. But I know I'm worried over nothing. I may be heavy, but his hold on me is solid and secure. I know that he'll never drop me.

He's got me. Momentarily, I enjoy being in his strong arms, committing the feeling to memory.

We reach the water, but he doesn't stop running. He continues splashing through the water, Max racing after us until we're deep enough for him to toss me into the air. My body goes flying through the air before cutting through the water's surface with a splash, the coolness enveloping me as I sink to the sandy bottom, finding my footing and pushing myself up.

I wipe away the water from my eyes, finding my daughter held in Declan's protective arms, matching broad smiles on their faces.

"You both are going to get it now!" I cup my hand and slice it through the water, sending a wave splashing at them both. This earns loud giggles from my little girl and promises of payback from Declan.

The three of us never stop laughing as we play in the water, splashing back and forth.

By the time the sun goes down, we're sitting on our towels around the fire Declan surprisedly built. Max fell asleep on her towel after eating her s'mores, melted marshmallows, and chocolate still on her face as she snores softly.

Eyes on mine across the blazing fire, Declan stands, holding his hand out to mine just as the song playing on his phone changes to "Touched By An Angel" by Charlie Wilson.

Though it's not a slow song, he still pulls me into his arms and holds me tight against his body as we slowly begin to sway, the low volume of the music filling the silence between us.

With our bodies pressed together, he presses his lips against my ear, softly singing the song's words to me, his voice causing a chill to race down my spine.

"I've been touched by an angel, but you've been touched by the devil," he whispers as the song fades, his lips finding mine.

In the pit of my stomach, I know that we'll never have another day like today. From this day forward, things will never be the same.

THIRTY-TWO

Declan

Tuesday morning is here. The day I've been dreading. I've been fucking sick about having to leave ever since Benny announced that Riot would be performing a few shows in Vegas.

I'm torn between desperately wanting to get back on stage in front of a screaming crowd, seeing the faces of our fans, and pouring my heart out for them. I like the rush that performing gives. I want to create magic with my brothers by my side because it's been too damn long. But I need to figure out how to do it sober.

I've never been sober while performing.

I'm afraid of the what-ifs.

What if I become so hopped on the after-show adrenaline that I need something more substantial?

What if my nerves set in, and I need a drink to calm myself down?

What are my fans going to think of me?

It's been over a year since anything new has come from Riot or since anything positive has been reported about us. The media surrounding Riot has been one negative story after the other.

I wish I could be stronger and believe that I'd be able to get through it. Wish I wasn't so fucking weak.

Lying in bed, I stare at the ceiling, one arm around Andy and the other propped beneath my head. The last time I checked the clock it was five in the morning, but I don't know how much time has passed. It could've been twenty minutes or two hours.

Thanks to Andy's blackout curtains over her window, there's no telling if the sun is up yet or not.

I'm lost in my head, replaying moments from my life when the ethereal woman beside me stirs, groaning as she rolls onto her back and stretches her long limbs, curly hair wild from falling asleep with it wet before she had a chance to put any product in it.

"Hey." She sighs. I look over at her, watching her roll back onto her side. "Are you okay?" she asks, noticing the somber look on my face.

"My mind is pretty fucked up this morning," I admit, wanting to be honest with her rather than lie about my feelings. For too many years during my marriage, I lied about my feelings so my ex-wife wouldn't have anything else to worry about when it came to me. Looking back now, I can admit that I was a horrible husband. I lied to her too many times.

In fact, every fucking day I lied to her.

Lied about being okay.

Lied about being sober.

I don't want to lie anymore. It's too exhausting, and I am so fucking exhausted.

"Talk to me," Andy whispers, placing a hand on my chest. I put my hand on top of hers, squeezing it. Hoping the touch will provide me with some sense of comfort. Taking one last look at her, I turn my head, my gaze returning to the ceiling.

"After my son died, I went down a dark path." I inhale, allowing myself to gather my thoughts and find the courage to speak the things I've never said out loud. What I'm about to tell her, I've never told anyone. "I've always been high or drunk.

Whether it was weed, pills, or coke, didn't matter. I was always on something, but I stayed away from the needle. My mother was a heroin addict, so I told myself as long as I don't become one, then I'm better than her." Andy remains silent, allowing me the time to compose myself as I begin telling her a story I know will be hard for her to hear. Especially when I know she has her own jaded feelings toward addicts, and for valid reasons, because of her mother, though she hasn't yet completely opened up and shared her story with me.

Andy turns her hand in mine to intertwine our fingers together and squeezes my hand, giving me strength to continue. "I was fucked up with grief and guilt after Luca's death. All I wanted was to be with my baby boy again. I was so fucking sick every day that I gave in to the one thing I never wanted to do." I swallow, my tongue feeling heavy in my mouth. "I left my ex-wife alone through her grief. I wasn't there for her because I was too busy hiding in the bathroom shooting up." Tears sting my eyes. Still, I force myself to continue. "I remember how it felt when I tied my belt around my bicep. I could barely see straight through the tears, but the moment the needle entered my vein, I felt free. So fucking full of relief. It didn't matter that my wife was in the next room planning our son's funeral." The first tear falls down my face, but I don't make a move to wipe it away.

"I was high on the day of the funeral. Can you believe that? I showed up to my son's funeral high as a fucking kite." I breathe out a humorless laugh. "The guilt was eating me alive, then one day, months later, while Camille was out of the house, I tried to end it all. Right there in our living room, I shot so much heroin that I overdosed. She'd buried our son that year, then came home to find her piece of shit husband dying. Turns out, she started keeping Narcan in her purse after she found out I'd been using again." Andy sniffles beside me, her grip on my hand tight.

"I'm alive because of her. She saved my fucking life that day. I went to rehab. Started seeing a therapist and going to NA meetings. I was doing good. The fog that was constantly hanging over my head was finally clear. She needed me, and it was my turn to be there for her. It took an entire year after Luca's death for me to get to that point. I was sober for nearly a year, needing to be there for Camille. Even after we decided to divorce and I moved back to New York, I was sober. She was going through some shit and went to a mental health treatment center, and I was there for her. Every fucking day. I'm ashamed to say that's the first time in our four-year marriage that I was there for her." Tears flow from my eyes, but not once do I attempt to wipe them away. Wishing they were enough to drown me, I allow myself to express the feelings of regret that I've kept to myself for far too long.

"A few months after our divorce, Riot went on tour. We had to fulfill the dates we'd postponed, so it was only a few shows. Everything was great until the last night on the road. I thought I was strong enough to have one drink. One shot, that was it. The next thing I knew, I was on a fucking two-week bender. Since then, I've been trying to get myself cleaned up." Finally, I roll over onto my side to face Andy, finding her tear-stained face staring back at me with sorrow-filled eyes.

Reaching out, I wipe the tears from her face with my thumb. "I'm trying so fucking hard. You have no idea how much I do not want to go back to being that person. I hate that version of myself. The one that is so wrecked with guilt that all I want to do is escape."

Finally, she opens her mouth and asks, "Why do you feel guilty?" The loaded question hangs between us.

Now is my chance to tell her my biggest regret. The worst thing I've ever done in my life. It'll likely mean the end of our short-lived relationship, but I need to tell someone. I've been slowly killing myself by keeping it inside.

"Because I'm the reason my son is dead," I admit, my chest constricting with the confession lingering between us. "I'd just snorted a line of coke before driving, and it must've been laced with some shit because it's never affected me the way it did that night. I was driving, it was raining, and the next thing I knew, my eyes were heavy, my vision was blurry, and then we were colliding with a semi-truck. It all happened so fast, and I don't remember everything. Just bits and pieces. I heard Camille scream for our son, and it all went dark. When I woke up in the hospital, I hated that I was alive." I've always been a fuck-up, but that was the night that changed me. The night that cemented my fate.

Andy's eyes widen in horror. Her bottom lip trembles as she abruptly sits up, tears rolling down her flushed cheeks. The look she gives me is enough to slice through my heart. It's the look that I've been dreading seeing on her face.

I knew her opinion of me would change after confessing my sins, and maybe that's what I wanted. Perhaps I don't want her to look at me with hearts in her eyes like she did last night when we were dancing on the sandy shore. She looked at me like she was falling in love, and I don't deserve that.

Perhaps in my fucked-up mind, I'm only telling her these things because I need her to hate me. I need her to give up on me rather than try to save me; there's no hope. I'll only break her heart, and I'm confident we both know it. I'd rather do it now than later.

"Declan." She says my name in a plea as if she's begging for me to tell her it was all a joke and it wasn't my actions that resulted in my son dying. Surprising the fuck out of me, she reaches for me, wraps her arms around me, and buries her face in my neck as tears coat my skin. She sobs against me, pulling back until we're face to face, and in her sad brown eyes, I see everything she's unable to say.

How could you drive while under the influence?

You're a piece of shit.

You don't deserve anything good.

Maybe those are her words, or maybe I'm imagining what I want her to say.

She was right when she said I was dangerous.

Like the selfish prick I am, I wrap my arms around her, holding her warm body tightly against mine one last time.

We both know this is it.

How would it be possible for her to carry on knowing what I've done and what I'm capable of?

We're ending before we've ever had a chance to begin.

We lie together, limbs tangled, for who knows how long.

"I don't know what to say," she confesses, and I appreciate her honesty. I'd never want her to say anything she doesn't mean.

"Don't say anything. I wanted you to know. Wanted you to see the darkest parts of me." So you can leave me without blaming yourself.

"My mom used to drive high while I was in the car," she confesses, wiping the remainder of her tears away. "When she'd start to nod off and swerve, she'd act like it was a joke and we were playing a game. It wasn't until she almost hit a car that I realized it wasn't a game." She takes a deep breath, finding her own courage before continuing. "She's an addict who was unable to take care of me, so I moved in with my grandparents, and they raised me for several years until they died. She lived there too, but she was like an absent older sister rather than my mother. The only time she was around was when she was fighting with my grandparents, begging for money. After they died, we moved into our car. We lived in it for about a week until I found an apartment and paid for it by selling my stuff. We never lived in one place very long because we were always getting evicted thanks to the company she kept." She pauses, eyes becoming unfocused as she loses herself to the past, and I get the feeling this is the first time she's been able to talk about it.

"By our third move, I stopped unpacking. I lived out of suitcases and boxes because I knew we wouldn't stay long enough to unpack. Most days, she ignored me. The only times she seemed to notice me was when she needed money. When I'd tell her no, we'd fight, and she'd tell me what a selfish, ungrateful bitch I was." She scoffs. "I paid for everything. The money she had went toward drugs, so I dropped out of school to take a full-time nanny job so I could pay the bills. I was fourteen and not old enough to have a regular job, but I did what I had to do." She brushes the loose strands of frizzy curls out of her face, tucking them behind her ears.

"I was sixteen when I got pregnant, and I knew I wasn't going to raise my daughter in that environment. Luckily, I was able to become emancipated and rented a basement apartment from a lady who also ran a daycare out of her home. She watched Max for me while I worked. We've lived there until she recently passed away, and well." She waves a hand around her bedroom. "Obviously, we moved."

"My point is, Declan, I know what it's like to watch someone you love battle addiction. We've both had a front-row seat to our mothers' struggles. The difference is you followed in your mother's footsteps. You became the person you never wanted to be." My jaw clenches, hands balling into fists at the brutal reality of her words.

I can't argue. She's right. I became the exact person I never wanted to become.

Andy continues as if her brutally honest words hadn't fazed me. "You don't have to be this person you hate. You are the only one in this world who can change. If you want to be sober, then do it. Figure out what's going to help you. Stop using guilt as an excuse."

"Do you fucking think I want to be this way?"

"You're making excuses. Figure your shit out if you want to be someone different." I sit up, my back against the headboard. "You said you've been an addict since you were thirteen, yet you're blaming it on the death of your son."

"I'm not blaming shit on him!" Who the fuck does she think she is? Angrily, I shove the blankets off me and climb to my feet. I don't fucking need this shit. I was honest with her, and now she's throwing it in my face, acting like I'm playing the victim.

"Dec, don't be mad. I'm only trying to help you."

"How the fuck do you think you're helping me?"

"Because you're not honest with yourself about when you started using drugs and why."

"Does anyone know why the fuck they do it?" I know why, but I'll never tell.

She nods. "A lot of people do. Many people use drugs and alcohol as a coping mechanism. You started at thirteen. That's awfully young." My hands ball into fists at my sides as she stares at me, keeping her distance from me.

Without taking her eyes off me, she slowly climbs off the bed and stands before me. "What happened, Declan? What were you trying to escape?"

"What are you? My fucking therapist?" I snarl, shaking my head as I stare at her from head to toe.

Fuck her. There's no goddamn way I'm going to stand here and allow her to continue going down this path that my therapists in the past have all gone down.

My answer has always been the same. For years, I've told the lie that I became hooked on drugs at thirteen because I was experimenting and decided I liked the high. For years, all I ever did was smoke weed and drink. To many, weed isn't considered a drug, but for me, it is.

I enjoyed the way it made me happy and temporarily forgot all that was happening around me. Made me forget about the foster home I was living in.

Made me forget the sound of the old creaking mattress I slept on and how the squeaks became louder with added weight.

Whenever I'd close my eyes, I'd see those hazel eyes staring back at me. For years, weed and vodka were my escape. The only thing that could calm me when the nightmares came.

The only thing I had that was able to drown him out.

Eventually, I found myself chasing a higher high, and that led me down the path of cocaine and pills.

Then came Luca's death, and to cope, I turned to heroin.

I'm so goddamn weak. So fucking pathetic.

Andy stands before me, her warm palms against my chest. "I want to help you, Declan. I care about you, and I don't want to see you do something you'll regret."

"You care about me?" I scoff. "You barely fucking know me." *Lie.* We've known each other for a few weeks, yet she knows me better than anyone. I've opened up to her and told her things I've never told anyone else. "Stop trying to fix me just to make yourself feel better." I pull away from her, grab my jeans from the floor, and quickly pull them on.

"Don't leave, please."

"Instead of trying to save me, call your mom. Maybe this tough love bullshit will be enough to save her." Needing to hurt her even further, I place the final nail in our coffin. "Your love will never be enough to save anyone." She rears back as if I slapped her, but I can't bring myself to look at her any longer.

Quickly grabbing my shit, I pull my shirt on and then stomp down the hallway with my suitcase and duffle bag.

I'm standing by the door, putting on my shoes and socks, when a small figure appears in the hallway, rubbing sleep from her eyes.

"Best friend?" Max calls out, her voice soft and her eyes filled with worry. "Why are you yelling at my mommy?" she asks, her bottom lip trembling.

My heart shatters.

Staring into her innocent brown eyes, I'm reminded of all the ways I'm a piece of shit.

"Goodbye, Max," I whisper, unlocking the door and rushing out of it before she can realize what's happening.

My ears perk up at the movement behind me as I hear Andy's voice fill the cracks in my heart as she pulls her daughter away from the door.

I don't look back as I carry my bags down the three flights of stairs, the pain in my chest increasing with each step.

I don't take a breath until I'm behind the wheel of the rental I planned to leave for Andy and pulling out of her apartment complex parking lot.

All she had to do was listen. I wasn't asking for her advice or for her to try and save me.

All I wanted was to confess. To tell her what a piece of shit I am. What a waste of space I am. How it's useless for her to love me because I'll never be worthy of it.

Instead of listening and keeping her mouth shut, she tried to fix me by figuring out what happened when I was thirteen that led me to need an escape from reality.

Fuck that and fuck her.

Some secrets are better left buried.

THIRTY-THREE
Declan

Tuesday 3:49 pm

ME

I'm so fucking sorry.

Baby, I'm so sorry.

You didn't deserve that shit, mama. I'm so fucking sorry.

Tell Max I'm sorry for scaring her.

Missed call to Andy

Tuesday 4:15 pm

ME

Please talk to me.

I didn't mean any of that shit.

Max's face is haunting me. I never should've left you two like that.

You didn't deserve that.

Missed call to Andy

Tuesday 11:23 pm

ME

Please call me. Need to hear your voice and apologize.

Baby, please.

Fine. I'll give you some time. Just know I'm sorry, and that shit will never happen again.

Missed call to Andy

Wednesday 10:30 am

ME

I miss you so fucking much.

Miss waking up next to you.

Miss having you in my arms.

Missed call to Andy

Wednesday 9:30 pm

ME

Please, mama. Talk to me.

> Please. I fucking need you. I'm sorry.

> I wish I could be the man that deserves to be in your and Max's life.

Thursday 8:30 am

ANDY

> Fuck you.

ME

> I'm so fucking sorry. Please answer the phone.

Missed call to Andy

ME

> Please.

ANDY

> Fuck you.

Thursday 9:30 pm

Incoming FaceTime from Andy

WIPING MY SWEATY PALMS ON MY JEANS, I LOOK AT MYSELF IN THE mirror of my backstage dressing room at The House of Carnage, where Riot will be performing tomorrow night.

We've been here all-day rehearsing, and I've been sitting in my dressing room taking a much-needed break when my phone began ringing.

Taking a deep breath, I click the green accept button, watching as my dark-eyed daydream fills my screen. It's been two days since I've seen her face, but somehow, it feels much longer than that.

All I wanted to do on Tuesday morning was hurt Andy so bad that she'd be done with me. Wanted her to block my number and remove me from her existence.

If she stays with me, I'll slowly suck the life out of her just like I did to Camille. Day by day I drained the life from my beautiful wife until eventually, she became so resigned that she no longer looked at me with anger or resentment. Her gaze was filled with indifference. The only time she was happy was when she was in the arms of another man. And that's because of me. I drove her to that point.

I wanted to save Andy the hurt of having to suffer the same fate as Camille. Save her from spending years of her life trying to save me, and pretending to be happy, all while I'm draining the life from her eyes little by little.

My plan backfired. Instead of her letting me go, I'm the one unable to let her go, which is not something I considered. I didn't realize how deeply she's worked herself under my skin, or how much of my heart she owns. Tuesday should've been the end of us, but I couldn't let that happen. Not when my heart is coming alive for her. Not when she's infiltrated my every thought.

Like a true piece of shit, I can't let her go. Even if that means destroying her in the end. She's mine until her very last breath. Until I ruin us both.

I've been beating myself up for two days over how I left things. All she was trying to do was help me, and instead of accepting or being willing to talk things out with her, I exploded. She didn't fucking deserve that shit.

"Hey." Her sultry voice fills the silence, her face stoic as she stares at me.

"Baby, words cannot express how truly sorry I am for everything I said. You didn't deserve any of that shit, and I'm sorry. And I'm so fucking sorry if I scared Max."

"Yup," she says with a nod. "I didn't deserve any of that shit. All I was trying to do was help. You tell me you want to be someone else, someone better, and yet you're not doing anything to accomplish that. I want to help you, Declan."

"Why? I'm not worth it."

Her eyes soften. "You are worth it, baby. I'm sorry that you don't think you are, but I promise you are. You are worth it, and you deserve it."

I shake my head, wishing I could believe in myself like she believes in me.

"I'm not giving up on you, Dec. I'm here, and you won't get rid of me that easily. But I'm also not going to allow you to treat me like shit either because you're triggered or whatever the fuck happened Tuesday."

"I know, mama. I'll do better for you. For both of you." Max's frightened face flashes in my mind, my heard aching at the memory of her standing there calling for me.

"Let's talk later, I'm going to bed."

"Will I see you tomorrow?"

She pauses, and there is a long silence between us before she finally shrugs and answers, "We'll see. I'm not ready to forgive you."

"Please, Andy. I really need you there. What can I do?"

"Nothing. I need to sleep." She sighs, turning to her side. "Goodnight, Declan." She ends the call, not waiting for my response.

"Fuck!" I roar, throwing my phone onto the vanity, my hands tangling in my hair and tugging at the roots.

I hoped hearing her voice would calm my storm, but I'm still wound up. For two days, I've been lying to myself, telling myself that even though she's angry right now, she cares about me and will show up for me tomorrow night.

After speaking with her, I'm not so sure of that anymore.

My phone rings, and instantly I jump up from my seat and grab it, answering the call without checking to see who it is, but praying like fuck it's her. The woman who is digging herself so deep into my veins that I'll never be able to cut her out.

"Andy?" I say wishfully, needing confirmation that she'll be coming.

"Who is Andy?" a feminine voice comes across the line, a voice I'm all too familiar with. Groaning, I scrub a hand over my face, attempting to find some sense of happiness.

"Hey, Spence," I greet, returning to my seat and throwing my head back as I speak to Spencer, my ex-sister-in-law.

"Wow, you are sure excited to talk to me," she says, her voice playful and teasing. Any other time, I would be happy to hear from her. We've always had a great relationship. I know things about her that she's never shared with Camille.

Usually, I tell her about things happening with me and my life, but I've yet to tell her about Andy. This is likely because I'm unsure how she'd react to hearing that I'm dating.

Lie.

I know exactly how she'd react. She'd be thrilled for me.

"Sorry, I'm just tired. We've been here rehearsing all day, and I'm fucking exhausted."

"Yeah, I heard about Riot having a comeback show. By the way, thanks for telling me," she says, voice full of sarcasm, and I imagine she's rolling her eyes.

"Fuck. I meant to. It happened so fast, and I spaced out on letting you know."

"Whatever. I'll forgive you because at least I was able to find out ahead of time." Her tone turns chipper, and I know she's about to drop some news: "It just so happens that I'll be in Vegas tomorrow. My flight lands in the morning." The thought of seeing her brings a smile to my face. It's been a couple of months since I've seen her.

After Camille and I divorced, Spencer made me promise that I wasn't divorcing their family and that we'd remain friends.

Spencer is practically my sister, so of course, I agreed, and she's been to New York many times to visit me.

I haven't been to Seattle in years, since the day I left mine and Camille's house and returned to New York.

Spencer often visits New York for work, and she stops to see me each time. We also text often. She's one of my best friends.

I need to tell her about Andy, but I'm not ready yet—not over the phone. If Andy comes tomorrow, I'll introduce them then.

"Fuck yeah, Spence. I'm stoked to see you."

"Better be," she teases. "I want to stay at the same hotel as you, so send me your info so I can book a room."

I roll my eyes. We both know I'll never let her pay for her own room. "Send me your flight info. I'll have my driver pick you up. I'll book your room, too."

"Thanks, Declan. You're the best."

"Really fucking excited to see you, Spencer. I mean it."

"Are you okay?" she asks, noticing that my tone isn't as upbeat as usual. Spencer always has a way of knowing when I'm down.

I sigh, not wanting to get into it right now, "Will be. We'll talk tomorrow."

"Alright, see you tomorrow."

"Tomorrow."

I end the call, feeling a little better than before.

Thank fuck I'll have another person showing up for me, making me feel a little less alone.

All I need now is the girl bringing my cold, dead heart back to life.

God. I hope she shows.

THIRTY-FOUR

Andy

Friday 8:30 am

DECLAN

I hope to see you tonight.

David will be at your apartment by 4 p.m. if you decide to come. I really hope you do.

Since Declan left Tuesday morning, I've been replaying our last conversation, trying to figure out where it all went wrong.

Had I pushed too hard when all I'd wanted to do was help?

My mother often accused me of trying to fix her, which Declan also said. Were they right?

Were they broken pieces that I've been trying to repair?

What choice do I have when I want to see the people I love in good health? If they continue going down the path they're on, I know how it'll end, and I refuse to watch someone I love die by their own hand.

For years, I've tried to make my love be enough for my mother. Foolishly, I hoped that if I loved her enough, that'd be enough for her to open her eyes and want to free herself of the constant drug-induced haze.

I've tried loving and supporting her. Then I tried tough love. None of my attempts so far have been successful, but like a fool, I'm hopeful for her.

Maybe that makes me an idiot. Or perhaps I'm just a desperate girl who desperately wants a mom who cares. A mom who loves me more than getting high. A mom who wants to spend time with me and cares about me.

I want the type of mother I saw my classmates have growing up.

Maybe that makes me a fool, longing for something I'll likely never have. My grandma had been like a mom to me, but she was too old and tired to do a lot of things, and she died when I needed a mother the most in my life.

Deep down, I'm just a girl who fantasizes over something she'll never have and lying to myself by saying it's possible.

One day, my mom will put down the pipe and choose me.

One day, Declan will have the strength to fight his demons.

They both have things in common. Neither of them feels worthy of anything.

My mom has told me many times how worthless she feels.

Declan has said the same thing to me nearly every day.

But how can you make someone feel like they deserve better, that they're worth living a good life, when that person doesn't believe it themselves?

When he left Tuesday, I swore I would block his number and move on with my life. I won't allow myself to be disrespected the way he did. The only time I'll allow myself to be disrespected is when I'm on my knees and going to be rewarded with an orgasm. He can disrespect me all he wants then as long as it's followed up with *good girl* and some dick.

I tried to be strong for a couple of hours until the first text came in. Then I caved. I'm still angry with him, but I'm not ready to toss in the towel like I'd been willing to do. He can grovel a bit, but I know that by the end of the night, his head is going to be between my legs, and I'll be screaming his name as I forgive him.

How fucking twisted is that.

It might make me weak or a pushover, but apparently, when trying to have a healthy relationship, you should work things out rather than run at the first sign of trouble. At least that's what Jenluv123 said on the Reddit thread I read about handling the first fight in a relationship.

Yes, I went to Reddit for advice. It's not like I have anyone to talk to for relationship advice.

All day at work, I'd been thinking about Declan's text this morning and whether I would attend his concert tonight. Even as I got off work early and went home to shower and get ready, I debated it.

Even now, while I'm in my bedroom packing my duffle bag with things I'll need for an overnight trip to Vegas, I'm still wondering if I'm making the right decision.

"Don't be a pussy. Just go and face him," I mutter, searching my closet for the perfect outfit for tonight. I woke up an hour earlier this morning to wash my hair, and it's been air-drying all day. Now that it's completely dry, all I'll have to do is fluff my curls, and they'll be perfect for tonight.

Lucy picked Max up from daycare and took the girls out for dinner, so once I'm finished packing, I'll need to pack a bag for Max and bring it to Lucy once they get home.

This will be my first time leaving Max overnight while I'm in a different city. I trust Lucy, or else I wouldn't be willing to leave my daughter with her, but that doesn't change the fact that I'm going to miss her like crazy and can't wait to get home to her tomorrow. Tomorrow, I'm taking my girl out and spending the day doing whatever she wants to do. Fuck the cost.

She was heartbroken when Declan left Tuesday. His raised voice had woken her up, and after he left, she was crying, wanting to know why he'd been yelling at me. I don't know why I covered for him and lied to my daughter, but I did by telling her that he wasn't yelling at me and that we weren't fighting. I told her that we'd just been talking in loud voices.

Bless her innocent little heart. She believed me, and for the rest of the day, she yelled everything she said.

Lying to my child isn't something I'm going to make a habit out of, and I'm not sure why I protected Declan. If I had to guess, it was because I was confused and unsure what to do. I was in shock and didn't want to ruin the image Max had of him, especially when I wasn't sure what I would do.

Leave him or work through it.

Considering I'm now dressed, and my packed bag is on the bed, I guess I made my decision.

I stand in front of the full-length mirror in the corner of my bedroom, giving my outfit a final look. I'm dressed in black ripped jeans that are so tight they look painted on, but they make my ass look incredible. My shirt is an old Riot t-shirt I splurged on and ordered on their website a few years ago.

Willing to step out of my comfort zone, I grab the hem of the shirt and bunch it up the smallest amount to reveal a minor sliver of my midsection, then tie it behind my back with a hair tie, rolling and tucking the extra fabric up.

I lean forward, shove my hands into my freshly washed hair, and ruffle my curls. Then, I stand back up, admiring how fluffy and full of volume my dark brown locks are.

My curls fall above my tits, perfectly defined and ready for a night out.

After spraying myself with my signature cherry vanilla perfume, I grab my bag, leave my bedroom, and enter Max's room.

There's a knock at the front door while I pack her backpack, so I abandon the pink backpack and rush toward the living room, knowing it's my daughter and Lucy.

Max rushes toward me with her arms open wide when I

swing the door open. I grab her in my arms, attacking her face with kisses.

"Mommy!" she squeals, her face scrunching up as I pepper kisses across her perfect little face. I'll never not be amazed by the fact that I made this beautiful little person. I'm sure most mothers feel the same way—amazed by the fact that they created an entire human being.

"Hey, girl. You look good," Lucy says with a whistle, standing in the doorway.

"Thanks." For once, I feel good about my appearance and don't feel the need to question her compliment. I accept it without overthinking it.

Regardless of what happens tonight, I will see my favorite band perform live and experience my first concert at twenty-one years old. Tonight is going to be a great fucking night, and I'm determined to keep a positive attitude and not let anything fuck it up.

Setting Max on her feet, I turn my attention to Lucy as my daughter runs down the hallway toward her bedroom.

"Thank you so much for watching her. I'll pay you tomorrow as soon as I get home."

"I've already told you not to worry about it, Andy. I'd love to have Max for the night. Haley is excited, too. She's over there trying to figure out which game they'll play first." She waves me off, but I know she's counting on the money, just like I am. Every penny you can get is essential when you're a single mom.

A faint smile brushes my lips. The fact Max has a friend means everything to me. She's too young to become an untrusting, jaded hermit like I am. Making friends was hard for me when I was always the girl with an addict for a mom that other parents liked to whisper about. It makes it hard when no one wants to sit with you at lunch or play on the playground. Everyone treated me as if I was contagious, like they were going to catch a drug addiction just by being near me.

Bastards.

It didn't help matters that I dropped out of school either, so that I could work full time.

"Give me just a minute to finish packing her bag. I'm almost done."

"Bring her over when you're done. I need to get over there with Haley." I nod, watching Lucy walk across the hall to the white door to the apartment directly in front of mine. Once she's inside, I close my door, quickly pulling my phone from my pocket to check the time.

3:58 p.m.

Fuck.

David will be here any minute if he's not already.

I step into Max's bedroom to find her digging through her bottom drawer, pulling out her tutus and princess costumes that she always manages to find at the thrift store. "Whatcha doing, baby girl?"

"Haley and I are going to be princesses tonight, so I'm bringing my dresses," she says, gathering the clothing into her tiny arms and taking it to the bed. She stuffs it in the open backpack and zips it closed.

I watch her in amusement. She pulls the straps over her shoulders and says, "I'm ready to go to my sleepover party."

"Are you forgetting anything?" She taps her chin, thinking momentarily. A second later, her face lights up, and she rushes to her toy chest and pulls out a silver and pink tiara, sticking it on her head.

"Now I'm ready."

"How about I finish packing, Princess Max?" I unzip her backpack and lead her toward the closet, where I quickly gather pajamas and clothes for her to wear tomorrow.

I fold the clothes before putting them in the backpack, her small body dramatically jerking with my movement.

Rolling my eyes, I lead her out of the room and into the bathroom. After packing her toothbrush and toothpaste, I zip up the backpack and grab my own bag.

"Time for our parties!" She jumps in delight, the straps falling off her shoulders with the movement.

"Be good and listen to Lucy, okay?" She nods, following me outside. I lock the door and then shove the keys into my purse.

We approach Lucy's door, and Max presses the doorbell. A second later, Lucy is there staring up at me.

My jeans make squatting difficult, but I do my best to hug and kiss my daughter.

"Do you know how much I love you?"

Max nods frantically. "With all your big, fat, purple heart."

"That's right, baby girl." I give her another kiss before standing and handing the bag to Lucy.

"Thank you again. Please call if you need anything."

"We're good here, girl. Go support your man." Lucy wiggles her eyes suggestively, shooting me a playful smirk.

Max rushes inside, yelling for Haley to look at her tiara.

Now that the time has come, my nerves are beginning to set in and make me anxious, but I remind myself that I can do this.

It's just Declan.

The man who spends his weekends at the park with me and my daughter.

The man who carried my daughter on his shoulders at the cherry festival and tried every chocolate-covered or infused item she wanted him to try.

The man who is making me feel safe enough to let my guard down and let him in.

With a sharp inhale, I waved goodbye to Lucy, taking the steps slowly and one at a time.

"It's just Declan. It'll be fine," I whisper to myself as I reach the bottom of the stairs. Instantly, I spot David in the parking lot waiting for me.

"It's just Declan. Sure, he's a rockstar, but he's your boyfriend," I tell myself out loud, needing the reminder. The word boyfriend has a smile curling on my lips and the butterflies in my belly flying away.

I'm going to see my boyfriend.

One look at him, and I'll feel better.

I'll feel at home.

THIRTY-FIVE

Declan

"Riot!"

"Riot!"

"Riot!"

The crowd chants like a mantra. My heart races in my chest, my palms sweaty, and my hands shake. In an attempt to calm my nerves, I shake my hands and jump in place, hoping the movement will get me hyped and prepared to go on stage.

It's been over a year since I've claimed the stage, standing in front of thousands of screaming fans and their cell phones as they record everything, ready to post any fuck-up on social media.

The last time I was on stage, I'd been so high that I forgot the lyrics. By the night's end, the video of me slurring and forgetting the words was trending on all social media platforms. Had I been sober, I could've played it off, but it was apparent I was under the influence.

That was over a year ago, and tonight, I'm determined to make my comeback. Determined to put on the best fucking show.

I've done many hard things in my life, fuck, my entire life has been hard, so I'm certain I can do this, too. At this point, I've got no choice. I'm not going to let Benny or my brothers down.

Adam, Damon, and Cole have been anxious to get back on stage, just like I have. We're all fucking ready for this. We need this. Need the music to remind us we're alive.

"Are you ready, man?" Adam asks, slapping a hand to my back. Looking at him over my shoulder, I nod, my eyes watching Damon and Cole as they approach us.

Huddling close, as we do before every show, Damon and Cole wrap their arms around mine and Adam's shoulders, and we do the same.

With a wide, confident grin, Damon speaks up, "Let's fucking do this shit! We were made for this."

"Let's make our comeback, baby!" Cole joins in, each of us doing our best to hype ourselves up before the show.

Feeling more confident than I had only moments ago, I chime in, "We're going to make that stage our bitch." Surrounded by my best friends, I take a moment to study each of them, noticing the worries swimming in each of their eyes. They have just as many fears as I do. Selfishly, I'd been so wrapped up in my own head that I hadn't stopped to realize that this may also be difficult for them. I'm not the only one performing again after a long hiatus.

Squeezing the shoulders of Adam and Cole, who are on either side of me, I give them all a look. "We've got this. For tonight, nothing else matters besides those screaming fans out there. They deserve the best show possible. Let's go out there and give them everything we've got." Our bodies come closer together, and the four of us embrace in a group hug that we have shared before every single show since the day we formed our band.

Rushed footsteps approach us, and we break away to turn our attention toward Benny along with Chelsea and Tyler, the sound manager and her assistant. She carries four mic packs, handing two to Tyler and keeping the other two for herself.

I take mine from her, hooking the audio pack into the back of my black jeans while my best friends do the same. We did a sound check earlier but took off our audio packs and earpieces afterward to get cleaned up for the concert and ready to go on stage.

Benny stands with his hands on his hips, looking over the four of us like a proud dad. When Cole steps close to him, he reaches a hand out and ruffles Cole's long, dirty blond hair. The only time Cole wears his hair down is when we're on stage. Any other time, he has his long locks in his signature man bun.

"I'm so proud of you, boys." Benny glances at me with glossy eyes that I'm sure I imagine. When I meet his gaze again, I notice they're clear but shining with pride. "You four are going to kill it. Go out there and give it everything you got. Tonight, you feel the music and remember why the fuck we're here. Nothing else matters once you step out onto that stage." We nod in unison.

"Five minutes!" someone in the distance calls, and we take that as our queue to hurry up. Damon pulls off his T-shirt, tucking part of it into his back pocket and allowing it to hang down.

He's your typical rock band drummer with a shirt hanging from his back pocket and drumsticks tucked into the other pocket. He and Cole have always been shirtless during our shows. I wear the same shit, too. All black. The only difference between Adam's attire and mine is that he wears a white T-shirt.

When we're like this, we look like four tattooed heathens ready to cause trouble. In a way, I guess that's true because once we get on that stage, we do fuck shit up.

"Show time, boys." Benny claps us each on the shoulder before leaving us to do whatever he does while we perform for two hours.

With our earpieces hanging around our necks, we share one final hug before following the stage crew and security out of the backstage area, making our way to the dark stage.

We stand to the side of the stage, the lights in the venue

dimming to the point the only light radiating is a soft glow along the stage for us to be able to see.

I stick my earpieces in each ear, watching as Damon and Cole walk to the stage first to take their place. Damon removes the drumsticks from his pocket before sitting behind his drum set. Next, Adam joins them on stage, and he and Cole grab the guitar and bass from the stands.

Per usual, I'm the last one to take my place on stage, and I do so after taking a few deep breaths, needing to calm my nerves.

As I stand behind the microphone, the lights go up, a spotlight filling the stage and illuminating my bandmates. The crowd goes wild at the sight of us.

I look out over the sold-out floor at the screaming crowds and take in the scenery.

Stage and camera lights are in my face, screaming faces huddled together and blurring as I frantically search the faces, desperate to find Andy, the only face I need to see.

My eyes snap up to the VIP section on the balcony above the general admission floor. Dark eyes stare back at me, a shy smile on her beautiful face.

Thank fuck. She came.

The sight of Andy dressed in a Riot T-shirt and ripped black jeans has my dick twitching in my jeans. She's bunched up the shirt and tied it behind her back, revealing the slightest sliver of silky brown skin above her jeans. A tease of flesh that has me wanting to run my tongue along her belly button.

Removing the wireless microphone from the stand, I hold it as I stand center stage, eyes never leaving Andy's dark pools as I become alive, feeding off her energy and strength. "Las Vegas, what the fuck is up!" I roar into the microphone, the crowd erupting into screams.

"In case you're living under a fucking rock and don't know why you're here, I'm Declan Valentine!" More cheers erupt.

"We've got the badass Damon Jackson over here on drums."

Damon throws his sticks into the air and, after catching them, expertly twirls them in his fingers.

"Cole Conrad on bass." Cole steps forward, strumming a single note on his instrument, smirks at the crowd, and slowly runs his fingers through his long hair. This guy.

Same routine, every show.

"On guitar, we have Adam Jones." Adam puckers his lips, presses a hand to them, and then mimes throwing kisses into the air.

More cheers erupt, and I swear I see a couple women jump to catch the air kisses Adam threw.

"We are Riot, and we are here to play some fucking music! Make some noise, House of Carnage!" I remove one of my earpieces to hear the full extent of cheers from the crowd.

The screams and chants of our fans are all I need. It's enough of a high for me to get through tonight. I can fucking do this.

"We're going to start the night off with the very first song we wrote together when we were eighteen-year-old shitheads daydreaming about playing music for a living. If you know the lyrics, I want you screaming them as loud as I'm going to make my girl scream tonight." My eyes connect with Andy just in time to see her matte red lips part and a blush color her cheeks. She glares at me, and I give her a playful wink.

Putting the earpieces back in, I prepare myself, listening to the beat as Damon begins hitting his drums, Cole following in on the bass.

Holding the microphone in both hands, I bring it to my mouth, close my eyes, and sing the words to "Rockstar," a song we wrote jokingly that led us to meeting Benny. The song is responsible for putting us on the map, and we begin every show with it as a reminder to always remember where we came from.

The words pour out of me, and before I know it, we're four songs into our setlist, and I feel more alive than ever.

I jump around the stage, interacting with the crowd between

songs, thriving on the comfort I feel about being back in my element.

As we begin our final song of the night, I drop to my knees, eyes closed, and sing the words into the microphone. The words to our newest song that I wrote with bloody knuckles in a hotel room in a strange little town, which seems like forever ago, when it was only weeks ago.

Tell me, baby, do you hate me?
Would you believe me if I said I was sorry?
That I never meant to hurt you.
Told you my love will be our downfall.
You shouldn't have tried to save me.
Baby, we're only going down, down, down.
You can't save me.
Save yourself.
Let me be free.

THE FINAL NOTE RINGS OUT INTO THE CROWD, AND MY EYES instantly find Andy's. As expected, she stares back at me with confusion evident on her face and no doubt a million questions racing in her mind.

As the crowd erupts into a final round of cheers, it takes her a moment before she joins in, but she finally does.

Andy cups her hands around her mouth and screams, eyes never leaving mine. Standing to my feet, I smack my fist against my heart, a gesture only for her.

The stage lights dim, and then we're exiting.

Adam, Cole, and Damon are fueled by adrenaline and already making plans to go out tonight to celebrate, but my mind remains on the brown-eyed beauty in the VIP section.

Standing there, I realized that I'd replaced one addiction with the other. One that'll kill me just the same.

Only this one, I don't mind dying for.

THIRTY-SIX

Andy

SEEING RIOT PERFORM LIVE WAS INCREDIBLE. IT WAS HONESTLY unlike anything I have ever witnessed. And I'll never experience anything like that again. It was my first concert, after all.

I'd been nervous going into the crowded venue by myself, especially after seeing the long line wrapped around the block, but to my surprise, there was a VIP line. I'd shown them the ticket Declan had emailed me, and next thing I knew, I was bypassing the line and being escorted to a private suite on the balcony with a security guard and five other women.

One of which was a tall redhead that I instantly recognized.

Cece.

We haven't spoken much since the barbeque, even though she texted me. It's primarily because of me. My time was spent focused on Declan, and then we had our fight on Tuesday. Since then, I have not felt like speaking to his best friend's girlfriend. But once she spotted me, she pulled me in for a hug, and we spent the entire show watching our men perform, screaming the lyrics along with the crowd.

After the show ended, Cece linked her arm with mine and had the security guard escort us backstage. She told me all about how she goes to find Cole after every show she attends.

Once we arrive backstage, she turns to face me. "If I don't see you again tonight, have fun. Text me, and we'll plan something when you're in Vegas again," she says, pulling me in for a tight hug. "Declan's dressing room is around that corner." She points ahead of us. "Cole is this way." She nods in the opposite direction, pulling away and walking toward her boyfriend.

After a quick wave, I follow her directions, weaving through the bustling backstage crowd, hoping to find Declan. I wasn't sure what to do after the show ended. He'd mentioned us getting a room and staying the night together, but that was before our fight. I'd considered texting him to see if he wanted to meet me somewhere, but I figured he'd be too busy to see his phone. People would be leaving, and I hadn't wanted to be the awkward girl standing around, so I'm glad Cece took charge and brought me backstage.

Although, now that I'm back here, I feel uneasy.

What if Declan hadn't wanted me to come back here?

What if he doesn't want me to stay the night with him anymore?

No, of course, he does. He wouldn't have texted me this morning to ensure I was coming.

Ugh.

Stop fucking overthinking, Andy. Just go find him.

Walking around the corner, a smile spreads across my face at the sight of Declan but quickly falls as I watch a gorgeous dark-haired woman step out of his dressing room behind him. They turn to face each other, a broad smile on her red lips as she talks animatedly to Declan.

He seems interested in what she says because he never takes his eyes off her and has a genuine smile. I stand frozen in place, molding my back to the wall as I watch them from around the corner.

The woman is dressed in sky-high stilettos, making her legs look even longer than they are. She's wearing fishnet tights and an older Riot T-shirt from their tour several years ago. Her black hair is pin straight and perfectly down her back without a strand out of place, unlike my hair, which I'm sure is now frizzy thanks to the humidity in the venue.

My heart stops beating while watching their familiar interaction. Who the fuck is she, and why is she coming out of his dressing room?

There wasn't enough time for them to have fucked, but I still have many questions. Did he think we broke up and this is my replacement?

Perhaps he's tired of slumming it with the fat girl and is returning to the type of woman he usually dates.

Oh, God. What if I'm the other woman?

What if this is his girlfriend, and I was the one he was using to pass the time while he was forced to be in Loganville.

I'm trying not to let my mind jump to the worst-case scenario, but it's hard when I've never been anyone's first choice, and I'm watching the man I'm falling in love with stand so close to the type of woman he's known to date.

Declan grabs the petite woman, crushing her against him as they hug. When they pull away, she kisses his cheek but keeps an arm around his waist while he wraps his around her shoulders and walks directly toward me.

Oh, fuck.

They haven't seen me yet, but the second they turn the corner, they will, and it's too late to hurry and leave.

Instead, I do something I'm not proud of. I act surprised, as if I've just got here. I quickly run backward, then step forward, just as Declan and the most gorgeous woman I've ever seen turn around the corner.

His reaction to the sight of me takes me by surprise.

Instead of looking guilty, his eyes flash with relief. It was as if he was relieved to know I had come even though he had seen me in the crowd minutes ago. Removing his arm from around the woman, he rushes toward me, hands around my ass as he picks me up, spinning me around.

Just like that, all the anger I've held onto for two days, and the insecurity I just experienced fades away, and I'm left with butterflies fluttering around in my stomach and true happiness on my face.

Declan sets me on my feet, his hands cupping my face as he crushes our lips together. He kisses me so deeply and intensely that it steals the breath from my lungs and turns my knees weak.

He pulls back and rests his forehead against mine. "I've missed you so fucking much." Then, he whispers only to me, "Thank you for coming, Mama." Before I can respond, a voice in the background clears, and I'm reminded we're not alone.

It's like a bucket of cold water is dumped over me. I remember seeing Declan walking arm in arm with the raven-haired beauty behind him.

Sheepishly, Declan pulls away, turning to face the woman. She pops her hip, arms crossed over her chest.

"Such a caveman." She scoffs, rolling her dark eyes. "You could at least introduce us before you attack her." She walks toward me, eyes full of warmth and kindness.

"You must be Andy. Declan was just telling me about his new girlfriend, which he's crazy about." I side-eye the man beside her, taking in his suddenly bashful expression. "I'm Declan's sister, Spencer." She holds her hand out. Despite being shorter than me, she has a very intimidating presence about her.

She's his sister, not a secret girlfriend. Thank fuck.

But wait. He's never mentioned a sister before. In fact, I remember Declan telling me he's an only child.

Wanting to be polite, I reach out and shake Spencer's hand, surprised when she pulls me in for a tight hug. "Take care of him," she whispers in my ear, so low that there's no chance of him overhearing. "Don't give up on him when he fucks up. Please be there for him." She pulls back, the smile never falling from her lips as if she hadn't just whispered in my ear.

"It's great to meet you, Spencer. I'm sorry. I didn't know Declan had a sister."

He opens his mouth to speak, but she cuts him off. "Technically, I'm his ex-sister-in-law. But Declan is one of my best friends, so it doesn't matter that he and my sister are no longer married. We're family," she explains, eyes bouncing from me to Declan. "I'm heading to the hotel now, but I hope we can meet for breakfast tomorrow. I'd love to get to know you better, Andy."

I look to Declan, waiting to see what his answer will be since I'm unsure if he has anything planned for us.

"Sure. Text me in the morning, and we'll have breakfast," Declan confirms, stepping away from my side to give Spencer another hug. "Be safe and call if you need anything. David is outside waiting. We'll see you tomorrow." Spencer gives me another hug, and then she leaves, strutting down the hall in heels that look entirely uncomfortable.

With her out of sight, Declan turns us to face each other, backing me up until my back hits the cement wall. "You came," he says breathlessly, hands gripping my hips firmly as if he expects I'll disappear if he were to let go. "Thank you for being here." He presses his lips against mine, forcing his tongue inside my mouth. He dominates the kiss. His body presses into mine, closing the space between us as he swallows my noises, practically fucking my mouth with his tongue.

"Holy fuck. I can't wait to get you back to the hotel. I've missed you so fucking much, Mama."

I take a much-needed breath. It's hard to breathe when he's around. He's suffocating, but I wouldn't have it any other way. "Me too," I agree, meaning what I say. I did miss him—a lot more than I'd expected.

"I need to finish up a few things here. You can wait in my dressing room, and then we'll go. We really need to talk." He takes my hand and leads me down the hallway toward the room where I'd seen him and Spencer exit.

Opening the door, he leads me inside the plain white dressing room, guiding me toward the black couch on the back wall.

"Relax. I'll be back as soon as I can. Just need to let the guys know I'm leaving and see if Benny needs me," he assures me, leaning down and pressing another kiss to my lips.

Declan walks to the door, looks over his shoulder, and gives me a lazy smile. "I really am happy you're here. I don't know what I'd do if you didn't show up." He turns away and leaves me in the room, his words lingering in the air.

What would he have done if I hadn't shown?

THIRTY-SEVEN

Andy

TWENTY MINUTES AFTER DECLAN LEFT ME IN HIS DRESSING ROOM, HE returned to get me. He held my hand and led me outside, using the back entrance to avoid fans. David had been waiting after just returning from taking Spencer to the hotel.

The drive to the hotel was short, and the ride was silent. We also rode the elevator in silence, and now we stand outside the door of the hotel room that Declan booked for us. After David dropped me off at The House of Carnage, he took my duffle bag to the hotel, so I'm not surprised when I see it inside the room once Declan unlocks the door, and I enter before him.

The door slams shut, and the deadbolt clicks into place as he enters. The space feels smaller with him inside—as if the walls are closing around us. My body is wound tight with nerves as Declan steps behind me, his chest bumping into my back. His warmth and amped-up energy from the show radiate around him.

He places his hands on my shoulders, squeezing them lightly, then runs his hands down my arms and to my hips. Gripping them firmly, he pulls me back against his body so we're flush together, his chin resting on my left shoulder.

"Thank you for coming tonight, Mama. You have no idea

how much I needed to see you when I looked out into that crowd," he rasps, voice low as he trails his fingertips along the bare, exposed skin at my midsection.

"Let me show my appreciation." My breathing hitches as he moves his hand to the front of my jeans and expertly unbuttons them, shoving his hand inside my panties. "Tell me to stop if you don't want this," he whispers, breath fanning across my neck before he places a kiss beneath my earlobe. His finger swipes through my slit, finding me wet and ready for him.

Traitorous cunt.

We really should be talking first, but at this point, I'm not willing to stop him. We can talk after he makes me come—hopefully a few times.

His finger swipes through me again, bringing the wetness to my clit before he slowly traces the sensitive bud with one finger.

"Don't stop," I say with a breathy moan, needing him to give me what I need right now more than anything.

Using the hand not in my pants, Declan shoves my tight jeans and panties down beneath my ass to allow himself easier access to my wet aching pussy.

Without warning, he shoves two thick fingers inside of me, instantly setting a punishing pace that has his palm slapping against my clit as he finger fucks me.

My body bucks forward against his hand. "Oh god." I gasp, my eyes closing as my legs become weak at the sensation.

He wraps an arm around my shoulders, keeping my back pressed firmly against his chest as his fingers curl upward, massaging my G-spot while his thumb rubs my clit.

"Oh, fuck," I whimper. My hands grab onto his forearm wrapped around me, head falling back onto his shoulder. He kisses my cheek, and I turn my head toward him, capturing his lips with mine.

"Come for me, baby. Let me feel you squeeze my fingers," he mumbles against my lips.

Declan adds a third finger that has my moans turning into

soft screams of pleasure. He captures my lips once more, swallowing my whimpers and pleas for more. He gives me what I want by picking up his pace and hitting the spot within me that has my toes curling in my shoes.

As he presses his hard length into my ass, I can feel it straining, trapped beneath his jeans. Knowing he's that hard just by fingering me makes me feral.

My pussy convulses around his fingers. Squeezing him tightly as he quickens the pace on my clit, sending me over the edge.

Fireworks erupt around me as I pull away from his kiss, my mouth open in a silent scream as euphoria fills my body.

"Fuck, you're such a good girl," he praises in my ear before kissing my earlobe. "Such a good fucking girl coming on my fingers." He continues rubbing me, forcing my body to ride out the wave of pleasure.

He removes his hand from between my legs, and I watch him through dazed eyes as he brings his fingers to his mouth and sucks them clean.

"Goddamn," he groans. "Your taste."

"How do I taste?" I ask breathlessly.

"You taste like you're mine." He wraps his wet fingers around my throat, squeezing slightly as he connects our lips, tongue invading my mouth. He's not squeezing enough to cut off my airway, but damn, I wish he was.

I've never been into choking during sex. Mostly because I never trusted anyone enough, but with him, I bet he'd be willing to do anything I asked.

While he ravages my mouth, I place my hand on top of his around my throat and urge him to tighten his fingers. Exactly as expected, he takes the hint and tightens his grip around my throat.

"Always fucking knew you'd be a dirty girl." He smirks, one hand slipping between us to undo his pants. "Continue being my good girl, and let me fill your sweet pussy with my cum." He pulls away from me, dark eyes focused on my pussy between my thick thighs.

Eyes never leaving my skin, he undresses himself until he's standing completely naked. His hard cock juts out, angry and heavy between us. His skin is so hot that I can feel the warmth radiating off him. He wraps a hand around his thick shaft, slowly stroking himself from base to tip.

With his dark eyes on me, I slowly remove the remainder of my clothing until I'm standing before him bare. My hands go to my heavy breasts, pinching and tugging my pebbled nipples.

A deep, throaty groan escapes him as he watches my movements, watching everything I do carefully.

"Bend over, now," he commands, stalking toward me. Not wanting to waste any time, I climb onto the bed on my knees and lean forward on my elbows, ass in the air for him.

He grabs something from the floor that I can't see before he approaches the bed. "Hands behind your back." I obey, placing my hands behind my back as I turn my head to the side to breathe.

He slaps my ass, the crack of his palm against my skin ringing out into the silence of the room, the pain causing me to hiss.

I watch over my shoulder as Declan grabs my hands and slips his belt around my wrists, securing them together. With my wrists bound, he uses his knee to spread my legs wider, the cool air causing a gentle breeze on my wet cunt as I reveal more of my core.

"I want to hear you screaming my fucking name. Scream it louder than my fans did tonight." He places a hand in my hair and grabs a fistful, using his grip to pull me up while his other hand wraps around my throat.

My lips part, my body shaking as my back arches to relieve some of the pressure from his grip on my hair. His cock brushes against my clit as he shifts closer to me, lining himself up with my wet entrance.

With one quick thrust, Declan enters me, seating his cock deep inside of me, already hitting me exactly where I need with this position.

We groan in unison at the feeling. He lingers a moment, allowing himself to relish in the feeling of being inside of me— the feeling of both my stomach and walls fluttering, loving the intrusion of him.

Having a dick deep inside of you is hands down one of the best feelings ever. I don't care what anyone says. I don't think it's talked about enough. Sex is considered a taboo topic when it shouldn't be. I'm not afraid to say it and will gladly scream it from the rooftops.

A cock gliding in and out of your slickness is the best feeling, and I will gladly accept it 24/7.

I've made the mistake of waking my inner hoe, and there's no way she'll go back into hibernation.

Declan pulls out to the tip, then slams back into me, his pelvis slapping against my ass with the movement. He pulls me up until I'm on my knees with my back arched, the new angle allowing his long length to hit the spot where I need him most.

"Do you know how much it killed me when you ignored me for two days?" he rasps into my ear. The grip around my throat tightens, and I take that as a sign that he doesn't want me to respond, so I give him my cries instead.

"You fucking ignored me." His pace quickens until it's punishing, his cock slipping deeper inside of me until it's borderline painful. But I accept it. He needs to get out of his frustrations, and I'll allow him to use my body however he needs to.

Moving his hand to the back of my head, he pushes me forward, my face buried in a pillow as he holds me down, taking what he needs from my body.

"Did my apology mean nothing to you?" he hisses, palm cracking against my ass. "God fucking damn, Andy. Do you see how crazy you make me?" My tits bounce with each thrust, the pillow cutting off my oxygen, but he doesn't allow me to turn my head to suck in any air.

With a roar, Declan pulls out of my weeping pussy and unbuckles the belt from my wrists. When he's off me, I lean onto my elbows and rub my wrists, inhaling the precious air.

I'm only given a moment before he's on me again. With a painful grip on my hips, he flips me onto my back, spreads my legs wide, and thrusts himself back into me.

"I need to see your face when you come on my cock like my own personal whore." His words shouldn't excite me, but they do. What does it say about me that I like him calling me his whore?

With his eyes on me, never once straying from my face, he reaches between us and finds my clit, rubbing it in sync with his thrusts.

"Declan!" I scream his name as I shake with my second orgasm of the night, the sensation rushing through me suddenly. He continues rubbing my sensitive clit, his movement never faltering.

His dark gaze never leaves mine, as if he's committing my face and this moment into his memory. His stare is intense, but I am staring back at him, unable and unwilling to break eye contact.

Declan stills, body stiffening as he fills my pussy with his cum deep within me. The warmth from his release flooding my body.

His heavy body collapses above me, caging me in with his forearms on either side of my head and cock still seated inside of me. My legs are still thrown over his thighs, but neither of us makes any attempt to move. We need this moment. We need to remain connected as intimately as possible.

And I'm not sure how much more intimately connected we can get since his cock is still inside of me.

"Don't leave me," he whispers, vulnerability clear in his words and eyes.

"Please, Andy. I need you. Don't fucking leave me." His words give me whiplash and send chills down my spine. His words are both desperate and ominous.

"Without you, I'm nothing." He presses a kiss against my lips. "Promise me you'll never leave me. Promise you'll love me no matter what." There's no point in being shocked or denying his mention of love. I'm in love with Declan Valentine; he knows it without me having to say anything.

I stare into his eyes, not straying from his gaze as I lie there, wishing I could see inside his head and read everything he's thinking.

"I promise," I whisper into the stillness of the room, too love-struck to comprehend the weight of the promise. And despite the knot in my stomach telling me not to make a promise I'm not sure I'll be able to keep, I do it anyway. Because right now, the only thing that exists is him.

No matter what the future holds for us, I'll forever remember this moment. The moment of him being vulnerable and begging me not to leave him.

If only I understood the weight of those words.

THIRTY-EIGHT

Declan

AFTER WE UNTANGLED OURSELVES, ANDY AND I SHOWERED IN THE massive ensuite bathroom. We took turns washing each other and getting nice and clean, only to get dirty again when she dropped to her knees and took my cock down her throat.

I'd braced my hands on the glass shower wall and watched her while she sucked me. To show my appreciation, I came into her mouth, and she swallowed my load. She even showed me her pink tongue to prove she drank everything I had to give her.

Such a fucking good girl.

Now, we're lying in bed. The only light in the room is coming from the floor-to-ceiling window, which gives us a view of the Las Vegas strip. Something about the city being alive outside the window calms my racing mind.

Andy is cuddled into my side, using my chest as a pillow as I trace slow, lazy circles over her bare skin, singing the words to a new song I've been working on. We couldn't be bothered to get dressed after the shower, so after drying off, we climbed into bed and haven't been able to stop touching each other since.

Knowing we need to talk about Tuesday, I clear my throat and dive in. "I'm sorry for blowing up at you." Her breathing is calm beside me, her body still, but I know she's not asleep.

She does make me wait a while before responding, but her response has me blowing out a breath of relief.

"I know you are. And I forgive you." She hikes her leg over mine. "Why did you get so angry when I asked about your past?"

My body tenses. She deserves the truth and to know everything that has made me the way I am, but I can't tell her. Not yet. Not when I haven't been able to accept it myself. "It's not something I want to discuss." I sigh.

Thankfully, she doesn't pressure me into telling her and spilling the secret I've buried the deepest since I was thirteen years old.

"Can you promise me that one day you will talk about it? Whether it's with me or a therapist, just please, Declan, talk to someone because it's affecting you." My jaw clenches, my hands stilling around her body.

I take a deep breath, count to ten, and then let it out slowly, the tension escaping my shoulders. "Yes," I grit out. "One day, I promise you." I'm not naive enough to think my secrets aren't controlling me, but I am stubborn enough never to share them. At least I'd never planned on it. Not until now, at least. For her, I'm willing to get help, even if that means sending myself down a dark path and a downward spiral.

"Where's Max's dad?" I ask the question that has been lingering on the tip of my tongue for weeks now.

Andy sighs, body pressing closer into mine. "I don't know," she confesses. "I'm not sure who her father is. I was a very promiscuous teenager and had slept with a few guys around the time I got pregnant. Once I found out, I told them all that I was pregnant and asked if they'd be willing to do a paternity test. Only one of them was willing. The other's denied Max was theirs and blocked me. The one guy who was willing to take the test was negative." I wrap both arms around her, holding her tight to my chest while she shares something that is not easy for her to discuss.

"When she turned one, I made a new social media account and found one of the guys. He was newly married and having a baby, so he told me never to contact him again." My eyebrows raise at her words, anger filling my veins at the fact the pieces of shit she fucked were man enough to fuck but were too cowardly to get a DNA test.

"Silly me." She scoffs. "I thought the guys would've been more mature than that. But I guess it's not a good look when you get a sixteen-year-old pregnant at twenty-six." What the actual fuck? That was not what I was expecting her to say.

"You were fucking around with grown-ass men?" I attempt to keep the judgment out of my voice, but I'm not sure I do a great job. And I'm the last person who should be judging anyone.

Besides, I'm ten years older than she is.

"Yup. Disgusting, right?" She sighs. "I'd been so desperate to be wanted. My dad left me before I was born. My mom was too busy getting high. I felt so alone, so I turned to men. No one my age held my attention, so I started talking to older men."

"I kind of figured you had a thing for age gaps, considering I'm thirty-one and you're twenty-one," I say playfully, shifting to look down at her. She tilts her head up to meet my gaze, a grin on her lips.

"Oh, yeah. I'm with you because I'm interested in those senior citizen discounts I'll get by being with you." A teasing smirk spreads across her face. "How does it work with AARP? Do you add me so I can take advantage of the discounts too?" She bellows with laughter, and despite her teasing me about my age, all I can do is smile because she's so fucking carefree right now. Her body is loose, and the tension she always carries is gone.

I love that she's getting a night off from worrying about everything and enjoying herself.

"Probably on our next date, I'll get to sit on your walker, and you can push me." She rolls onto her back, laughing so hard that her only sound is a near-silent wheeze.

"Alright, you're going to get it now." I quickly roll on top of her, caging her in with my arms.

Her eyes widen. "Oh no! Don't move too quickly, or you'll break a hip." Her eyes close as she laughs, her mouth open wide. God, I love her laugh.

Everything about this woman below me has my head all fucked up and in a tailspin.

"Andy." Hearing my serious voice, she calms down and looks up at me.

"What's wrong?"

A lazy smile spreads across my mouth. "You're in love with me," I say, admitting something that I realized tonight at the show. How she watched me on stage, unable to keep her eyes off me, tracking every movement—it made me realize something. This girl loves me. It was more than being awestruck by being at a concert. It's how she cares for me and allows me to see parts of herself that she doesn't show anyone else. Even the way she forgave me after being a dick was enough to confirm it.

She fucking loves me.

Her face goes blank, all laughter a thing of the past as she stares at me.

"You're going to break my heart." She whispers her fears into the silent, dimly lit room. The confession hangs between us, but I cannot deny it. Destruction is what I do best. I break all beautiful things, and her heart is the most beautiful.

"I don't want to," I whisper, my eyes softening. I hope she can see the fears and truth swimming in my eyes.

She gulps, her throat moving with the swallow. "I won't survive if you do."

I never want to hurt her, and all I can do is try not to. Considering it's me we're talking about, it may happen unintentionally.

Suddenly, I find myself asking a question that I've been

thinking about since the first time I shoved my dick inside of her. "Are you on birth control?"

She laughs. "You're asking me this just now? After all the times you've came inside of me?" I shrug, rolling off her and lying on my back beside her, turning my head to watch her. "Yes. I'm on birth control, but I haven't been with anyone since getting pregnant. My periods were bad after giving birth, so I got on it." Both statements excite me. It thrills me to know I'm the only man who has been inside of her for years and that I can continue coming inside of her without having to worry about accidental pregnancy. Not again.

"Do you want more children?" I ask, turning onto my side and propping my head up with a pillow. She mirrors my position, rolling on her side to face me.

Without taking the time to think, she shakes her head.

"Are you sure?"

She nods. "I've thought about it a lot, and I have the baby I've always wanted. I don't want any more. I'm not interested in being pregnant again, giving birth, or raising another child. Max is enough for me."

Each time I've come inside of Andy, I've thought of how she'd look with a pregnant belly growing my child, but as much as I like to fantasize, I have no intention of ever making that a reality. I'm not interested in ever having another child.

My, how the tables have turned.

Years ago, I was the one begging Camille for another child, and she was the one denying me. Now, she's pregnant, and I'm the one who doesn't want another kid.

"Do you?" she asks, teeth biting into her bottom lip nervously.

I shake my head. "Luca was enough for me. I don't want another. Marriage, either. I'm not interested in ever being married again."

"Good. I'm not either." That surprises the hell out of me. Most women are all about getting married and having a house full of children. She must see the surprise on my face because she grins before continuing to speak. "Marriage is a piece of paper. My grandparents were married for fifty years, and they had a once-in-a-lifetime kind of love. I love how they loved each other, but I don't want to be married to have that." She holds her left hand out in front of her face.

"Now, would I look good with a diamond ring? Absolutely. But I don't want the legal attachment."

"So, you wouldn't turn me down if I gave you a ring and asked you to be mine forever?" I cock an eyebrow, needing her answer for my next move.

Smiling, she brushes loose curls from her face. "It would have to be a pretty large rock for me to agree." Say less. I smirk, give her a quick kiss, then climb off the bed butt-ass naked and go toward the grocery bag sitting on the coffee table.

"What are you doing?" She sits up in the bed, pulling the white sheet around her beautiful golden body and leaning back against the headboard.

I rummage through the bag of candy bought for me until I find what I'm looking for, then quickly tear off the wrapper. Since I stopped smoking, my bandmates have been keeping my pockets full of hard candies. Apparently, having suckers around helped Cole when he quit smoking, so they've been doing the same for me.

Sticking the cherry-flavored candy behind my back, I approach the bed and sit beside Andy with a wide grin.

She eyes me suspiciously. "What's behind your back?"

Holding her gaze, I remove my hand from my back, revealing the cherry-flavored ring pop. I clear my throat before speaking. "Andy Harris—"

She cuts me off as she playfully shoves me away from her. "Are you proposing to me?" She scrunches her face, eyes shifting from me to the ring pop.

"No, because we're not getting married. But I'm giving you

my ring, and you will agree to be mine." Her eyes soften, and she pulls her bottom lip between her teeth.

"Declan." My whispered name is full of awe.

"Andy, I'm a fuck-up that doesn't know how to love. Everything I feel is intense. My highs are high, and my lows are low. I can only express my feelings when I'm writing songs. Other than that, I'm shit with words." She holds my free hand, the ring held between us in offering. "I'm not asking you to marry me, but I am asking you to not give up on me and to love me with all you've got. I'm asking you to be by my side as I become a better man. The type of man that you deserve. You're the one I want by my side when I look at my life tomorrow. I would say in the future, but tomorrow is as far ahead as I can promise because I'm not good at making plans." Her brown eyes shine with unshed tears as she looks at me.

"You are becoming the very best part of me, Andy. You're already the best part of my day. You're the light to my darkness." How have I known this woman for less than two months, yet it feels like we've shared a lifetime together?

"I want you to spend all the tomorrows with me." I reach out, and she places her left hand in mine. I can't give her a future, but I can give her tomorrow.

Slowly, I slide the cherry ring pop on her left ring finger, admiring the way it looks. One day, I'll replace it with a real diamond the size of the moon, but for right now, tonight, this will do.

"I'll spend all of the tomorrows with you." She wraps her arms around my neck, lips finding mine in a slow lingering kiss. She pushes me back, then climbs on top of me and rides me slowly until we're both yelling our releases. Then we kiss, portraying all the love we have for each other. My kisses tell her everything I need to say but fail to find the words for.

The only thing I can commit to is the ink on my skin.

Right now, all I can promise her is tomorrow and another orgasm.

THIRTY-NINE

Andy

Saturday 9:14 pm

DECLAN

I'll be there Monday when you get off work, but I have to be back Tuesday morning. The next shows will be Wednesday, Friday, and Saturday.

ME

Can't wait to see you.

DECLAN

Me too. Miss you so fucking much, Mama.

Sunday 8:30 a.m.

DECLAN

Good morning, Mama. I hate waking up without you.

Send nudes. I miss your body.

ME

Haha. No way.

DECLAN

Please. I miss your tits.

ME

sends a tit pic

DECLAN

incoming dick pic

I just came all over my phone on the tit pic you sent. Thanks, baby. I can't wait until you're in my arms and I'm inside you.

Next time, it'll be your tits I'm coming on.

Monday 9:47 a.m.

DECLAN

By this time tonight, we'll be together. You have no idea how badly I need to hold you.

ME

Me, too. Are you okay?

DECLAN

We'll talk tonight.

You'll always have my tomorrows.

WAKING UP IN VEGAS IN DECLAN'S ARMS SATURDAY MORNING WAS everything I hoped it could've been. We showered together, got ready for the day side by side at the double vanity, and then went to a restaurant in the hotel for breakfast with Spencer. I thought it would've been odd having a meal together and getting to know his ex-wife's sister, but it wasn't. Spencer had been genuinely interested in me, and the way she and Declan spoke to each other eased my fears about anything intimate happening between them.

But that didn't stop me from asking him if they'd ever fucked, and he laughed so hard at the question I swore he was going to piss himself. That also calmed my fears.

Unfortunately, right after we ate, I had to leave. Declan had to work, and I missed Max and was ready to get home to my baby girl.

Since then, I've been texting as much as possible and waiting to see him again. We never mentioned what we discussed Friday night, and he never said anything when I took the ring pop off. I'm sure his declaration had been pillow talk, but I won't be the one to bring it up. He doesn't owe me anything.

Logically, this wouldn't work out long-term between us, but I'm fine remaining in my delusional bubble for as long as possible.

Today is Monday, and I've been watching the clock since I arrived. Declan wants to be with me, even just for one night. He's taking time away from his busy schedule to be with me.

The true definition of if he wanted to, he would.

By the time 3:30 p.m. arrives, I clock out and practically run out of the hotel. I'm not sure what time he'll arrive, but I will be ready for the moment he does.

On the way home, I stop at the daycare center to pick up Max. I haven't told her that her best friend will be here tonight, but she'll be thrilled to see him. Not a day has gone by that she hasn't asked about him. I swear she misses him more than she missed me while I was away Friday night.

"Mommy! Look at my drawing." Max calls out once we're inside our apartment, rushing toward the kitchen table. She sets down her pink backpack and unzips it, pulling out a piece of paper that she delicately placed inside. She carefully carries it in both hands like it's her most prized possession. She hands me the paper, and I take it, looking over the three stick figures inside a house.

My eyes flick between her and the paper. "Tell me about your drawing."

Her brown eyes shine with excitement. She reaches up on her tiptoes, grabs the white piece of paper from my hands, and points to the smallest figure. "That's me." She points to the figure with long black hair and red lips. "That's you, Mommy." She points to the following figure. "That's Declan. And that's our house and our doggie." Her finger moves over the page.

"We have a dog?"

She grins, rocking on her heels. "I'm asking Santa for a doggie this year. I've been so super-duper very good." She clasps her hands, placing them beneath her chin. "A doggie will make me so, so, so, *sooooo* happy."

Hard to argue with that. Although I thought we were past the dog discussion, or at least I was hoping we were. Every once in a while, she becomes fixated on us getting a dog. I'd get her one in a heartbeat if I could afford it.

"One day, Max." I pick her up in my arms, kissing her round little cheek, carrying her toward the fridge. Grabbing a magnet, I hand it to her and hold the paper to the refrigerator, allowing her to set the magnet on top, securing it to the front of our fridge.

"Do you promise?" she asks, holding up her pinky. I hook it with mine and give her another kiss.

"One day, baby girl. Mommy never lies to you." She smiles brightly at me, her wide eyes full of trust. I do my best to give my daughter the life my mother was never able to provide me with. To give her everything she wants and needs. I don't want her to grow up and have trauma like mine.

I may not be able to buy her everything she wants or fill our house with brand-new name-brand items, but I'll do anything to ensure she never goes a day without a warm meal or clean clothes and never has to question whether she's loved.

My girl will always know she's loved and so very wanted.

Setting her on her feet, I glance at the drawing once again. "Max, why did you draw Declan in your picture?"

She looks at me, rolling her eyes and giving me her teenage attitude. "Because he's our family," she states, matter-of-fact, as if I should've known that.

I've wanted to keep her from becoming attached to him, but I know it's pointless because she already is and has been since they met.

Over the past month and a half, my girl and I have fallen in love in different ways.

Pulling Max into my arms, I hug her close, inhaling the sweet scent of her shampoo. "Yeah, baby girl, you're right. He is our family," I say in a low tone, a smile of contentment tugging across my lips.

Three hours later, Max and I are dressed in pajamas, clean from a shower. She chose her green and white *Princess and The Frog* pajamas, while I wore an oversized white T-shirt and black sleep shorts.

Typically, I'd be getting ready to put her down for bed, but considering Declan will be here tonight, I've decided to keep her up a little later than usual. He's only going to be here for one night, and she's been missing him like crazy.

I'm in the kitchen cleaning up our dinner mess while Max is in the living room sitting at the coffee table with her coloring book when there's a soft knock at the door.

My ears perk up, and my heart skips a beat at the noise. A second later, there's another soft tap, followed by my phone pinging with an incoming text. Drying my hands, I quickly grab my phone from the counter, grinning at the sight of Declan's name.

DECLAN
Open the door, Mama.

I'm sure he thinks Max is asleep, which is why his knocks are gentle, so I choose to surprise him.

"Hey, Max?" I call out, looking toward my daughter, who sits on the floor in the living room with a crayon in each hand.

399

Her wide eyes meet mine, "What, Mommy?"

"Can you open the door, please?"

Her face scrunches up in confusion, knowing she's never allowed to answer the door, "Why?"

"Because there's a surprise for you outside." She sets the crayons down and stands to her feet, eyes wide with excitement.

"A present? For me?" I nod.

"Yay! I love presents!" She runs toward the door, tiny hands reaching for the locks.

She huffs in annoyance as she struggles with the deadbolt but eventually gets it to turn. Once the door is unlocked, she yanks the door open, revealing a sexy-as-fuck rockstar standing on the other side.

Declan.

The black strap of his duffle bag is over his shoulder, and he's dressed in his typical black ripped jeans and a plain black T-shirt.

His brown eyes meet Max, his face shifting into pure adoration at the sight of my daughter.

Max blinks rapidly, trying to comprehend what she's seeing. The moment her mind catches up with her eyes, she's a bouncing ball of energy and excitement.

"Best friend!" she yells, throwing herself at him with her arms wide. She wraps herself around his legs, hugging him tightly.

"I missed you so very much!" Declan leans down, picks her up into his arms, and steps inside while she clings to him, small arms wrapped around his neck.

"Hi, Max. I missed you too." Kicking the door shut, he reaches back and engages the locks before shifting Max slightly to remove the bag from his shoulder and drop it. It falls to the floor with a thud. Then, both arms are wrapped around my daughter.

Her eyes close, a tear rolling down her smiling face as she soaks up every second with her best friend whom she hasn't seen in what she claims is forever.

Declan's eyes find mine from where I stand across the room, an easy smirk playing on his lips at the sight of me. He holds an arm out to me. I don't need to be told twice, and I've missed him like fucking crazy, so I walk toward him, falling into the comfort of his arms.

I'm aware it's only been a few days since we were together, considering I saw him over the weekend, but I'm becoming used to having him around.

For once, I feel safe.

Declan wraps his arm around me, hugging me tightly against his body while he holds Max in the other.

"Missed my girls so much," he mumbles under his breath.

His girls.

Swoon.

Max pulls back to look at him. "Best friend, are you back and staying with us forever?" I raise my hand and wipe the tears from her round pink cheeks.

Before answering, he looks at me, and I see the dread in his eyes about having to respond and risk making my girl sad with his answer.

"Sorry, Max, I'm leaving tomorrow. I have to get back to work in the morning." His words are laced with regret, and I get the feeling that if he could stay here with us, he would. He doesn't want to leave us as badly as we don't want him to leave.

Max's shoulders fall, and her pouty lips curl into a frown. "Oh." She lays her head on his shoulder, one arm still wrapped around his neck. "That's okay, best friend. Mommy and I will be here waiting for you."

"I have something for you." I step away from him, allowing him space to bend and set her down.

"What is it?" she asks, suddenly interested in what he has.

Declan reaches down into his duffle bag, pulls out a rolled-up poster, and holds it with a grin. "We have to hang it in your room. Come on." She grabs his hand and leads him down the hallway.

"Andy, do you have tape or thumbtacks?" he asks over his shoulder, following Max's lead. They're out of sight before I'm able to answer. In the kitchen, I pull open a drawer and grab a roll of Scotch tape. I carry it as I head toward Max's bedroom, curious about what Declan brought for my daughter.

They are standing by the wall across from Max's bed. He unrolls the rolled-up poster in his hands, revealing a US map.

Max stares wide-eyed, interested but unsure what she's even looking at. "Woah! What is it?"

"This is a map for you to mark every state I visit while I'm away. That way, you know where I am," he explains patiently, taking the tape I hold out to him.

My heart skips a beat as I watch the two of them hang the white map on the wall. The thoughtfulness of it has me choking up, unable to believe the man did something so adorable for my daughter. But I shouldn't be surprised. This is the type of person he is.

I sit on her bed across from them, watching them together. Max grabs her set of markers, and Declan chooses a blue one. He explains to her what he's going to do.

"These are all the states, and I'm going to write the cities I'll visit inside each one." The large white map poster is blank except for the abbreviations of each state. He points to the shape of Washington. "This is Washington, where my first show will be, so I will write it here." He points out, making sure Max understands everything he does.

Inside the sizable blank shape, Declan writes *Seattle* and *Auburn*, the two cities he'll be playing while there. Then, he moves on to the other states he'll be visiting.

Arizona, New York, and Pennsylvania.

Four states.

Seven cities.

"You can have your mom show you where I'm at each day. That way, you'll always know." Max nods in understanding, looking between Declan and the map.

"Where do we live?" she asks. He points to the shape of Nevada.

Max takes a purple marker and draws a massive heart over the state, turning to him with a smile when she's done. "There. Now I can see how far away from me you are."

They spend the next hour talking and playing, and I leave them to it while I finish cleaning the kitchen.

Eventually, Declan comes to find me, wrapping his arms around me when he sees me in the kitchen going through the mail I'd brought in earlier but had yet to sort through.

His chin rests on my shoulder as his arms wrap around my waist from behind.

"She's knocked out. She was falling asleep while we were playing with her dolls, so I helped her into bed while she protested and told her that we were playing hide and seek. She closed her eyes to count, then started snoring." He chuckles, the deep, raspy sound sending a wave of lust through me and vibrating against my back.

I'll never get tired of hearing the sound of his voice.

"Good. I'm glad she's asleep." Setting the mail back down on the counter, I turn in his arms to face him, wrapping my arms around his neck. "Thank you for being here." He steps into me, pressing our bodies together.

"No place I'd rather be," he mumbles, crushing his lips against mine in a heated kiss that sends warmth through my bloodstream and a wave of moisture to my core.

Fuck.

His lips are magic.

No one has ever had the ability to turn me on with just a kiss as much as he does.

"Fucking missed you," he mutters against my lips, forcing his tongue inside my mouth and tangling it with mine. One hand slips beneath my T-shirt and grabs my breast, a strangled groan leaving him when he realizes I'm not wearing a bra. His fingers stroke over my already hard nipples, pinching and rolling the pebbled peaks in his fingers.

His other hand slips between us and dips down into my sleep shorts, instantly finding my wet core and clit.

"Fuck. You're not wearing panties." He groans, making me gasp as he spreads my arousal to my clit and begins stroking it in slow lazy movements.

"Don't tease me. I'm too fucking horny for that."

He laughs, teeth sinking into my neck as he continues playing with my nipples and clit, making me gasp against his kiss.

"Let's go to your room so I can spend the night fucking you." He pulls his hand away, sucking his fingers into his mouth. An unladylike growl climbs up my throat at the sight of him sucking his fingers clean, watching the way his eyes roll as the taste of me hits his buds.

Grabbing his hand, I nearly drag him down the hallway toward my bedroom. Once we're inside, I lock the door, and in a matter of seconds, I have myself stripped bare of clothing and am climbing onto the bed, spreading my legs to give him the perfect view of my glistening pussy.

"I need you now," I whine, reaching a hand between my legs, and begin playing with myself. Two fingers disappear inside my pussy for a moment before I drag them up to my clit, rubbing it slowly as I work myself up while watching him.

A smug smirk spreads across his mouth as he takes his time undressing himself. Black briefs are the final clothing item to fall from his magnificent body, revealing his hard cock pointing straight toward me like it knows its way home.

The third arm between his legs is pointing home, and that home is inside of me.

Declan lies down beside me, his large hand wrapping around his shaft as he tugs at himself.

"Get on top of me, Mama. Right fucking now. I need you to

ride me and bring those tits to my face." My stomach fills with nerves at the mention of riding him.

It's not my favorite position, and this'll only be the second time I've ever done it. Vegas with him was the first.

"I want you on top fucking me," I say, continuing to rub my clit, hoping to entice him.

"If you want this dick, you'll climb on it."

When I don't move, he continues pumping his dick, eyes never leaving me, daring me to give in before he does.

Fuck that, and fuck him.

If I weren't a horny hoe right now, I'd call his bluff, but I guess he's calling mine instead.

Swallowing down my fears of not looking good enough, I climb onto my knees and swing a leg over him so he's positioned below me, my legs on either side.

Declan guides his cock in as I slowly lower myself, the same way I've seen in porn videos.

The tip meets my slick entrance, a groan leaving my lips as I continue lowering myself until my ass meets his thighs, and he's seated deep inside of me.

"Holy fuck." I gasp, nipples becoming so hard they can cut glass. This position has him sliding deeper into me than ever before. I'm sure I can feel him in my throat, but I love it. It's equal parts pleasure and pain.

I move slightly onto my knees so he's not as deep, then I drop back down. His head is angled where I need it, rubbing against the spot within me that'll have me soon seeing stars.

"Bring those tits to my face." He groans, one hand on my hip while the other slips between us and rubs my clit.

Giving the man what he wants, I lean forward until his lips wrap around one of my nipples, sucking the pebbled peak and flattening his tongue over it.

We fall into an easy rhythm, with me bouncing on him and him fucking me from below, all while he continues rubbing my clit.

Before long, we're both reaching our climax and falling over the edge, gasping and crying our release into each other's mouths.

After cleaning up, we lay naked beneath the sheets, limbs tangled together as we listen to the sounds of each other breathing, taking comfort in the fact we're together.

Declan is the first to break our silence.

"I'm leaving next week. This is our final week before we head to Seattle to prepare for our first show. We'll be there for a few days beforehand, then two weeks of shows before returning to Vegas." I knew this was coming. I knew our two months was coming to an end, but that doesn't keep my heart from dropping.

"Fuck," I whisper, closing my eyes and hoping he doesn't hear the hurt in my voice. I get the feeling that our lives are about to change forever. Once he leaves, we'll never be the same again. Call it intuition, but I know something is going to change us.

"I know." He tightens his arms around me, pulling my back against his chest as he molds us together. "We're heading out next Monday." This is our last week together.

One week from today, we'll be faced with the ultimate test of whether our relationship can withstand a tour.

"Since we haven't toured in a while, everything is getting fast-tracked. Our label and Benny want us out there performing as much as possible." His arms tighten around me. "I'll be gone for about two and a half weeks, then once we get back, we'll instantly be diving into rehearsals for our upcoming tour. It'll likely be six months before we leave, but until then, the days will be long and busy." I've seen the joy on his face when he's in front of a crowd. Despite his fears, I know how much performing means to him, and I'd never want to keep him from doing what he loves or make him feel bad about it.

I will support him no matter what because that's what good girlfriends do. That's what you do for the ones you love.

"We'll make it work." I force a smile, wishing I could ignore my gut feeling and believe my lie.

"Yeah, Mama. We will." He kisses my shoulder and up to my neck, causing a soft groan to escape. He grabs my leg and raises it to give him better access to my still-wet pussy. Slipping a hand between us, he lines himself up and pushes inside of me.

Declan fucks me slowly from behind while holding me and whispering promises in my ear that I pray he'll be able to keep.

"I'll come back to you."

"You're my everything."

"I want all your tomorrows."

FORTY

Declan

ONE WEEK.

I've spent one week going back and forth between Las Vegas and Loganville. Riot performed at The House of Carnage three nights a week, and after those shows, I was hopping in the car with David and being driven to Loganville to spend the night with my woman, only to go back to Vegas the next day.

Most nights, I got to Andy's apartment after two a.m., and she was always waiting for me despite having to be up for work at six a.m.

I'd bury myself inside of her always wet and ready pussy, then we'd fall asleep in each other's arms, only to wake up hours later and have to part ways to return to work.

By the third day of going home to her, she surprised me by giving me a key to her apartment so I could let myself in and out. Since then, I've been letting myself in so she can sleep.

On the days I didn't have to be in Vegas until later, I'd hang out in her apartment after she left for work, catching up on as much sleep as possible before using her shower and heading to Vegas.

One week of being tired as fuck, but damn, it's been a great week.

I've remained sober after every show, I get to fall asleep with my woman in my arms at the end of the night, and for once, I'm fucking happy.

I know it's only temporary because that happens to people like me. To pieces of shit who cause destruction. Happiness is temporary.

Until my time comes to an end, I'm going to soak it all in and enjoy every fucking second that I can.

It's Monday now, and I'll be in Seattle by tonight. A city I haven't returned to since my divorce.

Camille has already been texting me, thrilled to see me, but I can't say the same. I've been thinking a lot and reading many posts from online support groups, and I've decided that I need to confess. The secret of that night has been weighing heavy on me for so many years, and I can't continue living with it anymore.

Maybe that's selfish, and maybe I'm only trying to make myself feel better. I'm not sure, but I know that Camille deserves to know.

She's been trying to make me feel better about what happened for years, but that's impossible when she doesn't know the truth. She'll hate me, but it's what she deserves. I can't stand her trying to help me and make me feel better when I'm the reason she has to live with her grief.

I've already called her, told her I'd be in Seattle tonight, and asked to meet her tomorrow, but she's away on business for a few days. She owns a successful lingerie company and has been trying to get as much done as possible before going on maternity leave.

It's a good thing, too. It gives me a few more days to get the nerve to see her while I'm back in Seattle.

I'd never believed places could be a trigger, but I was wrong as usual.

New York City and Seattle are my trigger cities. And, of course, we'll be going to both of them within the next two weeks.

There's nothing like being forced to face your demons head-on.

I'm not looking to rid myself of guilt because that's impossible. All I want is to tell her what happened.

If she hates me, that'll make me feel better. I can return to hating myself, too, rather than liking myself as I have been this past week.

For the first time, I really fucking liked myself this week.

My mind has been clear, my heart has been full, and I've been with Andy and Max playing fucking house, which is something I don't deserve.

I only recognize who I am when I hate myself, and that's what I need.

Mostly, I just want Camille to know. It's not right for her to continue living without knowing what I did. What type of person I really am.

Andy took today off work and kept Max home from daycare so the two of them could accompany me to Vegas this morning. She wanted to spend as much time with me as possible, so she's coming to the tour bus with me.

Since David has been driving me all week, I left my Range Rover with her to use. It's Andy, so of course, she protested at first but quickly caved when she realized she'd be getting to drive her dream car.

As soon as I get home, I'm taking her to Vegas and letting her order her very own custom Range Rover or any other car she wants.

We've been driving in a comfortable silence, the car filled with Max's soft snores from the backseat and the low hum of the radio playing a song I don't recognize. My hand is on Andy's thigh while she sits in the passenger seat, her hand on top of mine, needing to touch me as much as I need to touch her. This morning, she woke me up by choking on my cock. The moment my eyes sprung open and I caught sight of her, I was dragging her up by the hair to sit on my dick and ride me until she was shaking with multiple orgasms.

When the trembles faded, I rolled her on her back, buried my head between her legs, and ate my new favorite breakfast. Once she was sensitive and begging me to stop, claiming she couldn't take anymore, I hooked her legs over my forearms and fed my dick back inside of her tight cunt.

Despite taking a shower and cleaning herself, I'm confident her cunt is still dripping with my cum. The mental image makes my lips twitch as I hold back a smirk, my grip on her thigh tightening.

The closer we get to Vegas, the more nervous I become. I've stepped onto a tour bus countless times. It's second nature at this point, but I've never done it while in a sober and clear headspace. I've always used a shot of vodka to take the edge off, then snorted a line the moment I reached my bunk.

This time, I can't do any of that. I can't partake in any of my typical pre-tour routines. Now, with the building anticipation of seeing Camille, my chest is tight.

"Are you okay?" Andy's low voice fills the car, her brown eyes looking at me with concern.

Glancing at her for a moment, I offer a small smile before turning my focus to the road. "I'm seeing Camille in a couple of days," I confess, unsure why I haven't thought to tell her before now.

"You saw her before you moved here, right?"

I nod. "When I lived in New York, we'd meet anytime she came for business. Also, every year for Luca's birthday." His birthday that's also his death date because the universe isn't fucked up enough.

The devil had to punish me for my actions, and because I chose to get high before getting behind the wheel, my son will forever be four years old. He'll never get to grow up or celebrate another birthday.

"This will be different, though. It might just be the last time I see her." I sigh, glancing at my woman beside me once again.

It takes her a moment to realize what I mean by that, but then her eyes widen once it clicks. "You're going to tell her," she says with a gasp. "Holy fuck." She squeezes my hand reassuringly.

"For years, she has helped me while I've spiraled, which she assumes is because of grief. It is grief, but it's also guilt. She deserves to know what happened and what I did. I hate myself every time I look into her eyes and allow her to comfort me because I don't deserve any comfort."

"Dec, that's not true. He was your son, too, and you deserve to grieve and feel whatever you need to feel. Just because you made a mistake doesn't mean you get to continue hating and blaming yourself."

"Who else can I blame? He'd still be here if I had given her the keys. We argued about her wanting to drive because she assumed I was tired. She was ruining my high, so I didn't want to hear her complaining. I jumped into the driver's seat without giving her a choice." I've shared pieces of that night with Andy before, but as I reveal new information, I can only hope she doesn't use it against me to leave me. She cannot fucking abandon me, not now when I'm barely holding on and need her the most.

Two months was all it took for her to become my anchor—the bright light in my darkest days.

"What if you don't tell her? Does she really need to know?" she asks, the worry she feels for me evident in her rushed words. She's worried about me. I love her even more for that.

"I have to, baby. She deserves to know." My whispered words hang in the air, coating us in fear for the future.

We remain silent for the remainder of the drive. Before long, we're pulling into the studio parking lot, where two large tour buses are currently parked. Several people are already outside the buses, loading them with all the supplies we'll need over the next two weeks.

At the sight, Andy squeezes my hand tighter. A quick look over at her reveals her scrunched face. Eyes focused on the busses, lips parted as her chest rises and falls rapidly.

Her plump bottom lip trembles, and she bites down on it to hide it.

Letting go of her thigh, I move my hand to the back of her neck and pull her over to me, crushing our lips together in a bruising kiss. One hand on the back of her neck, the other cupping her face, angling her so I can plunge my tongue into her mouth and stroke it over the roof of her mouth, desperate for another taste of her that'll last me the next two and a half weeks.

Initially, we were going to leave Wednesday since our first show isn't until Thursday, but Benny wanted us to be in Seattle earlier to allow for more rehearsal time since we haven't had as much as we'd usually have before shows.

Pulling away, I rest my forehead against hers, staring into her glossy brown eyes. "You have my heart and all of my tomorrows," I whisper, pressing another lingering kiss against hers.

Outside of the car, I hear loud catcalls from familiar voices. One look out the windshield has me rolling my eyes at the sight of Adam and Damon, whistling and yelling at the sight of me kissing Andy.

Rolling my eyes, I flip them off, a grin on my lips as I turn my attention back to my girl.

"Guess it's time to go." Stealing another quick kiss, I pull away and climb out of the car. Opening the back door, I lean in and kiss a sleeping Max on the forehead.

"You can wake her up. She'll want to see you," Andy says from the passenger seat as she gets ready to get out.

"Max," I say, taking her small hand in my large tattooed one and stroking her soft skin with my thumb. "Wake up, best friend." I give her a little shake.

She groans, dark lashes fluttering as her eyes begin to open. Recognition sets in at the sight of me, and a sleepy smile spreads across her face.

"Hi, best friend. Are we there yet?" she asks with a heavy sigh, arms and legs stretching as I unbuckle the clips of her car seat.

"We're here. You can get out now." I step back to give her some space, holding a hand out as she climbs out of her seat and then jumps out of the car.

She squints against the sun, cupping her hands over her face like a visor.

"I forgot my glasses." She sighs, shielding her eyes as she turns into me, using my large frame to block the sun.

"Diva," Andy mutters from where she now stands beside us. Giving her a wink, I walk to the trunk and open it, grabbing my bags.

It's been a couple of weeks since I returned to the hotel. The last time I was there, I took all my belongings, and since then, I've been staying with Andy each time I've been in Loganville. I still have the hotel room, although I make a mental note to check with Andy and see what she thinks about me checking out of the room once I get back. I'd love nothing more than to continue being with her every chance I can get.

If I knew she'd say yes, I'd get a place for us here in Vegas right fucking now and move her in with me. But Andy is too independent to be taken care of. She'd rather budget than accept my help. Which I can applaud her for, but I hate that she's turned down my help the multiple times I've offered this week.

Giving her money isn't going to break the bank—not when I have millions of dollars that I'll never spend. The most she's been willing to accept is using my rental car and the food I pay for when the three of us go out.

My girl is so goddamn stubborn.

"Hey, Andy!" Adam calls out as we approach. "Hi, Max!" Beside me, Max waves with one hand while the other rubs her tired eyes.

"Sup, guys!" Damon rushes toward my girls, pulling Andy in for a tight hug, then ruffles Max's hair.

"Where's Cole?" I question, noticing he is nowhere to be seen.

Adam and Damon exchange smirks. "Inside saying goodbye to Cece," Damon says, waggling his eyebrows suggestively.

Lucky fucker.

If I could steal Andy away for five minutes in private, I would. I'm dying for another taste of her, but it'll have to wait. This morning will have to be enough to hold me over until I'm able to sink inside her sweet pussy again.

Adam and Damon hug Andy and Max goodbye, and she wishes them good luck before they leave, giving the three of us privacy to be together.

"Max," I squat in front of my mini best friend, "Be good for your mom, okay? Listen to what she says, clean your room, and keep track of the map." She nods, throwing her arms around my neck and hugging me tight.

"Do you promise to come back, best friend?" She sniffles, "If you don't, then I will miss you so super much."

"I promise, Max. I'll be back in two and a half weeks, and the three of us will be together again," I assure her, rubbing her back as I hold her in my arms. No matter what, I will return home to my girls.

When Max lets me go, I kiss her forehead before standing, turning my attention toward Andy.

"You can kiss my mommy," Max says, surprising the hell out of me. "You can be her boyfriend, too." She nods, satisfied with herself.

A grin tugs at the corner of my lips while Andy stands there, speechless. "Why do you say that?" I ask.

"Because you're my best friend and nice to me and my mommy. You should be my mommy's boyfriend, then you'll have to come home to us because you can't leave if you're dating," she says, staring up at me with her wide innocent eyes.

Who am I to argue with that logic?

"Okay, Max, your mom can be my girlfriend." Andy snickers but remains silent.

"No, you have to ask her," Max says, looking at her mom over her shoulder. "And then, Mommy, you'll say yes."

"Andy, will you be my girlfriend?" She looks at me with eyes full of humor, going along with whatever her daughter wants to make her happy.

"Yes, Declan. I'll be your girlfriend."

Max giggles, clapping happily. "Yay!" She shouts, smiling wide as she stares up at us with eyes full of awe.

Andy steps toward me, wraps her arms around my neck, and presses her lips against mine. Her body softens in my arms and melts against me. I'm aware we have the eyes of a child on us, so I don't take the kiss any further despite my cock pressing against my zipper as Andy brushes against me.

Pulling apart, she gives me a slow smile, heated eyes full of lust. "Be safe, and come home to us."

"Always, Mama," I say, resting my forehead against hers. "I will be back." I seal the promise with a kiss.

After another hug and kiss for both of my girls, I load Max back into her car seat, open the door for Andy to climb into the driver's seat, and then watch as they leave, taking my heart with them.

The countdown is on.

Two and a half weeks until I get my heart back.

FORTY-ONE
Declan

Thursday 8:15 a.m.

ME

Does it make me a simp for saying these past few nights without you feels like it's been months?

I miss you, Mama.

ANDY

Absolutely, but I love that you miss me. I miss you too.

ME

Our first show is tonight.

Two weeks, I'll be back with you and Max.

ANDY

We can't wait.

How'd you sleep?

ME

Like shit. I'm going to see Camille today. We're meeting up before I head to rehearsal, and my anxiety is high.

ANDY

You got this, baby. Be honest and let her know how sorry you are.

ME

Sorry doesn't begin to describe what I feel. I don't deserve her forgiveness, and I know I won't get it. I'm not looking for forgiveness, either.

ANDY

Tell her that. Let her know why you're telling her what happened years later.

ME

I'm scared. Wish you were here with me.

ANDY

Me too, baby. Call me if you need me.

ME

You're everything to me, Andy. All of my tomorrows belong to you.

ANDY

Mine too.

SEATTLE.

The city I've been fucking dreading.

It's been years since I've been back here—since my divorce.

The city is as toxic to me as New York. Filled with memories and all the people I let down.

As if fate wanted to fuck me, Seattle is the first city we're stopping in. We'll be here a few more days before moving on to the next.

I've been dreading this day since I knew it had to happen. Always known it was inevitable, and many times over the years, I'd planned to tell Camille but was always too fucking weak. Too much of a coward to confess my sins to the woman I spent four years married to.

The woman who will forever be one of my best friends and have a special place in my life because of the bond we share. Camille will forever have a piece of my soul.

As much as I love her, I'm about to break her heart and destroy the relationship we've been building since the day we divorced.

I'm going to destroy everything... it's what I do.

When we arrived in Seattle on Monday night, Damon, Cole, and Adam had already booked us a penthouse suite to stay in during our time here, which is typical. Every tour, we're only on the bus while traveling, but once we reach each city, we get a hotel room during our stay there.

This time, we're staying together rather than in separate rooms, a decision I've already regretted, considering Damon has had a woman in his bed both nights we've been here.

Leave it to Damon to find the two loudest women in the city and bring them back to our penthouse to fuck. And, of course, I'm the lucky fuck that has to share a wall with him.

Bastard.

After showering and pulling on a pair of black briefs, I walk out of the ensuite, using one of the white fluffy cotton towels to dry my hair. I return to the bedroom as my phone pings with an incoming text.

Looking at the screen, knots return to my stomach.

Fuck.

I have no choice but to suck it up and face her.

I can do this. I have to do this.

She deserves it.

♪ ♪ ♪ ♪ ♪ ♪

BY TEN, I'M SITTING AT A TABLE IN THE BACK OF CARLIE'S CAFÉ, A local place Camille and I would often come to when I lived here, when she comes waddling in, her large pregnant belly perfectly round and protruding.

Seeing her makes my skin pale and my mouth dryer than the Nevada desert. I knew she was pregnant, but the sight is still shocking, especially considering she was always against having another child. Even before Luca died, she never wanted another one. A decision that was cemented by his death.

No matter how in love I am now, it's still jarring to see a woman I used to be in love with move on and be happy. Especially because she's getting everything I couldn't give her. I'm thrilled for Cam because she deserves it, but it's still a shock to the system and enough to send a punch to the heart.

She rushes toward me, dressed in her typical attire of stilettos and a form-fitting dress, lips painted a deep red, and black hair pin straight down her back. Her lips are spread in a wide smile, and her emerald eyes shine in delight at seeing me. Soon, the light in her eyes will be extinguished.

"Declan!" She wraps her arms around me, pulling me down for a hug the best she can around her pregnant belly.

I return the embrace, lingering longer than I should to inhale her sweet, familiar scent and remember what it feels like to have her in my arms.

"Hey, Cam." I exhale, squeezing her a little tighter. We break apart, and I help her into her seat before sitting across from her.

"Hope you still like the lavender honey lattes because that's what I ordered for you." I gesture toward the steaming coffee mug in front of her. I'd ordered as soon as I got here, and our drinks had been delivered moments before she arrived, so they're both still piping hot.

She grins, picks the mug up, and blows into it before taking a careful sip. "Of course I do." She licks her top lip where the milk clung to it. "I've obviously had to limit my caffeine intake, but when I do drink coffee, this is what I get." She takes another sip before setting the cup down, her eyes focusing on me.

Her head tilts to the side, and her bright-green eyes study me, no doubt taking in the dark circles beneath my eyes, disheveled hair from nervously running my fingers through it the past few hours, and hands in a white-knuckle grip holding onto my own coffee mug.

"What's wrong?" she asks, already knowing something isn't right with me. It's amusing that she couldn't tell when something was wrong with me for so many years. Only after we divorced did she begin to notice when I wasn't okay.

All the times I did drugs right under her nose or lied unconvincingly to her face, she either didn't care enough to try and notice or was that blind when it came to me. I'll admit I did try to hide the drug use, but there were many times when I was sloppy, and it was evident that I was using.

When she saw me with red eyes, dilated pupils, or slurred words, she never called me out. Now, I wonder why. She must have known.

Clearing my throat, I decide to dive head first into the year's past due conversation rather than begin a meaningless conversation. "Cam, I need to tell you something."

Her eyes widen, and her posture straightens as she raises her guard, already on high alert by the tone of my voice. "Are you using again?" she asks in a pained whisper.

She knows about my relapse a few months ago and knows exactly how long I've been sober this time around, so her question isn't surprising, but for once, I wish everyone wouldn't expect the worst from me.

Guess I can't blame anyone when the worst is all I've ever given them.

Shaking my head, I shove my fingers through my dark hair, needing to do something with my twitching fingers. "No, I'm still sober. I have been doing really good, actually."

A proud smile crosses her face. Camille leans forward and places a hand on mine, giving me the strength to speak. "Tell me whatever you need to tell me."

Taking a deep breath, I hold it and count to ten, then slowly exhale. Holding her gaze, I confess my biggest sin to her before I can think better of it. "Camille, I want you to know that I'm so fucking sorry and that I know what a worthless piece of shit I am. I've been beating myself up daily for years, and I've wanted to tell you so many times, but I couldn't." She shakes her head in confusion, opening her mouth to speak, but I cut her off, needing to say what I've got to say before she responds. "I'm the reason Luca is gone."

Pity fills her green eyes. "Declan, we've discussed this. What happened that night was an accident. I know I blamed you in the past, but that was just because I was angry and grieving. I know it was an accident." For a long time, she blamed me, and one night, during a fight, she told me that she blamed me because I was the one driving. That should've been when I told her what happened, but I didn't. Instead, I let her be angry and then apologized for being angry and for every hurtful thing she said that I deserved.

She fucking apologized and felt like shit, and I still kept my mouth shut.

What the fuck is wrong with me?

"I was high," I confess, rendering her speechless. "Before I got behind the wheel, I'd just snorted some coke. I wasn't tired from working. I was out of it because I was high." She pulls her hand away from me, face paling as she stares at me across the table, green eyes shining with tears that spill free and cascade down her pale cheeks.

"You're lying. You wouldn't do that when our son was going to be in the car." Before that night, I never had. Luca had never even seen me high or drunk, but something changed in me that night. The voices became too much, and I wanted to feel free, so I gave in, not considering that my family would soon be in the car.

Tears fill my own eyes as I stare at my ex-wife, seeing the emotions that fill her eyes and change her face. Her features switch from confusion to anger to denial.

"You're lying." Her eyes beg me to tell her I'm lying, but I can't. "Why are you lying?"

"I'm not lying, Cam. The accident was my fault. I was high and didn't see the red light." I was under the influence, ran a red light, and ended up in the intersection where we were hit by a semi-truck. Had I been sober, I would've noticed the red light and stopped.

Had I fucking been sober, my son would still be here. He'd get to grow up and celebrate every birthday. He'd get to experience what tomorrow will bring.

A strangled sob escapes her, earning curious glances from other patrons in the restaurant, but I don't pay them any attention. My sole focus is Camille.

A public space wasn't the best place to have this conversation, but I can't change it now. We're already here.

"You—" She chokes on her words, mascara-coated tears running down her face, leaving black streaks. "You killed our baby." Her red bottom lip wobbles and my heart fucking breaks at the sight of the strongest woman I know falling apart in front of me.

"How could you?" She hiccups, mouth open as she sucks in air. "How could you?" she repeats, voice louder.

When I open my mouth, she raises a hand to silence me. She abruptly stands, the chair falling back with the movement. "I need to get out of here." Not bothering to wipe away the black stains, she rushes out of the café, and I follow right behind her.

Once we're outside, she places one hand on the brick wall of the building and the other on her pregnant belly, shoulders shaking with her loud sobs. "How could you!" she screams, anger and so much fucking pain swimming in her now dull green eyes.

"You have no idea how much I wish I could return to that night and change what I did. Or how many nights I wish it were me that died instead of him." Tears sting my eyes as they roll down my cheeks. My heart breaks at the sight of her, and I ache to hold her, but I remain rooted in place, knowing her well enough that she'd never let me touch her.

Steeling her spine, Camille narrows her eyes into a glare at me, using the back of her hands to wipe her face, eyes never leaving mine. "Yeah, you should've." Her words strike me like a fist that just delivered the first blow. "You're right, Declan. You are worthless, and it should've been you." Her words are delivered with so much venom that it catches me by surprise. I stumble back, catching myself before I trip, but the venom continues to spill from her lips, "You just can't seem to stop hurting me, can you?"

She steps toward me, fury in her eyes. If looks could kill, I'd drop dead on the sidewalk. Without warning, her palm strikes my cheek, forcing my head to jerk to the side, leaving my cheek stinging.

"Go to hell," she says through gritted teeth before disappearing from my sight.

Too late, babe, I'm already there.

FORTY-TWO
Declan

My hands shake as the final lyric and strum from the bass ring out into the air. Droplets of sweat line my forehead, dark strands sticking to my face. My T-shirt is damp with sweat, clinging to my skin. My heart races as I stare into the crowd of blurred, screaming faces that blend through my dazed vision.

Camille's words have been playing on repeat in my mind all night long. Throughout the entire show, all I've heard is her voice.

You killed our baby.

How could you?

You are worthless.

Go to hell.

Too late, babe. I'm already there. Been there since my son died on that dark rainy night four years ago, all because I decided to get high before getting behind the wheel.

Nothing she says to me could ever be worse than what I tell myself daily.

My vision is blurred as I drag myself from the stage. The typical rush of adrenaline I feel after performing is missing from my veins. Instead, all I hear is the voices in my head telling me what a fuck-up I am. Telling me how better off I'd be if I were to numb the pain.

Just numb it.

You can do it.

You know how.

Time seems to pass me by. I don't remember getting in the car with my bandmates and going to the after-party in the penthouse suite we rented for the nights we were here.

The suite is already blaring with music when we arrive. Someone must've given them the key to enter, but I don't pay much attention. My bandmates rush in, oblivious to my inner turmoil as they rush across the threshold, joining the groupies that are desperate for Adam and Damon's dick.

Two blonde women rush to my side at the sight of me, their hands on my body, stripping me from my black leather jacket, and I let them, not looking at either of them. The woman on my right slips a hand beneath my T-shirt, raking her acrylic fingernails along my stomach. The sensation causes my stomach to twist.

Disgust fills me as my dark gaze turns to her. I straighten my spine, my height towering over her petite figure as I stare at the woman. Two months ago, she would've been the type of woman I'd be attracted to. I would've had her bent over the closest surface by now, pumping my cock into her, but staring at her now, even as she tries to push her fake tits against me, it does nothing for me.

All I feel is disgust.

Every fiber of my being, mind, body, and soul, is claimed by a mouthy, curly-haired woman who agreed to give me all of her tomorrows. I don't want the two girls in front of me, no matter what filthy promises are spilling from their overfilled pink lips.

Their mouths are moving, but I don't register what they're saying, though the implication is clear.

Shoving them aside, I walk toward the kitchen, ripping open

the fridge and grabbing a water bottle. I twist the lid with force, and the cool liquid spills from the bottle's jostle down my hand.

Bringing the bottle to my lips, I take a long drink, the coldness calming my raspy throat and cooling my heated skin.

Setting the bottle down, my eyes flicker to the liquor bottles spread along the counter. Across from me, I spot a woman snorting lines of white powder from her friend's cleavage.

You know you want it.

Numb the pain.

Numb the pain.

Numb the fucking pain.

My hands curl into fists, lips parting as my breathing becomes heavy. Chills trickle down my spine, the liquor and drugs calling to me in the sweetest siren song that has me aching to answer.

Adam had assured me this would be a drug free party, but clearly didn't get the fucking memo.

With every ounce of willpower I can muster, I swipe my water from the counter, shoving my way through the crowd as I stalk toward my bedroom, needing to get away from all the half-naked bodies and temptation.

Temptations that have me aching to give in and allow my mind to be free from everything that taunts me. Free from the haunting past that I can't seem to escape, no matter how many years have passed and how much numbing I've done.

Escaping is all I want to do. It's all I've ever wanted to do.

It's all I wanted when I'd be forced to watch my mother shoot drugs into her veins.

It's what I wanted when he would enter my bedroom each night with whiskey on his breath.

It's what I wanted when I lay helplessly listening to my ex-wife scream while our son died.

Escaping reality is what helps me. It's what I need.

Do it.

Do it.

Just fucking do it.

You know how.

I slam the bedroom door behind me, leaning my back against it as I stand there, heaving, unable to capture enough air into my lungs.

What I need is to be saved. Saved from myself. Saved from the destruction that follows me.

Making my way toward the king-size bed in the middle of the room, I sit on the white sheets and reach into my pocket. Pulling out my phone, I scroll my list of favorites until I land on my girl.

My saving grace.

The one I don't deserve.

Andy.

Selecting her contact, I press call and bring the device to my ear, silently begging her to answer.

Come on, baby.

I need you.

I fucking need you.

The ringing stops, the robotic answer of her voicemail filling my ears.

No, baby, no.

With a bottle in my hand and tears in my eyes, I bring my phone to my blurred line of sight and lock the screen.

Calmness washes over me as I allow myself to give into the demons that constantly whisper in my ear, telling me how to ease the pain. Even if it's just for tonight, I want to end it.

I want to drown out the look in Camille's green eyes when I revealed what I did that night and the feel of her palm against my cheek.

Want her voice to fade away as she told me she'd never forgive me and wished it was me who died that night.

I've felt dead for years, but Andy has slowly brought me back to life, not that I deserve it. She's made me feel alive for the first time in years.

She's responsible for waking my soul, but I don't fucking deserve it.

Don't deserve a woman like her.

Don't deserve to feel anything other than misery.

A life of living in hell on earth is what I deserve.

I knew my time with Andy was temporary, and I'd been right.

She's too good for me, and it's time to let her go.

Let her go.

Let him go.

Let go of it all.

Finding myself back in the kitchen, I grab the bottle of vodka from the counter, twist the cap off, and bring it to my lips, pausing momentarily before it touches my awaiting mouth.

Tears burn my eyes.

I'm tired of fighting. Tired of being strong when I know what a failure I constantly am.

"I'm sorry, baby," I whisper, wishing my words would carry to Andy so she knows how I feel.

Pressing the cool rim of the bottle to my lips, I tilt my head back and have my first drink in nearly three months.

The smooth liquor slips down my throat, burning my stomach as it settles, filling me with warmth and an all too familiar feeling.

I chug until my throat burns and the voices in my head disappear.

A woman appears at my side, hands roaming over my body as I fuel myself with liquor, needing relief more than I've realized.

But it's okay. I'll be alright. I'm only letting loose for tonight, and I'll be good again tomorrow.

I promise. I'll remain sober after tonight.

I've been sober for a while, and I deserve this. Just a little reward to myself. I fucking deserve it.

The woman wraps her small pale hand around the bottle and pulls it away from my mouth, the liquid spilling down my chin and the front of my shirt with the movement.

My eyes flicker down to hers, a smirk on her lips as she brings the bottle to her lips and licks over the opening where my mouth had been before drinking.

I'm sure she's trying to be seductive, but even in my drunken state, I don't want her. I won't touch anyone else, no matter what. My dick belongs to Andy. Regardless of if she knows it or not, she's the only one that will ever be on my cock again.

How can I prove that my dick is only for her?

My tattooed fingers drum along the cold marble countertop, the ink catching my eye. A smirk spreads along my lips as a lightbulb clicks inside my vacant head.

Got an idea.

I'll get her name tattooed along my shaft.

Fuck yeah.

I'm going to do it.

Laughter spills free from my lips at my latest idea.

"What's so funny?" the woman asks, standing so close to me that I can feel the warmth from her body.

"I'm getting another tattoo," I tell her, a broad smile across my lips.

She smirks. "Oh yeah? Where?"

"My dick," I confess, turning away from her and searching the cabinets for another bottle of vodka. There's no way I'm putting my mouth back on that bottle as she's touched it.

My girl wouldn't like that. I wouldn't want that.

Glee sparkles in my eyes the moment I spot the unopened bottle of vodka in the cabinet, and I pull it out, cracking open the sill before taking a quick swig.

"Can I watch you get it? Never seen anyone tattoo their dick before."

I shrug, not sparing her a glance. "Know anywhere that's open tonight that'll do it?"

I half expect her to say no, but to my surprise, she nods. "Actually, I do know a place. Let's have some fun, and then we'll go."

"I have a girlfriend, and I'm not fucking you," I blurt out, needing her to know instantly. I'm already crossing lines by standing close to her and talking.

She laughs. "Good, me too." Then she reaches inside her bra, pulling out an all too familiar little baggie containing white powder that instantly has my heart racing and palms sweating.

Fuuuuuuck.

My gums ache for a taste.

The short brunette opens the baggie, dumps some out on the counter, pulls out her wallet, and begins cutting lines with a credit card.

Meanwhile, my eyes remain fixated on the powder, desperate for my chance to soothe my racing heart and mind.

She rolls up a dollar bill, snorts a line, then cuts another before offering it to me.

Who am I to say no when she's being so polite?

"Don't mind if I do." I grin like the fucking Cheshire cat. Leaning toward the counter, I grab the rolled bill and quickly snort the line. Not bothering to ask permission, I cut a second, then snort that one instantly.

My nose tingles and my body expels energy as I let out a weird sound, a mixture of moans and laughter.

Perspiration lines my forehead, and my body suddenly feels overheated. I tear my T-shirt off, grab the bottle of vodka, and take another long drink.

The feeling that courses through my body is a feeling I've missed. So fucking much.

Finally, my mind is clear. I'm free from the pain that has me in a chokehold every day. Free from the voices in my head telling me what a fuck up I am, as if I wasn't already aware.

From across the room, I look up to see Adam staring back at me with disappointment.

Fuck him.

Fuck anyone who is trying to ruin my high.

Flipping him off, I return to my new friend beside me.

Before I have a chance to make my lips move, my body begins to vibrate.

"Holy fuck." I gasp. "I'm vibrating." I place a hand on her shoulder, wondering if she can feel it.

I've never felt this before.

Shiiiiit. I'm vibrating.

What the fuck?

I laugh, chugging another mouthful of liquor.

The vibrating continues until I realize something. "Can you hear me vibrating?" I chuckle. "I can hear my body vibrating." I sway with the movement.

"It's your phone." She reaches into my front pocket, pulls out the magic vibrating device, and sets it on the counter beside the white lines she cut.

When did she cut those? I don't remember seeing her do it.

Fuck, she must be magic and did it with her mind.

Magic. Wow. My mind is blown.

The vibrating continues, my red eyes looking down at the screen. "Is that your girlfriend?" the woman without a name asks, looking between me and my phone.

Andy's calling. My favorite photo of her on display. I'd taken that photo before I left while she'd been in bed, naked and wrapped in sheets. Her curly hair is thrown over her pillow, the sheet is low enough to reveal ample cleavage, her eyes closed with long dark lashes, and the slightest smile is on her lips. I'm unsure what she'd been dreaming about, but it was enough to cause the most angelic smile.

I'm glad her eyes are closed. That way she can't see me through the magic vibrating device and judge me.

Holy shit.

Andy is calling.

Fuck me. I can't answer like this.

Not when I've broken my promise to her.

Sorry, baby. Give me tonight. Tomorrow, I'll return to trying to be the man you deserve. But for tonight, I'm escaping.

Looking away from my phone and ignoring the woman's question, I lean down and help myself to another line.

"What's your name?" I ask as I wipe away the cocaine residue from my nostrils.

"Amber."

"Well, Amber. Are you coming with me, or what?" She raises her dark brows in question, so I clarify, "To get my girl's name tattooed on my cock. You can't watch, but you can come."

Her face lights up, and quickly nodding, she claps her hands together. "Yes! Let's go."

"Will your girlfriend have a problem with it?"

A mischievous grin spreads across her lips. "My girlfriend will be the one tattooing you."

What the actual fuck?

"No. No way." I may be a fucking idiot, but I'm not stupid enough to let another woman touch my dick and stick her face in it. Maybe that's sexist, but I'd rather have someone with a cock doing the tattoo. That way they know what it feels like.

Amber rolls her hazel eyes and pulls off her sweater, revealing two colorful arms full of beautiful designs. "Mora is the best in the fucking state. She's done all my tats, and she's tatted and pierced a couple dicks before. Promise you'll be in good hands." She takes my lack of protest as my consent.

"Glad that's settled. Finish up. I'll call to give her a heads up." She removes her pink phone from her pocket, walks away, and leaves me with my little white best friend.

Turning to the marble countertop, I smile at the drug. "Sorry for breaking up with you. I'm back now," I whisper, dipping my finger into the powder before rubbing it across my gums.

Tomorrow, I'll have regrets.

Tomorrow, I'll repent for my sins and return to my life of hell.

Tonight I will have fun with my old and new friends.

Tonight I'm free.

After taking another shot of vodka, I replay my conversation with Amber and burst out laughing when I realized what I had agreed to.

Holy shit. I'm getting my fucking dick tattooed.

FORTY-THREE

Declan

I HAVE THREE THOUGHTS WHEN I WAKE IN THE MORNING.

First, why does my dick hurt?

Second, why does my head hurt?

Third, why the fuck is it so bright?

With a groan, I pry open my heavy eyes, squinting against the sunlight shining on my face. Blinking rapidly to clear my vision, I stare at the window from where I lie. "Where the fuck am I?" I wipe my eyes, groaning in pain at the stiffness in my aching body.

My vision clears enough for me to see where I'd slept. An ugly, small green couch is below me, which explains why I'm stiff. One leg is thrown over the back of the sofa, and the other hangs over the arm of the couch, my body too long for the small space.

Rubbing a hand down my face, I move my hand down my chest, desperate to ease the discomfort of my aching dick. The moment my fingertips touch my bare cock, I freeze.

Holy fuck.

Why the fuck am I naked?

I sit up quickly despite the protest of movement from my throbbing head and tighten the blanket across my lap.

I'm in an apartment; the space is an open floorplan with a kitchen directly in front of me. The coffee pot on the counter is the first thing to draw my attention, making me desperate for the bitter taste of caffeine.

Elbows on my knees, my head falls into my hands, and I take a moment to remember where I'm at and what happened last night.

Closing my eyes, the memories seem to rush back to me.

The meeting with Camille.

Drinking a bottle of vodka.

Snorting coke in the kitchen of the penthouse.

Leaving with a woman I had just met despite Adam's protests.

The tattoo.

Holy fuck. The tattoo.

Shoving the blanket off my lap, I stare down at my exposed cock with wide eyes.

Oh my god, I tattooed my fucking dick.

Along the shaft, in bold black letters, is a name.

Andy.

Shiitttt.

Somehow, I don't think she'll find it as funny as I had last night. Especially when she finds out the reason I did it was because I was out of my fucking mind with drugs and alcohol.

"Good—" a familiar voice catches me off guard. "Oh, god! Put your dick away!" I scramble to cover myself with the blanket, looking up to see Amber standing there with her eyes closed. Peeking through her fingers, she gives a nod once I'm covered.

"Good morning," she says, entirely too fucking cheerful. "Coffee?" She makes her way into the kitchen and begins preparing a pot of coffee.

"Yes, please," I mumble, my voice raspy. My tongue is heavy in my dry mouth, my head throbbing. Every part of me aches, but what hurts more than the physical pain is my heart.

My heart fucking aches at the memory of seeing Camille break down and everything she said to me afterward.

"Do you have Tylenol?" I ask, finding my jeans on the floor and pulling them on, followed by my shirt. I don't see my boxer briefs anywhere, but with how tender my dick is, I don't want any more fabric rubbing against me than required.

"What happened last night?" Reaching the island, I sit on one of the stools, graciously accepting the bottle of pain reliever and water that Amber passes toward me.

"Well, my girlfriend tattooed your dick, we came back here, and the two of you decided to see who could drink the most. She's already left for work this morning, so clearly, you're the winner." She clicks her tongue, looking me up and down.

Shaking three pain pills into the palm of my hand, I pop them into my mouth and then wash them down with a glass of water. The cool liquid slides down my throat, easing my dry mouth.

Amber continues explaining our night. "You were complaining about your dick hurting, so you took your clothes off and then passed out on the couch. Neither of us wanted to move your naked ass." She grins, grabbing two mugs from a cabinet as the bitter aroma of coffee fills the air.

I watch silently as she pours two mugs and then slides one over to me. Thanking her, I lift it to my lips and slowly sip the burning liquid, needing the caffeine in my body as quickly as possible.

Glancing at the clock on the stove, I groan at the red light displaying the time.

10:37 a.m.

"Fuck, I need to go." I'm late for rehearsals, and no doubt Benny is going to have my ass for it.

"I'll take you wherever you need to go," she offers.

"Thanks, but I'll call a ride."

"Up to you, but it might be quicker if I drive you." She's right. Plus, I don't have anyone to call for a lift, considering everyone I know is likely at the venue already for rehearsals. And I'm not about to call an Uber and risk having my photo all over the media, being shown leaving a random apartment building in the morning. Andy would see that shit and get the wrong idea.

Andy. Fuck.

She will never speak to me again once she finds out what I did last night. After I promised to fight for her, she'll never forgive me for relapsing.

Fuck it.

It'll be okay.

It has to be.

It's fine.

I'll do what I've always done in the past. Have fun and party for two weeks, then when it's time to return home, I'll clean myself up and get sober again.

Nothing I haven't done before.

Fuck it. I deserve it. Just a little fun, a little pick me up to get through the next two weeks to make myself feel better.

It'll be okay. I can control myself.

As if reading my thoughts, Amber holds up a familiar baggie in front of me. "Is coffee good enough for you, or do you need something stronger?" She smirks, my hand already reaching out to grab it.

This time, I don't bother cutting lines. I pour some out on the back of my hand and snort, needing the instant boost it will give me.

Inhaling, I wipe away the excess powder from my nostrils and lick off the residue from the back of my hand.

The drugs hit my system, my body becoming free from worry and aches. "Fuck, that's good. Can I have this?" Reaching into my pocket, I grab my wallet and tuck the baggie inside, tossing some cash onto the counter before she has a chance to answer.

"It's a pleasure doing business with you." She grins smugly, scoops up the cash, and tucks it into her bra. "If you need more of that, or anything else, let me know. I can help you out while you're here."

"You a dealer?" I chug the rest of my coffee, then shove my wallet back into my pocket, standing to my feet.

"Don't ask questions, Declan. Just give me your phone so I can give you my number, and text if you need me." Considering she was at the party in the penthouse last night and came with drugs, I'm sure the answer is yes.

Good to know. I'll see her before I leave. I know that for sure.

Pulling my phone from my pocket, I unlock the screen, ignoring the notifications, and slide the phone across the table toward her. She picks it up, yellow-painted fingernails flying over the screen as she types in her number and saves her contact. Once she passes it back, I check the notifications, cringing at all the messages and missed calls. Rather than reading and responding to the individual messages from my friends and Benny, I send a quick text in our group chat.

ME

Overslept. On my way to the venue.

Exiting the chat, I slip my phone back into my pocket, giving Amber my attention. "If you don't mind, I'll take a ride."

"Grab your shoes, and let's go."

By the time we reach Amber's car, a sleek back BMW SUV, I return my phone to my hand after giving her the address and read over the messages from Andy, sighing at the words on my screen.

I'm so fucking sorry, baby.

ANDY

How'd it go with Camille?

You okay?

I'm here if you need me.

Have a great show tonight.

I watched clips of the show online. You were amazing, Dec. Wish I could've been there with you.

Good morning. I hope today is great for you.

I know you're busy. Sorry if I'm texting a lot.

We'll talk when you can. I don't want to be that girlfriend who blows your phone up daily.

While she's been worrying about me, I've been out all night with a woman I just met, getting a tattoo and getting high.

Boyfriend of the fucking year.

I send Andy a quick text just as we arrive at the venue Riot will be playing at tonight.

ME

Sorry, Mama. Busy as fuck. You have no idea how much I miss you.

ANDY

I miss you, too.

ME

You have all of my fucking tomorrows, I promise you that.

Got to go. Know that I'm thinking about you and can't wait to get home to you.

"Thanks for the ride. We'll be having another party tonight, so you should come." I offer, taking my seat belt off and opening the door.

Amber smirks. "Alright. I'll bring the party favors and see you tonight." With a grin, I climb out of the car and then make my way inside.

Before going to find my manager and bandmates, I make a brief pit stop in the bathroom long enough to splash water over my face and appear more alive than I am. Since I wasn't able to brush my teeth, I pop in a piece of gum and cut a line on the side of the bathroom sink.

With the drugs coursing through my veins, I feel invincible. My mood has already improved, and I feel strong enough to put on the best fucking show possible tonight.

Staring at myself in the mirror, the sight of my wide eyes makes me chuckle. "I'm back, baby!" I yell at my reflection, daring the unrecognizable person in the mirror to say something.

Backstage, I find Benny pacing as he speaks on the phone, his left hand on his hip while his right has a white-knuckle grip on the device. The moment he notices me, his dark eyes narrow into a scowl, and he abruptly ends the call, smashing his finger against the end call button.

"Where the fuck have you been?" He holds his arms out, demanding an answer.

A lazy smile crawls across my face. I won't let him ruin my buzz. Not when there's nothing to worry about. I feel energized and ready to give the best show and have the best night possible.

"Overslept." My answer comes easily since, for once, I'm telling the truth.

"Where were you?" I open my mouth to lie, but he must sense that's my plan because he cuts me off by pointing a finger in my face. "And don't fucking lie and tell me at the hotel because I know you weren't there." Of course, he knew I wasn't there. He probably had someone check my room and found my bed empty and cold.

"Out with a friend. Passed out and overslept."

His eyes narrow as he studies me, but I keep my gaze on him and a smirk on my lips.

Benny is like family to me. He's been cleaning up my shit for far too long and only wants the best for me. I know this. He jumped through many hoops to make these shows happen and to fast-track our upcoming tour, so I'm not going to disappoint him by allowing him to find out I'm using again.

Besides, it's only temporary. Just long enough to keep my energy up for these next two weeks and the demons at bay. Then I'll be better.

"Relax, Benny, I'm okay." I release a breath. "Saw Cam yesterday and needed to clear my head after that. Really, I just had a late night with a friend. Won't happen again." Seemingly convinced, he nods, then pats me on the shoulder.

"Get out there and don't be late again."

"Yes, sir!" I run away from him and make my way toward the stage, arms outstretched as the beat of Damon's drums syncs in tune with my heartbeat, the two of us becoming one.

Stepping behind the microphone, I jump in with vocals at the exact moment I need to, falling quickly into place beside my bandmates.

I ignore Adam's gaze, not wanting to hear anything he says. He's the only one who saw me last night, but it isn't the time for a lecture.

Right now, I need to let the music feed my soul and soothe me in the way only it can.

WHEN THE CONCERT ENDS, I'M THE FIRST ONE OFF THE STAGE, rushing into my dressing room to get my hands on the mini bottles of vodka I'd taken from the bar and hid in here for after the show. My thirst is too intense, and waiting until I return to the penthouse is too far away.

I need a drink now.

Locking the door to my dressing room, I dig in the back of the cabinet where I hid my treasure and pull out the four mini bottles. Victory shines on my face at the sight, my mouth watering for a taste.

Twisting off the top, I toss the lid behind my back, then bring the bottle to my mouth and swallow it down in one gulp. The vodka is the cheap shit that tastes more like rubbing alcohol, but it does what I need it to do, which is calm my mind and give me the warmth in my veins I've been needing.

Once one bottle is finished, I repeat the process by gulping down the other three, warmth settling in my stomach.

I hide the bottles in the bottom of the trash can after popping a piece of gum into my mouth, hoping it'll be enough to get the scent of liquor off my breath.

When we return to the penthouse, another party is happening when we enter our room. I make a mental note to ask who is allowing these people into our room and arranging for the parties, but it'll have to wait for another day.

Girls swarm to me the moment I enter, but I shove them all aside, pushing through the crowd until I reach my temporary room. I've been dying for a shower, and before I can relax and enjoy myself, getting under warm water is exactly what I need to do.

Locked safely in my bedroom, I remove my clothes, letting them fall silently to the floor. Reaching into my duffle bag, my hands close around the small familiar bottle of cherry vanilla-scented body wash, the same one Andy had on the shelf in her shower. I took it the morning I left, wanting her scent while we were apart.

Besides, I'd bought a new bottle of soap for her while we were at the cherry festival, so I took it upon myself to steal the half-empty bottle she'd had in her shower.

With the soap in one hand and my phone in the other, I step

inside the glass walk-in shower and set my phone up on the little shelf on the opposite side of the shower head.

Turning the water on, I let the cold water rush over my heated body, sending chills down my spine as I bring up my contact list and FaceTime, my girl.

Five rings pass before she answers, and her smiling face fills my phone screen.

"Hey, Mama," I rasp, relief rushing over me at the sight of her. The purple glow from the hanging lights in her bedroom illuminates her face, cascading her in the soft purple hue.

"Hi, baby." The sound of her voice has my heart racing. She's the calm to my storm. She's all I needed—this moment, right now. She'll be all I need, and as I stare at her beautiful face, I promise myself to do better—to be better—because that's what she deserves. "Are you in the shower?" she asks, bringing the phone closer to her face to study the background.

I chuckle, "Yup. Just got back to the hotel a little bit ago. I was sweaty as fuck and needed a shower." She nods in understanding. "Plus, I was hoping to see your tits to help me take care of this." Grabbing my phone, I tilt it downward until she's able to see my hard cock jutting between my legs.

Taking my phone from the shelf, I move it up to the higher shelf so she has the perfect view of my face and dick in the same frame, double-checking the image. A slow smirk spreads across my mouth once I confirm she can see all of me. The distance is far enough away that she won't be able to spot my tattoo, especially once my fist is wrapped around my cock.

Grabbing her soap bottle from the lower shelf, I squirt some shower gel into my palm, put it back down, and rub my hands together to lather it up.

Andy notices the familiar bottle and clicks her tongue. "I knew you stole my body wash."

I shrug. "What can I say? I wanted your scent with me." I wrap my hand around my shaft, lathering the hardness up with the cherry-scented soap, the smell invading my nostrils and making my dick ache even further. Thankfully, she won't see my latest tattoo from this angle with the suds. Thank fuck. I'm waiting until I see her in person to show her.

With the tattoo still fresh, I'm probably not supposed to jerk off or fuck with it yet, but I have to do something to relieve the ache between my legs.

"Wish you were here in front of me, down on your knees, taking me down your throat like the good girl you are," I say, groaning, my fist pumping over my length.

At the sight of me pleasuring myself, her lips part, breathy sounds escaping her. "It's not very nice to tease me when we're not together for me to do anything."

"What would you do, Mama?" My strokes are slow, and groans caught low in my throat, "Get naked, then tell me."

Andy sets the phone down long enough to remove her clothing and then returns the camera to her face. There's some shuffling, then the click of a switch. The warm glow from the lamp on her nightstand illuminates her body, revealing bare, soft skin. She lowers the camera until her tits come into view, showing nipples as hard as my dick.

"I'd let you lie back while I get on my knees and take your cock in my mouth all the way to the back of my throat." She lowers the camera until her pussy comes into view. Spreading her legs wide, I'm given the perfect view of her glistening cunt.

"Fuuuuck, baby." I groan, tightening my fist as I continue stroking myself root to tip, squeezing the crown. "Look how wet you are. Touch yourself."

Like the good girl she is, she obeys. Using two fingers, she spreads her pussy lips open to reveal her wetness. Two fingers press against her entrance, then slowly sink inside of her. Bringing the wetness up to her clit, she slowly begins massaging herself, moans filling the speakers.

"Yeah, baby, you'd swallow my dick so good, but I want you on my face as you suck me off. Let me fuck that sweet pussy with my tongue and fingers until you're drowning me with your juices."

She adds a third finger, alternating between rubbing her clit and fucking herself with her fingers. "Not enough. I need your fingers on my clit and your cock filling me."

"Soon, baby. The minute I get home to you, I'm going to fill your pussy every chance I get." My balls tighten, and my movements quicken, warm tingles settling at the base of my spine. "Fuck, I'm close."

"Me, too." She gasps, thighs beginning to tremble with the onslaught of her upcoming release.

"Let me see your face as you come," I grit out with a clenched jaw as I chase my climax while inhaling the sweet scent of cherries.

She brings the camera to her face, revealing curly hair spread across her olive-green pillowcase, mouth open with soft cries, eyes hooded with pleasure.

I know the moment she gives in and falls off the edge of the cliff she's been climbing because her eyes roll in the back of her head before closing, her mouth widens, her back arches, and her cries become almost silent whimpers.

The sight of her giving into euphoria is what sends me over the edge. I give in, and with a long groan of pleasure, I release warm ropes of cum shooting across my hand and the shower wall.

"Fuck," we say in unison, sated smiles spreading as we come down from our release.

I quickly rinse off my hand and the wall, watching as my cum circles the drain before disappearing.

"Thanks for that, baby. Two weeks, then we'll be together."

She flips onto her side, pulling the blankets over her naked body. "Two weeks," she agrees with a yawn.

"Get some sleep. We'll talk later," I say, quickly washing the rest of my body.

She hums, eyes closed and already giving into the lure of sleep.

With her sleeping face on my screen, I mute myself so any noise in the background doesn't disturb her, and I watch her while I finish my shower, get dressed into a pair of black boxer briefs, and climb into bed.

Despite the party going on outside my bedroom door and the loud bass of the music, I ignore it, focusing solely on the angel sleeping on my screen.

My body fills with torment. "I'm sorry, baby," I whisper. "Please forgive me."

FORTY-FOUR

Andy

DECLAN

We made it to AZ last night. I'll call you after tonight's show.

ME

Can't wait to hear from you. I miss the sound of your voice.

DECLAN

Me too, Mama. Been so fucking busy.

ME

Don't forget about me tonight. I want to talk if you can.

DECLAN

I could never forget about you. You're forever marked on me. Mind, body, and soul.

ME

I got your gift last night ;) Thank you for it
photo of purple rabbit vibrator

video attachment using purple rabbit vibrator

DECLAN

Fuuuuuck baby.

Now I'm sitting here hard as fuck about to jerk off and imagine I'm balls deep inside of your tight hot pussy.

ME

Soon, baby.

DECLAN

Not soon enough.

IT'S BEEN OVER A WEEK SINCE DECLAN LEFT, YET IT FEELS MUCH longer with the lack of communication. His texts throughout the day are rare, and at night they become nonexistent. I've tried calling and texting when I know he's likely to be at the hotel after the show, but every call goes unanswered. Sometimes, he'll respond and say he got held up having to do something with his bandmates after the show; other times, he's too tired to talk.

I hate that I've become the clingy girlfriend who waits beside her phone waiting for the moment it beeps with a new message. My phone has been glued to my hand since he left.

Declan is doing what he loves. Singing the songs he wrote that mean everything to him and being swarmed by fans every night. Of course, his days no longer revolve around me, but I wish they did. I miss the man I've fallen in love with.

Negative thoughts often creep in.

Declan's one of the most famous rock stars in the world; why would he waste his time with me?

Everyone outside of small-town Loganville seems to know who Riot and Declan Valentine are. Thankfully, he hasn't been recognized during the almost two months he's been here, which, if I'm being honest, is surprising as fuck.

But what do you expect from this small religious town hidden in the Nevada desert? Their only version of acceptable rock music is Christian rock and church hymns that are slightly faster-paced than others.

It's Saturday, which means I didn't have to work today. Usually, my Saturdays consisted of breakfast and park dates with Declan and Max, but today, it consists of lunch with the woman who gave birth to me.

Diane Harris wears her short, thin brown hair in straight strands down to her shoulders. Her bright-blue eyes are clear from the fog that is typically present, and for the first time in years, she looks alert and present—aware of her surroundings and what is going on.

It's been nearly two months since I've last seen her. I had been okay with that and wouldn't mind going another two months, but she'd been blowing up my phone recently, asking to meet. She claims she's sober, but obviously, I don't believe her.

How can I? Many times in the past, she's told me that she's sober and promised to stay that way for me. Every promise she ever made to me was broken. I've given up on the fantasy that I'd ever have the type of mother I desperately want. Part of me will always ache for a loving parent to support me and guide me through this big, scary world, but I'm also aware it'll never happen.

I grew up hearing that God had a plan for everyone, and apparently, his plan for me was to be alone. I must've fucked up big time in a past life.

As I approach the back table where Diane is sitting, my eyes never leave hers, searching for any sign that she's under the influence.

"Hi, Andy. Thanks for coming." Her thin figure stands, fingers nervously playing with each other. She's uncertain about hugging me, and I can't blame her because so am I.

I don't remember the last time I hugged my mom, but I'm not

ready to take that step today, so I sit across from her instead. She sits back down, a small smile curling on the corner of her lips.

"It's so good to see you."

"You wouldn't stop texting, so here I am." My words come out harsher than expected. All week, she's been texting and calling, claiming she's sober and begging for another chance with me. Promising to be the mother I deserve if I just give her a chance. After a week of deleting the texts and ignoring the calls, I agreed to meet for lunch. I'm unsure why, but I did, and here I am.

"I know you hate me, but I'm glad you came. Where's Max?"

"At the park with her friend." Lucy was all too happy to take Max to the park with her and Haley while I came to lunch with my mom. I didn't want Max around unless I knew what I'd be walking into. My guard is up, and I don't trust Diane. Not when she's spent years lying to me.

We sit silently for a few minutes, staring at each other, unsure what to say. The awkwardness creeps in until she finally decides to put us out of our misery by speaking.

"I'm sober now, Andy." I resist the urge to roll my eyes. I've heard this so often that I'll never be able to believe her. She's sober for at least one week every month when she's out of money. She'll spend the week withdrawing, and then the moment her government assistance check hits her account, she's calling her dealer. She used to ask me for money when she was out, but she quickly learned that I'm not willing to give her a single penny, not when I know what'll happen the moment the cash touches her hand.

I'm not a heartless monster. I have helped her in the past, so I know what happens with any money she receives. The same day after giving her twenty dollars, she smoked it away. I know this because I passed her dealer on the way out of her trailer. That's when I swore I'd never help her again. I work hard for what little I have, and I'm not going to waste it by allowing her to smoke it away or shoot it in her veins.

"Been nearly two months now. Haven't touched a single thing since the week you walked out of my house." she intertwines her slim fingers, hands resting on the table. Her pale skin is ghostly compared to my brown skin. "You have no reason to believe me, but I swear to you on everything. I am clean." She's saying everything she's told me many times before, only this time, she's holding eye contact, and her eyes are clear.

I'm not sure if she's telling the truth about being sober for the last two months, but I know that right now, she is sober. I can tell by the lucid look in her eyes.

It's a look I've spent years wishing to see daily.

"One day, I hope you'll be able to forgive me for everything I've done to you. I wasn't a good mom, and you didn't deserve that. You were my innocent little baby who loved me so much and just wanted me to be present and be there for you." Emotion clogs her throat, and tears fill her bright eyes, but she doesn't allow them to fall.

"You didn't deserve any of that shit, Andy. I'm so fucking sorry, but I know it'll never be enough."

"Why should I believe you? What's different this time compared to all the others? You've said this all to me before."

"I know I have. This time is different, but I don't know how to make you believe it. I'm done with the drugs. I'm forty-seven years old and have been an addict since I was eighteen. I'm so fucking tired of this life and all the shit I've wasted and missed out on. Didn't get to be your mother because drugs controlled me. Didn't get to meet a good man and get married because who would want an addict?" She laughs humorlessly, wiping her snotty nose with a napkin. "I don't want to miss any more of my granddaughters or your life. I've missed enough, but I'm begging you, please give me another chance. Please allow me into your life to be there and get to know you." How sad is it that she's asking to get to know me after twenty-one years?

"You've let me down so many times, and I promised myself

I'd never let you do to Max what you did to me. You're not going to disappoint her the way you disappointed me."

Her head hangs. Sniffling, she brings the Kleenex to her nose and blows it. "I know." She sighs. "I don't deserve your forgiveness or another chance, but I'm begging for it. I'm begging you to get to know my granddaughter."

"You weren't there when I needed a mom. Grandma had to be that motherly figure for me because you were too damn high all the time. I'm twenty-one, and I don't need a mom anymore. It's too late for you to swoop into my life and suddenly want to become a mom to me." She'll always be my mother, but I don't have space in my life for her to claim that role. Not when I spent years begging.

Her head pops up, blue eyes full of pain and sorrow staring back at me. Her bottom lip trembles. She opens her mouth to speak, but I cut in before she can say anything.

"It's too late to be a mother to me, but maybe we can be..." I say, thinking about what role she can play in my life. She stares at me with hopeful eyes. "Friends. Maybe we can be friends and get to know each other."

Relief washes over her. Shoulders that were raised to her ears in tension and worry lower in relief, "Friends," she parrots. "We can be friends." A small smile curls on her thin lips.

I nod my confirmation.

"Thank you. I'm not going to let you down this time." She straightens her posture. "Shall we order? Lunch is on me today." It's on the tip of my tongue to ask her how she can afford it, but I refrain from any snarky remarks that'll likely make her feel bad about herself. Especially when we're both trying.

Instead, I nod, and she waves for the waitress to come over and take our order.

After we ate and she paid the check, I grabbed my purse and stood beside her outside.

As I approach my car parked at the curb, I ask, "How did you get here?"

She shrugs, tucking her hair behind her ears. "I walked." My eyebrows raise in surprise.

"You walked twenty minutes to get here?" That's not long, but considering Diane Harris has never been willing to venture into town alone, let alone on foot, I'm surprised. She once asked me for a ride to the gas station across the street from her trailer park.

A pink hue tints her cheeks. Is she embarrassed? I don't think I've ever seen her be embarrassed about anything. "Yeah, well, I've been walking a lot lately. The fresh air has been nice. I go out for a walk about twice a day. One in the morning, and then one at night to my meeting at the community center."

She's never gone to meetings before. I hope she's telling the truth and that this time will be different, but I'm also not holding my breath because I'm tired of being let down. It's better not to have expectations; that way, you're less likely to get hurt when someone inevitably lets you down.

A proud smile lights up her face, and I return it for the first time since meeting her here. "That's great. I'm happy for you." Pulling the keys from my bag, I click the button to unlock my car. "Get in. I'll give you a ride home."

"Are you sure? I don't mind walking."

"Yeah, Mom. I'm sure." Tears fill her eyes again, and I can only assume it's because I called her *mom*.

She opens the passenger seat and climbs into the car without saying anything else.

For once, I'm hopeful for the future with her. I'm still guarded, but I pray this time will be different.

I need this time to be different.

ME

You'll never guess what I did today.

I had lunch with my mom.

She's been sober for two months. For once, I believed everything she said to me. It was a good day, and I'm happy I went. I want to tell you about it, so call when you can.

I miss you.

FORTY-FIVE
Declan

"Goodnight, Phoenix! Thank you for the best two fucking nights!" The crowd erupts into a chorus of applause as our second show in Phoenix ends. We performed two shows here, and tonight, we'll hop on the bus and head to Pennsylvania for three shows.

We've been away for a week, and in that time, I've easily slipped back into old habits. Night after night, it's been the same shit. Party at our hotel after the concert ends and fill my system with the same shit I spent too fucking long detoxing from.

Withdrawal fucking sucks. That shit is brutal. I'll have to endure it after our time on the road ends, but until then, I will enjoy doing anything I can get my hands on. The high keeps me going. It mutes the voices in my head that constantly tell me what a fuck up I am.

Silence is all that I need.

Once I'm backstage, I first send a text to my woman and then snort a line of blow that I hid in my shoe.

ME
Show was fucking epic. Miss you, Mama.

Busy as fuck, but I will call as soon as I can.

The moment the drug hits my system, I feel invincible. My pulse races, and heat pounds in my chest, filling my ears with the music of the rapid beat.

More drugs are the last thing I need, considering I haven't slept since we left Washington three days ago. Besides a twenty-minute nap on the tour bus, I've been awake.

My sleep schedule is all fucked up. I'm tired at the worst possible times. When my energy gets low, and my eyelids become heavy, I turn to the baggie in my hand for energy. Which results in my staying up all night long and repeating the same unhealthy cycle.

Oh well.

I'll sleep once I return to Loganville. Hopefully, the lack of sleep will catch up to me, and I'll be able to knock out for several days and blame the withdrawals on being exhausted rather than from coming down.

Andy's not stupid. She'll notice, but fuck, I pray I'll be able to play it off. No way am I going to lose her over something as silly as using coke.

Laughter tears free from my mouth at the thought.

No way is she going to leave me over coke.

I'll be fine. I've got this. It'll be okay.

Two hours later, the stage is torn down, and our equipment is loaded into the buses and trailers that travel with us.

Since we'd already checked out of our hotel and had no place to host an after-party, Damon took it upon himself to allow a few groupies backstage to party with him and Adam. Cole's been off somewhere on the phone talking to Cece. I should've done the same. It feels like forever since I've heard Andy's voice, but I can't speak to her like this.

Not when she'll be able to take one look at me and know I'm

not okay. She'll see my red eyes and slurred speech and will ask if I'm on anything.

I'll lie.

She'll know it, then she'll be angry for rightful reasons, and that'll be the end. Not fucking happening. I'm not dumb enough to call my girl when I'm all fucked up.

Instead, I've been sitting backstage with Damon and Adam while they entertain the two women they invited back.

I sit in an ugly red leather recliner, my legs spread wide as I hold a water bottle full of vodka in one hand and a cigarette in the other.

Moans fill the air as two of my friends fuck their nightly girls on the couch. They both standing on either side of the sofa with their cocks buried in pussy, while the two women are on all fours on the sofa facing each other, their tongues tangling with each other as they get fucked.

My dick jerks in my pants at the sight and scent of sweat and sex in the air.

I've been so horny that I'm worried my dick will fall off. I've watched Adam and Damon tag team a new woman every night while I've sat back watching, wishing Andy were here to hop on my dick.

I wonder if she'd be willing to ride me while my friends watched. Knowing her, she'd probably be shy at first, but she'd soon become putty in my hands. She always gives me what I want. And I'll be honest. She fucking surprised me. I had not expected her mouth to be so filthy and for her to be so open and willing in the bedroom.

Fuck. Now my cock is hard as stone and painful thinking about her.

Taking another swig of vodka, I stand, bring the joint to my lips, and inhale the smoke deep into my lungs. Holding it in, I set the bottle down and stub out the ember, exhaling the smoke as I step into the bathroom, needing privacy away from the orgy currently happening.

Pulling my phone from my pocket, I FaceTime Andy and make quick work of pulling my dick out while the phone rings.

I know I said I wouldn't talk to her like this, but I'm too desperate right now. As soon as I come, I'll hang up.

I angle the camera on the counter so she cannot see the tattoo along the left side of my shaft. Wrapping my fist around myself, I groan as I pump my fist.

The call connects seconds later, and Andy's gorgeous face fills the screen. Brown eyes widen at the sight of my cock filling her screen, a slow smirk spreading across her face.

"Fuck, baby. Hello to you, too." She giggles, propping her phone up on a pillow, then quickly pulls the gray T-shirt over her head to reveal her perfect heavy teardrop-shaped tits.

"Goddamn, I miss you and that sweet pussy." I've heard stories about guys not being able to get it up while under the influence. Luckily, that's never been the case with me. Regardless of the conditions I've been in, I can always perform.

Andy lies back, spreads her legs to give me a view of her already glistening pussy, then a buzzing sound fills the speaker as she brings her new toy into view.

Licking my lips, I keep my focus on her core as I pump my first. "What's got you so wet?"

She brings the purple rabbit to her clit, moaning softly as pleasure courses through her body at the contact. "I was lying here thinking about you and was getting ready to watch the video you sent of yourself jerking off the other day."

"You were going to watch it while you played with yourself?"

She gasps. "Yes." The length of the purple toy slowly disappears inside her body, and I watch—transfixed—as her greedy pussy sucks it in. The silicone glistens with her arousal as she pulls it out, then slowly pushes it back inside her tightness.

"Tell me how it feels." A moan slips free from my throat, eyes heavy as I keep my focus. My fist tightens around my shaft, pumping myself quicker, squeezing the tip with each stroke. I use my precum as lube, gliding it down my shaft as I speed up.

My balls tighten, ass cheeks clenching as I fuck my fist.

From this angle, she's unable to see my face, which I'm thankful for.

"Feels so good, but you'd feel better. Your cock is what I need." She quickens her pace, fucking herself faster with the toy. Her pussy makes a squelching noise, arousal dripping down onto the bed.

"Oh, fuck." She cries out in pleasure, hips jerking and raising to chase her orgasm as her movements become frantic.

"Fuck yeah, Mama. Just like that. Fuck that little pussy and imagine it's me destroying it." My breathing becomes heavy. Lips parted as I chase my release. "Imagine it's my cock sliding in and out of you, pounding you so fucking hard that your eyes roll into the back of your head. Picture it, baby. Your nipples in my mouth, my tongue teasing them. Thumb rubbing your little clit. Your body at my mercy as I fuck you how you need to be fucked."

Her legs shake as she reaches her climax, pussy visibly throbbing with the sensation. She slaps a hand over her mouth, muffling the cries of pure pleasure.

I follow seconds behind her, cupping my other hand below my crown and using it to catch my release.

My warm cum fills the palm of my hand. Our heavy breathing mingles together, a slow grin spreading across my face.

"Fuck, baby. I needed that." I turn on the faucet and wash my hands before pulling up my boxer briefs and jeans, quickly fastening them.

"One week until you're here. Then you can fuck something other than your hand." She removes the rabbit from her pussy, bringing the glistening toy to the screen to allow me to see it.

"You drenched it. Now suck it clean."

She obeys, sliding the toy inside her mouth, moaning as the taste of her orgasm explodes on her taste buds. I groan, watching her tongue slide along the rabbit, licking every drop of the cum that I wish I was getting to lick clean.

I know one thing for sure. I'm going to fucking devour her the moment I get home.

A knock at the door momentarily steals my attention from the screen. "We're heading out! Hurry the fuck up!" Damon yells, pounding his fist against the door once more.

Sighing, I say, "Be right out!"

"Guess you gotta go."

"We're heading out to our next destination. The drive to Philly is over thirty hours, so we're leaving now."

"Holy shit." She sits up, bringing the camera to her face. "That's a long drive. Why wouldn't you guys fly?"

"Since we're only away for two weeks, we decided to drive along with the rest of the crew. Usually, we would fly, but not this time. We'll fly out of New York and back to Nevada, though." I wouldn't be able to bring my drugs if we were to fly.

She nods in understanding. "Go do your thing. Be safe, think of me, and send nudes later," she says with a playful smirk.

"You know it, Mama." I end the call, grateful she didn't mention anything about being unable to see my face.

I'll make it up to her by FaceTiming one of these days when my eyes are a little clearer.

♪ ♪ ♪ ♪ ♪

WE REACHED PHILADELPHIA TWO DAYS LATER, AND ON THE THIRD day, we performed flawlessly in front of a sold-out crowd. Thankfully, we got separate hotel rooms this time, so my room was empty when we got to the hotel after the show.

Tonight's party is hosted in Damon's suite, but I do not want to be around strangers. I want to have a party of one tonight.

I still haven't slept, and I'm so fucking exhausted.

Dark circles have taken residence under my eyes. Before

tonight's show, a makeup artist had to apply concealer under my eyes before I stepped underneath the harsh stage lights.

When I don't sleep, the voices in my head become louder. Insomnia has never hit me this hard before. Usually, I'm able to get myself to sleep eventually without much effort, but this time, I just can't seem to fucking do it.

There's a solution.

I've been avoiding it because I'm terrified of stooping that low again.

In the bottom of my duffle bag is a parting gift from Amber. A little something she gave me before I left Seattle in case I needed it.

It's been taunting me since then, but I've been strong enough not to give in. But now, I want it more than anything. I want the relief it'll bring.

I want to feel absolutely nothing.

No voices.

Freedom.

I want fucking freedom.

Grabbing the bag from the floor, I dig around to the bottom until I find the red T-shirt my gift is wrapped in. Carefully, I set it on the coffee table in the living room of my suite and unwrap the shirt, revealing my shiny friend that nearly claimed my life years ago.

"I've been thinking about you," I mutter, sitting on the floor in front of the table once I've collected everything I need.

Taking the metal spoon I swiped from backstage, which I found in someone's lunch box. I waste no time melting down the black tar and adding water as my stomach twists in knots. My mouth salivates at the sight of the flame from my lighter burning down the poisonous drug that I can't wait to inject into my veins.

It's been too fucking long.

Carefully setting the spoon down, I tear a piece from a cotton ball and drop it onto the spoon. Grabbing the syringe, I watch the tip disappear into the dark substance and slowly pull back on the plunger, watching with wide eyes as the liquid is sucked up and loaded into the syringe.

Once ready, I set it down, rip off my belt, and tie it around my arm. My teeth bite into the leather of my belt as I tighten it, using it as a tourniquet.

A couple slaps to my skin has a blue vein popping, rising to the surface and practically begging to be injected with the poisonous tar all loaded and ready to go.

You can do it. Don't stop now.

Once you do this, there's no going back.

You want this. You need this.

Don't do it. You'll never forgive yourself.

The little angel and devil sitting on my shoulders argue with each other, sending me mixed signals.

But my mind is made up. It's too late to turn back and allow a perfectly loaded shot to go to waste.

Don't do it.

Fucking do it.

With my eyes focused on my forearm, I carefully glide the beveled tip into the most prominent blue vein, drawing back until I see crimson, then slowly press down on the plunger.

The dark liquid disappears from my sight as it's injected into my veins.

I set the empty syringe on the table, unfasten my belt, and lay my head back on the couch as I stare at the ceiling with an open mouth, gasping for air.

The room spins around me, my vision becoming blurry as the drug invades my system, awakening a craving that I've suppressed for far too long.

Relief washes over me as my body becomes limp, eyes struggling to remain open and focused on the ceiling.

I did it.

I did something I promised I'd never do again. I'm a liar, so I've always known I'd return to this life.

My mother made this life look too impressive all the times that she'd inject herself with the black tar and then give in to the euphoria.

Drugs have always been my destiny. The path in life I've always been meant to take.

I'm doing what I do best.

Escaping reality when the going gets rough, giving up, and giving in.

So fucking weak.

My heavy eyelids finally close, a smile on my lips as dark brown eyes infiltrate my thoughts.

Andy *fucking* Harris.

The girl I never saw coming. The girl that has no idea how much this worthless junkie loves her.

I want to pick up my phone and tell her how loved she is, but my limbs are too heavy, and my eyes won't open. Instead of fighting it, I give into the sensation and continue thinking about those pouty lips and dark eyes.

She's my last thought as darkness creeps in, and everything becomes numb and goes blank.

FORTY-SIX

Andy

Tuesday 3:43 a.m.

DECLAN

dick pic with the New York sunrise in the background

Good morning, Mama. We're both thinking of you.

ME

Wow, that's just what every girl dreams of. Waking up to a dick pic.

Not even mad about it.

DECLAN

Send nudes.

ME

sends tit pic

DECLAN

Fuuuuck those tits. Can't wait to smother myself in them. I'll be home soon enough.

ME

Four days.

DECLAN

Four days too fucking long.

ME

Put your dick away and send me a picture of the sunrise.

DECLAN

sends pic of New York sunrise

One day, I will bring you here, and you'll get to try that smash burger.

ME

Can't wait.

DECLAN

A future with you is all I want. I may not deserve it, but goddamn, I fucking want it.

ME

Stop saying you don't deserve it.

DECLAN

My head has been a mess lately.

ME

Talk to me.

FaceTime?

DECLAN

Later, Mama. I don't want you to see me when I'm like this.

ME

Like what?

DECLAN

When my head is a mess, and I can't fucking find relief.

ME

Did something happen?

DECLAN

This fucking city brings out the worst in me.
Every fucked up memory I have is here.

ME

Tell me three positive things about New York.
Good memories you have from living there.

DECLAN

My son was born here.

Riot started here.

I got out. I got to leave the city that houses my
demons, but they've been waiting for me to
return.

Sometimes I think everyone around me would
be better off without me.

FaceTime call to Declan

DECLAN

Not now, baby.

Me

You promised me all the tomorrows. That
means I'm here for all the good, bad, and ugly
that tomorrow may bring.

I am here. Don't shut me out.

DECLAN

Tell me something good.

ME

I love you.

Incoming call from Declan

"I LOVE YOU, ANDY." HIS RASPY VOICE FILLS MY EARS WHEN I CLICK accept, not waiting for me to speak. His voice sends chills through my veins, my heart pounding at the soothing sound. It's been too fucking long since I've heard him.

I know he loves me, but hearing him say those three words is different. It's everything to me, yet it isn't enough to explain my feelings for him.

Before I can respond, he continues, "Tell me something to keep me going. Something to motivate me to get on that stage tonight."

My heart clenches at the desperate plea in his tone. I'm not sure what's going on with him, but the pain in his voice tells me he's not okay. He needs me.

Without thinking what to tell him, I open my mouth and tell him something he asked me for weeks ago when he was in Vegas. He told me to tell him when he needed a reminder of why he gets on that stage, so I tell him the reason "It's Over Now" is my favorite song.

"When I was fourteen, I tried to kill myself." I let the confession hang between us, gathering the courage to discuss something that I've never shared with another soul. "I took some vodka from the family I babysat for. Filled my water bottle with it, then went home and locked myself in my room. I put my earphones in, started drinking, and then swallowed a bunch of sleeping pills. All I wanted was to be free. Every day was a struggle, and I was tired. Exhaustion consumed every ounce of me, and I was done. I was ready to end it all. I didn't want to be here anymore. Everything inside of me ached. After I swallowed the pills, 'It's Over Now' began playing." His heavy breathing fills my ears, sounding so close to me that I imagine he's here with me when I close my eyes.

Lying beside me in bed with his calloused fingers trailing

softly over my skin, looking at me with those brown eyes that could set my soul on fire given the chance.

"The moment you began singing, it felt like you were speaking to me directly. You put lyrics to everything that I had felt and was going through. You understood me." I remember that day like it was yesterday, alone in my bedroom. My knees to my chest, rocking back and forth as my body shook with silent sobs, my soul crushed, and my body physically aching with the internal pain I'd been holding and keeping to myself. I never had anyone to talk to. Never voiced how I felt. But then I heard Declan's voice for the first time. "You made me feel seen. Like it was okay to break down as long as I got up, brushed myself off, and continued living because tomorrow will always be better, and I need to be alive to see that. Maybe not tomorrow or the next day, but one of these days, my tomorrow will be better."

I'd been drowning, screaming for someone to reach out a hand and pull me up from under the water. But no one heard my screams. I'd given up hope of someone ever hearing them... until him.

"Andy," he rasps, voice full of emotion.

"You saved me, Declan. I was sick for several days, and while I was stuck in bed, I listened to all your songs on repeat, watched videos, and memorized the lyrics. And you were right, because one day, my tomorrow was better. I didn't want to die anymore. I'm glad I didn't because I would've missed out on so much."

Pain is temporary. It may not feel like it now, but one day, it will get better. And I'm so fucking happy that I am here to see better days. I am so fucking happy that I didn't give in to the darkness that crept into my mind during those darkest days.

I survived.

I'm alive.

Everyone is fighting a silent battle; unfortunately, many people give in to the pain of not wanting to be here anymore. Some succeed, others fail.

I am one of those people who gave in. Who so desperately

wanted the pain to end. All I could think was how much happier I'd be once dead. I'd get to see my grandparents again.

Be free.

"I am just one person out of your millions of fans. You have no idea how many other people you're helping by pouring your heart onto the page and giving a piece of yourself to your fans. If it weren't for you, Declan, I wouldn't be here. I would've tried again. And again. And again. However many attempts it would've taken to become successful."

"You're giving me too much credit, Andy."

"No, I'm not. When you put that pen to paper and write the thoughts in your head, it's poetry. You may not see it as art, but it fucking is, and you're saving lives by doing what you do. I can promise you that. I'm not just stroking your ego, Dec."

His breathing hitches, and for a long minute, he's silent, so I continue, "Don't ever doubt yourself. When you step onto that stage tonight, I want you to remember that you are saving lives."

"Thank you, Andy. I needed to hear that." His exhale is heavy. "I was twenty-one when I wrote that song one night. My depression was worse than ever, and I'd been going through some shit. The only way I could express what I was feeling was by writing it down. My mind was a constant mess, and I wanted to escape. I wanted to be out of my skin and be someone else. The only way I escaped was by doing drugs." He clicks his tongue. "Look how well that turned out for me."

"I wish you could see yourself how I see you," I say, throwing the words back at him that he once told me. "Wish you could see what a beautiful mind you have and how incredible you are. You are truly fucking amazing, Declan." Once, I thought he was a selfish prick, but I've quickly learned that Declan Valentine is anything but selfish.

"Apart from Max, you're one of my favorite people," I admit, my voice low.

His deep chuckle fills the line. "Considering you hate people,

I'll take that as a compliment." We sit in silence, listening to the other breathing.

When I think he's fallen asleep based on his low, steady breathing, he says, "Say it, baby. I need to hear those three words, even if it's a lie." I know what he wants to hear—what he needs to hear—so I tell him easily. No lies are required.

"I love you." The words slip off my tongue easily, hanging heavy in the distance between us. He's the first man I've ever said it to, and I know without a doubt in my mind he'll be the last.

Declan Valentine will forever be the only man I will ever love.

One day, forty years from now, I'll tell my grandchildren the story of us and the summer I spent falling in love with the man with haunted brown eyes and demons in his beautiful mind.

"Go back to sleep, Mama. We'll talk when you wake up." We disconnect, but I don't go back to sleep.

Instead, I call Adam.

FORTY-SEVEN

Declan

I'D LIKE TO CONSIDER MYSELF A HIGH-FUNCTIONING ADDICT.

I've never traded favors for drugs or lost my livelihood like I've seen happen to others. Even when I'm high, I still show up for work and put on the best show possible.

Those two hours I get to be on stage are an escape all by itself, and I don't need drugs to get through it. Hearing my fans scream my lyrics back at me is enough.

I may not be able to get through my day without the frequent bump of blow, but at least I'm lucid and able to show up for the things I need to do.

I don't have a problem. I'm fucking fine. Something I assure myself numerous times a day.

So fucking fine.

Being in New York again makes my skin crawl. The moment we crossed the state line, the demons and baggage I left behind welcomed me home, clinging to me like a second skin as if I'd never left.

When we arrived last night, I was so desperate to escape the memories haunting me that I called a number I had saved in my phone for years. Part of me hoped the number would no longer be in service, but while I sat there praying, my prayers were ignored and cut short when Tommy's voice came on the other line.

Two hours later, he was meeting me at my hotel room, and then I spent the night passed out.

This morning was supposed to be better, but I woke from a dream about Luca. The memory that had played in my mind was so vivid, and when I opened my eyes, I could still hear his voice in my ears as I tore my hotel room apart, searching for him and screaming his name.

I'd fallen asleep after that, my dream long forgotten. When I woke for the second time, my mind was consumed with thoughts of Andy.

Andy's naked body writhing beneath me.

Andy's lips pressed against mine.

Andy's laughter in my ears.

She tore herself apart for me during our conversation on the phone, reliving a traumatic moment in her life to make me feel better about myself. Hearing that I saved her made me feel like scum because all I wanted was to tell her that she saved me too, but that would be a lie.

A lie I desperately want to be true.

I've realized the only person who can save me is myself. How ironic is that? I have to save myself from myself.

The biggest threat to me is me.

The fucking irony.

Hearing Andy's story should've been the moment that I decided to clean up my act and get myself better, but that would be too easy, and apparently, I like doing shit the hard way.

Instead, I loaded a spoon with powder and water and cooked it with my lighter until it was bubbling. Then I added the cotton and loaded my syringe, keeping it steady so the needle didn't touch the spoon. Instead of shooting up on my arms and risking anyone noticing the fresh track marks, I wrapped the belt around my calf and shot up in the vein at my ankle.

I've always preferred the white powder over the black tar I

got from Amber. The white powder is purer, and the high seems to hit differently.

The high hit instantly, relief washed over me, and I was fucking floating. Mind free from worrying about everyone that I was letting down.

I was floating.

Down, down, down, into the darkness I went.

The high wore off too quickly, but I hadn't shot as much as usual, considering I needed to be ready for my show.

See?

I'm responsible and perfectly fine.

I'm functioning.

Sure, I may have been late to the venue, but I'm here.

After a shot of vodka and a line of blow, I'm bouncing back-stage, mumbling lyrics to myself as I prepare for our first show in New York. It's been years since we've performed here, and despite my feelings about this goddamn city, I'm determined to make this the best show yet.

"Hey, Dec." Adam approaches me, eyeing me cautiously. "You good, man?"

I stop moving, standing still as I stare at the man who has been my best friend and been by my side since I was sixteen.

An easy smile spreads across my lips. "Of fucking course, man. I'm great!" That might've been a little enthusiastic, but I'm excited. Anxious to get on that stage and give our fans the best night of their lives. My foot taps, arms wrapping around myself as I scratch at my forearms.

Adam stares into my eyes, shaking his head at what he sees in me.

I wonder what he sees when he looks at me.

Does he see what a fuck up I've become? Or have always been? I'm sure I've always been this way.

I've always been nothing.

A waste of space.

"You're high, aren't you?" He shakes his head, shoving his

hands in the front pockets of his jeans. After that night in Seattle, he never said anything to Benny, Cole, or Damon when he caught me partying. He's tried talking to me about it, but I've avoided him as much as possible. Luckily, he hadn't tried talking to me while on the tour bus either, considering we didn't have privacy.

I click my tongue at his question, rolling my eyes at the accusation. Before I can tell any lies, he interrupts, "You are. We both know you are." He sighs, yanking a hand from his pocket and shoves it through his hair. "We're going to have a talk once you're sober because I refuse to talk to you when you're like this. Just know, you're letting yourself and everyone around you down. You're fucking better than this." Sadness fills his eyes, and I know he's disappointed.

I am, too.

"Don't do anything else tonight. You need to sober up and then be sober after the show. Please, Declan. Be fucking sober after the show."

I hold up my hands in mock surrender. "Yes, Dad." I salute him. "I'll be sober. Whatever you say."

He doesn't look convinced or amused by my response. "I'll be watching you tonight. Just—" He groans, running his fingers through his year once again, something he does whenever he's feeling frustrated. "You have to be sober tonight. It's important. Please." He pleads with his eyes. I get the sense that he's not telling me something, but I don't push for answers.

Instead, I nod, then follow him to where Damon and Cole stand beside the stage, waiting for the lights to lower to illuminate the stage which will be our signal for us to come out on stage.

The moment we make our appearance, the crowd goes wild, "Hello, New York! Welcome to our show, thank you for fucking being here!" I place my finger against my lips to silence the roaring, sold-out crowd.

"Tonight, we're going to do shit a little differently. As

everyone knows, we always begin every show by playing 'Rockstar.' Tonight, though, I want to kick us off by playing a song we haven't performed in years." More cheers erupt, and I wait, letting the noise fade before I continue speaking. From the side, I can see my bandmates glancing at each other, unsure what to make of this sudden change.

I should've warned them ahead of time.

"I wrote this song when I thought that was the lowest point of my life." I chuckle, shaking my head at the memory. Back when I was twenty-four, battling depression and swearing that was the lowest point in my life, little did I know that one day I'd tumble even lower and fall into darkness that made my struggles at twenty-four seem easy. "You all know that I've struggled with shit in the past, and I know that many of you have, too." Screams fill my ears, and they are so loud I can hear them through my earpieces.

"Someone recently told me that this song saved her. So, I'd like to sing it for you tonight in hopes that it can help anyone out there who is struggling. I know it's hard, but fight to live another day because brighter fucking days are ahead!" I turn to face my bandmates, and they each give me a nod, knowing exactly what song we're about to play. "This song is called 'It's Over Now', and as we play, I want you to imagine I'm speaking to you directly rather than a crowd of people." I remove the microphone from the stand, walk toward the edge of the stage, and then jump down.

Security wrangles the jumping crowd as they rush toward me, arms outstretched and attempting to grab hold of any piece of me they can. I stand in front of the metal gate barrier, one hand gripping the mic and bringing it to my mouth while my other hand reaches out into the crowd, grabbing the outstretched hand of the boy in front of me.

The dark-haired boy can't be older than twenty-one, his shaggy hair sticking out of the red beanie. His black Riot T-shirt is faded, with holes lining the collar. There's a sadness in his teary eyes that calls out to me, tugging at my heart as I feel his pain.

Looking over at him, I notice the too-short jeans he's wearing and the checkered vans with a hole on the top that his sock-cockered toe peeks out of.

Staring into his eyes is like staring into the eyes of my younger self. Based on his appearance, I'm guessing he's either homeless or living in a less-than-ideal situation. Instantly, I'm curious how he managed to get tickets to our show, but that's an answer I can get another time.

Keeping his hand held firm between mine, the first note of the bass rings out into the screaming room, but I remain staring into the eyes of my younger self as I begin singing.

What's the point of being here if all I feel is pain?
Am I living, or am I existing?
The demons in my mind call out to me, promising sweet serenity.
A bullet to the brain can provide relief.
Sweet, sweet, relief.

As expected, the show is fucking epic.

After we finished our first song, I'd told one of the security guards to bring the kid backstage after the last song, so I wasn't surprised when I walked back and found familiar wide brown eyes staring at me like I was the reason for the stars in the sky.

The kid rocks on his heels, hands buried in his pockets, jaw dropped as he watches the four of us step backstage.

"What's up, man?" Damon greets him, a smile on his face as he embraces our fan in a hug. Every tour, we do meet and greets at as many shows as possible. This time, since we only have two weeks of shows lined up, no meet and greets were scheduled. And I'll be honest, I miss the close connection with our fans.

Luckily, my best friends know me well enough that they know I won't bring someone backstage unless I feel it's important, so they don't question me. Not yet, at least. I know they'll have questions once we're alone, but right now, in front of the kid, they're fulfilling his every fantasy, judging based on the look in his eyes.

I join them after my three best friends introduce themselves. "What's your name?" I ask, stepping into their circle.

"Aiden," the kid says. Deep dimples pierce his cheeks when he smiles.

I return his smile. "Thanks for coming to our show, Aiden." He holds his hand out, unsure if he should shake my hand or greet me in any other way.

Just like my friends, I open my arms for a hug, and the kid nearly knocks me down as he rushes toward me, his arms tight around my bare torso as he hugs me, shoulder shaking with silent sobs.

He's nearly as tall as me, though his build is much smaller. He's tall and lanky, and his baby face shows how young he is.

Adam pats me on the back, disappearing from sight with Cole and Damon by his side as he allows us a moment, sensing that Aiden is clearly going through some shit and needs this moment.

I don't rush him or say anything. I let him hug me with silent cries and hold him right back.

When he's ready, he pulls away, wiping away the tears from his face. "Sorry about that," he says, shyness creeping in as he looks everywhere but at me.

"Don't be sorry for needing a moment. Want to go sit?" I nod toward the black leather sofa. When he nods, I lead him over, pulling two bottles of water from the mini fridge and tossing him one. He catches it before sitting on the sofa while I drop myself into the chair across from him.

"What's your story, kid? How old are you?"

"Nineteen, today, actually." He shrugs. "It's my birthday. Riot has been my favorite band for years, and when I heard you guys were coming, I had to come to see you." He removes the beanie from his head, showing his fingers through the damp sweaty strands. "I won tickets on a radio show. Took three days of calling, but I won. Then, I camped outside for eight hours to ensure I'd be the first one in the door. I love the way you capture the crowd and tear open your soul each time you perform. One day, I want to be just like you." The majority of our shows are general admission, and every time, there's a line of people who arrive early for the chance to be in the front row when the doors open.

I'm not a fucking role model, but damn if I didn't wish I was worthy enough to be one. "Happy birthday," I say, choosing to not acknowledge his comment about being like me. I unscrew the lid off the bottle and chug half at once, the bottle crinkling and popping with my suction. Once I'm done, I screw the lid back on and wipe the water from my mouth. "When I saw you out there, you reminded me a lot of myself at your age." His eyes widen in surprise.

There's not much posted online about my past. No one knows about my life prior to forming Riot and blowing up what seemed like overnight. The only pieces of my story I've given anyone are in my lyrics, and speculation formed from that, but I've never confirmed anything.

Something about this kid has me wanting to share, so I open my mouth and do just that. "I had a pretty fucked up childhood. Mom was an addict. Dad wasn't around. Foster care and group homes were my life until I met Adam, and we ran away. We were homeless for a while until we met Cole and Damon. Cole lived in his dad's garage then, and he moved us all in. The four of us have been through a lot of shit, but we believed in ourselves, and one day, it paid off."

He stares intensely at me, soaking up everything I have to say. "I know a little something about addiction," he mutters, staring down at his hands in his lap. I lean forward, elbows resting on my knees, waiting for him to continue. "My dad died of an overdose, and my mom kicked me out when she found out I was using. I've been staying with friends and on the streets." My assumptions about him being homeless are confirmed.

Fuck. This kid is too damn young to be doing drugs, but who am I to judge? I've been using since I was thirteen. "What are you on?" I ask, swallowing as my throat becomes dry at seeing him. Taking in his disheveled appearance and long sleeves, I realize the answer is pointless. "You're on H, aren't you?" The whispered words hang heavy between us.

Aiden's head pops up, pulling the frayed sleeves of his shirt down over his pale hands. The fact that he's wearing long sleeves in summer should've been a good indicator, along with his itching and twitches. I'd be the one to know, considering I'm on the same fucking shit.

"I don't want to be, but it's the only way to escape reality. My life is pretty fucked up." Fuck, he even sounds like me. I've used the same tired excuses time and time again.

"Drugs are not the solution,"

I realize I'm a walking fucking advertisement for D.A.R.E. I have no room to give anyone advice when I've never been able to take my own. "No matter how big your problems are, kid, you can't risk your life by doing that shit. H will fucking kill you, and you have your entire life ahead of you."

He pins me with a dark stare. "You did. You were on drugs, so don't tell me that they're not the solution. You wanted to escape just like I did." He refers to my use in past tense. Little does he know, I'm currently in active addiction. I have a baggie of coke in my shoe right now, and H is sitting in my duffle bag at the hotel.

"You're right." I run my fingers through my hair, tugging at the roots. Standing, I make my way over to the couch where Aiden is and sit down beside him. "I made a lot of fucking mistakes. Even overdosed once, too. Had it not been for my ex-wife carrying Narcan and getting home in time, I wouldn't be here right now." He turns his head to look at me, eyes widening at the confession I've never shared with anyone apart from family and close friends.

"I don't want you to be like me. Be better than me. Clean up, believe in yourself, go home to your mom, and have a future. Put this shit behind you and live your life. You're too fucking young to be willing to throw it all away for a temporary high." His eyes fill with tears, the tip of his upturned nose turning red.

"I'll help you, Aiden, if you let me."

"You would do that for me?" he asks in a small voice.

I nod. "It's fucking hard and may feel like it's impossible, but I will help you. You can go to rehab and take it day by day." He scoots closer to me and wraps his arms around me, giving me another tight hug.

Wow, look at me. Sponsoring a nineteen-year-old kid for fucking rehab.

The hypocrisy isn't lost on me.

I'm willing to help him, but not myself.

I need to help myself.

Like Aiden, I can't spend the rest of my life being this person.

When my friends eventually return, Aiden sticks around for a while with us, and we load him up with all of our band merch. We paid for one of our drivers to take him to a hotel for tonight since he didn't have a place to go, and then I called Benny to fill him in about the kid and ask for help getting him into a rehab program.

After Aiden left, I went into the bathroom, dug the baggie of white powder from my shoe, and flushed it down the toilet.

How can I make someone else see their worth if I can't see mine?

I watched the drugs disappear until there was nothing left.

Wish it made me feel better, but it didn't. I felt numb as I hoped this would be it.

This has to be the end.

I can't take this life anymore.

FORTY-EIGHT

Andy

Navigating the Las Vegas airport and then JFK was a terrifying experience. Before today, I had never been on an airplane or even outside of the state of Nevada.

After my call with Declan this morning, I knew I needed to be there for him. The tone of his voice told me that something was going on with him that he wasn't admitting. The feeling in the pit of my stomach had fear creeping in as I assumed the worst.

Had he relapsed?

Was he drinking or using again? He hadn't sounded drunk or high over the phone, but that doesn't mean that he hasn't done something he'll regret.

I've been reading a lot about addiction online, and I've learned that when addicts are recovering within the first year of sobriety, it's advised to refrain from starting a relationship because you're at risk of creating codependency. Without the drugs, it's easy to turn your addiction elsewhere.

Is that what Declan has done?

Is our entire relationship one of codependency because he's newly sober and trying to fill one void with another? I'd like to think not, but the insecure thought still lingers.

Regardless, I needed to see him. I called Adam after getting off the phone with Declan and told him I wanted to surprise Declan while they were in New York. He didn't ask questions, just asked for my email, then ten minutes later sent me a first-class plane ticket for a flight leaving after work. I couldn't miss any more days, so I had to go to work, but afterward, David picked me up and drove me to the airport. I'll miss work tomorrow, but losing a day of pay is obviously better than two.

Thankfully, Lucy was happy to keep Max until I return home tomorrow night. I know I shouldn't rely on her as much as I do, but she always tells me how much Haley loves having Max over to play with. Lucy had been worried when Haley wasn't making friends, but now she and Max are inseparable. Plus, the money I pay Lucy for babysitting helps her greatly. She works from home, so she's always around for the girls. I hate leaving Max, but I'm learning it's okay to take time for myself and have my own identity outside of being a mother.

Once I landed at JFK, Adam had a driver there waiting for me, my name on his handwritten sign. The sight made me laugh, and I almost reached for my phone to take a picture.

Look at me, Andy Harris, from a small town to being in New York for the first time with a personal driver dressed in a black suit, holding a sign with my name. That's something I'll only experience once in this lifetime.

It's nearly midnight when I arrive at the hotel where Declan is staying. I'd texted Adam to let him know I'd arrived, and he gave me the address of their hotel and assured me Declan was in his room. He, Damon, and Cole went out, but Declan stayed behind.

Knowing he chose to stay in over a night out fills me with hope. I'm not sure what I'll be walking into, but at least I feel better knowing he's not out somewhere surrounded by temptation.

The hotel they're staying at is a luxurious five-star hotel. A doorman dressed in a green uniform opens the door for me with a nod, and suddenly, my mind is racing as I step inside the lobby. The marble floor is in pristine condition, and briefly, I wonder how often they have to clean it to keep it looking as shiny and neat as it is. Above me hangs a massive chandelier, the reflection sparkling in the marble.

There's a line of guests at the front desk, but I bypass it and head directly for the elevators, wanting to get away from the guests dressed in their designer attire. I'm dressed in leggings and an oversized Riot T-shirt that Declan gave me. My curls are piled on my head in a messy bun, and my secondhand duffle bag is over my shoulder.

I do not belong in a place like this. One look at me is enough to determine that. There's nothing designer about me, not that I'm complaining. I've never been the type of girl to care about labels and name-brand anything.

Sure, it must be nice to step into a designer store and purchase anything without looking at the price, but even if I had the money, I wouldn't be that type of person. I'd never waste money on material objects. If I were rich, I'd use my money to secure a comfortable financial future for Max, and then I'd get us both a passport and explore the world with my little girl.

The elevator dings as I reach the top floor, and I roll my eyes at the pretentiousness of it. Of course, they're staying on the top floor. Why am I not surprised?

The moment the doors open, a security guard dressed in black turns his stoic gaze toward me. Taking in my appearance and duffle bag, I watch as he raises his cuff to his mouth and mumbles something, dark gaze never leaving mine.

Stepping onto the carpeted floor of the hallway, I notice two other security guards spread along the hallway. I'm willing to bet this entire floor has been reserved only for Riot.

"Ma'am, stop right there." The large man stops me, the reflection of yet another chandelier shining on his bald head. "You have the wrong floor." He eyes my T-shirt, likely thinking I'm an obsessed fan who found out this is where Riot is staying, and I came here to stalk them.

Straightening my posture, I refuse to be intimidated. "I'm on the right floor. Declan Valentine is my boyfriend, and I'm here to surprise him".

He laughs a full belly laugh, taking me by surprise.

Damn.

Is it that hard to believe I'm dating Declan?

He scoffs. "Yeah, okay. And I have a full head of hair."

Asshole.

A second security guard joins us, looking between Baldie and me. "There a problem?"

"My name is Andy Harris. I'm here to see my boyfriend. Adam told me that he put my name on a list with security."

The second guy nods, turning to look at Baldie with a red face. "She's right." He faces me. "Do you have identification?"

Reaching into my purse, I let out a huff of annoyance as I grab my wallet, taking out my driver's license and show it to the new guy. He takes a photo of it before handing it back while Baldie continues staring at me, shooting daggers.

What the fuck is his problem? I'm not the typical model type that Declan used to date, but come on. I'm still a person with feelings. He's making me feel insecure and like a joke for being here.

"Do you know which room he's in?" I return my wallet to my purse.

"Yup." My eyes roll as I shoulder past Baldie and walk down the hall until I reach room 9038.

Standing outside the door, I inhale, giving myself a pep talk. My body filled with nerves and excitement over seeing Declan for the first time in two weeks.

Reaching up, I remove the satin scrunchie from my hair and shake out my curls.

You got this.

You can do this.

He'll be thrilled to see you.

With a smile on my face, I knock on the door.

The door flies open, stealing my breath away.

The sight before me freezes me, my heart beating rapidly as I stare into the brown eyes I've been dreaming about.

"Andy?" his whispers, his eyes wide as if he's unable to believe it's really me standing here before him.

A slow smile spreads across his face, and I'm not sure which of us moves first, but suddenly, the door is closed, my bag has fallen to the floor, and our arms are around each other as our lips meet, further stealing the remaining air from my lungs.

God. His kiss feels like heaven.

Kissing him feels like my own form of heaven, created just for me.

Being with him feels like coming up for air after drowning for so long.

"You're fucking here." He pulls back, looking me up and down, before tangling his hands in my hair, angling my face how he wants it, then devours my mouth once again.

Warm hands slip beneath my shirt, trailing up my back until he reaches my bra. With a flick of his wrist, the clasp comes undone, and my heavy breasts sigh in relief.

Our kiss is broken long enough for Declan to remove our shirts. The bra straps slide down my arms until it lands on the floor beside our feet and shirts.

Grabbing the waistband of my leggings, he slides them down my ass, grabbing a fistful of each cheek in his hands, yanking my body closer to his as he grinds his hard cock against me, making a groan rise from the back of my throat.

Pulling back, I wrap my arms around his neck, taking a moment to look at him. He presses our foreheads together, strong arms wrapping around me, making me feel the safest I've ever felt. With him, I can breathe a sigh of relief because, for once, I don't feel alone.

"I can't believe you're here. Was this already planned when

we spoke this morning?" he asks, minty breath warm across my lips.

I pull my head back enough to look at him clearly, needing to take in his appearance and memorize every feature. Shaking my head, I explain how I came to be here with him. "After we got off the phone, I called Adam. Told him I wanted to surprise you and what he thought about it. He said it was a great idea and that he'd take care of everything. He got my ticket and arranged my ride to the airport in Vegas and from JFK to here." His eyebrows raise. "Something about your tone on the phone made me feel like I needed to be here with you."

His shoulders lower with his exhale. Bringing my body flush against his, he buries his face in the crook of my neck, lips meeting my skin. "Thank you for knowing I needed you and coming. You have no fucking idea how much I needed this. You in my arms. Your scent in my nose. Your body against mine." Pressing his nose into my skin, he inhales, humming his response to my cherry scent.

"What's going on with you, baby?" I ask, fingers mindlessly rubbing over the bare skin of his back.

He's silent for a long stretch of silence before answering, "I've been fucked up since seeing Camille. I know we haven't talked about it, but seeing her didn't go very well." He pulls away from me, pressing a quick kiss to my lips, then lowers to his knees in front of me, pulling my leggings and panties down my body until I'm standing there naked.

"As much as I really want you to fuck me, I wouldn't mind a shower. It's been a long day, and I'm sweaty," I say, fingers running through his soft hair.

"I haven't showered yet, either. We got back from the venue not that long ago. We'll go shower together, but first, I need to talk to you, and I want to look at your beautiful body as I do." His lips press against the pale marks on my stomach, his warm tongue poking out and swiping along each one.

Once he's licked every stretch mark, he stands, takes my

hand, and guides me to the couch. He sits down, pulling me onto his lap so I'm straddling him and facing him, my naked body on top of him.

He grips my thighs, head resting on the back of the couch as he stares at me with half-hooded eyes. "Talk to me, Dec." I urge him on, doing my best to remain confident as I sit butt naked on his lap, legs spread on either side of him.

"I told her everything. She yelled at me and said shit that I deserve, but fuck, it still hurt hearing it. Everything she said to me is shit I've already told myself a thousand times. Didn't make it any easier." I remain silent, allowing him to take his time and get whatever off his chest that he needs to. "She now blames me, just like I blame myself. The friendship we've built is fucking ruined, and all I can think about is that look in her eyes. She fucking begged me to tell her I was lying, Andy. Fucking begged." He scoffs, shaking his head in disbelief.

"No matter what we've gone through, she's never looked at me with hatred. But that's all I saw in her eyes after I told her. She will never forgive me." I've selfishly avoided this topic because I don't know how to feel or what to say. His actions played a direct role in the death of his child. We'll never know what would've happened had he been sober because he wasn't.

He made a choice that had deadly consequences.

"One thing about Camille is she always needs space to process shit. I know she'll be ready to talk to me one day because she'll have questions. She's always been quick to lash out, but she'll have more to say."

"Are you sure about that?"

He nods. "Positive. When she's ready, she'll reach out. She might never forgive me, but I will get another chance to apologize to her. It might be two months or two years, but it'll happen. I don't even want her to forgive me because I'll never forgive myself."

My heart aches for him when he talks this way about himself. "You can't go back in time and change anything. Yes, what happened was fucked up and devastating. Fucking tragic actually, but you can't change anything. Eventually, you're going to have to forgive yourself."

His head tilts up, eyes staring into mine as he whispers a question. "Do you think I deserve forgiveness for killing my son?"

I swallow thickly, eyes softening as I stare at the beautiful, damaged man beneath me.

Does he deserve forgiveness for driving while under the influence, which resulted in death?

"Yes," I whisper, my hand pressing against his racing heart. "You deserve grace, and to stop punishing yourself. You're human, and we all make mistakes. You didn't know what was going to happen that night. It was dark and raining, and anything could've happened."

He stares at me, unblinking, for what feels like forever, but since I don't know what time it is, I'm not actually sure how long we're stuck in this staring contest.

Finally, he says, "There's no such thing as forgiveness for a sinner like me. The only one who will ever want me is the devil himself." Before I can respond, he grips my wrist and yanks me toward him, lips attacking mine. I fall into his bare chest, body colliding with his as he claims the air in my lungs.

Slipping a hand between us, he finds my pussy, spreading my lips with two fingers while a third swipes through me.

"Fuck, baby, you're soaked. This all for me?" I nod frantically. He groans, taking a deep inhale as if he expects to be able to smell my arousal. "Mmmm." A sinister smirk curls on his lips. "Smells like desperation." Without warning, he shoves two fingers inside of me, curling them upwards and jackhammering inside of me without allowing me a second to catch my breath or adjust.

"Is this pussy desperate for me?" Fuck. I've missed his mouth. "God, yes."

"God's not here with us, baby. It's just you and me. The only name I want to hear you screaming is mine. I am your God, now." His thumb presses against my clit, moving it in sync with the fingers inside of me.

My eyes roll into the back of my head, going so far back in pleasure that I'm almost certain I see my brain. He leans forward, lips wrapping around one of my nipples, tongue flattening over the pebbled peak.

He adds a third finger. The stretch is delicious and welcome. Curling them upward, he massages me in that spot that has my body climbing high and shaking with anticipation of release.

"Fuck, fuck, fuck!" I cry out, eyes squeezed shut as I place my hands on his shoulders and ride his hand. My pussy squeezes his fingers, inviting them deeper inside of me.

"Eyes on me, baby," he rasps, biting and sucking my tits so roughly that I'm sure when he pulls away, I'll have dark marks left behind.

Yes, baby. Leave your mark on me.

My eyes fly open, watching the way his tongue laps at my skin and nipples, loving the feeling of him flicking them with his tongue.

Keeping his rhythm, he reaches a hand between us and unfastens the button and zipper on his jeans to relieve the strain against his hard cock.

"You're suffocating my fingers," he says, teeth biting into his bottom lip as he pumps me harder.

Harder, harder, harder, until I'm falling over the edge.

White lights explode in the back of my eyes as I give into the release I've needed from him for over two weeks. My body shakes and jerks with the climax, head becoming lightheaded.

It's only after I float back down to earth that I notice his soaked hand, dripping with my release, and the wet puddle I made on his jeans. It's hidden on the dark fabric, but still noticeable when you look close enough.

A blush climbs up my cheeks at the sight, embarrassment setting in. Squirting is not something I'd ever done before him, but now, I manage to drench him every time we have sex or he plays with my pussy.

Breathing heavily, I watch as he raises his hips, then lowers his pants and boxers enough to free his aching cock, hand instantly wrapping around the shaft. In his grasp, his cock is long and hard between us, the heat radiating off of it making my pussy clench in anticipation, slowly stroking himself a few times, squeezing the tip until beads of precum are displayed and dripping down.

Groaning at the sight, I raise myself onto my knees, allow him to line himself up with my drenched pussy, then slowly sit back down, seating him inside of me.

We moan in unison, eyes connected with each other as I hold him inside of me, clenching my walls around him.

He grips my hips in a bruising grip. "Need you to move, baby." He says it through gritted teeth, his jaw clenched tight.

Keeping his tight grip on me, he guides me up and down his length, meeting me thrust for thrust from where he's seated, our eye contact never breaking as I ride him.

Even as I soak his cock and he fills me with his warm cum, our eyes never stray from each other. The intensity of his gaze sets my soul on fire, filling me with emotions I've never felt before.

The intense feelings I have for Declan scare me.

Two months, and he's already becoming the air in my lungs I need to breathe.

My life raft to save me from drowning further.

I wonder if he feels it too, how deeply in love with him I am.

And how desperately I wish there would be a happy ending for us.

FORTY-NINE
Declan

Mornings are better when waking up with a curly-haired bombshell in your bed.

Andy's dark curls are spread over the white pillowcase as she lies on her back, dark nipples visible beneath the thin white sheet.

She'll be leaving today, and it would be a waste if I didn't give her my dick once more as a parting gift. Lifting the sheet, I slip beneath the covers until I'm nestled between my woman's legs, her perfect pussy in my face, begging for me to enjoy my favorite meal.

After she rode me on the couch last night, we fell asleep before we had a chance to take a shower or go another round. I'll rectify that situation today because she's not leaving here until we're both thoroughly fucked.

Last night had been a mind fuck when I opened my door to find Andy standing there. For a moment, I had wondered if I was high and imagining shit, but then I felt her warm skin against mine and knew that my angel was real.

She was real and came for me because she knew I needed her. She has no idea how right she was about me needing her. It's like

507

she heard my silent cries for help all the way across the country and answered my plea.

Fucking Andy.

The girl who is too damn good for me.

Spreading her pussy lips apart, I slide my tongue up the length of her, flattening my tongue against her hardened clit, and suck it into my mouth, easily sliding two fingers inside of her as she grows wetter beneath my touch.

Andy moans, fingers coming down to tangle in my hair as she wakes, becoming aware of what I'm doing to her body and how only I can make her feel.

I'm addicted to her.

Her taste.

Her smell.

Her presence.

Everything about her enthralls me.

Her legs widen, hips raising to my mouth as I continue the combined assault of licking and sucking her sweetness into my mouth.

Suddenly, the sheet is removed from our bodies, and brown eyes stare down at me, a smirk on her lips. "Best way to wake up," she says breathily, followed by a gasp as I slide a third finger inside of her.

Humming against her cunt, I give her another slow lick before pulling my head back, fingers still buried deep inside her and pumping slowly as I gaze up at her. "Morning, baby." I press a kiss to the soft dark curls between her legs. "Do you trust me?" She nods quickly.

Smirking, I pull away from her body, get off the bed, and walk toward my duffle bag. Reaching inside the side pocket, I pull out a cherry ring pop, the same as the one I'd put on her finger weeks ago.

Her eyebrows raise in question, and I remove the wrapper, sticking the cherry-flavored candy into my mouth. I suck it for a couple of seconds before climbing back onto the bed, then hold out the candy for her.

Andy parts her lips and then closes her mouth after I stick the candy inside. She sucks it, then I pull it out. She lets go with an audible pop.

Smirking, I reclaim my space between her legs, tongue licking over the sucker as I spread her pussy, then drag the candy along her wetness.

She props herself on her elbows, and her eyes are focused between her legs as she watches me drag the candy through her slit until it becomes coated in her wetness. Pulling it away, I lick over her pussy, humming at the sweetness that explodes on my tongue.

"You taste just like you smell." I lick her again, lips closing around her clit, then pull back.

"Oh, fuck," she mutters, wide eyes still taking in my every movement.

Returning the candy to her pussy, I rub it along her clit, moving it in slow massaging circles as I lower my mouth and shove my tongue inside of her tight little hole while keeping the sucker moving along her clit.

Her head falls back, chest rising and falling with heavy breaths as her climax builds.

Within seconds, I have her coming into my mouth just by thrusting my tongue inside of her and using the sucker to circle her clit.

I lick up her release, sitting up with a smug grin on my lips. Reaching forward, I shove the candy into her mouth, forcing her to taste my new favorite flavor.

Cherry mixed with Andy's cum.

"So fucking dirty." I grin, kiss her cheek, then climb off the bed. "Let's go take a shower, and you can wrap those lips around my cock while we're in there." She doesn't need to be told twice. She loves sucking my dick as much as I love her sucking my dick.

She hops off the bed, removing the sucker from her mouth, and shoves it into mine, before racing into the bathroom.

In the shower, she obeys like the good girl she is and sinks to her knees, eyes level with my aching cock.

At the sight of me, her eyes widen, her mouth popping open, as she finally notices the tattoo on my shaft.

"What the fuck?" Her eyebrows furrow in confusion, fingers carefully touching my heated velvet skin. Shifting my cock to the side, she stares at her name tattooed in bold black letters along the shaft.

Brown eyes flick up to me, a smirk on my lips as I stare down at her smugly, my chest flexing as I stand there, proud to show off the latest ink marking my body for the rest of my life.

"Do you like it?" I ask when she remains silent, eyes bouncing between me and my cock. Her expression isn't one of horror, but there's no doubt she does have some thoughts in her pretty little head about it.

Licking her lips, she sits back on her heels, hand falling away from my length. "Why did you get my name tattooed on your dick?"

Because I was high as fuck.

I can't tell her that, so I shrug. "I don't want anyone else, Andy. You are it for me. You love my cock, and it's yours, so why not?"

She throws her head back, exposing her neck, and lets out a full belly laugh that has her body shaking. "You're fucking crazy." She climbs back to her knees, wraps a hand around my hardness, puckers her lips, and presses a kiss to the tip. Her tongue pokes out, licking the bead of precum that slips free from the slit.

With her eyes on me, she swallows me down until my length hits the back of her throat, triggering her gag reflex. Drool drips from the sides of her mouth as she gags on me, but that doesn't stop her from tightening her lips around me and sucking me as fiercely as she sucked that cherry ring pop I used to make her come.

Andy sucks my dick until I'm shooting thick ropes of cum into the back of her throat, and she's swallowing like the good girl she is.

Fresh from the shower, and after drying off, I walk my naked ass into the bedroom, grab my duffle bag from the floor, and set it on the bed. I grab a pair of jeans and boxers from the top of the pile and pull them on.

Andy mimics my actions by bringing her duffle bag onto the bed and dressing in a matching lace bra and panties set that has my cock already straining against my zipper.

When she catches me staring at her, she raises an eyebrow in silent question. The corner of my mouth lifts in a half smile, "You're gorgeous, do you know that?" I step toward her, placing my hands on her curvy waist and bringing her body flush against mine. "When I look at you, I see someone too good for me. I'm amazed that I get to call you mine." I kiss her lips, my tongue taking advantage of the momentary gasp and slips inside of her warm, wet mouth.

I hold her against me like she's the most precious thing in the world.

Brushing the dark strands of hair from her face, I stare down at her. "I love you, Declan." she whispers, the words filling my ears along with the rapid sound of my heart beating. "I'm not lying to you, either. You have my heart, and I'm sure you've had it since that day in the thrift store." I get the sense it's not easy for her to reveal her feelings or allow herself to be this exposed when it comes to her feelings. Andy has had walls around her heart for too long, and she's finally letting me in.

"You don't know how lucky I am to be loved by you." A knot forms in my stomach as I stare into her trusting brown eyes, now feeling like a piece of shit for keeping secrets from her.

If she knew how weak I was and that I'd given in to the demons haunting me, her brown eyes, which shine with love and adoration, would look at me with anger and possibly hatred. I don't want her to ever lose that spark in her eyes when she looks at me. It's a look I want to see forever. Even when we're old and gray, I want that spark to remain.

I'm selfish, I know this. And I know I won't be able to keep it a secret from her for long. Soon, she'll find out just how far down the rabbit hole I've fallen, but I'm not ready for that. When I get back to Loganville, I'll sit her down and explain.

Until then, I will take advantage of my time with her this morning.

Besides, I'll be quitting soon.

I've already flushed the coke I'd been carrying with me, and soon, I'll get rid of the half-empty bottle of liquor in my mini fridge along with the H. I need a little bit more time.

Having it there within arm's reach provides me comfort, just like with my cigarettes. I carried them with me after I quit, just in case I needed one.

I can do the same with my stash.

Keep it around just in case, but not actively seek it out.

Yup. I can fucking do it.

It's fine. I'm fine.

My addiction could always be worse.

Forcing a smile, I press another kiss to Andy's lips. "I love you, Mama. Let's finish getting ready, then we'll go grab something to eat before I have to take you to the airport." She nods, kissing my lips, then pulls away. Grabbing the bag of toiletries from her duffle bag, she returns to the bathroom to finish getting ready for the day.

While she's there, I grab a T-shirt from my bag, carefully avoiding the rolled-up red shirt hiding my H and everything I'd need to shoot up. Luckily, I'd managed to conceal it before last night's show, or Andy might've spotted it when she surprised me in my room.

Thank fuck it wasn't sitting around. So far, I've done pretty good at hiding it. Especially considering Adam and the others aren't aware of how far I've fallen. Adam knows I've relapsed, since he witnessed it when it happened. As far as he knows, I'm only smoking weed, drinking, and occasionally snorting a line.

He doesn't know that I snort a line any chance I can get or shoot up the moment I return to the hotel.

I'm pissed he knew Andy was coming but hadn't warned me.

Fuck it being a surprise.

What would've happened if I shot up last night after the show like I've been doing? She would've found me high and left.

It was too close of a call.

Even now, it's a close call having her in the same room with my hidden drugs and liquor. Sure, if she found the bottle of vodka, I could easily lie and tell her one of the guys left it, but catching me with H buried in my bag would be harder to explain.

Fuck, now I'm reeling out of control.

My mind is racing with too many what-if scenarios, unaware that I had even begun pacing back and forth, scratching at my chest and forearms.

Last night, I'd been riding the high of performing. Now, I was stone-cold, sober, and desperate for a small bump to get me through the day. I don't need a lot, just a little bit of something. Fucking anything that'll keep my skin from crawling.

Fuck.

My palms are sweaty—the desperate need for another hit is choking me.

"Declan." Andy's stern voice cuts through my racing thoughts, and I turn to look at her, saying a silent prayer that she hasn't been standing there long. I'm perfectly aware that I look every bit like a preening drug addict with the way I'm pacing and mumbling.

One look at Andy has my heart dropping into my stomach and my throat constricting at the look in her eyes. "Want to explain?" Between her fingers, she holds up a little orange sealing cap that I'm all too familiar with.

Fuck. Fuck. Fuck.

No. No. No.

To most people, the bright orange syringe cap would've been easily overlooked, but when you have experience with drugs, you know what it means.

How could I have been so careless and stupid? Big fucking mistake not making sure I'd cleaned up after coming down from my high. Each time I bit the cap off the needle, I'd spit it across the room, not paying attention to where it landed because my attention was too focused on getting the drugs into my veins.

Stupid. Stupid. Stupid.

I'm a fucking idiot.

The used syringes are in my bag, along with the new ones, but who knows where else the other caps have landed. If she finds those, too, she'll know exactly how many times I've shot up since being here.

How did she even find it? Was she fucking searching the carpet? Trying to catch me doing something I shouldn't?

My eyes narrow, and she mirrors me, already preparing herself for what I'm going to say, "Are you fucking searching my shit?"

Wrong thing to say.

She throws the cap at me, the small plastic object bouncing painlessly off my chest and onto the floor.

"I stepped on it in the fucking bathroom!" She points as if I'm not aware where the bathroom is in my hotel suite.

The bathroom. Fuck. I remember now.

My second time shooting up here was while I was in the bathroom. I'd gone into the bathroom to get water from the sink to mix with the white power before cooking it, but I had been so desperate for an immediate fix that I ended up sitting on the floor and shooting up.

Shoving my hands into my damp hair, I tug at the roots, eyes wide as I stare at her, willing my brain to devise a plausible excuse.

I have two options.

Lie. Or tell the truth.

If I lie, I could say one of the guys has diabetes and used the syringe for insulin while in my room.

If I tell the truth, she'll leave me.

She can't fucking leave me.

As if sensing that I'm trying to figure out a way to explain, she snaps her fingers, bringing my focus back to her. "Don't you dare fucking lie to me." Her hands find her soft hips, her foot tapping expectantly as she waits for an answer that I'm not prepared to give.

This isn't how the day was supposed to go.

I had planned on telling her about the relapse once I got back to Loganville, but not right now. Not yet.

Fuck me.

Fuck my life.

Fuck Andy for finding that cap.

She's expecting a lie, and I want to give her one, but she knows what happened. So, I don't insult her further and give her the truth.

"I'm fucking sorry!" I yell, dropping to my knees, burying my face in my hands. "I fucked up! Is that what you want to hear?" I remove my hands, allowing her to see the look of devastation on my face.

At the sight of me, her face softens. She approaches me, taking my face in her hands, "What happened, Dec?"

Now is my chance to tell her everything. Tell her I've been using since Seattle. Tell her about meeting Amber and getting drugs from her. Tell her about the vodka and coke.

I have to be honest. I do. I will. Yes, right now, I'll tell her everything. I open my mouth, and words spill out before I can register what I'm saying. "The first night here, I ran into my old dealer, and I was so fucked up about being here that I bought heroin from him and used it once." Lies.

All I fucking do is lie.

"Now is your chance to be honest with me, Declan. How many times have you used?"

"Once." Another lie.

"You haven't used since Monday night?" I shake my head.

Another fucking lie from my sinful lips.

I used yesterday morning, but the truth doesn't fit my narrative.

"My head has been fucked up since seeing Camille. Then being here, I fell further down the rabbit hole, but I hated being high on that shit again." I fucking loved being high on H, "I'm done, Mama. I fucking promise. I flushed the rest after that." Lie. It's in my duffle bag.

She blinks, lips pressed together as she remains silently studying me, so I continue speaking, "I hated the feeling of being high. All I could think about was you and how much I let you down." I hate that I'm not high right now.

"Declan, I think you need to go to rehab. You need more than NA meetings."

Fuck rehab.

Been there, done that, and failed every time.

I know you need a positive mindset and want to recover to be successful with their program, but it didn't work for me. And I know why.

I'm not willing to share the reason why I began using in the first place. Until I'm willing to remove the skeletons I've buried deep in the back of the closet, I'll forever be stuck in this fucked up cycle, constantly teetering on the edge of sobriety and relapse.

Right now, I'm willing to tell Andy anything to get her off my back.

"I can do that." I nod, licking my lips. "I met this kid at my show yesterday. He's nineteen and on heroin. He has been homeless ever since his mom kicked him out of the house for doing drugs since his dad died of an overdose. We invited him backstage, and I fucking helped him," I say, hitting my fist against my chest. "I'm fucking paying for that kid to go to rehab because he has his entire life ahead of him, and I don't want to read about his death one day. He inspired me so fucking much." I'm a piece of shit for bringing up Aiden and using him to convince Andy that I'm willing to get help.

"I'm so fucking sorry, baby. Please don't give up on me. That kid opened my eyes, and I don't want to be like this." Emotions clog my throat, tears filling my eyes, as I say something honest for a change.

I don't want to be this way. I hate myself.

"I hate my addiction and the person I am because of it."

Andy's eyes soften, and slowly, she sinks to her knees in front of me, holding my face between her warm hands. "You are worth more than your addiction, Declan. I love you, and I'm here for you. We're in this together, and I'm not going to leave you. I'll help you." My shoulders sag with relief.

She's not leaving me.

"When you come home, we'll figure it out. But please, do not take anything else because I will not give you another chance." She closes her eyes, taking a slow and steady inhale. "I will not be with you while you're using. Drugs will not be a part of my life any longer, or my daughter's life." When she opens her eyes, I see the fear lurking beneath. I see the scared child she once was who begged her only parent to put drugs aside to be there for her. I know everything about her past and how she grew up, yet here I am—dragging her down that same path filled with lies and broken promises.

Staring at her, I nod frantically. "I promise, baby. Monday was the first and last time." I wrap my arms around her waist, burying my face in her soft curls, inhaling the faint cherry scent lingering on her silky brown skin.

I'm lying to the woman I love.

I'm lying to myself.

All I do is lie and destroy.

She'd be better off without me.

Everyone would be better off without me.

I'm nothing.

I'm worthless.

I'm a liar.

I'm a fraud.

I'm an addict.

I will never be anything other than this.

My mind is racing. Uncertainties fill my brain with fucked up notions of what I should and shouldn't do.

Of who I should and shouldn't be.

Regardless of how much I want to keep her, I only know that Andy is better off without me.

Our lips connect, each of us desperate for the connection and feel of each other. She lets me strip her bare and lay her body out on the floor beneath me.

When I sink my length inside of her body, tears roll down the corners of her eyes, and I kiss them away, whispering apologies in her ear as I fuck her slowly, savoring the moment of having her warm pussy wrapped around my cock for the last time.

This is goodbye.

It has to be.

She's better off without me.

FIFTY

Andy

Wednesday 10:15 p.m.

ME

Just landed. David is here to pick me up and take me home.

11:45 p.m.

ME

Made it home safe.

1:13 a.m.

ME

I love you, Declan. We'll get through this.

Missed call to Declan

Thursday 5:45 a.m.

ME

Good morning, baby. You didn't answer your phone last night, but I hope you're feeling better today and slept well.

You're probably still asleep. Call when you can.

I love you. Remember that.

8:35 a.m.

ME

Miss your voice. Call me when you wake up.

12:58 p.m.

ME

Hope you're okay. Call me when you can.

6:39 p.m.

ME

I just finished having dinner with Max. I hope you're okay. Please call me. I'm worried.

11:30 p.m.

FaceTime Unavailable

12:14 a.m.

ME

Worried about you, Dec. Please call.

Friday 7:30 a.m.

Missed call to Declan
Missed call to Declan

ME

Please call. Tell me you're okay.

12:00 p.m.

ME

Dec, I'm really worried about you. Please
answer the phone.

Missed call to Declan

3:30 p.m.

ME

If you used again, don't be scared to tell me.
We're in this together. Just talk to me.

If you're busy or need some alone time, there are better ways to do it. At least text back so I know you're okay.

4:30 p.m.

ME

Please.

Please, baby. Tell me you're okay.

Saturday 11:14 a.m.

ME

If you need space, at least have the balls to tell me. I can leave you alone. I just want to hear your voice so I know you're okay.

2:47 p.m.

ME

You're coming home today... right?

11:11 p.m.

ME

Please, Declan. You're really scaring me.

11:14 p.m.

FaceTime Unavailable
FaceTime Unavailable
FaceTime Unavailable
FaceTime Unavailable

Sunday 9:12 a.m.

ME

I hate being the type of girlfriend to blow up your phone, but I'm worried as fuck.

2:30 p.m.

ME

I need to know you're okay and not dead somewhere.

You don't have to say anything. Just answer the phone and let me hear you breathe.

Missed call to Declan
Missed call to Declan

6:00 p.m.

ME

I'm calling Adam if I don't hear from you tonight. You should've been home by now.

9:58 p.m.

ME

All you have to say is you're okay. That's it. Two words are all I need. I promise I'll leave you alone after.

Don't speak. Just pick up.

Please, Declan. I'm freaking out.

Missed call to Adam
Missed call to Damon
Missed call to Cole
Missed call to Cece

11:45 p.m.

ME

I'm freaking out. No one is answering.

I'm starting to think your plane crashed, and you all are dead.

If that's the case, then don't cross over. Ignore the light. Your ghost can come to me.

Maybe I've been watching too much Ghost Whisperer, but if there was a plane crash, I hope your spirit comes to me.

Sorry. That was morbid. I want you to be alive. I need you to be alive.

12:40 a.m.

ME

I don't care if you did something you think I'll be angry about. All I need is you and to know you're alive.

Monday 8:00 a.m.

ME

I love you, Declan. Please don't do this to me.

Fuck you.

Fuck you for making me love you.

527

FIFTY-ONE

Declan

I fucked up.

FIFTY-TWO

Andy

WEDNESDAY MORNING, I WAKE WITH DREAD IN MY STOMACH AND AN ominous feeling surrounding me. I've gotten used to Declan going silent on me for hours, sometimes an entire day. I understand he was traveling and busy, and I've never wanted to be the girlfriend constantly nagging him and begging for attention.

No matter how busy he's been, we've been in contact every day, no matter the time. Not hearing from him for nearly a week has me on edge, yet I get the feeling he's been avoiding me for a reason.

It's been a week since I've heard from him, and with each passing day, my anxiety increases, especially considering I know that he relapsed. For a week, I've been replaying our last conversation.

Had he said something that I missed?

Did he break up with me, and I missed it?

After we made love on the floor of his hotel room, we talked and made a plan. When he came home on Saturday, I would help him prepare for rehab. We were going to find the best program for him, and he was going to go, and I'd be there waiting for him once he got out.

He rode with me to the airport, hand on my thigh for the

531

entire silent journey. When we'd arrived, he'd kissed me so deeply that it left me lightheaded and nearly gasping for air.

Was he telling me goodbye?

Had he known he was going to ghost me?

It's been a week of radio silence. A week of texting nonstop and checking my phone every time it dings, desperate to see his name across the screen.

I've tried calling and texting his friends, and each attempt has been a failure. I even tried calling Cece, and just like the others, there's no response.

I just need someone to tell me he's okay.

I'm ashamed to admit it, but I even called Declan's manager's office and left a message for Benny. When he didn't return my call, I figured they were avoiding me for a reason.

This must be how they treat the girls Declan decides to toss to the side when he's done with them.

I was right all along. I was just a warm pussy to pass the summer with. I was never meant to be anything more. He wouldn't have ghosted me if I had been worth more.

If he's still using, that's fine. We'd get through it. All I wanted to know was that he was alive and okay, but clearly, I'm so insignificant that I can't be given that single courtesy.

Fuck him.

I have a bad attitude when I go to work Wednesday morning, and working is the last thing I want to do. All I want is to sit in my pajamas, stuff my face with ice cream, and eat my feelings away all day while rewatching episodes of *One Tree Hill*.

I was tempted to call in, but I needed the money, so I had to suck it up and be an adult.

Even had to lie to my daughter when she asked about Declan.

Max asks about him every day. Asking me to show her on their map where he currently is, when he'll be back, and when she can talk to him.

Eventually, she'll realize that he's not coming back to us, and

I'll have to prepare her for that moment. She loves him so much that I know it'll break her heart when I have to tell my innocent child that Declan's no longer going to be in our life.

The sad thing is, if he were to call me right now, I'd forgive him for anything. That's how hopelessly in love with him I am.

I'm sitting at my desk in the back office, sorting through the papers from the nightly audit, when my phone rings.

At the sound, my breathing stops, hope filling my body as I pray to anyone who will listen that Declan's voice will come through the speaker.

Sinking my teeth into my plump bottom lip, I reach inside the pocket of my black work pants and pull out my phone, checking the name on the contact.

Adam's name displays on my screen, and my heart stops. Dread fills my body, ice chilling my veins. There's only one reason he'd be calling.

"Hello?" I answer too quickly, waiting for his voice on the other end of the line, waiting for him to confirm the horrific feeling I have deep in my gut.

"Andy." He sniffles. The way he says my name has me holding my breath, my fingernails digging into the soft flesh of my thighs.

"Say it, Adam. Tell me what happened," I say sharply, desperate for information.

"It's Declan." He hiccups. "God, Andy. Declan fucking over-dosed. He's in the hospital right now, and we don't know what's going to happen." I fucking knew there was a reason he hadn't been answering me. Nausea fills my stomach, bile rising in the back of my throat at the thought that the man I love could die.

My bottom lip trembles as I force myself to ask the question, "He's alive?" Emotion clogs my throat, but I force myself to swallow it down even though my throat feels like sandpaper and the motion is painful. *He's alive*, I remind myself.

That's all that matters.

"Can you come, Andy? You need to be here. I can send a car for you."

"What? How?"

"We're back in Vegas. We got in on Saturday."

They've been in Vegas since Saturday. They're all safe and arrived precisely when they were supposed to.

Did they fucking know Declan was using again? Is that why they didn't answer the phone?

I'm unable to keep the venom from my tone as I ask, "Did you fucking know he was using again?" Right now, I don't care that he's upset about his best friend.

Adam sighs, and that's all the confirmation I need. I grit my teeth, pinching the bridge of my nose as I take slow and steady breaths. "What happened?"

"We've been trying to help him since you left last week. We didn't know he went out that night, but when he came back to the hotel, he was fucked up. I moved his shit into my room and made him stay with me until we got home. He's been so fucked up, Andy." He sniffles and I can practically feel everything he's feeling through the phone. "I've never seen Declan so fucked up. When we got home Saturday, I brought him home with me, and we've been keeping him clean. He's been detoxing for a few days. I left him alone for thirty fucking minutes, and when I came back, he was passed out, needle still in his arm." I don't realize that tears are streaming down my face until I lick my dry lips, tasting the saltiness. Wiping my face with the back of my hand, I stand from my desk, gathering my purse and car keys with one hand while holding my phone with the other, needing to hear everything Adam has to say.

"Send me your location. I'm on my way." He says something in response, but I'm already hanging up before I can hear him.

My phone chimes a second later, and I open his text, clicking on the location pin that brings up the map and directions to the hospital where the man I love is.

I rush out of the back office, attention turning to Eliza, my employee that's working the morning shift with me today. I stop long enough to tell her there's a family emergency and I have to go, then I'm running to my car, jumping in, starting it, and speeding out of the parking lot.

Lucy answers my call instantly, and as soon as I tell her I'm headed to Vegas to the hospital, she agrees to keep Max as long as needed.

I've just turned onto the freeway when a painful sob rips through my chest, tears burning my eyes as they spill down my face like an endless waterfall. The pained sobs rip my chest apart, somewhere between screams of anguish and heartbroken, painful, wrenching sobs.

Declan is in the hospital.

Declan overdosed.

Declan is alive.

The moment I enter the doors at Sunrise Hospital, I'm hit with the nauseating smell of antiseptic and death.

Memories of being here when my grandpa died assault me, grabbing me by the throat and suffocating me. I grip the wall to steady myself, breathing through my mouth in a desperate attempt to rid myself of the smell.

The elevator takes me to the third floor, then dings open, revealing the somber waiting room.

At the sound of the elevator, Adam's head pops up, sad eyes locking on me as he stands from where he was seated beside Cece and Cole.

Damon and Cole turn their gaze to meet mine, wearing the same matching expressions as Adam and Cece.

I'm so fucking pissed at them that I pull my gaze away, attention turning toward Adam as he greets me. He instantly pulls me into his arms, and his sniffles are loud in my ear as he hugs me tight, shoulders shaking with a silent sob.

There are no more tears left in my body. I cried everything out during the drive. I am so fucking angry with every single person in this room right now.

How long had they known Declan was using again?

At this point, I'm certain he lied to me when I was in New York; I feel like he's been using longer than what he claimed. I'm just not sure how long. Likely since the day he left.

That second night in Seattle seems to be when everything changed for us.

Had he been high each time we spoke, and I didn't notice?

Was he using each time I tried to FaceTime or call him, and he had an excuse?

Was he partying with them after each show?

Is that why he tattooed my name on his cock? Because he was high and did it for whatever reason?

I'm doubting everything and replaying every conversation we've had.

How could I have been so fucking blind? He's been suffering in silence for much longer than I'd realized. I'd been foolish to think a few months of sobriety would make him strong enough for a relationship. I should've focused on being his friend rather than a girlfriend.

If I'd been only a friend, I wouldn't have been blinded by him going on a downward spiral.

Fuck, Declan.

What did you do, baby?

Damon, Cole, and Cece hug me after Adam steps away.

I sit down, and my leg bounces nervously as I stare at the four with narrowed eyes.

"What has the doctor said? Is he okay? Can he have visitors?" I ask as a million questions jumble together in my mind.

Damon clears his throat, fingers scrubbing over his exhausted face. "We're waiting for clearance to go back to see him. The doctor was out here before you arrived and said they're going to keep Declan for a few days."

"Andy, he told them that—" Adam chimes in, but Damon gives a subtle shake of his head, his eyes pleading with his friend not to tell me whatever he was going to say.

Instantly, my back straightens, and I'm on high alert. "Fucking tell me," I demand. "I think enough secrets have been kept. Don't you?" I snark, lip curling in a snarl as I stare between the four of them.

They all fucking knew what was going on, and none of them thought it would be a good idea to answer my calls or send a simple text to let me know what was going on.

"He told the doctor it wasn't accidental." Adam's whispered confession hangs in the air, sucking the air from my lungs as I struggle to understand what he's saying.

Shaking my head, I stand, needing to do something over than sit and hear what they're trying to tell me. But as much as it hurts, I need to hear it. "What do you mean it wasn't accidental?" I enunciate the words slowly in attempt to hide the tremble from my voice.

"He was trying to overdose," Adam explains while I watch Damon wipe a tear away from his face. Watching these three big, rough rockstars cry over their friend softens my heart a little, but it doesn't take away any of the anger and confusion coursing through my body. "Declan was trying to kill himself." He chokes up as he struggles to speak.

The realization that Declan intentionally overdosed has my knees giving out on me. I collapse into a chair, lips parted and mind racing as I try to make sense of his actions. "He did it again," I whisper, eyes stinging with tears that refuse to form.

"What do you mean again?" Cole asks, eyes pinning me in place.

Declan trusted me with his secret, but considering we're sitting in the hospital waiting room because he once again tried to take his life, I don't feel the need to keep it to myself. His friends should know. "His first overdose wasn't an accident, either. When he was married to Camille, he tried to kill himself then, too. She saved his life. But it wasn't accidental."

"He told you that?" Cole asks, blinking rapidly to keep his tears from falling. Cece sits beside him, knees hugged to her chest with one arm while the other rubs Cole's back. I nod in confirmation.

Having revealed enough, we fall silent and take in the new information.

Twenty minutes later, the doors open, and a nurse in baby-blue scrubs steps out, walking directly toward us. Her eyes are focused on Adam, and I'm assuming they've spoken before.

Adam stands, leaving the rest of us sitting. "Can we see him now?" he asks, voice full of hope.

The blonde-headed nurse looks over each of us with a sad smile. "He's asking for you, Adam, and only one of you can go back." Adam nods, looking over his shoulder at me. I was hopeful that Declan would ask for me, but why would he? He doesn't know I'm here.

As if reading my thoughts, Adam says, "Don't worry. I'll let him know you're here." He follows the nurse, and I overhear her telling him to empty his pockets and remove his shoes before going into the room because he's being held on suicide watch.

My poor, broken boy.

How long has he wanted to die?

How long has he felt worthless?

Eyes still stinging, I stand after watching Adam disappear between wooden double doors. I decide to walk down the opposite side of the hallway, needing space away from his friends who failed to fill me in on what's been happening.

Stepping into the restroom, I lock the door behind me, lean against the wall, and bring my phone to my face.

A red *alert* icon that I've never noticed before stares at me.

When did I receive a voicemail? I don't remember ever missing a call.

With shaky fingers, I click on the phone app, selecting the option for voicemail.

Declan's name pops up, showing a voicemail from 10:14 a.m. this morning.

I gasp, hands shaking and eyes becoming blurry as I struggle to realize what I'm seeing. Declan called me this morning before he overdosed, and I missed it. I missed his fucking call.

Frantically, I press the voicemail and bring it to my ear, placing a hand over my mouth to muffle the choked sobs that threaten to rip free.

At the first rasp of his slurred voice, I lose my balance, collapsing to the floor with a heavy thud, but I don't feel the pain. I'm too focused on the sound of my beautiful boy's broken voice.

"Hey, Mama," he slurs, voice raspy as if he just woke up. "I wanted to hear your voice, but you're not answering. I think it's because you hate me." He sighs. "That's okay because I hate me too. I want you to know that I've been thinking about you and Max, and I'm so fucking sorry. So fucking sorry that I made you love me because you gave your love to someone that doesn't deserve it. I'm going to fix things for us, baby. You'll both be able to free yourself of me because all I'll ever do is drag you down. You were too fucking good to be ruined by me, but I'm selfish and did it anyways." His words are slow as if he's nodding off between each word. "I love you, Andy Harris. It wasn't until I met you that I realized I'd never truly been in love before. You were it for me. I fucking love you. You deserve better than me. I'm sorry, Mama. So fucking sorry. Forgive me." There's a long silence, and I pull the phone away to see if the voicemail has ended, but I see a few seconds remaining. Bringing it back to my ear, I continue listening.

"I love you, Mama. Tell Max I love her, too. You're in my fucking veins. I just wanted all of your tomorrows. I'm fucking sor—"

The message cuts off just as a loud muffled sob escapes me, tears once again streaming down my face.

Curling into the fetal position on the cold bathroom floor, I rest my cheek against the tile, my body numb, heart aching as I place the phone on speaker, set it beside my head, and listen to the message on repeat.

My poor, poor, broken man.

What happened to him to make him this way?

No matter how much I love him, it'll never be enough if he doesn't believe he's worth it.

Declan, what happened to you?

Why are you so broken?

FIFTY-THREE

Declan

I FAILED.

Just like I fail at everything else in my sorry excuse for a life.

My demons were calling me home, so I surrendered.

What the fuck is the point of carrying on living like this?

All I've ever done is ruin those I love.

I leave destruction in my wake everywhere I go.

All I'd wanted was for the darkness living in my head to consume me, so for once in my miserable life, I could be at peace.

Andy would mourn me, but she'd eventually get over it and find someone better suited for her.

This is the second time I've tried to kill myself by overdosing on heroin, and it's the second time I've been unsuccessful.

Unfortunately for me, both times, there's been someone within arm's reach who could save my life.

Why won't they let me be happy?

First, it was Camille, then it was Adam saving me.

Don't they understand I'm not worth it?

They don't understand that my brain hurts. Twenty-four *fucking* seven, my mind is telling me how worthless I am and how I should end it.

I hear fucking voices in my head.

"Hey, man." Okay, that voice wasn't in my head.

Turning my head to the side, I look into my best friend's eyes. The tired and defeated look on his face guts me.

I wasn't supposed to be around for this part. I wasn't supposed to be alive to witness my friend's tears as they struggled to understand my reasons for doing anything that I did.

Adam steps into the room, and I notice his bare feet. My eyes roll at the sight, a dry chuckle leaving my dry, cracked lips. I'm assuming they took his shoes to ensure I wouldn't use his shoelaces to finish the job.

He walks into the room and takes a seat beside the bed.

"Is she here?" I ask, voice dry and scratchy. I don't need to say her name, I can't say her name, because he already knows the she I'm referring to.

He nods.

Fuck.

Just another glimpse into my fucked-up mind.

"She shouldn't be here."

"She loves you, man. Of course, she wants to be here."

I pin him with a look. "I don't want her here."

His eyes narrow, and he leans forward, hands balling into fists as he stares at me through the slits of his narrowed eyes. "I don't give a single flying fuck what you want anymore. From this point forward, you're my bitch, and what I say goes." Pleased with his growled words, he sits back in the seat, making himself comfortable. "First, you will go to rehab when you get out of here." He holds up a finger, counting off a second one. "Second, you will work the program this time and be there as long as they fucking say you need to be there. I don't care if they say you have to be there for five years. Your ass will be there."

I scoff, lips curling into a dry smirk. "You're not going to become my fucking parent, man. Watch yourself."

"Someone has to!" He raises his voice, jumping to his feet. "You tried to fucking kill yourself. For the second time." My fingers twitch as he throws that in my face, but otherwise I don't show that it bothered me.

Fucking Andy.

Of course, she told him.

Can't blame her either.

She's probably in the waiting room, terrified, waiting for her chance to see me. It was a dick move ghosting her like I did. I read every single message. Watched my phone light up with every phone call and FaceTime request.

I could've answered, but I had to create distance between us because there was no fucking possible way I could tell her goodbye to her face.

I took the coward's way out.

It's easier this way.

She can hate me and will be able to move on from me. I'm not going to drag her down any fucking further. I'm done taking from her and ruining her.

Turning away from him, I face the white wall. "I'm tired. You should go." I hear him sigh, and then he steps around my hospital bed to face me, giving me no choice but to look at him.

"You're my best friend, Declan, and I thought I lost you. You've been by my side since I was sixteen, and finding you like that, unconscious on the floor with a needle in your vein..." He shakes his head as if attempting to rid the image from his mind. "You've been selfish long enough, so now it's my turn to be selfish. I need you, man. You can't leave me. I will make you stay and get better, whether you want to or not." He waits for a reaction, but I don't give him one. Sighing, he walks off like a scolded child, head hung between his broad shoulders.

I don't let the first tear fall until he's gone from my sight.

I thought my death would make life easier for everyone. Didn't think that anyone would be sorry to see me go, but I'm starting to see how wrong I was.

Why am I like this?

Why can't I be normal?

Free from the memories that haunt me.
Free from the voices.
All I want is peace.

♪♫♪♫♪♫

THREE DAYS LATER, I WAS RELEASED FROM THE HOSPITAL ONCE THEY were confident that I wasn't going to off myself while in their care. Adam was there to pick me up, filling me in on everything Andy has done, as he drove me to his and Damon's house.

Apparently, Andy has been calling and texting daily for an update, waiting for the moment she's allowed to see me.

He's such a little pussy. He never told her I didn't want to see her while in the hospital. Instead, he told her I wasn't allowed any other visitors besides him.

She believed him and has been waiting for the day I get released.

While I was in the hospital, I realized how fucking stupid I'd been and how much I miss her. I should've brought her closer instead of pushing her away and trying to protect her from me. She's already promised not to leave me, and I know she'll forgive me.

She has to.

She's my angel. My personal piece of heaven on earth.

Something I'll never get to experience in the afterlife.

Adam has plans for me to go to rehab, and I've gone along with it, but I also have a plan for myself, and it doesn't include fucking rehab.

I was sick as fuck in the hospital, and I'm glad Andy didn't get to see me that way.

All I need is another bump, and I can forget everything and will feel better. I've got to learn to manage my addiction better.

I'd been telling myself that I could only have one or the other, but I realize now that I can have both.

I can have both the girl and the drugs. I'll have to be careful, but I can do it.

A smile spreads across my lips at the thought.

The moment we pull into the driveway, I spot Andy sitting on the front steps of Adam's house. Damon must not be home if she's sitting outside.

I climb out of Adam's SUV, and at the sight of me, my girl comes running over, brown eyes full of unshed tears.

Her warm body collides with mine, arms around my waist as she buries her face in my chest. Wrapping my arms around her shoulders, I hold her close to me, cherishing the feel of her against me.

She lifts her head, and our lips connect. "I'm so fucking sorry, baby," I mumble against her lips, angling her face upward so I can devour her mouth like the starved man I am.

I hadn't noticed it at first, but now that I look over my shoulder, I spot the white Range Rover parked at the curb. I smile at the fact she's still using my rental and make a mental note to order her car as soon as possible.

A throat clearing has us pulling our lips away and turning to look at a grinning Adam, "Hey, Andy," he greets, hands in his pockets.

"Hi, Adam. Thanks for letting me come over."

He smirks. "Did I have a choice?"

She shrugs. "Nope. I was going to be here with my man one way or another." He chuckles, the sound fading as he walks toward the front door, unlocks it, and then steps inside, leaving me and my angel behind.

"Let's go talk? I have a lot to apologize for." She nods, takes my hand, and allows me to lead her inside the house.

Once we reach my bedroom on the second floor, I lock the door behind us, step out of my shoes, then go toward the bed and stretch out. The hospital bed was scratchy and stiff. I've been dreaming about getting back to this fucking bed and attempting to get more than three hours of sleep.

She sits beside me, crisscrossing her legs, hands in her lap as she watches me. "I'm glad you're okay. You have no fucking idea how scared I've been." I roll onto my side, propping myself up with my elbow. I grab her hand with the other and intertwine our fingers.

"Do you think you'd ever be able to forgive me? Simply saying sorry isn't nearly enough for what I owe you."

She squeezes my hand, a faint smile dusting her pink lips. "I've already forgiven you, Declan. There's no point in holding onto anger. You have an addiction, and no matter what you do, you always will. Every day, you are going to have to make the choice to remain sober. I've told you once, but I'll tell you again, I won't give you a second chance. Next time I find out you're using, that's it. I will never again be the person that has to compete against drugs. I've done it my entire life with my mother, and I will not do it with the man I love."

I see the sincerity in her eyes, and God, I wish I could promise her that I don't want this addiction or to be this person who relies on it. This isn't what I want out of my life.

"For you, Mama, I'd do anything. I'm going to try so fucking hard."

Infamous last words.

FIFTY-FOUR

Andy

I'VE ALWAYS BEEN ABLE TO TELL WHEN SOMETHING TERRIBLE WAS about to happen.

Call it the calm before the storm.

Instinct.

A gut feeling.

I've always felt it before destruction hit.

It's the same feeling I have now as I walk into Adam and Damon's house. Declan has been staying here the past two weeks. When they got tired of getting up to open the door, Damon had a key made for me, so I've been letting myself in each time I come over—which has been often.

Declan has been out of the hospital for two weeks and doing great. Twice a week, I drive him to NA meetings and sit across the street at the café until he's done. After each meeting, he's in a better mood than when we left the house. He'll soon be going to rehab. We've been waiting for a spot to open at the facility Benny recommended to us.

He's alive, his energy is high, and he's starting to remind me of the version of him that I met and fell in love with three months ago.

It's crazy to think that three months ago, we were strangers, and now he's everything to me. So much has happened in such a short time, but I believe in our love. I believe in us. Some days are better than others, and I'm not going to say that Declan and I have the perfect relationship, but we're trying every day.

He's fighting for himself to become sober, and I'm standing beside him.

I've been driving back and forth to Vegas to see him every day, and each time I leave, Max asks about him. She's so confused, but I've told her that Declan is sick, and when he's better, he'll be back home with us.

Since then, she has made him a get-well-soon card I bring to Vegas daily.

As for Diane, she received her three-month chip, and I've been enjoying getting to know her. Our relationship is still strained, but Declan had once asked me, *How can you forgive one addict, but not the other?*

I'd wanted to argue at the time, but then I realized he was right. I love two addicts, both in different ways.

I grew up with an addict for a mother, and now I'm in love with an addict that I'm trying to save.

The irony isn't lost on me.

Letting myself inside the house, I use my foot to shut it as I carry the newest get-well card from Max, along with two iced coffees that I grabbed on my way over.

Choosing to ignore the nagging feeling I've had all day, I force a smile on my face as I shift the second coffee to hold in the crook of my arm as I reach Declan's bedroom.

Grabbing the door handle, I twist it, and the moment I push it open, horror washes over me, the feeling of anger and dread seeping into every pore of my body.

Declan sits on the bed, a belt wrapped around his calf, a loaded syringe with dark liquid in it bit between his white teeth as he slaps at his ankle, trying to find a suitable vein to shoot up in.

I stand there stunned, fury consuming me as I watch him. I

must make a noise because his head pops up, eyes wide as he stares at me with red eyes and blown pupils.

He's fucking high.

I want to scream because what the actual fuck? Here I am, driving two hours a day to support him. Meanwhile, he's not even trying.

What a fucking fool I am.

Walking toward him, I keep my face stoic as I set the coffees on his nightstand, along with the homemade get-well card from Max with a purple heart on the front that she proudly drew herself. As I set the card down, I notice the white powder residue left behind on the dark-stained nightstand.

"I'm done," I whisper, my eyes stinging with hot, angry tears. I turn to look at him, shaking my head in disappointment.

Carefully, he removes the syringe from his lips, sets it on the bed, and then stands, belt still wrapped around his bare leg.

"I'm sorry, baby." He whines, arms reaching for me, but I step away.

"How fucking long?"

"Baby, it's only sometimes. Just a little bit more before I quit. Come on, I promise. You know that I'll go once a spot opens up in rehab. I'm just getting it out of my system until then."

At this point, his excuses no longer surprise me. He's had one excuse after the other prepared, but I've been the dumbass who has believed him.

He reaches for me again, and I take another step back, furiously wiping away the tear that slips down my cheek.

Anger flashes in his dark eyes, his lip curling in a snarl. "Fuck you, Andy. You act like you're so fucking perfect. Looking down your nose at everyone who struggles because you're too perfect to ever have an addiction." I don't recognize the man in front of me. Right now, he's not the man I fell in love with.

"I'm done, Declan. You've broken my trust, and I can no longer do this." I throw my arms up in disbelief, my heart shattering as I continue staring at him through my teary eyes.

His shoulders sag, and when he reaches for me this time, I don't move or push him away. Instead, I let him hold me, trying to find safety in his familiar touch that used to set my soul on fire.

Instead, his touch feels empty, and when he kisses me, I can taste the lies on his tongue.

"I'm sorry, Mama. I fucked up. This is it. I'm done. I mean it."

Finding my voice through the overwhelming emotions threatening to suffocate me, I speak my words firmly, "Let me go. I warned you, and now I'm done. I mean it."

"No! You're not leaving me!" He collapses to his knees, arms wrapping tight around my waist.

"I love you, Declan. So fucking much. But I am not going to watch you self-destruct anymore." The tears I've been holding back spill over my lashes, trailing down my cheeks. "You'll never love me more than you love your addiction."

His arms tighten around my waist as he stares up at me from where he stands on his knees before me, eyes red-rimmed, tears flowing down his face. "Please, baby. I'm sorry. I'll change. You don't deserve this. I love you. I'll get help." He hiccups on a sob. "Please, don't leave me. I need you." He shakes his head. "You promised me all your tomorrows."

"There won't be a tomorrow if you don't get help." I inhale, my body aching with heartbreak. "You need help, Declan, but it's not my help you want. I can't fucking do this anymore. I love you too much to have a front-row seat to your downfall." He buries his face in my stomach, his shoulders shaking with sobs and his muttered pleas for me to stay.

"Please, baby. You promised you'd never leave me." He looks up at me through his blown pupils and tear-stained face. "If you leave me, I'll kill myself. I'm nothing without you, remember?"

"Dec, if you don't get help, you are going to die. Don't make me receive that phone call again. If you love me, you won't do that to me. Please, get some help. Not for me. For yourself."

"I'll do anything for you." His shoulders shake with his sobs.

His tears seep through my shirt, forever staining my skin with the memory of this moment. "Whatever you want, I'll do it if you tell me you won't leave me."

With my eyes closed, I force myself to be strong, running my fingers through the greasy strands of his unwashed hair. How could I not have noticed before today that he's still using? Am I that blind, wanting to see the best in him, that I overlooked what was right in front of me?

The man before me is someone I don't recognize. The version of Declan I fell in love with would never let himself go this way. He would never be okay with his hair being greasy, clothes stained, and skin smelling of body odor from being unwashed.

It's been over twenty-four hours since I've seen him, and this isn't the man I left behind.

Despite the grease on my fingertips, I can't stop touching him. My hands grip any part of him I can reach, desperate for the comfort he once brought me.

"I love you," I say, emotion clogging my throat. "But I can no longer watch you kill yourself. One day, I hope you realize that you're worth more than this. I hope you choose to get help because you want to. That'll never happen as long as you believe this is what you deserve." His arms tighten around me as if he can sense I'm ready to pull away.

"You were worried you'd ruin me. You were right. You ruined me for any other man," I whisper, fingers trailing over his heated skin.

As tightly as he's holding me, desperate to keep me with him, I force myself away. He lets me go, remaining on his knees as he stares at me with a heartbroken look on his face that'll forever haunt me.

I stare back at him through my tears, forcing my legs to remain strong and keep my body upright despite the numb feeling that makes me want to buckle and fall apart. No matter how much I love him, I can't follow him down this path any further. I can't follow him into the darkness slowly consuming him.

There is something deeply broken inside of him, and until he's ready to talk about it, he's never going to heal and move on from this life.

His screams fill my ears, but I can't bring myself to turn around. I don't dare face him, afraid of what I might do if I see that heartbroken look in his eyes again.

In the end, it doesn't matter how much you love someone.

Love isn't enough to overcome addiction.

It will never be enough.

FIFTY-FIVE

Andy

Two months later

UP TO SIXTY PERCENT OF PEOPLE RELAPSE WITHIN THE FIRST YEAR OF sobriety. I know this because I've spent hours online looking for answers I knew I'd never get, but I'd been desperate to understand what made a person turn to drugs for comfort.

I've been trying to find answers since I received the call in the middle of the night a week ago.

Why do people with an addiction relapse after completing a treatment program?

After going through all the steps, attending the meetings, experiencing life sober, and fighting every day for months to recover, what makes them turn back to doing drugs?

What makes them decide to pick up the bottle or load the needle?

I've been searching for answers, hoping to make sense of this, but no matter what, I can't.

Months of sobriety were thrown away in a matter of seconds.

Why? Was the momentary high worth it?

"I'm sorry, there was nothing we could do. It was a heroin overdose."

That emotionless voice on the phone, delivering the worst news of my life, has been haunting me all week.

I slide my hands down the front of my black dress to smooth out the wrinkles as the pastor speaks about life, death, and some other bible verse that I've tuned out long ago.

Beside me, my daughter wears a matching black dress, arms wrapped tight around the stuffed animal she brought as she stares at the cream-colored coffin in front of us.

She's too young to understand death. All she knows is that she will never see someone she loves again, and it makes her sad, but it isn't completely understood.

There are sniffles from one of the people around me, and I'm tempted to turn around and ask them why they're crying.

Are they suffering this loss?

No, I'm the one suffering, but you don't see me blowing my nose loudly, sniffling, and sobbing.

Instead, I stand stoic, eyes fixated on the casket that holds someone I love.

Someone I loved.

As if the day couldn't get any worse, the skies mourn with me and become as gray and gloomy as my mood. Though, unlike me, the sky cries.

Heavy raindrops fall on my skin, but I don't move to seek shelter or wipe them from my face.

Instead, I let them fall upon me, welcoming the chill that sets in the empty pit of my dark, tainted soul.

Why is it that it always rains during funerals? Is it the universe ensuring you remain in a gloomy mood? As if it were possible to be happy when you're burying someone you love.

Diane Harris gave in to her demons, and her addiction consumed her and stole her life.

Drugs stole my mother.

What was her final thought as she lay there dying?

Did she think of me?

Did she regret what she did?

Was she scared?

Why did she decide to load that syringe?

Why wasn't I enough for her?

I'm mourning, but not in the way everyone expects me to.

I mourned the loss of my mother long ago. She was dead to me long before she took her final breath, but this is final.

Unlike most children who lose a parent, I'm not left with fond memories. Which is why when the pastor asked if I wanted to say a few words, I declined.

My mother wasn't friends with any of the people around me. Most of them talked shit about her, yet here they are, standing beside me and crying as if they have anything to miss.

Diane and I were never going to have that mother-daughter relationship.

When we met at the café that day months ago, I agreed to a friendship. That's the only capacity she's ever had in my life. It was too late to become the mother I needed. We were friends getting to know each other. Over these months, I realized that not only did she not know me, I didn't know her.

Diane Harris was more than an addict.

She was a daughter who had dreamed of becoming an artist and sketched every chance she got. She had notebooks full of incredible drawings she'd kept over the years.

She attended community college but dropped out after meeting a boy who promised her the world. Desperate to leave our small town, she moved to Texas with him.

He was the one who got her hooked on drugs, and a year later, she was back on her parent's doorstep as a drug addict, someone they hardly recognized.

From that point forward, her life was full of ups and downs, struggling to get sober but giving up after weeks. The longest she'd been sober was while she was pregnant with me.

But I wasn't enough to keep her that way. She returned to her trusted pipe when I was barely a few months old.

Losing her has made me reevaluate the way I think about people with an addiction.

I've thought of them as weak.

They're not weak. They didn't choose that life.

Addiction is a disease.

It's not a choice.

No one wakes up one day and thinks, *You know what, today is a great day to become addicted to drugs.*

No child in school is telling their classmates they aspire to become an addict when they grow up.

All it takes is once to become addicted.

One hit from the pipe.

One drink from the bottle.

One pill prescribed by a doctor.

One shot with the needle.

Your life can change in a matter of seconds.

Everyone views drugs as hard shit, but what some don't realize is that you can become addicted to the legal opioids you receive from the doctor. It happens too often.

My entire life, I judged my mother for her addictions. I considered her weak because she gave in to the devilish lure of drugs instead of being strong enough to fight it.

The lure of heroin doesn't discriminate.

My mother wasn't weak.

Declan wasn't weak.

People with addictions are *not* weak.

They're victims.

They're fighting a silent battle that many people battle every single day.

They're not weak because they're addicted.

One thing I'll never forget about my mother is the days she went without food because of me. Many nights I listened to the sound of her stomach rumbling with hunger. Each time I offered her food or asked why she wasn't eating, she'd say she wasn't hungry or her stomach was making that noise because she had a stomachache. As a kid, I never thought too much of it and didn't question it as I ate my frozen microwave meal.

Using her last few dollars, even digging for change in the bottom of her purse to buy me food from the dollar menu. One night, I remember sitting at a table in the park during summer because our power was cut off, and that damn Nevada heat was no joke. Being inside was hotter than being out. We'd taken my piggy bank with us, and there on the park's picnic table, we laid out a piece of cardboard so the change wouldn't fall through the holes in the metal table, and we counted the change. It was less than five dollars, but it was enough for two cheeseburgers and a drink from the dollar menu.

After we got our food, she sat and watched me eat with a smile, all while her stomach rumbled in hunger. When I tried to offer a bite or a drink, she denied me each time, an excuse ready to go.

There were moments with my mother when her true self peeked out, but it was hard because so many of those moments were drowned out by her addiction. Every selfless moment was followed by something unpleasant.

I remember the rare nights she'd tuck me into bed, kiss me on my forehead, and say, "I love you with all my big, fat, purple heart." Apparently, when I was younger, I'd thought hearts were purple, so it had stuck.

I'll remember the times I sat in the backseat while she drove, and we screamed along to Hinder, Nickelback, and Faith Hill.

She knew all the words to every Nickelback song.

And "Breathe" by Faith Hill was her favorite song.

I remember my fifteenth birthday. She hadn't said anything to me all day long, and I was afraid she'd forgotten what the day was, and I didn't want to remind her. When I came home from my *date* with whatever grown man I had no business being with, she surprised me with a chocolate ice cream cake. We didn't have money, so I knew she stole it, but I didn't care, because at that moment, I was all that mattered to her. She'd stuck a large yellow plastic spinning candle in the center, and neither of us suspected it was a sparkler when she lit it. The plastic melted and set off the fire alarm, but our laughter drowned out the sound. It was the best birthday I'd ever had with her. For that moment, I was what was important to her. Not her friends waiting in her bedroom with a loaded pipe, me. I was her priority. Even as I sat in my bedroom eating cake alone twenty minutes later, I still cherished those moments.

I wouldn't say I hated my mother, but my anger toward her has always clouded my judgment and feelings toward her. Most days, I found it impossible to forgive her.

Impossible to forgive her for robbing me of the chance of having a mother. Of having a *normal* childhood. One that wasn't filled with fear, packed bags, and worrying about where I would sleep or how bills would be paid.

At the same time, I've learned to understand that her addiction robbed her of a life, too.

Diane Harris wanted to be someone.

She wanted to be an artist and travel the world.

She wanted the kind of love you see in movies.

And she wanted to be my mom.

Diane Harris wanted a lot out of life, but drugs stole her future.

I'll never know what led her to relapse after five months of sobriety.

Those five months with her are months I will forever cherish.

I remain standing above my mother's casket long after the crowd leaves, Max safely in the car with Lucy, waiting for me to join when I'm ready.

Reaching down, I grab a handful of dirt. The rain begins pouring, drenching me, and my dress sticks to my skin as chills take up residence in my numb body.

The cold dirt turns into mud in my hand, falling in clumps on the casket that lowers into the ground.

"I forgive you," I whisper the words that my mom had desperately wanted to hear while she was alive. Every time she apologized to me, I brushed it off, waiting for the moment she'd fuck up and break her promise, and the apology would become meaningless.

The first tear falls down my cheek, mixing with the heavy rainfall.

"I forgive you," I repeat, increasing the volume of my voice. The anger and resentment I've been carrying for years lifts from my shoulders, my heart aching.

I've lost everyone I have ever loved.

As if the angels above heard my confession, the rain stops, sunlight peeking through the dark clouds, shining its warmth down on my cold skin.

Turning away from the hole in the ground, I catch sight of a broad back several feet away, and without even seeing his face, I know it's him.

Declan.

Every instinct inside of me wants to run to him. To fall into his arms and cry and beg for him to help me through this pain, but I don't. I remain standing on the damp grass with my heels sinking into the earth where my mother will forever reside.

I watch him as he creates distance between us, and I let it happen.

I let him walk away while I stand rooted in place, watching him go.

He never looks back.

FIFTY-SIX

Declan

I STAND BENEATH THE LARGE MAPLE TREE, CAREFUL NOT TO TOUCH the sticky sap. With my sunglasses on and hands shoved in my pockets, I watch Andy from afar as she stands in front of the crowd gathered at the cemetery to lay Diane Harris to rest.

Two months ago, before Andy walked out of my life, she'd told me about her time with Diane and getting to know her as they navigated their strained relationship. She'd been uneasy and rightfully skeptical, but I saw the excitement in her brown eyes. Although her mouth said one thing, her eyes never lied, and I know she was still a scared little girl, desperate for her mother's attention.

I don't know where it went wrong. The moment Diane decided to give drugs another try, rather than remaining sober for Andy and Max.

Part of me is furious with a dead woman I've never met because now Andy is alone.

But hadn't I done the same thing?

I fucked-up, broke her heart, betrayed her trust, and I know it's not likely I'll ever have it again.

I wish I could say I cleaned myself up since she walked out on me, but the truth is, I've fallen deeper. I'm not proud of my life and how I live, but I'm glad that Andy had the strength to walk away from us. From me. I never would've been strong enough, and I'd have dragged her down for as long as she allowed it.

The crowd begins to leave until Andy is the only one remaining. She stares down at the casket, watching as it's lowered into the ground. All I want is to wrap her in my arms and be a strong shoulder for her to cry on, but I can't. I'm not strong. The truth is, I'm fucking lost right now. Floating through my life, no longer caring if I live to see tomorrow.

Right now, I should be sober and preparing for tour, instead, I'm the reason for yet another delay with my band.

One of these days, I will get my shit together.

My focus had been solely on Andy, that I hadn't noticed the small figure walking toward me, until she's standing right in front of me.

Max's big brown eyes stare up at me, a brown bear hooked beneath the crook of her arm, pouty lips downturned into a frown. "Declan?" It's the first time she's used my name. She's always called me *best friend*, but I guess she's figured out I'm no longer worthy of that title.

I stare down at the little girl, guilt swallowing me over the fact it wasn't just Andy that I fucked over. It was her innocent daughter, too.

"Hi, Max," I croak, voice raw with emotion.

Tears roll down her round cheeks, but she stands strong. She is a brave girl, just like her mother.

"Mommy said you were sick. Are you still sick?" I nod, already knowing what Andy had told her months ago. "Will you come home after you get better?" she asks, eyes full of hope. All I want is to tell her yes and run off into the sunset to live happily ever after with her and Andy, but that time has passed. I fucked it up, and I'm not going to get another chance.

Instead of lying to her, I shake my head.

"You're not my best friend anymore. You left us." She sniffles, bottom lip jutting out and trembling. "I thought you wanted to be my daddy." Her whispered words break what's left of my heart, and her gaze falls to the ground as she kicks at a nearby rock.

Beneath my dark glasses, tears fill my eyes as I lose my balance at the words that feel like a punch to the gut. I stumble back, falling against the sappy tree.

Max turns away, running toward the blonde woman waiting for her in the distance, who I assume is Lucy. She pins me with a look but doesn't say anything.

With my head held high, I turn and walk away.

The feeling of familiar eyes on me sends warmth through my body, the hair on my arms standing. I already know Andy is staring at me without looking over my shoulder. As much as I want to turn around and see her beautiful face, I force myself to continue walking, staring straight ahead as tears freely slip beneath my glasses, landing on my white dress shirt.

Keep walking.

Don't look back.

I force myself to continue, knowing I don't deserve to look Andy in the eye.

This is me.

This is my life.

Destroying everything I touch.

I'd always known our time together would be temporary.

No matter what happens in life from this point forward, I'll never stop loving the girl who set my soul on fire and made me feel worthy of her love.

Every tomorrow I'm given, she will be the one I think of.

FIFTY-SEVEN

Declan

Six months later

"My name is Declan, and I'm an addict. Today marks six months of sobriety." I wipe my sweaty palms along my jean covered thighs.

A round of applause fills the otherwise silent room. Faces I've come to know stare at me, each set of eyes filled with hopefulness.

When I arrived at Greenview Rehabilitation Center in Arizona six months ago, I was at the lowest point in my life.

The love of my life walked out on me, and all I wanted to do was further numb myself. I had been desperate to rid my brain of the look in her eyes as she left, so I did. I went on a two-month-long bender until the day I found out that Andy's mother, Diane Harris, had died of a heroin overdose.

I'd gone to the funeral but was too chicken shit to stick around and talk to Andy, so I left before she had a chance to see me.

That night, I'd gotten so high that I'd vomited in my sleep and pissed myself. The next morning I'd woken up covered in dried vomit and piss.

Never in my life had I thrown up on myself or pissed myself, but I was lying in a puddle of the proof of what my life had come to. I was a disgusting mess haunted by the face of the woman I let get away.

After I'd cleaned myself up, Adam drove me to Arizona for rehab, and I've been here ever since, actively participating. I've even been speaking with a therapist who has forced me to confront the skeletons in my closet.

I wish I could pinpoint a specific moment in my life that made me decide to get sober, but I can't. It's easy to say I took a long look at my vomit and piss-soaked self and decided to change, or that I see the face of my girls every time I close my eyes, but that's only part of it.

Truth is, I was so fucking tired. Tired of living in the past and constantly thinking about my next fix. My life revolved around drugs and alcohol, and I couldn't take it. Eventually, I was going to be the one that my loved ones buried six-feet under.

Everyone here knows my story, and I've learned that the more I share it, the more comfortable I become. I don't try to hide it anymore because what happened to me at thirteen wasn't my fault, and I shouldn't be ashamed. It's what led me to use drugs, and I've spiraled since then.

I've put a lot of work into myself over these past six months, but I still have a long way to go. I'm not anywhere near the man I want to be. The man I know I'm capable of becoming.

"I've made many mistakes in my life and have many regrets. There are many people that I need to make amends with, and I plan to do that today after leaving here." Another applause. "Thank you all for welcoming me here these past six months and for helping me. Without you, I wouldn't have a future to look forward to."

After group is over, I have a final session with my therapist, then say bye to all the people I've become friends with and who have helped me while I've been here.

The program allowed me to remain inpatient for six months,

but now it's time for me to return home and apply everything I've learned to my daily life when temptation is around every corner.

I'll always be an addict because that doesn't change once you're sober, but I know that I will try my best every single day. The chains that kept me buried in the past have been set free, and for the first time in years, I truly feel free.

I've never been so excited about living and getting to live to see another day. I once lived in the moment, day to day, but now, I want to live for the future. I want to plan for the future and know I'll be around for it.

"This is familiar. We've been here before." A familiar voice catches my attention as I walk out the front doors of Greenview. I smirk at the sight of Camille standing beside her rental car, arms crossed as she waits for me.

Four months ago, when Camille found out I was in rehab, she began writing me a weekly letter. Eventually, we began speaking on the phone, leading to her wanting to pick me up once I was released.

We've avoided the subject of Luca and what we discussed at that café months ago in Seattle. She's sent lots of pictures of her little family. Ironically, her daughter Lilli, was born the same month I went to rehab. She's a chunky six-month-old baby who resembles Luca so much at that age despite having Dean's DNA.

As for her and Dean, they're living together now, but there are no immediate plans to get married. They want to enjoy life with Lilli before tying the knot and being swamped with wedding planning.

I've enjoyed her weekly letters and calls. Seeing her happy in her life has been amazing and gives me hope that I'll be able to have the same experience one day. However, I'm not in a rush. My priority right now is myself.

A slow grin spreads across my mouth as I approach her. She's right. We have been in this exact situation. She was there to pick me up from rehab in Seattle after I'd completed a ninety-day program.

A few years later, here she is again, picking me up from rehab. I'm choosing to find the humor in it rather than dwell on the past and things I can't change, because it won't do me any good. All I can do is take it one day at a time.

I'm not proud that I've been to rehab multiple times, but I know that this was the very last time. The voice in my head is gone, and instead of wanting to hide away and escape reality, I want to face what each new day will bring.

"It's good to see you. You look good," I compliment, stepping into her open arms when she pulls me in for a hug. My arms wrap around her small body, and I inhale her scent, which no longer smells sweet and familiar. Instead, she smells like baby powder and remnants of Dean's cologne.

Dean and Lilli came to Arizona with her to pick me up, but they must be waiting at the hotel since Camille is the only one here.

Releasing me from the hug, she pulls away, a smile still spread across her signature red-painted lips. It's hard to remember a time when Cam wasn't wearing her signature red lipstick.

After tossing my bag in the trunk, I climb into the passenger seat, and then we're off, kicking up dust as we drive away, leaving Greenview in the rearview mirror.

They saved my life, and I'll never forget my time there, but as I watch the large white building become smaller and smaller in the rearview mirror, I can't help but smile as I put them in my past.

An hour later, we're sitting in the hotel room Camille booked for me in advance and sipping on the coffee we'd stopped to get along the way. We've been swapping stories the entire time, her sharing about Lilli and me telling her about the things I've learned at Greenview.

I'd just told her about Aiden, the nineteen-year-old boy I

helped nearly nine months ago, when she asked, "How is he doing now?" A proud smile curls on my lips at the question. I was thrilled to learn that he had successfully completed his program and went into a sober living house. Two months ago, he was able to return home to his mother's house, and she'd welcomed him with open arms.

I was surprised to receive a letter from him one day while at Greenview, but after that first one, I received a new one from him every week. He told me all about his program and new sober life and how he hopes I get to enjoy the same things he gets to experience by being sober.

Seeing him thrive was part of my motivation.

I realized that I had a lot of people in my corner who were rooting for me to succeed.

"He's doing great. He'll be enrolling at community college and one day wants to focus on his music, but for now, he's content with getting his education." I don't share that I'm paying for his schooling because that's private. Aiden doesn't even know. As far as he's aware, he received a grant.

"I'm so happy for him. You did something amazing for that kid, Declan. You gave him a future."

I shake my head. "What I did was easy. It's all him. He's the one who will have to go through the hard shit every day. He's the real badass here, not me."

Camille clicks her tongue. "Always so modest." She stands, grabs her laptop from her bag, sets it on her lap, and begins typing, her fingernails tapping against the keys.

"I want to tell you something, and then I want to show you something." She sets the laptop on the coffee table in front of us; the screen pauses on a dark video.

"What is it?"

Bright green eyes meet mine, her hands reaching across for mine.

"Declan, I want you to know that I am sorry for how I acted that day at the café when you told me what you'd done that night." My lips part, breathing labored as I remember that day. That was the day I used as an excuse for myself to fall to the one thing I've always run to whenever the going got rough.

Shifting to face her, I take her hands in mine, "You are not the one that has to be sorry, Cam. I do. That night fucking haunts me." Her emerald eyes swim with unshed tears. "You're the one I need to apologize to. I was the worst fucking husband to you. I lied to you, left you alone when you needed me the most, and was a selfish prick. You didn't deserve any of that. And for that, I'm sorry. It makes me so happy that you have Dean now."

"We were both too young to be married. I've forgiven you a long time ago, and I've never once regretted our time together. Sure, we had our ups and downs, but for four years I had my best friend by my side. It wasn't a waste, and I don't regret it." I bring our hands up to my lips and place a soft kiss on the backs of her hands.

"I've been working on forgiving myself for a lot. I'm not there yet, but one day, I'll forgive myself for being a bad husband to you."

She shakes her head, one hand moving to my face, her thumb stroking my cheek gently. "You have so much to forgive yourself for." She inhales, eyes closing, as she says, "You are not responsible for what happened that night. Dean hired someone who could obtain the traffic footage from that night. It wasn't your fault, Declan. The other driver ran a red light and hit us. It was an accident." Her eyes open, bright green hues staring back at me as I absorb her words.

"What?" My mouth hangs open, head shaking as I attempt to comprehend her words, "Why?"

"Because I've been angry with you for so long. I've blamed you, and ever since that day we met up in Seattle, Dean had wanted to look into the accident, but I wasn't ready. After I gave birth to Lilli, I decided it was time to confront the past and let go of my anger. So, I let him look into it, and you need to see what happened."

I shake my head, my heart beating in my chest. "No, Cam. I can't watch it. I can't watch myself destroy our lives again."

"You need to see this," she says, pulling away from me, and reaches toward her laptop, pressing play on the paused video.

It begins to play, our SUV from almost five years ago coming into view. Despite the rain and dark skies, the footage is clear.

Sinking to the floor in front of the coffee table, I bring the laptop closer to my face, eyes wide as I watch, not wanting to miss a moment.

I watch as our car travels through the intersection, the green light shining bright. The moment our vehicle goes through, the camera angle switches, revealing a glow from a red light and a semi-swerving through the lanes at an increased speed.

The semi collides with our SUV, causing us to spin before flipping, my limp body flying away from the destruction as I land on the pavement, away from the car that held everything precious to me.

I hadn't realized I was shaking and had tears streaming down my face until Camille sits down beside me and wraps her arms around me. "It wasn't your fault. You thought you ran a red light, but you didn't. The other driver did. There was no way the accident could've been prevented. You are not to blame," she whispers slowly, her voice filled with emotion. "If I'd been paying attention, I would've spotted the semi and could've yelled or done something. Anything." She sniffles, regret of her own shining in her green eyes. Luca had been whining about getting to open one of his new toys during the drive, so Camille reached back to grab the firetruck from him, and that's when we collided. Seconds her eyes were away, but mine never left the road. For years I've tortured myself, blaming myself for running the red light, when I hadn't.

My heart hammers in my chest, and my body shakes as I replay the video, reviewing it carefully to ensure she's right.

After the sixth time watching it, I shut the device, bring my knees to my chest, and bury my face in my hands as I allow sobs to wreck my body.

It wasn't my fault.

I didn't kill my son.

It was an accident.

I didn't fucking kill my boy.

"I'm so sorry I ever blamed you," she says through sniffles, rising on her knees beside me as she wraps her arms around me, holding me tight against her warm body.

"Forgive yourself for everything, Declan, because I do." Her head rests against mine. "It was an accident. You are not responsible for what happened."

Her words replay in my mind long after she's gone.

You are not responsible for what happened.

FIFTY-EIGHT

Andy

A year and a half later

"THANK YOU ALL FOR BEING HERE. IF YOU'D PLEASE FORM A SINGLE-file line this way, Andy will be happy to sign your book." The redhead guides the crowd to line up, her smile never leaving her face as she handles the rowdy crowd of readers who are anxious to meet me and have their books signed.

Brooke has been the most incredible personal assistant, and I don't know what I'd do without her. It's been over a year since we began working together, yet it still feels strange to say I have a personal assistant.

Some days, I feel like I'm living someone else's life. Never in my wildest dreams could I have imagined I'd be where I am now.

At a book signing.

Not just any book signing.

My book signing on *my* book tour.

Two years ago, after the worst heartbreak of my life and choosing to put myself first, I sat down at my laptop and poured my heart and soul into writing a book that I considered my trauma dump. I shared the story of the little curly-haired girl who only ever wanted love and acceptance from her drug-addicted mother. And how, one day, she met a boy who changed her life. They fell in love, and it was toxic and beautiful and consumed that girl's soul.

She needed him as much as needed to breathe.

His words saved her life. But her love couldn't save his.

Before I knew it, I had written my story.

Mine and Declan's.

One year after reaching out to as many agents as I could, I found Quinn Black with T House Publishing. Before I knew it, I had an agent, a book deal, and a personal assistant.

My life has changed, and I am now living my wildest dreams.

My debut novel is a deeply personal story of my life. It was released two months ago, and I have been on tour ever since.

It became one of the greatest love stories, instantly hitting all the charts. It's a story that shares that even in the darkest of times, love finds a way to prevail. I may not have gotten my happy ending, but the characters in my book did. They got the best ending possible for their situation.

Sometimes, the imposter syndrome attacks me, leaving me feeling like I'm living someone else's life. Some days, I wake up and pinch myself, unsure if I'm in a dream because, surely, it cannot be real.

Max has enjoyed traveling to all the new cities with me. For her seventh birthday, I took her to Disney World. It was the one thing she'd been asking for, and thanks to our new financial situation, I no longer have to deny her the things she wants in this life. Thankfully, it's summer, and she's out of school, so she's been able to travel with me.

She'd been excited to visit New York with me. She's currently with her nanny, exploring the city while I'm here at my signing.

Can you believe it? I, Andy Harris, of small-town Loganville, the girl who used to grocery shop at the Dollar Store and eat mystery meat packets for a dollar, has a fucking nanny.

Talk about a mind-fuck.

Did I mention we no longer live in Loganville? We moved to Las Vegas when I received the first check for my book. I enrolled my girl in private school, started a savings account, and now we travel as much as possible.

We have yet to leave the country, but that's on the list. Max made a list of places she wants to go, and so far that list consists of visiting every Disney location worldwide.

When it's time for me to come out, Brooke gestures me over and introduces me to the crowd, giving me a round of applause.

I smooth my clammy palms over my black and white jump-suit. Taking a deep breath, I hold it for a few seconds to calm myself. No matter how many of these signings I've done, it still feels like the first.

Sometimes, I feel like I don't belong and must look around to ensure security isn't hiding somewhere to escort me out.

That hasn't happened yet, so this must be real life.

The line of people spreads throughout the entire bookstore and out the door. Every stop on this tour has been like that. Countless faces. Countless books signed.

I'll never be able to wrap my head around the fact these hard-working folks are spending their money on my book and taking time out of their day to come and see me to get the book signed.

That's fucking crazy!

Do they know I'm just an ordinary person?

When Brooke recommended that I create a social media account for my writing career and a reader group for a place where my readers can interact, I swore no one would want to join or follow me.

Damn, had I been wrong.

Every time I open my social media, there are endless messages from readers telling me how much they loved the book and how they were able to relate. The fact anyone can relate to my words is a feeling I'll never be able to describe.

People have shared their own stories with me about either themselves having been an addict, or someone they love.

I'm just a small-town girl who doesn't feel worthy of having such an incredible reader base. But I'll never take a single moment for granted.

Taking my seat behind the table, a bright smile lights up my face as the first person steps forward, and I grab a book from the stack and personalize it to her before signing my name at the bottom.

An hour later, my hand is aching, but I'll never tire of doing what I do.

Before the next person steps forward, I grab another book from a box underneath the table. Sitting up, I set the book on the table without looking up, grab my marker, and open to the title page.

I look up, ready to greet the next person and ask who they'd like me to make it out to, but words fail me at the sight of the person I least expected to see.

My heart skips a beat.

Declan stands in front of my table, tattooed hands in his pockets, a grin on his lips as he stares down at me with that same intense gaze he's always had.

"Hey, Mama," he draws out, his voice raspy as if he hasn't spoken in a while. Chills race through my body at the sound of his voice, and goosebumps form on my skin.

God damn, he looks good. The pictures I've seen didn't do him any justice.

I've followed his career since our break-up. Since it was made public and all over social media, I also know he went to rehab.

Eight months ago, Riot finally went on tour. I'd be lying if I said I hadn't watched videos online and followed Declan closely, needing to know how he was doing with the tour and hoping I wouldn't find a video or news article about him relapsing again.

I'd also be lying if I said I hadn't known Riot had performed in New York last night. I knew they were here.

Knew he's here.

But I also knew it didn't matter because I couldn't go to him.

It's been two years, yet I've never stopped loving him, and I don't think I ever will.

No matter what we'd like to believe, love doesn't always come with a happy ending. Sometimes, you put in the work and do everything you can, but in the end, it doesn't matter.

Our relationship wasn't for nothing. There were things I learned from it. But in the end, it wasn't our time.

Declan and I had a whirlwind romance. He will forever be the first and only man I've ever and will ever love. But we met at the wrong time.

His love for me wasn't enough to steer him away from his path of self-destruction. The demons that haunted him were too strong, and he wasn't able to fight them.

In the end, I had to choose myself and let go. No matter how much my soul ached, I had to let him go.

Foolishly, I wanted to be the one to save him, the one to rid him of his demons. But the only one who could save him was him.

I wanted someone to love me more than they loved getting high. More than the feeling you'd get after the first hit from that little glass pipe, those little white lines, or even the needle in the vein. I wanted to be the only drug he'd ever need.

In the end, I realized I couldn't be anyone's savior.

I needed to save myself.

I let him go.

Finding my voice, I whisper a breathy, "Hi." My eyes wide, unwilling to blink and risk this being an illusion.

Declan pulls a hand from his pockets and rakes it through his dark hair, now longer than he used to wear it.

"You can make my book out to Declan. But you might need to get a new one." My brows furrow as I look down to see what he's looking at. On the front page is an ink stain from where I'd been holding the metallic marker tip against the page.

Groaning, I set the book to the side, grab a new copy, then quickly sign it before sliding it across the table toward him.

Declan grabs the book, a grin on his lips as he salutes me with it, then walks away backward, eyes on me for several steps until he turns, facing forward, and disappearing into the crowded line at the register at the front of the store.

What. The. Actual. Fuck.

By the time the signing is over, my heart is still racing at remembering the sight of Declan standing there. One look into his eyes had stolen the air from my lungs.

After helping Brooke clean up our signing area, I grab my purse and pull the strap over my shoulder before stepping outside. Phone in hand, I send a text to Molly, Max's nanny, to find out where they're at.

Spotting the shadow of a figure near the entrance, I look up, eyes widening at the sight of Declan. One hand was shoved in his pocket, the other holding the shopping bag from the store. He leans against the brick building, a smirk on his lips.

"You're still here." I exhale. Shoving my phone into my pocket, I walk toward him until we're standing toe to toe.

"I wanted to wait until you were done." A slow smile spread across my lips, heart pounding in my chest. "Want to grab a cup of coffee?"

My mind is racing. The sight of him mixed with the spicy, woodsy scent of his cologne sends mixed signals to my brain.

The chime of my phone breaks our staring contest, and I quickly pull it from my moment, seeing a new text from Molly.

MOLLY

Back at the hotel. Max is passed out in my room. Want me to bring her over to yours?

ME

No. Keep her with you. I'll see you both tomorrow.

Attention back on Declan, he nods toward my phone. "Gotta be somewhere?" he asks, dark eyes full of questions and something else I can't quite make out. I feel his eyes on my body, taking in every soft curve of my body that hasn't changed much over the last two years.

Suddenly, it doesn't matter that we've been apart for two years. This is the man I've loved every second of every day, and if we only have one night together, I don't want to waste it.

"I know a place that has the best coffee."

"Oh, yeah? Where?"

"My hotel room," I say bluntly, watching his surprised reaction.

Pushing off the building, he steps toward me until my breasts are brushing against his chest. "Let's go then, Mama."

He hails us a cab, and an hour later, we're tumbling into my hotel room, lips locked, hands grabbing at each other.

Declan doesn't waste a second, slipping his tongue between my lips and ravishing my mouth while our hands furiously tear at each other's clothing.

He only breaks our kiss once we're both naked and standing in front of each other, my eyes instantly going down to his stiff cock between us, a smirk on my lips at the sight of my name still tattooed along his shaft.

Reading my expression, he wraps a fist around himself and strokes. "Did you think I'd get rid of it?"

Eyes finding him, I shake my head. I wasn't sure what he'd do, but removing it never crossed my mind. Besides, I'm not sure if it is possible to remove a tattoo on a penis.

His dark gaze roams over my body, eyes savoring every groove of my figure. A growl escapes his throat, hands grabbing my waist and pulling me into him, hot, wet kisses trailing along my neck.

When he raises his hands to cup my face, the flash of purple

587

captures my eyes. I grab his left wrist, turning it over to see his newest tattoo.

On the inside of his wrist is a purple heart, the drawing familiar. Beneath the heart, is a semi colon.

"Oh my God." I gasp, eyes finding his, needing an explanation.

A shy smile creeps over his lips. "It's the purple heart Max drew on all of those get-well cards she'd made me. I got it tattooed after I got out of rehab as a reminder of what I lost and that my time with both of you was real. It's my reminder to keep going." Just when I thought I couldn't love him more, he says that.

I grin, turning my back to him, and pull my hair away from my left shoulder. The same tattoo is on the back of my left shoulder.

"I got it after my mom died," I confess, heart aching at the memory.

Declan doesn't say anything as he steps toward me, warm lips kissing over the purple heart. His arms wrap around my waist, fingers tweaking my nipples as I become putty in his hands. Familiar calloused fingers trail down my body and to my pussy, a finger circling my aching clit.

My head falls back on his shoulder, tilting to look up at him as he plays with my body. His lips connect with mine, and our tongues tangle as he plunges two fingers inside of me and fucks me with them until I'm crying out my release.

I've no sooner come down from the high of my release when he picks me up, carries me to the bed, spreads my legs, and buries his cock so deep inside my pussy in one thrust that I see stars.

My pussy is still spasming from my orgasm as he fucks me, our eyes never leaving each other, each of us savoring this moment.

Unspoken words hang in the air.

Where do we go from here?

Is there a chance for us?

Do you still love me?

I swallow the questions I want to ask him, choosing to be in the moment rather than worry about the future and what this moment means.

For tonight, he's mine.

Declan raises my legs, ankles on his shoulders, as he stands at the edge of the bed, fucking me with everything he's got. The roughness has screams falling from my lips, eyes threatening to roll into the back of my head permanently.

We come together, my release drowning his cock while his cum floods my pulsing pussy.

My legs slip off his shoulders as he lies on top of me, still buried deep inside of me.

"So, want to grab some smash burgers?" he asks, a loud laugh escaping me.

He's still buried inside of me, and our cum is dripping out of me, and he's asking about getting food.

God, I fucking love this man.

"Yeah, that sounds good."

FIFTY-NINE

Andy

DECLAN WORSHIPPED MY BODY A SECOND TIME BEFORE WE FINALLY unwrapped ourselves from each other and left the hotel, hand in hand, to visit one of his favorite food trucks to get smash burgers near Central Park.

He'd always promised to bring me to New York to get one, and here we are, over two years later, finding ourselves in New York at the same time. Not exactly ideal, considering the plan was always to come together, but nevertheless, here we are.

Had I been a fool to allow Declan into my bed and body without at least pretending to be hard to get and making him grovel a bit for the things he's put me through? Probably. But do I regret it? Absolutely not.

Two years later, he still knows my body like the back of his hand.

After getting our food, Declan carries the plates while I carry two water bottles, following him toward an empty bench.

Sitting beside him, I pass him one of the waters, exchanging it for a plate containing a burger and fries.

We eat silently, the air thick with awkwardness and tension.

It was easy jumping into bed with Declan, but now that it's time to talk, I'm unsure how to act.

He still resembles my Declan, but we've been apart for two years. We're different people now. I'm not the same naive girl I'd once been, desperate for a man to make her feel special. I've learned my self-worth and am not defined by a man anymore.

Declan takes our empty plates over to the trash as soon as we're done eating, then returns to my side, leg bouncing nervously. Finally, he breaks the silence, putting us both out of our misery.

"Andy," he turns to face me, taking my hands in his, "I'm embarrassed and unsure where to begin. Saying sorry to you isn't enough for all the shit I've put you through." I mirror him, moving one leg onto the bench between us, "I want you to know I'm sober now, and I understand that may be hard for you to believe because I've lied to you so many times." I remain silent, allowing him to work out the thoughts in his head.

"I've been following your career. You fucking did it, Mama. You accomplished every dream you had." The corner of his mouth curls up in a half smile. "I'm proud of you. And I may have a dozen copies of your book already."

Warmth fills me when he tells me he's proud. I'm proud of myself, but it's different to hear that from someone else—from someone who, after two years apart, still means everything to you. "Thank you," I mutter bashfully. "Have you read it?" I'm nervous about his answer, unsure if I want him to have read my book or not, considering it's our story.

Declan nods, surprising the fuck out of me. When I give him a wide-eyed look, he chuckles before clarifying, "You wrote our story." His thumbs stroke over the back of my hands. "I'll admit, it was hard to read about how much I hurt you. You always forgave me and rarely told me how you truly felt. You poured your heart into that story, which helped me understand you a lot more."

My eyebrows furrow. "How did it help you to understand me?"

"After the night you came to New York to surprise me after

my show, you stopped letting me in. Stopped sharing your feelings." I shake my head, pulling my hands away from him.

"No," I close my eyes. "That's not—" I pause, letting out a heavy breath. Looking back, I think he might be right. That moment in our relationship had us heading downhill to our fatal ending.

"You're right," I admit, letting my leg slide down from the bench as I turn away from him to face forward. "I was afraid to say anything that would set you off. You were fragile, and I didn't want to push you over the edge. You tried to kill yourself, Declan." My voice clogs with emotion, and I swallow it down. Tears sting my eyes, but I refuse to let them fall. The memory of getting that phone call from Adam haunts me. For months, the what-ifs had haunted me.

What if Adam hadn't gotten to Declan in time?

What if Declan tried again?

"I didn't want you to try again. You have no idea how much it killed me to be there at the hospital. So close, yet so far away from you. Even when you were released and I could see you, I was constantly afraid. Every time my phone rang, I stopped breathing because I didn't want to get the call that you were dead." I lose my fight with keeping my tears at bay, and the first one rolls down my cheek.

Declan moves from the bench and squats down in front of me, arms wrapped around my waist as my legs spread to make room for him. Glossy brown eyes stare back at me.

He opens his mouth to speak, but I press my finger to his lips to silence him. "Walking away from you was the hardest thing I've ever done. I wanted my love to save you, and for a long time, I couldn't understand why it couldn't. It wasn't until my mom died that I realized it wasn't about me not loving you enough. It was you who needed to love yourself and fight your demons. You needed to realize that you were worth more than the life you were living. You needed to confront your fears, and my love would never change that." Gentle, familiar fingers caress my skin, wiping the fallen tears from my cheeks.

"I love you, Declan. I have always loved you," I whisper. "But I couldn't watch you kill yourself."

"My demons had nothing to do with you, Andy. What I was going through, that was all my own shit. You loved me so fucking much, and I took it for granted. At that stage in my life, I was the only one who could save me, no matter how much you loved me." he buries his face in my lap, shoulders shaking with silent sobs, the warm tears seeping through the fabric of my jeans. "I'm so fucking sorry for everything I put you through. I don't know how you can forgive me, but I need you to know that I will spend the rest of my life making it up to you if you allow me a chance," he says, words muffled by my lap.

His red-rimmed, teary eyes stare at me. His grip around my waist is secure, and for the first time in over two years, I feel safe again in his arms. My hands slide up his arms, leaning forward until I can tangle my fingers in the hair at the nape of his neck.

"I don't deserve your forgiveness, so I won't ask for it. And instead of making promises, I'm going to show you how fucking sorry I am and how much I've changed. You are my light in the darkness. You were what helped me find my way out of the darkness that surrounded me for too fucking long." I rest my forehead against his as my heart pounds in my chest, aching at the sincerity of his words. "I don't know if you have room for me in your life, and even though I don't deserve it, I'm begging, please give me another chance. Let me make it up to you. Let me love you how you deserve to be loved. Let me love you how I should've instead of taking you for granted." His warm, minty breath fans across my lips, tears running down both of our cheeks.

I've always loved that Declan was never shy about showing his emotions. While many men consider it weak to cry, I love that Declan wears his heart on his sleeve and isn't afraid to cry. It shows his humanity.

"Declan, I don't know what I can offer you. You broke my trust, and I don't know how you can get it back. I gave you a chance to come clean to me about your drug use, and instead of being honest, you lied and gaslit me. Then you ghosted me, tried to kill yourself, lied again about being sober, and then again gaslit me. I was fucked up for a long time after that." It took months of therapy and writing for me to be able to unwrap and understand everything that we went through in our three-month relationship.

"We went through a lot in a short amount of time." He sighs. "I put you through a lot, and take full responsibility for everything. I'm not going to blame it on my addiction either." He pulls back until he can look into my eyes. "Please, Andy. Give me another chance. Let me prove to you that I am better than that. Let me prove that you are safe with me and that I can be the man you deserve. I've been working on myself every day for two years, hoping and praying I'd have this chance. I know I don't deserve it, but I'm begging."

When I stare into his eyes, I find the truth reflecting in his dark brown hues. It's too easy to fall under Declan's spell, but I'd like to believe I'm stronger now and won't fall for the devilish lure of his lies.

I choose to believe him and give him another chance without any conditions or ultimatums. Maybe I'm a fool, but I love him. And if I end up a fool in the end, then jokes on me. However, something tells me that he won't let me down this time.

"Friends," I say, watching as he sucks his bottom lip between his teeth. "We can be friends. Take things slow and go from there." His eyes light up, and he stands, pulling me up.

Declan slips his hands into my hair, tugging on my curls to tilt my head back. Then his mouth devours mine, and I'm melting in his arms.

I taste him. The man I love. The man I'm choosing to trust with my heart.

"Friends," Declan confirms breathlessly, and then his lips are back on mine.

His kiss sets my soul on fire and repairs my broken heart.

For the first time, I don't taste bitter lies on his tongue.

SIXTY

Max

Six months later

I LOVE SUMMER.

I love playing with my friends whenever I want without being stuck inside a classroom listening to boring Mrs. Wilson blab on and on about gross math.

Yuck. I hate math.

Luckily, I'll go to third grade soon and have a different teacher. I'm hoping for Mrs. Bee because she's the coolest teacher ever! Everyone likes her, and she doesn't give a lot of homework.

Unlike Mrs. Wilson, who thinks we should never get to have any fun and should do homework every night.

Gross.

I hope she retires soon because she's mean, and I'm happy I'm not in her class anymore. My best friend Ella says she's a witch because of her pointy nose and wrinkly face. I think she's right because she loves Halloween and dresses up as a witch every year. I'd wanted her to like me and not pass out homework over the weekend, so I dressed up as a witch princess for our classroom Halloween party last year.

When I showed her my costume, she clicked her tongue and

said I can't be a princess and a witch. It made me sad, and I told my mom when I got home.

Mom called her a bitch when she thought I wasn't listening, but I heard it. I'm always listening, even when I know it's wrong to eavesdrop on adult conversations.

But if I hadn't been eavesdropping, I wouldn't have known that Mom has a new boyfriend. Well, not a new boyfriend, but he's not old, so I'm not sure what to call him. Regardless, Mom is dating Declan again.

My Declan.

The man I deemed my best friend the day I met him at five years old.

The man who would crawl around on the floor on his hands and knees with me on his back because I wanted to play horse. I was always the princess, and he was the horse I rode on.

Molly, my nanny, often tells me I have a wild imagination, but it was never too wild for my best friend—Declan. He always played with me, but he got sick and went away.

I used to ask my mom about him every night, but then she'd cry herself to sleep when she thought I was in bed and unable to hear her. After that, I stopped asking about Declan, and eventually, she stopped crying.

I used to ask Molly about him, too, but she'd tell me he was away getting better.

What did that mean?

When Ella was sick, she was back at school three days later.

Once, Molly had a cold but was back at our house two weeks after her cough had gone away.

I wanted to know what kind of sickness made Declan be away for so long.

One day, while I was at Ella's house, we asked her older brother Jacob to look up photos of Riot online to see if I could spot Declan. The pictures had been recent, and he didn't look sick as he stood in front of the crowd singing the songs that Mom cries to.

I don't think he's sick.

I think I'm the reason he's gone.

I've never told Mom what I said to him the day at grandma's funeral, because I don't want her to be mad at me. I didn't mean what I'd said to him. I was just sad about losing my grandma and not being able to see him like I used to.

One day, he was there promising he'd come home to me, and the next, he was gone without saying goodbye.

It's been a really long time since I've seen him, and I miss him.

Especially since finding out Mom still talks to him and sees him.

Thanks to my eavesdropping skills, I heard Mom talking to Aunt Lucy on the phone. She told her that she reconnected with Declan while we were in New York, and they were going to give their relationship another chance. She said she forgave him for the shit that happened, but what does that mean?

What *shit* happened?

I asked Ella if she knew what it meant, and she said it meant "stuff happened." But that didn't bring me any closer to the truth.

Sometimes Ella doesn't know shit.

I've been at the park all day with Molly while Mom went to "visit a friend." I'm not a baby. I know that's code for *going to see Declan* because every time she says she's going to "visit a friend," she comes home smelling like a guy.

I still remember what Declan smelled like. I'd inhale his smell every time he hugged me because he made me feel safe.

When I was a kid—well, a little kid, because I'm still a kid now, I'm just an older kid—I wanted to be like my mom. I was happy to be like her because she didn't have a dad, and neither did I.

But then I met Declan, and I no longer wanted to be like my mom.

I wanted a dad, but I never told her because I didn't want her to be sad.

I wanted Declan to be my dad.

Then he left. He forgot about me, and dads aren't supposed to do that.

Ella's dad never forgets about her.

I've been at the park with Molly all morning, the two of us seeing who can swing the highest on the swing set. I always win because my legs are shorter. Hers are long, and she has to kick them funny, or they'll drag in the sand.

When Molly gets off the swing to answer her phone, I don't pay her any attention. Instead, I start singing the words to my favorite Taylor Swift song. One day, I'm going to be just like her because I can sing just like her.

Mom says it'll happen, and I believe her.

Moms know everything.

Just like when I stole a cookie from the package while she was making dinner. She wasn't even looking at me and knew what I was doing. When I asked her how she knew, she said it was because she had eyes in the back of her head.

I think those eyes see the future.

"Max, start slowing down so you can get off," Molly says, interrupting the chorus to "Shake It Off." Rolling my eyes, I stop pumping my legs and allow my bare feet to drag beneath me, feeling the warmth of the sand spread between my toes.

Giggling, I come to a stop and climb off the swing, watching as Molly picks up my sandals from where I'd kicked them off the moment I got on the swing.

"Can we get ice cream?" I ask, sticking my face in my shirt to wipe away the sweat lining my forehead. I've been playing hard today and could use a cold treat.

Molly opens her mouth to speak, but no words come out as something in the distance steals her attention, a small smile spreading on her pink lips.

Curious, I turn around to see what she's looking at, and my jaw drops.

Oh. My. God.

I'm seeing shit.

I blink rapidly, my mouth open and closing like a gaping fish.

My mom and Declan are walking toward me.

I take a hesitant step toward them, arms wrapping around myself as I stare at him, tears stinging my eyes.

His brown eyes stare back at me, and I watch as he wipes a fallen tear from his cheek. Oh no.

I frown. Is he not happy to see me?

I bury my toes in the sand, keeping myself standing in place instead of running to him like I want to.

Suddenly, he's in front of me and squatting until we're eye to eye.

"Hi, Max." He smiles, his voice the same as I remember.

"Hi, Declan." I attempt to scowl, but I'm so happy to see him that my lips curl into a smile. Hesitantly, I take a step closer. "Are you better now?" I ask, crossing my fingers behind my back.

He wipes another tear away, a smile on his face as he nods. "Yeah, Max. I'm better now."

"Did you come back to be my daddy?" I blurt the question, instantly shrinking into myself, afraid of his answer.

Before I can take it back, his face lights up with a smile. "I did, Max. I'm all better, and I'm here to stay. I'm here for you and your mom. I'll never leave you again."

With my arms spread wide, I throw myself against him, and he catches me.

Declan stands with me in his arms, rubbing my back as I cry into his shoulder.

My best friend is back.

EPILOGUE
Declan

One year later

WHEN I WAS THIRTEEN YEARS OLD, MY FOSTER FATHER RAPED ME FOR the first time. Multiple times a week, while I was living under his roof, he'd sneak into my bedroom and touch me. It started three weeks after moving into his home and continued for months until I was eventually moved into a group home for being labeled "problematic" after breaking his nose.

After it started, I was constantly angry and disgusted with myself.

Angry at my mother for turning her back on me.

Angry for living the life I had to live.

Angry at everyone around me for failing me.

The first time I smoked weed, I felt free. My mind and body were numb, and when my foster father came into my room, I barely registered what was happening because the high was soothing me.

After that, I realized I could make the pain go away.

Vodka. Weed. Pills.

I took anything I could get my hands on because it helped me through the nights.

After I'd turned fourteen, he tried touching me, but I was stronger then. I fought back and punched him in the nose. A few days later, I was removed from his care after he called the case worker to report the assault and tell her all about my drug use.

It was okay to rape me when I didn't have the strength to fight, but once I was able to fight back, I was no longer wanted.

Thank fuck.

Getting away from him was the best thing that could've happened, but it was too late by then. The memories of him sneaking into my room haunted me every time I closed my eyes.

Every time I tried to sleep, my mind would replay the sound of his grunts, my struggling cries of pain, and the squeaks of the old bed I slept on.

The only way possible for me to escape the memories was with drugs. As the years went on and I became older, I was too reliant on the drugs to ever seek help because I liked that I could forget.

Before Greenview, I'd never told anyone what had happened to me and why I began using in the first place. My therapist while I was in rehab, Dr. Leerman, was the one to get me to open up and share my story. He made me realize that I'd been so trau-matized by that event that it was impacting me into adulthood.

Drugs were the only thing that had been there for me, so I clung to them and relied on them for every difficult moment in my life. It was easier to get high rather than deal with whatever was going on in my life.

Since going to therapy and talking about my painful past, I've learned how to handle those stressful situations life will inevitably bring without turning to drugs.

Dr. Leerman diagnosed me with PTSD and prescribed me antidepressants that I take religiously. We have virtual meetings once a week, sometimes twice if I need him, but I've been doing great for the most part.

Today marks three years of sobriety, and I feel better than ever.

I will always be an addict, but I'm lucky that I'm alive and get to have a choice, and I choose to fight every day to remain sober.

Two weeks after seeing Andy at her book signing a year ago, I told her everything. It took me some time to be able to confess my secrets to her, but I did. Told her everything about my foster father, and she's been my rock ever since.

We've been together ever since that day in New York. I fulfilled my promise to her about getting smash burgers, and ever since then, I've kept every single promise.

We dated for six months before she fully allowed me back into Max's life, but after that, we bought a house together in Las Vegas and have been living together ever since.

Max forgave me for leaving her, and one day, when she's older, I'll share my story with her, but for now, I'm here to stay.

My girls keep me grounded.

This morning, I woke up wanting to do something I once swore I'd never do again. Surprisingly, it didn't take anything to convince Andy. As soon as I told her, "Let's get married today," while my head was between her legs, she smiled at me, said to give her an hour to get ready, and that was it.

Now, three hours later, we are standing in the little white chapel, waiting for Elvis to pronounce us man and wife, surrounded by our family: Max, Lucy, Adam, Damon, Cole, Cece, Benny, and Camille and Spencer on FaceTime. It's just us and the people who mean the most in the world to us.

We didn't have time to stop and get rings, but that doesn't matter. I don't need a ring to prove I'm committed to this woman for the rest of my life.

I've spent nearly three and a half years loving her every day, and I'll continue to do so until my dying breath.

"I vow to love you unconditionally. I'll love you when you don't love yourself, and I'll be by your side for every struggle you may face. You are my heart, my soul, the air I breathe. I've never been more in love than I am with you. You, Declan Valentine, saved my life. You were the life raft when I was drowning. My saving grace. My happy place. I love you and can't wait to spend all of my tomorrows with you." Andy stares into my eyes as she says her vows, our fingers intertwined as she stands before me dressed in a white mini dress with white Chuck Taylor high-tops.

Max stands beside her in a purple dress—it's her new favorite color—and flowers in her hair that Cece helped her pick from who-knows-where.

I'm dressed in black pants and a matching dress shirt and wearing the same shoes as my bride. Great minds must think alike because we both came out wearing the matching shoes we bought together.

When the Elvis impersonator instructs me to share my vows, I slide the cherry ring pop onto her left ring finger before speaking. "I vow to give you not only all my tomorrows but my future as a whole. You, Andy Harris, are love. Knowing you and loving you has changed my life. It wasn't easy convincing you to let me in, but for some crazy reason you did. Now I'm the luckiest man in the world to be loved by you. Your heart is gold, and I want to spend the rest of my life having the honor of calling you my wife and best friend. We have been through a lot, and I'm going to spend the rest of my life making it all up to you. It's you, Mama. It'll always be you."

When it's time to kiss my wife, I take her face delicately in my hands, holding her like the greatest treasure to ever exist. I press a slow kiss against her dark-painted lips, savoring the feel of her lips against mine. Kissing her feels like we're the only two people to exist. It's only us.

Me and my wife.

My Andy.

My saving grace.

My sunlight.

Clapping erupts around us as our family cheers and whistles for us.

Andy pulls away with a grin, happiness shining on her face as she stares at me, eyes full of love. Holding her hand in mine, I lead her down the rose petal aisle, then pull her into my body before we exit the building. "I love you, wife."

"I love you, husband." She lifts her left hand between us, a devilish smirk darkening her features as she looks between the cherry ring pop and me. "Let's go home and put this to use?" she says in a low, suggestive tone.

Unable to keep the easy grin from spreading across my lips, I give her another slow kiss. "Anything for you, wife."

Our friends take Max for the night to give my new wife and me privacy on our wedding night. When we arrive home, I carry Andy over the threshold into our bedroom, lie her body out on top of our bed, and put her new ring to use.

I give my wife multiple orgasms until she's a sweaty mess and begging me to stop. Only then do I pull her into my arms and savor the feeling of her pressed against me, head on my chest, listening to my heart beating for her.

Just when I think she's asleep, she tilts her head up and looks at me, lips upturned into a smile, but she doesn't say anything.

We don't always need words. I know what she's thinking because it's the same thing I'm thinking.

Despite everything we've been through, we're getting our happy ending.

Through depression, insecurities, lies, and active addiction, we made it.

We made it through the storm.

"Because of you, I'm alive," I confess, fingers tracing random shapes over the soft skin of her back. Because of her, I live to see another day.

Loving an addict isn't easy, and for that, she's the strongest woman I know.

I'll always be an addict because I'll always have an addiction. There will never be a time in my life when I'm able to drink or use drugs and not spiral and fall off the deep end. I used to think addict was a dirty word, but it's not. There's nothing wrong with me, and I'm not less than because of my addictions.

I'm human.

I'm worthy.

I deserve to live.

I deserve to forgive myself.

I shouldn't be defined by my addictions because I, along with every other addict, am more than that.

We're people who are struggling.

Many of us are fighting a silent battle.

We are worthy.

We can recover.

THE END

SIGNED COPIES

Do you want to own a signed copy of this book?

Order yours today:

www.kylafayebooks.com

ACKNOWLEDGMENTS

Thank you for taking the time to read Andy and Declan's story. I have poured my blood, sweat, and tears (literally) into this story.

Many tears were shed during the process of writing this story, and many times I doubted myself. Many times I told myself to stop writing because no one would want to read something sad that could potentially hit close to home for some. I'm so glad that I pushed and forced myself to continue telling this story even though it was painful.

Thank you to my lover for being there and always supporting me. You made me feel safe as I wrote a story you knew was hard for me. You're my shoulder to cry on, my biggest supporter, my sounding board, and always quick to give me ideas. I love you forever.

Thank you to everyone who played a role in bringing Because of You to life. Emily, my incredibly talented cover designer. My amazing editors who clean up my mess. My alpha/beta readers, ARC readers, and everyone else who read this story and helped me along the way as I brought it to life.

Special thanks to Amanda, Gabby, Kelsey, Mikaylah, and Rae Ann, for sharing their stories and crying right along with me. You ladies are incredible, and I couldn't have done it without each of you.

Thank you to my PA Martha for being there 24/7 whenever I need to flood you with messages. You make my life so much easier and I appreciate you soooo much!

Because of You will forever be the book I am the most proud of in my career.

Thank you for giving it a chance and allowing me to share my story.

ABOUT THE AUTHOR

Kyla Faye is a twenty-something author of dark, adult erotic, and contemporary romance. When she's not reading about romance, she's writing about it, trying to give a voice to the characters that live inside her head. She has a caffeine addiction and always has a candle burning.

Keep up with her on social media

Join Kyla Faye's mailing list for exclusive material: https://bit. ly/41blIFl

Readers Group: Kyla's House of Whores
Instagram: authorkylafaye
TikTok: authorkylafaye
Website: https://kylafaye.com/

Printed in Great Britain
by Amazon

44285808R00354